BUTCHER'S BILL

C.J. &
   Burl,
HOPE YOU ENJOY THIS.
IT'S NOT JUST A STORY...
IT'S AN ADVENTURE.

11/01/202

C.I. 4

Burl,

Hope you enjoyed this.
IT'S NOT JUST A DREAM...
IT'S AN ADVENTURE.

[signature]

BUTCHER'S BILL

Eric W. Herbert

TATE PUBLISHING
AND ENTERPRISES, LLC

Published by Tate Publishing & Enterprises, LLC
127 E. Trade Center Terrace | Mustang, Oklahoma 73064 USA
1.888.361.9473 | www.tatepublishing.com

Tate Publishing is committed to excellence in the publishing industry. The company reflects the philosophy established by the founders, based on Psalm 68:11,
"The Lord gave the word and great was the company of those who published it."

Book design copyright © 2013 by Tate Publishing, LLC. All rights reserved.
Cover design by Rhezette Fiel
Interior design by Caypeeline Casas

Published in the United States of America

ISBN: 978-1-62994-771-6
1. Fiction / Thrillers / Crime
2. Fiction / Thrillers / Suspense
13.10.18

DEDICATION

For Cindy
"You will never be lonely or friendless
as long as you have a book."

ACKNOWLEDGEMENT

James Tcherneshoff for being my personal photographer.

CHAPTER ONE

Rosie's tail bounced randomly about his hundred and ten pound frame as the black and tan German shepherd trotted down the muddy path. It was the first time in five days that the rain stopped falling from the Washington winter clouds. Humans smile, dogs do not. Nevertheless, John Beam swore his canine companion wore an ear-to-ear grin on his face. Master and mutt were happy to be outside, inhaling the cool, damp air.

Beam loved to study history, especially if it involved his favorite president, Theodore Roosevelt. He held the conservationist in such high esteem that he had named his black and tan companion Roosevelt. However, instead of calling him Roosevelt, the insurance underwriter shortened the pooch's name to Rosie most of the time. Only when the dog found mischief did he invoke a thunderous "Roosevelt!" to startle the dog back to reality.

For Beam, living on the tiny island in the Puget Sound was his fortress of solitude. Camano Island held a mysterious and shrouded air about it. Mist and fog perpetually shrouded the island in the winter. Island people gladly suffered through the ninety-minute commute to Seattle every day, just for the peace of living in woods, where broad winged bald eagles nested in the trees above their homes. Camano Island held its true charm in the summer, when the brilliant sun was the orb commanding the sky. During the winter, it was a different story. Instead of snow blanketing the forest like what was experienced in much of the state's interior, the coastal regions were doused with rain, mist, and fog making it the only "rain forest" in North America.

The ground was perpetually wet. The long winter walks through the damp forest ended with hiking boots caked with black mud and Rosie needing a good bath before being allowed back inside their home. Neither man nor beast cared, though. Beam regularly bought new hiking boots every two months, and Rosie patiently suffered through a dousing of cold water, just for the opportunity to romp in the forest and follow strange scents to their root. Rosie and Beam were best friends, just as a man and his dog should be.

Rosie trotted ahead of his master, darting in and out of the damp foliage, searching for unseen critters that left fresh traces. Beam often wondered what the black and tan canine searched for when he brought his big dog out to explore. It could have been one of a large array of animals. Normally it was a deer, fox, coyote, rabbit, woodchuck, or some sort of fowl. When Rosie locked onto a scent, he always wanted to find its source. This time was uniquely different from the many times Beam watched his dog track his prey. The scent Rosie followed baffled Beam. His dog was acting differently. Rosie sniffed the ground and then bounded down a steep embankment. The dog would rustle around a bit, come crashing out of the underbrush, and sprint back to the top of the hill. Beam sensed Roosevelt was trying to tell his friend something.

Over the last two years, Beam learned to understand how his dog communicated. He knew Rosie found something the dog wanted him to see. There were so many thickets where Rosie went that Beam believed he could not make his way through to discover what he had found. Rosie had probably found another deer carcass. John knew if he did not go and see what the pooch had discovered, he would be letting his friend down. Plus, he was curious about what captured the dog's attention.

Beam checked the ground to make sure it was firm enough to hold his weight, and cautiously inched his way down the hill through the thicket. Pine boughs, ferns, dead leaves, and rotting timber grabbed at his legs and ankles, slowing his trek. The dog waited at the bottom near a rotting log. "He found another dead deer," Beam breathed out, as he descended through the bramble. Rosie barked once, ordering his master to quicken his pace.

Beam cautiously approached the black shape. Only twenty paces away, Beam realized it was not a rotting log or a dead deer Rosie had found. Lying in the pine-bow-covered ravine was the naked body of a young, black woman, whose angelic face was spotted with cold raindrops. Beam snatched his cell phone from its holster and nervously stabbed in 9-1-1. There was nothing else he could do. One look at her pretty form confirmed she was no longer with the living.

The dispatcher called Deputy Monroe twenty-three minutes before his shift ended. For a day shift, he was busier than usual. He responded to three domestic disturbance complaints, arrested a local lawyer for DUI, served four subpoenas, and testified in court against a teenager running a bicycle theft ring. He wondered if it had anything to do with the full moon commanding the night sky.

Monroe started the day knowing he was pulling his fourth twelve-hour shift. His wife was home pregnant with their second child, and they needed the overtime money. Diapers and a new home were expensive. Their three-bedroom townhouse was quickly becoming too small for their needs.

The dispatcher apologized to Monroe before she gave him the assignment. Nancy Kard, the county's police and fire dispatcher for the last twenty-five years, had seen many young sheriffs cut their teeth as deputies. She subconsciously pondered their safety whenever she assigned them a call. Sometimes she saw one or two she really liked, and forwarded the more career-enhancing incidents to them. Nancy knew Deputy Monroe was planting his roots on the island, so she made sure he caught the better cases to prepare him for his life on the island, and to help him establish roots in the community. He was honest, happy, calm, and a real family man. She liked his kind of people.

It was not often Camano Island had a report of an unnatural death. Only three had been reported in the past five years. There was the thirty-something hunter who suffered a heart attack in the woods. The second was a scuba diver who panicked exploring Puget Sound's waters. He drowned in thirty feet of water. The most tragic involved a six-year-old girl chasing her kitten into the street. Both kitten and kid were crushed by a logging truck. Nevertheless, the appearance of a body dumped in the middle of the woods was something completely unexpected. Not to mention eerie.

Monroe drove his county-issued green 2006 Chevy Blazer, with a silver star emblazoned on its hood, doors, and roof. The powerful eight-cylinder engine bucked the truck when the deputy drove his foot down on the accelerator. Monroe needed to get to the site quickly. Cold drizzle fell upon the Washington earth. Soon, rain would start falling from the clouds washing valuable evidence into the rainforest's decay.

The truck's emergency lights threw red and blue flashes into the fine mist. The location was thirteen miles away, but the curvy country roads impeded his progress. Luckily, old lady Kard knew to dispatch crime scene technicians, an ambulance, and firefighters. It was lucky that she located a forensics team who was only twenty minutes away in Stanwood, conducting field training. Having the forensic team so close helped to capture clues at the scene, before evidence melted away with the rain.

Monroe spied the old man and his dog huddled underneath a mammoth pine tree. The pine boughs provided them a modicum of protection from the raindrops. He pulled up alongside and noticed the man's ashen face.

Mrs. Kard reported a guy walking his dog had discovered the body. He knew from his six years of experience and training that more times than not, the person making a report was involved. He had to be on his toes when he talked to the dog lover. The detectives assigned to the case would crucify him if he bungled the initial interview. After announcing his arrival at the scene over the radio to old-lady Kard, Monroe stepped down from his SUV, donned his neon orange rain slicker with "Sherriff" written on the back, and headed over to listen to the man's tale.

Deputy Monroe did not have to ask any questions to start. The man introduced himself as John Beam, who lived a mile down the road. In his excitement to tell the deputy what he had found, Beam kept gesturing with his hands towards the logging road. He quickly explained what he was doing and that he found a young girl dead in the woods.

After Beam finished his story, Monroe asked him more questions. "How did you know she was dead?"

"Because I couldn't see her breathing. Plus, she just looked dead," replied Beam.

The deputy machine-gunned his questioning: "What were you doing in the woods?" "What time did you find her?" "Was anyone else with you?" "Where is the body?" "Did you move her?" "What did you do after you found her?" "Did you know her?" It took less than a minute. The man told Monroe everything he knew. The last question was designed to throw Mr. Beam off his story, to determine if he had anything to do with the death. Monroe quickly realized Beam was telling the truth about taking his dog for a walk and stumbling upon the horrible discovery.

Another set of emergency flashing lights appeared at the entrance to the muddy road. A white van emblazoned with an Island County seal approached quickly. Inside sat two men who looked remarkably alike. Both sported sun-blond hair. The one on the right had his cut short just below the ears and pulled back over his scalp. The other let his grow down past his shoulders with its edges curling outwards. Besides that, the crime scene technicians were identical.

The two men in the van were Israel and Ishmael Colby. They were twin brothers, whose father had a love for all things nautical. He named his boys after characters in Stevenson's *Treasure Island* and Melville's *Moby Dick*. Both possessed the same passionate interest in forensic science. Their combined talents were renowned throughout the west coast forensic community. The duo was single-handedly responsible for the capture of a serial rapist preying on teenage boys in Seattle and who evaded capture for three years. The perpetrator was thorough in his attacks. The boys never saw his face, never heard his voice, and he always used condoms when he sodomized them. The two-brother team knew science eventually triumphed over most mysteries. Criminals always left traces when they committed a crime. The hard part was knowing what to look for, where to search, and connecting the dots. The rapist struck thirteen times in a thirty-seven month period. Parents were horrified to let their kids out alone.

The Colby twins patiently collected bits and pieces of evidence, researched each piece, looked for singularities, and put the puzzle together. The pervert turned out to be a landscaper. He picked his victims among the neighbors of his clients. The case was such a tough nut to crack because the attacker's pattern seemed random. His clients were scattered about the city and had no connections to one another. The Colby's tenacity proved overwhelming. Quickly convicted by a jury of his peers, the judge sentenced the pedophile to serve thirty years in a maximum-security prison. It was rumored he was being raped daily by the Aryan Brotherhood. Sometimes, justice is served.

The twins rolled up and parked next to Deputy Monroe's patrol truck. They immediately donned their fluorescent orange rain suits and asked the officer for a report.

"Not much yet, I just arrived a few minutes before you. This man is John Beam. He was walking his dog up the logging road and stumbled across a young African-American woman's body," replied the deputy sheriff. "I haven't seen the body yet. Beam says the body is a half mile up the muddy road and lying in a gully." He pointed towards the dirt path.

"So no one has been up the road since it's been reported?" inquired the short-haired Israel Colby. "That's good. I imagine you have more officers coming. Can you block off this road? We want the entire entryway blocked off. No vehicles can pass and muck up the tracks in the mud. We want to keep the scene as uncontaminated as possible."

"That's not a problem. Take a radio with you. I need to know if the girl is dead. I have an ambulance on the way, just in case," replied Deputy Monroe.

"Roger that. Ishmael is going to go look at the woman. I plan to scout around here." He motioned with his arms to encircle the surrounding area.

The brothers slipped black vests over their rain suits. The vest pockets housed instruments used to collect evidence at crime scenes. Most of the county's Crime Scene Units used standard evidence collection cases. The vests were their own creation. A professional quirk they developed. The twin towheads liked to have their material ready and at hand, instead of lugging around the heavy cases, or schlepping back to the van to retrieve special collection devices. This was especially important with the rain falling on the crime scene. The impending rain showers demanded haste, coupled with efficiency.

Before moving off, the brothers gathered at the foot of the logging road and discussed their collection scheme. Israel chose to canvass the road, hoping to isolate foot impressions, tire tracks, or animal traces on the pathway. He would look for telltale signs about who dumped the murdered girl in the isolated forest track. Meanwhile, Ishmael would carefully make his way towards the girl, determine if she was dead, take photographic evidence, and establish an evidence grid.

Both men carried nylon numbered flags. The twins used different colored pennants to distinguish who identified a piece of evidence. This came from working side by side at numerous crime scenes. Israel used red flags embroidered with black numbers. Ishmael's flags were yellow with red numbers.

Ishmael started out first. Deputy Monroe watched the technician intently, as the young man moved up the road, planting flags as he went. Monroe knew from working with the two men before that when more police officers showed up, the flag trail marked a path to follow without trampling over potentially valuable evidence.

Israel commenced his work at the lower left corner of the road and walked across the road. Reaching the other side, he walked down the road. Effectively, he executed a ladder search of the muddy road for any type of trace evidence. He worked fast. Every so often, Israel knelt down on the soggy ground, planted four red flags in a cross pattern, laid down a waterproof placard with a letter etched onto it, and snapped digital photos. Once finished, he recorded the picture's frame number, subject, time, GPS coordinates, and date in his logbook. The information logged would be used when they started the real analysis work back at their lab. It was a tedious process. Good forensic science takes time and patience.

Ishmael walked quickly up the logging road. Attached to his hat was a miniature digital video camera. The idea to attach a camera to his hat came from watching the Seattle Seahawks play. The referee had installed a tiny camera to his hat so ESPN could show football fans exactly what he saw when he made a call. For the forensic scientist, it allowed him to later study a crime scene for evidence he may have overlooked during the collection process. The hat-cam was critical in today's work, when Mother Nature threatened to ruin the crime scene.

They had to work quickly. Taking as much photographic evidence as possible helped them in the long run. Making his way up the path, Ishmael noticed boot prints, dog prints, deer tracks, coyote tracks, and tire tracks in the muddy road surface. Rosie the dog, he surmised, made the dog tracks. The tire tracks were not from a single vehicle. There were tracks upon tracks. It was getting more difficult to ascertain which tracks were fresh and which were old.

Ishmael told himself he did not need to focus his concentration on the road. His brother was on top of his game. He needed to find the body and process it and the immediate surroundings. The forest became thicker and thicker during his hike up the road. His first thought was that unless there was another path leading to the crime site, the killer drove this patch of road to the site where the victim lay.

The man with the dog said he found the body on the right side of the road in a shallow gully. If the dog had not found the body, the man would have walked right by it. However, he said a large stand of Douglas fir trees marked the corpses' locale. Beam told him to look directly across from the trees and down the hill. The girl lay at the bottom. Reaching the trees, Ishmael peered through the mist of the rain-dampened forest. He noticed the bramble pushed down from its normal erect posture. The tech scanned the area, planted yellow flags, and anchored the end of a crime tape roll to a flag. After snapping digital images of the site, Ishmael slowly hiked down the embankment, streaming the crime scene tape as he went. After two or three steps, he scanned the area side to side, up and down, and turned in a circle, so his hat-cam captured the scene.

The only plants he could make out being disturbed were those that recently were forced downward. The crime scene investigator continued planting flags and taking pictures. Whenever he found a footprint, he planted a flag marking its location. Ishmael recorded its exact position with GPS coordinates and took more photos. Just like his brother, he would eventually measure the footprint's length. That would have to wait for the time being. His first priority was to locate the dead girl.

The embankment leveled off thirty yards down the slope. The younger Colby, younger since he was born thirty-six seconds before his brother breached his mother's womb, sighted the victim. His immediate reaction was to rush to the girl to see if she was breathing. He resisted the temptation. If he did not, he might trample critical pieces of evidence into oblivion. It would take an extra five seconds to map the route he wanted to traverse to the girl. He stepped forward with stealth and with purpose.

Her long, delicate, ebony fingers caught his attention first. Inching forward, her body came into full view. From her waxen appearance, Ishmael knew life had exited her body. *She's more girl than woman*, thought the investigator, as he panned the scene slowly with his camera. From a distance, any sure signs showing brutalization were absent. Rather, she was dumped to remain lost and to decay, along with the rest of the fallen leaves and tree limbs.

He acknowledged her death was far from her peaceful appearance. It was not up to him to determine how she died. That job belonged to the coroner. His job was to process the evidence and to assist in apprehending the person responsible for dumping her in the woods, where forest animals and bugs could feast upon her lifeless corpse.

Ishmael heard voices coming from police officers, detectives, and the emergency response crew following his flag trail. He would have to work quickly, because he could hold off the detectives for only so long. They wanted to get on with their work as well. And he knew detectives sometimes didn't like working with crime scene investigators too much. Hopefully, he and Israel would get matched up with a detective who appreciated their skills and the intricate science involved.

"Colby! Where are you?" beckoned an unseen caller.

"Down here! The victim is not alive. Send the EMS personnel back before they trample over anything else," ordered Ishmael.

"Give me ten more minutes to survey the scene and then you can come down."

"Okay, this is Detective Hendricks from the Seattle PD."

"What else do you need?" questioned the unseen plain-clothes cop.

"Ah…it's Hendricks…that is a good thing," whispered the younger Colby. "He's a guy we can work with. Thank God we didn't get a rookie detective."

"Nothing down here, thanks…all I need is time. When you come down, make sure you follow the marked trail. Where is my brother? Do you see him?"

"He is almost here. Another five minutes and he'll reach us," replied Hendricks. "What do you have?"

Rain beaded on Ishmael's rain suit. He snapped photos of the immediate area and the girl's body. There was not any blood or signs of a struggle. Nevertheless, it was obvious it was a homicide. His initial assessment led him to believe the African-American female was laid to rest there. Not unceremoniously dumped following her murder.

He reported his findings to the detective on the hill above the site. His best approximations concluded the victim was between nineteen and twenty-five. Ishmael judged her height to be about five foot six. She weighed close to 120 pounds. Thin, but not overly so. Athletic was a better description. She had runner's legs. Her hair was stylishly short, soaked from the rain, and unkempt. She was not dirty, except for a few leaves lying on her naked brown body. Her legs lay side by side. Her left arm extended down her side. The right limb seemed to reach towards the sanctity and safety of the woods. Despite being African-American, her lips were a harsh shade of gray. It happened when a dead body lay prone for a while. The heart no longer pumped blood through her arterial highways. As a result, gravity pulled the blood to the body's lowest point. In this case, it pooled in her backside.

She is a great looking girl. She really took care of her body. What a shame. Obviously, the killer saw something he really liked in her. If he did not, he would not have stalked her, the forensic specialist thought.

Ishmael stepped closer, searched the immediate area around her, and found a shoe imprint near the body. Ishmael staked the imprint with flags, measured it, and documented it with photos. A broken branch in the nearby woods caught his eye. He would have to remember to investigate it after he turned the body over to the police. For now, he concentrated on the girl. He knew she was dead less than twenty hours, because rigor mortis had not set in yet.

He wanted to place plastic bags around the girl's hands and feet to preserve any DNA evidence under her nails. Softly lifting her right wrist, the criminal scientist discovered something curious. Her wrists were gummy and tacky. The murderer used tape to bind her.

Reaching into his vest, he pulled out a clear plastic Ziploc bag. He slipped a bag over each hand, making sure he protected the glue residue on her wrist. Ishmael did the same to her feet, and did another once-over of the scene, to make sure he did not miss anything. Nothing captured his attention. It was time to bring the troops in to help search the surrounding area.

"Detective Hendricks, it's okay to come down now," yelled the crime scene analyst. "Only bring one or two people with you. I have to search the crime scene's outer perimeter."

"Okay, I'm bringing down one policeman and the coroner," replied the lean detective sergeant.

Hendricks was known throughout the Seattle Police Department for being thorough, fair, and extremely competent in his police work. Most of the force believed he would make Lieutenant next year, Captain in another five, and Chief of

Detectives ten years after that. He was the type of leader people liked to follow.

Sergeant Hendricks started down the hill, following Colby's yellow flag trail. A water-resistant blue hiking coat protected him from the elements. His mountain boots provided the traction he needed to traverse the slippery slope. He learned early in his career to wear comfortable clothing. Wearing the rugged gear allowed him to stay warm and dry during the winter rains. Plus, if the occasional perp ran away, he could still keep up without having to worry about cumbersome clothing or horrible shoes hampering his ability. Running three miles a day helped, too.

The detective never grew accustomed to homicide scenes. He told himself the first time his empathy or compassion for a victim or their family disappeared; it was time to quit the force. The feelings he felt made him effective at his job. He wanted to solve the case. He wanted the victim's family to receive the closure they yearned for desperately. Most of all, he wanted the victim's soul to rest in peace. Hendricks did not think of himself as overly religious, but he firmly believed there was something beyond man's terrestrial existence. If the death was unnatural, the crime had to be solved, to allow the dead person's soul to be released from its agony of being murdered. This was not a feeling he ever shared with anyone, nor did he ponder it too often. It sat in his brain, which he gladly accepted. It made him more human.

Just like Colby, the six-foot-two police officer approached the scene cautiously, with his instincts fully tuned. Approaching a few steps at a time, he stopped and surveyed the area for things out of the ordinary. Homicides discovered outside proved the most difficult to solve. Nature had a tendency to cleanse critical evidence away quickly. Now that it was raining, nature multiplied its efforts to thwart his study of the crime scene. He worked briskly.

Hendricks liked collaborating with the two brothers. Knowing they were extremely competent, though their twenty-something age embodied a different first impression, he learned to implicitly trust their judgment. There was no need for him to take photos or instruct them on how the crime scene was processed. They knew exactly what to do without his interference.

Reaching the body, the girl's beauty made Hendricks pause. She was not a very dark African-American. She was more like half Black and half something else, maybe Asian. Whatever she was, she received the best traits of her races.

Hendricks spotted Ishmael, who briefed the homicide detective on what he knew so far.

"She is a nineteen to twenty-five-year-old woman, with no apparent cause of death. There are no marks of physical confrontation, rape, beating, or mutilation." He continued after catching a breath. "She was placed here. She was not dumped. Notice the way her legs are positioned together. If the murderer wanted to show disrespect, he would have tossed her body down the embankment. No, this murderer had a passion for his victim. Almost remorse for doing what he did."

Ishmael let the thought sink into Hendricks's mind before he continued. "However, she was bound. There is a sticky residue on her wrists and ankles. Tape was used to bind her limbs. I'll be a hundred percent sure after Israel and I analyze the residue I found."

Detective Hendricks nodded his head, showing Ishmael that he understood what he said, and was waiting for the rest of his assessment. Hendricks' reputation rested on his willingness to be patient.

"There are a few footprints that Israel and I need to analyze. Obviously, there are prints of the guy who found her, but there is another set leading back through that patch of woods," Ishmael said, as he pointed. "I want to follow the tracks before the rain comes down anymore, okay?"

"If you're done here, go ahead," replied the detective. "When can I expect your report?"

"Once Israel and I are finished here and we get back to the lab, we can give you a preliminary report within twenty-four hours."

"Thanks. I will meet you and your brother shortly to discuss what he found. Leave me a trail of flags through the woods, too. I want to walk the path too."

That was why the Colby brothers liked working with Hendricks. He let them do their job. However, Hendricks liked to review the crime scene himself. Both brothers had to admit they perceived a crime scene differently than the police officers. Putting the pieces together was Hendricks' job after all, and he did it well. The crime scene investigator's science mixed well with the detective's street education. It was an effective combination to solve crimes.

Detective Hendricks gazed upon the lifeless, yet pretty, corpse. He wanted to get inside the killer's head, to understand what the murdering beast wanted to express. Murder contained emotion. Some were extremely cold, brutal, and ugly. Others were somehow peacefully serene in the killer's eyes. A person could gain insight into a murderer's motives, mind-set, and emotional well-being, simply by studying how he left his victims.

This unknown killer cared for his victim. It was a crime of passion between two lovers, or the killer was transferring pent-up emotions through this girl, who served as his conduit for him to express his anger. Murders ultimately boiled down to raw anger and rage. The way she died was by suffocation, strangulation, or poisoning. The lack of blood or bruising, signs of torture, or battering, ruled out all other forms of death from the equation.

Like Ishmael, Hendricks deduced she was carried there. It was clear the killer did not expect discovery so quickly. He picked his dumping ground carefully. The surrounding trees, the soft gurgling of a nearby stream, and the seclusion made it a peaceful resting place in the killer's mind. The killer chose it because he wanted his victim to rest well for all eternity.

Hendricks noted the woman was not buried. The architect behind her murder did not have the luxury of time. He wanted to get rid of her, but in a place where she would not be quickly discovered. If not for the nose of Rosie, the curious canine, the girl's remains might never have been found at all. The police got lucky. A month from now, the rainforest and wild animals would have left nothing for them to examine except a rotting pile of bones.

Hendricks crouched and examined her features more closely. Just as Ishmael observed, she was in extremely good physical condition, besides the obvious fact of her being dead. This girl worked out and took care of herself.

Leaning in, the detective gently lowered the woman's jaw to expose her teeth. Her teeth were in great shape. Straight, white, and healthy. From these few observations, Hendricks further concluded the woman came from a middle- to upper-class family. She probably attended college, or worked in a white-collar office.

Shifting his focus, he observed her hands through the clear evidence bags. The girl kept her fingernails cut short. Most women working in offices keep their nails short, so they can use the computer keyboard efficiently and quickly. This lent credence to his initial observations.

His forty-five years made the rise from his perch over the body slow. Hendricks was getting to the point where his body was starting to send him messages. He was not as limber as he was twenty years ago. Upright, he resurveyed the scene. The plain-clothes cop had no way of telling if a sexual crime had occurred. The coroner's report would shed light on that subject. Hopefully, the report would tell him who the girl was. There was a 30-70 percent chance she had fingerprints on file somewhere. The FBI's new updated database combined fingerprints from all fifty states and American territorial criminal databases, Department of Defense records, driver license files, school records post-1992, and employees who were required to have background checks accomplished for their jobs. The only good thing that came out of the 9/11 tragedy was it was easier to keep track of people. If Hendricks had his way, the entire nation would possess national identification cards. It surely would make his job easier.

Finished with the site examination, he jotted his observations in a black notebook. The department had issued him an electronic tablet, but he seldom used it, except for playing chess and keeping up on his email. He preferred the old-fashioned method, paper and pencil. It let him flip quickly between the pages and let him mentally outline his thoughts.

He waved for the coroner to collect the body for transport to the morgue. Hendricks started following Ishmael's flag trail into the woods. Every twenty feet he noticed Colby had posted another cross-like flag diagram. Encased within the imaginary lines of the flag cross was a single shoeprint.

A good thing about a rainforest was everything left a track. Small birds, coyotes, rabbits, deer, mountain lions, and people left a trail in the decaying forest. Under the tree's green canopy, Hendricks scrawled more notes in his pad.

The footprints were deepest in the heel as they approached the body. The footprints leading away were shallower. Whoever made the tracks supported a heavier weight as he went into the woods than when he came out from it. This trail surely was the one used by the murderer to dispose of his victim.

The Colby boys, with their scientific bag of tricks, would give him a composite of the culprit he was now pursuing. From their measurements, the young mad scientists were able to determine an approximate height and weight of the murderer. Sometimes, if the criminal had an extraordinary gait, they could determine if the man they were searching for was a couch potato or someone active. They normally did this by measuring the distances between footprints. Over many cases and after much evidence collected, crime scene analysts could determine the probable inseam of their target. Based on this, it was basic mathematics to postulate how tall an individual was. Most of the time, people who were not physically active took much smaller steps than those who liked being on the go. Therefore, naturally, it would add more evidence in building the profile of their subject.

After examining the corpse, the forty-something cop madly craved a cigarette. He had quit the habit ten years ago, but discovered he desired the comfort given from puffing on tobacco after he saw a homicide victim. It provided him a bit of relief in stressful situations. Resisting the urge, he practiced relaxation techniques to settle his mind. Halting, he shut his eyes. His ears and nose took over for his eyes. Hendricks listened and tasted the forest sounds and scents. In his mind, he identified everything he heard and smelled. Raindrops landing on tree leaves. A small animal scurrying in the brush to his left. Wind whispering through the trees. The technique worked. The nicotine craving disappeared, and his focus returned to the horrible job at hand.

Stooping over one of the best tracks left by the culprit, Hendricks noticed the shoe's tread design. It appeared the shoe trace mimicked the pattern on hiking or work boots. The killer's profile had begun to take shape.

He continued down the path until the sloped terrain leveled off and intersected the logging trail. There, Hendricks found the Colby brothers deep in conversation over their respective discoveries. They both turned and watched the police officer emerge from the wooded cover.

"That is some path our quarry took through the woods," Hendricks stated. "He certainly wanted to hide his accomplishments. I bet he did not count on us finding his dastardly deed so quickly. Thank the Lord for the intrepid John Beam and his German shepherd Roosevelt," he commented, as he hiked to where the crime scene investigators stood. "What have you two discovered that I haven't seen so far?"

"Besides our perp weighing approximately one hundred and seventy pounds, he stands roughly five foot six to ten inches tall, and is in good shape," Ishmael reported. "He drove here in a truck, a sports utility vehicle, or a van. Only one vehicle has recently been down the road to this point."

Israel chimed in seamlessly after his brother. "I have some good tire track photos and casts of the vehicle's wheels." He displayed the photos through the digital camera window to the detective. "I'll narrow down the type of vehicle in three or four days, once we get back to the lab. We got lucky on this one. If we had arrived an hour later, we could not have collected as much as we did. Washington rain has a way of making things disappear."

"What's your theory about our victim?" The officer was busy making more notes in his worn notepad.

"Detective Hendricks…when are you going to migrate to the twenty-first century?" chided Ishmael. "You know, you can store a lot more info in an iPad than you can in that caveman notebook of yours."

"I'll get rid of this notepad and switch to the digital age when you two get respectable haircuts," replied Hendricks with a sly smile, knowing his notebook was quite safe from ever being thrown in the trash.

Returning to the subject at hand, Ishmael took the stage. "We think she knew her assailant. We did not find any signs of a struggle or defensive wounds. The County Coroner will determine her time and manner of death. Nevertheless, we can tell the killer restrained her with tape. Our guess right now is her assailant used duct tape. It is strong as hell, and it is almost impossible to break free if the legs and arms are bound. That's why we bagged her hands and feet."

"Yeah, I noticed you covered more of her hands and feet than you normally do. Our perp definitely knows his stuff, though. He removed all of her clothes, left her in this desolation, and probably would be lost until the forest was logged again. We got to her just in time, where we could possibly get her identification from her fingerprints and a photo. Make sure you two spend some time on her dental work. She is not a crack whore or a prostitute, picked up from the street at random. Her teeth tend to make me believe she was a college girl or came from a good family. When I get back, I will canvas the missing person's reports. Someone is going to report this pretty girl has gone missing."

The three-man investigative team charted their course back to where the logging trail met the paved country road. Each walked in silence enveloped in his own thoughts. The coroner's team loaded the black-bagged body into the plain white van. It was now well past lunch, and by the time the body got to the county morgue, the day shift would be ready to leave for home.

Hendricks made a mental note to call the county coroner to accelerate the autopsy's completion. Quick answers allowed Hendricks to pursue a hot trail. He did not want it to go cold. Once it did, it became near impossible to solve the crime. He needed information fast, and lots of it. He would take over where Rosie the German shepherd left off.

CHAPTER TWO

Onboard a navy vessel, a whistle controls all the action. There are special tunes a ship's boatswain's mate pipes to call the crew to eat. He pipes a tune when the captain wants to speak to the crew. His instrument sounds when the ship's company starts cleaning the mighty warship. The evening prayer recited by the ship's chaplain is even prefaced by a shrill tune from the bos'n pipe. Using tones instead of speech has been a tradition in the United States Navy ever since its birth in a candlelit chamber in Philadelphia in 1775. The fledgling country's new laws and customs came from its English roots. So too did its naval mannerisms.

At sea, time is a variable, constantly monitored and announced. Every half hour in a four-hour span, a single ring from the ship's bell signified another thirty minutes passing into extinction. It told the men when to shoot a sextant star fix and when the crew changed the watch. Most of all, subconsciously, it reminded the sailors they worked as a team instead of as individuals.

This morning was no different onboard the United States Navy Aegis destroyer, the *USS ILORETA*. Many of the traditions observed in the seventeenth and eighteenth century continue into the twenty-first century. Instead of using wind to propel themselves through the oceans, the modern warship uses immense jet engines to turn its cambered six-bladed propellers. Instead of using cannonballs and gunpowder stuffed down the muzzle of cast iron cannons, the destroyer fires automated guns. A destroyer armed with a powerful radar, carrying missiles capable of striking the enemy hundreds of miles away, and possessing rapid firing guns engaging an enemy force ten miles down range is a vast improvement from firing a close quarters cannonball every two minutes at an enemy warship that had to be closer than a thousand yards.

Naval tradition is still tradition. It is the glue keeping the nautical service potent.

Without prompting, the seasoned tattooed bosun's mate picked up the microphone that would carry his tune throughout the entire warship's steel structure and played his high-pitched melody for a full minute. Before he finished the first ten seconds of the high-pitched melody, the ship's crew sprang to action. Their coordinated reactions resembled bees swarming in the hive. No one needed direction about where to go or what to do. Eighteen months of intense training and six months' sailing through hostile seas seasoned the crew to react without thinking. Each sailor knew his or her duty and carried it out efficiently.

The tune being piped signaled the crew to man their sea-and-anchor detail stations. On the bridge, the quartermasters plotted the ship's position every three minutes. The destroyer's normal watch team turned over their positions to seasoned officers and enlisted sailors more accustomed to sailing in perilous waters. In the engine room, the ship's engineers started redundant turbine engines, oil pumps, and electrical generators. In the Combat Information Center, operational specialists plotted their navigational track by using the vessel's surface search radars. Every station backed up another station. Redundancy kept the ship from running aground.

On the forecastle and fantail, sailors in starched white uniforms pulled three-inch thick mooring lines onto the main deck from hidden storage spaces below deck. Their efforts were so honed; dirt or grime soiled not a single white uniform. They wore their dress white uniforms for the most special and momentous occasion of the deployment overseas. *ILORETA* was finally returning home after serving in the Persian Gulf and Indian Ocean for five months.

Smiles beamed from every face. Laughter and singing told the joy the crew was feeling. They were proud of their accomplishments. Now, it was their time to receive the hearty martial welcome awaiting them. It would be a traditional naval welcoming staged on the pier for a naval ship returning from battle.

Wives, husbands, children, parents, grandparents, girlfriends, and boyfriends anxiously awaited their return. Many brought their children to see their long-lost Mommy or Daddy race down the brow to scoop them up and shower them with love once again. The media was there, too. San Diego was a naval town after all. One out of four people living in San Diego owed their livelihood to the United States Navy. They either worked on the sprawling naval base, worked as a private contractor supporting the nautical operations, or were part of the service sector, gleaning the tertiary benefits from having the Pacific Fleet stationed in Southern California. It was big news when one of San Diego's own returned from afar.

Chief Boatswain's Mate Andrew Sherman was just as thrilled about being home as the rest of the crew. Not expecting any lavish welcome ashore by loved ones, Sherman was anxious to throw off the sheepskin clothing he wore for the past eleven months. He would become Agent Andrew Sherman once again. Ever since the Navy Criminal Investigative Service discovered a plan by some of the ship's crew to smuggle large quantities of heroin from Thailand, Agent Sherman of the Federal Bureau of Investigation worked undercover as a sailor to thwart their reckless ambition.

Thailand had become the main rest and relaxation port for many United States' naval ships needing a break from The Global War on Terrorism. Cheap booze, countless brothels, pristine white sandy beaches, inexpensive hotels, and spicy food helped sleep-deprived and overworked sailors feel human again. Sex was just a matter of going to a bar and picking a partner from a live menu paraded in front of them. The soft sandy beaches with a warm ocean to swim in made it a perfect place for sailors to unwind from the rigors of being at sea. Thailand was an excellent place to get illegal drugs, too.

For now, all Sherman wanted to do was to get off the ship and make his report to his superiors. Stationing himself near the anchor windlass, he still played his part as the ship's Bosun. Tattooed on both arms, darkened by the countless hours of toiling in the scorching Arabian sun, and a physique hardened by manual labor made him a sailor few wanted to challenge. It also made him the ideal candidate for the assignment. After his initial six-year enlistment in the Navy as a boatswain's mate, he went to college and studied Criminal Behavior. He defrayed the educational cost by staying active in the Navy Reserves. The undercover assignment was tailor-made for the FBI Agent.

Typically, narcotic rings were the responsibility of the Drug Enforcement Agency. However, the government's law enforcement and intelligence realignment after the 9/11 terrorist attacks forced the agencies to work together. His naval experiences made him the ideal choice for the covert operation. When the mission was assigned to him, all he did was don the uniform he used to wear, deposit his FBI badge in his dresser drawer, walk out the front door, and report for duty onboard the ship.

The ship's captain was the only person onboard who knew his real identity. He never had a conversation with the ship's CO about the mission during the deployment until recently. Not once did Captain Smythe let on that he knew of the agent's identity until two weeks before they planned to return home to San Diego, when Sherman met with the captain to discuss his annual military performance evaluation.

The meeting started out smoothly. The captain discussed the sailor's performance. Sherman had gained the respect of the sailors under his charge and he led by example. Exactly the way the Navy expected their senior enlisted members to perform.

"You really came aboard and squared your division away, Chief," announced the old man during the meeting. What really blew Sherman away was when the captain rose, shut his state-room door, sat down at his desk, and plainly asked, "Chief…so… have you found out who is smuggling drugs onboard my ship yet?"

The bluntness momentarily knocked Sherman off his guard. He focused his eyes on Captain Smythe, while a small lump magically appeared in his throat.

Smythe continued speaking, knowing he had caught the agent unawares. "Did you really think I was not aware of you and your mission? The military's culture may have changed a bit over the years, but we still honor the notion that a ship's captain must know everything going on in his command. The commodore briefed me on your mission a few days before you arrived."

Searching for something to say and before he could get it out of his arid lips, the captain continued: "I was told because it was necessary. Someone had to watch your back while you were executing your mission. Sending someone out into no-man's land is a cruel thing to do. Your superiors thought it best that you were unencumbered to do your mission. You needed a safety net if things went south. Plying the oceans deep is a lonely and dangerous business. 'Always best to have a friend in hostile waters' is my motto. Plus, if you cannot trust the captain of his own ship with this type of information, why should he be made the captain in the first place? Don't you agree?"

Agent Sherman found his tongue. "Captain," he bluntly started. "Your ship is transporting two tons of pure grade heroin. The dope is stored in your aft supply rooms." Thinking the statement would stun the salty officer, Sherman watched for an emotional response. None came.

He continued. "Your supply officer, supply department senior chief, and a first class petty officer received the drugs from a gang in Thailand, just prior to our departure from Phuket. The dope was loaded onboard, with the rest of the supplies your ship received, while the crew was on liberty. They have been planning it for fourteen months, through a member of the senior chief's family, who lives in Thailand."

"Go on," remarked Smythe, steadfast and emotionless.

"That much pure heroin is worth millions on the American and Canadian streets. They intend on removing it from the ship this weekend, while the bulk of the crew is on leave," reported Sherman. "For four months I didn't have any luck, and I was starting to believe our intelligence was bogus. Then, when we were in Thailand, I noticed the senior chief supervising a bunch of crates being craned onboard your vessel. The crates resembled those used to bring spare parts onboard for the helos. I would have never thought twice about it, until I realized there were not any aviation crewmembers helping him. Typically, if aviation parts come onboard, the helicopter mechanics swarm over them, to make sure they received everything they requisitioned. Not this time. It was just the senior chief. The boxes were stowed quickly, before anyone noticed what was going on."

Smythe nodded his head, signaling the agent to continue his tale.

"I found where the boxes were stored, waited until we departed for sea, and broke into the supply storeroom. Sure enough, when I peeled back the crate's lids, there was the dope. There are eight heroin-filled crates sitting back aft, waiting for distribution in the United States.

"It was a good scheme if you stopped and thought about it. Customs officials perform minimal inspections on U.S. warships returning from overseas. With the ship practically deserted after the first couple of days upon returning home, it gave the three sailors a perfect way to smuggle drugs into the country and make a lot of money. Their plan is to offload the junk by crane to a truck late Thursday afternoon."

"How do you know the three sailors you've identified are the criminals?" inquired the ship's skipper.

"That was easy. Once I figured something was askew, I contacted my FBI contacts on the beach. They followed the paper trail back to the chief's cousin in Thailand. The Thai police arrested the Thai man and interrogated him most effectively. He quickly spilled the story. You see…Thailand has much stricter drug laws than the United States. Once he learned he was going to a Thai prison for a very, very long time, he was more than cooperative. Prisons in Thailand are not the Hiltons we provide our criminals."

"I want to be there when they are arrested. What's your plan for that?"

"Captain, it's already arranged. We have surveillance teams established ashore. We want to follow the heroin to its ultimate destination. I have installed GPS tracking devices on the crates. Besides tracking it electronically from an eye in space, a team will track the shipment on the ground. The goal is to seize as many in the ring as possible. It is too dangerous to take you with us when the arrests occur; however, we can have you at the station when we book them. How does that sound, sir?"

Captain Smythe mulled over the agent's recommendations. Navy captains were used to being decisive and not used to being told "no." They make so many decisions a day, ranging from the most inconsequential to some having immediate and life-impacting effects. Smythe decided quickly.

"It's a sound plan, Chief," using Sherman's naval title, instead of calling him "Agent." He made a mental note to make sure he started the process of giving BMC Sherman an award from the ship and U.S. Navy. To him, Sherman would always be an *ILORETA* crewmember. Having crewmembers who were traitors and criminals did not bode well in his mind. The treachery was committed under his watch. If it had not been for good intelligence, having the crime go undiscovered would have been an even greater atrocity. Without an inside guy like Sherman, he may never have found out a crime was being committed on his ship. Smythe admitted it was a clever plan, using his warship to smuggle drugs. Nevertheless, it left a bad taste in his mouth. His three sailors became traitors and criminals for the sake of money. The allure of making a small fortune overnight supplanted their sense of right from wrong. Once again, greed and evil overcame the power of good. Some humans were so weak. However, truth always breaks out in the end.

Watching the special agent from the destroyer's bridge while the ship made its way to port, Captain Smythe recalled the meeting with Sherman. He was anxious to see the expressions on the three traitorous sailors' faces when they were captured and booked. First things first, though. Smythe snapped his attention back to the destroyer when a young lieutenant saluted and reported all preparations for entering port were completed. The officer was twenty years junior to the salty captain, but the officer had confidence of youth, and knew when to ask for advice. Officers like that would go far in the naval service.

"Very well. Pick up the harbor pilot and order the boatswain's mate of the watch to announce to the crew to man the rails," ordered the CO.

"Aye-aye, Captain," was the only reply necessary, as the Officer of the Deck turned and carried out the orders quickly.

USS ILORETA made her grand entrance into San Diego harbor. The ship churned ahead at ten knots navigating the channel to the home of the United States Pacific Fleet. A harbor patrol boat, with a sailor manning a machine gun, escorted the ship through a throng of pleasure craft and sailboats, which filled the narrow channel to welcome the crew home from war. A slight fog encapsulated the low-lying regions of the harbor. In no time, the hot Southern California sun would dissipate the mist.

ILORETA's crew smartly assembled at the sides of the ship. Normal protocol called for the crew to remain motionless at the position of attention. Arriving home from war was different. It was a time for celebration. The sailors strained their eyes against the rising sun in search of familiar faces. Faces brightened as the crew found their loved ones waving frantically to their returning heroes. The Pacific Fleet's Navy band floated musical notes across the bay, creating an upbeat stage for the ship's long-anticipated arrival.

ILORETA's engines churned the harbor's muddy bottom with its strong propellers. The nine thousand-ton ship inched towards the pier to moor on American soil for the first time in six months. Mooring lines were heaved to sailors on the pier at the command of the officer of the deck. Anyone who had ever served aboard a large ship knew how dangerous mooring evolutions were. In a moment's notice, a strong breeze could apply a deadly force upon the ship, and stretch its mooring lines to the point of separation. Or, the ship's steering hydraulics could fail, leaving the ship rudderless and adrift. *ILORETA*'s motions were fluid. It glided alongside the pier, using a combination of rudder and engine changes.

The captain took great pride in his crew. During the two short years he commanded the warship, he relentlessly exercised his officers and sailors seamanship skills. Normally, he used tug boats to moor the ship. Today, he wanted his officers to demonstrate their expertise in handling an American destroyer, in full view of the military brass, press, and their families. The lack of tugboats assisting the ship would go unnoticed by the bulk of the crowd. However, the officers and enlisted sailors who came to greet the ship certainly noticed the change in paradigm. Smythe had his ship's nominee for the Junior Officer of Year giving the helm orders to bring the ship into port. The destroyer squadron's commodore was watching, and he knew that ship-handling prowess was the main event in the stiff competition. Demonstrating that his chosen officer could bring a ship into port unassisted was a big feather in the young man's cap. An *ILORETA* warrior would win the coveted Squadron Seamanship Trophy today.

When all of *ILORETA*'s mooring lines were made fast, the engines were stopped and powered down. A heavy metal brow was lowered into place amidships. Commodore Perry, a fifth-generation naval officer, came aboard and happily greeted the captain and his crew. Knowing they were eager to go on a much-needed respite, the commodore kept his comments short, to "Welcome Home, *ILORETA*."

Captain Smythe nodded to the vessel's senior enlisted man, Command Master Chief Hickey, who took charge of the crew and dismissed them from their military duties for a much needed and well earned respite. Following tradition, the first off the ship were the sailors whose wives gave birth while they were out to sea. The new babies and young mothers waited anxiously at the bottom of the brow for their fathers to gaze upon their child's face for the very first time. Sixteen sailors hustled down the metal steps to embrace the new additions to their families. Fast on their heels were the rest of the crew, except those chosen to stay behind to man the ship while the rest of the crew was on leave and liberty. Like any other naval vessel, the ship breathed and demanded constant attention. So, the crew elected to hold a lottery to determine who would leave first and who would stay behind. The sailors going ashore cleared away, quickly carrying their sea bags and numerous gifts purchased overseas. Then the tide of people reversed, as family members came onboard to welcome home those left behind to tend to the ship.

The pier rapidly emptied of spectators and sailors. Families wanted their husbands, wives, boyfriends, girlfriends, sons, and daughters home so they could start catching up on six months' lost time. Those who went to sea as pilgrims returned seasoned sailors and accomplished warriors who knew how to work and fight. They launched their missiles against the enemy. They captured pirates trafficking in human slaves. They eliminated terror-ists attempting to sneak through their blockades. They showed their country's strength, honor, and fortitude throughout the Pacific Rim and Middle East. Now, each carried their own sea-faring stories home. None would ever again take for granted what America truly had to offer.

The last to leave was Captain Smythe. His wife and kids sauntered aboard to welcome him home. His mission was com-plete. He had done his job. The captain would be transferring to a desk job at the Pentagon in two months. He left satisfied, knowing he trained his crew well. His reward for his hard efforts was returning home without losing a single soul. What remained was simple. For the next month, the ship would do little else except minor maintenance. Following the post-deployment leave period, he planned to prepare the ship to turn it over to her new commanding officer. But, before he altered his focus, there was one last task to complete. Captain Smythe wanted to witness the three traitorous sailors who dared to use his decorated vessel to smuggle death into his beloved country. While his wife herded their five kids off the ship, the CO glanced in Chief Sherman's direction. Sherman was one of the few who volunteered to stay aboard the *ILORETA* when she returned home. Everyone knew he was not a married man. He told those who asked that he was an only child to long dead parents. No one suspected he wanted to stay onboard to watch the only other three sailors who volun-teered to stay on the ship. The crates loaded with the heroin sat on the flight deck, waiting transfer ashore. There they sat without anyone, except him, the captain, and the three criminals knowing what was stored in the wooden crates.

Sherman caught the captain's vision and saluted smartly, silently wishing his commanding officer farewell as the CO left the ship. The undercover agent quickly shifted his eyes from the captain to the crates. Smythe recognized the agent's signal in his mind's eye, but gave no other recognition than that. The two had worked out a plan earlier that would summon the captain for the drug peddler's arrest. The CO returned the salute and marched off the ship, hearing four distinct tolls on the ship's bell, followed by a single chime as the quarterdeck watch announced, "*ILORETA* departing" over the general announcing circuit. Soon, his brief stint commanding an American Man-of-War would end. The ride was too short, Smythe thought.

It was ironic that BMC Sherman's duties for the rest of the afternoon included making the crates holding the drugs ready for transfer ashore. He noticed Storekeeper First Class Lopez hovering about the area, keeping vigil on the illegal cargo.

The crane lowered chains to lift the crates up and off the ship. A flatbed tracker-trailer rig waited to receive the cargo. It was unknown if the truck driver was involved, so the FBI planned to pick him up after he delivered his load.

The crates were bound for a warehouse on the other side of the base. So many crates, boxes, packages, and stores arrived at the warehouses every day. Each package was quickly cataloged and stowed according to the shipping instructions and follow-on destination. The crates were to be stored overnight in the warehouse and shipped to another loading facility in the morning. Sherman's team ashore inspected the logistics paperwork to determine the cargo's destination. All Sherman could do now was to wait and to do his naval duties.

Captain Smythe rose from the chair perched next to his backyard pool after he received the text message 'batteries release' on his cell phone from a blocked number. It was the reckoning moment for his disloyal sailors. He knew Sherman had sent the message to summon him to the base brig. They had prearranged this signal days before. By now, the drugs were off base en-route to their final distribution point. *Hopefully,* Smythe thought, *the FBI was*

able to capture the whole drug ring. This was not how he envisioned ending his first ship command tour.

The graying naval officer walked into the dull tan building housing the navy brig. Military and civilian police officers worked without regard for the uniformed naval commander. They were used to having officers picking up sailors from the jail cells. He approached a bulletproof glass window where a Marine police corporal was sitting.

"I'm Commander Raymond Smythe, Captain of the *USS ILORETA*," he stated to the corporal, who stood to acknowledge the officer's authority.

The police man found his voice. "Yes, sir. I have been instructed to escort you back to the booking room when you arrived. No one has arrived yet, but we expect them any minute." He opened the door that led to the station's holding area.

The corporal led Smythe through a narrow fluorescent-lit hallway, opening into a sterile-looking room. Bench seats lined three of the walls. Each had steel rings embedded so the police officers could handcuff their charges to it. A waist-high table built into the wall stood ready for fingerprinting. A digital camera stood on a tripod near the room's fourth corner. Processing alleged criminals was a simple, but efficient task. A surveillance camera mounted in the ceiling maintained constant surveillance over the room and its occupants.

"Captain, you can wait here." The corporal waved to a bench where the officer could sit. "Would you like a coffee or a soda, sir?"

Smythe would have responded until the booking room's door swung open and a group of police officers with three men immobilized by hand and ankle shackles, shuffled into the room. The handcuffed men immediately recognized the man standing in their way.

Sherman pushed his way to the front of the crowd to put himself between Smythe and the shackled men. "Captain Smythe, I am Special Agent Andrew Sherman of the FBI."

Lieutenant Baylor, Senior Chief Black, and Petty Officer Tu stared openmouthed at whom they believed was the ship's Bos'n.

Before Sherman could continue his statement, Smythe sternly stated, "That's right, you filthy traitors. Chief Sherman is really a special agent from the Federal Bureau of Investigation. He has been tracking you three degenerates for the last eight months. You are now under arrest and will face a military court martial. I guarantee each of you will be making little rocks out of big rocks in less than a month. You screwed with the wrong people."

Smythe's voice remained calm while his fingers twitched from the obvious rage he held back. "Military justice is swift. I understand you were all surprised when the police stormed into your homes to arrest you. You were all keeping such low profiles. Your entire drug ring has been arrested, too. Agent Sherman and his team collected enough evidence for you to spend the rest of your petty, miserable, puny lives in prison. I suggest you cooperate or, we could extradite you back to Thailand for trial. I am sure the Thai government would jump at the chance to try three American sailors for smuggling narcotics across their borders," he added. Their eyes inflamed with fear. American jails were bad. Thai jails would be a living and everlasting hell.

Unable to control his anger anymore, Smythe moved into the supply officer's face and shouted, "Did you really think you can smuggle that crap aboard my ship traitor? Baylor, you are the worst of all. You sat at my table and broke bread with your shipmates for almost two years. You had such great potential, and this is the path you chose, instead?"

Baylor raised his eyes to meet his. "I don't owe you anything, Captain. Going to sea for months on end, knowing a job in the Navy would never make me a rich man was not a comforting thought. It was worth the risk, Smythe," he replied unremorsefully.

Not deterred by the young officer's insolence, Smythe continued to berate the sailors. "You three are cheap drug pushers and traitors to your country." Letting the thought that they betrayed their nation soak in a bit, Smythe lowered his voice and continued. "So…because you choose to betray your nation which is at war…the United States Navy is going to push for execution by firing squad." *ILORETA's* commanding officer knew the threat of execution was hollow, but he wanted them to have an imaginary sword dangling over their heads as they paced their tiny dimly lit concrete cells while awaiting trial.

Sensing the CO was finished, Sherman moved in and barked orders to the police officers to start the booking process. Sherman clasped his hand on the naval officer's shoulder and steered him towards the exit. Smythe and Sherman departed the room in silence and walked outside, where the sun disappeared behind the desert hills. The two men turned, shook hands, and walked away in opposite directions. Smythe received what he wanted, and Sherman finally shed his veil to exit the shadows again.

CHAPTER THREE

It took sixteen years. Ignacio Xavier Medina finally earned his promotion to Chief Petty Officer in the United States Navy. He had taken the exam once before, but the Navy's budget was too tight to promote him. Too many Electricians' Mate CPOs were on the accounting books. Last year, only twenty percent of those eligible received promotion. This year was different. The Navy lost many senior sailors from fighting the Global War on Terrorism. For many, this made their choice to leave active naval service easy. Many did not want to see their families torn apart from their constant absence. Many just got tired of having to keep going back to sea while they witnessed other sailors parking their butts behind desks and enjoying life ashore.

The great exodus from the enlisted ranks offered him a perfect opportunity to reach his lifelong dream of wearing the senior enlisted sailor khaki uniform. The initiation ceremony was a bit of a letdown for him. For the last five years, the Navy cracked down on hazing. Therefore, the new chiefs celebrated with a watered down and agonizingly boring initiation ceremony. Nonetheless, Chief Medina stood skyscraper straight while his fellow chiefs placed the coveted khaki Chief's hat upon his head as his Commanding Officer sealed the promotion with a handshake and a signature.

Medina loved the Navy. He joined sixteen years earlier in the Philippines. Back then, the United States Navy still recruited sailors from his islands. He took their tests, passed with high scores, and chose his rating as an electrician. Once he signed the final papers, the Navy whisked him away from the archipelago to attend boot camp in wintery Michigan.

At first, Medina underwent culture shock when he reached the States. Standing only five foot eight inches tall, he stood in his American counterparts shadows. To a degree, it was something he had grown accustomed to being surrounded by American soldiers and sailors most of his life. In Manila, he used to fetch drinks, cigarettes, and launder their clothes while they screwed his whore Mother. If he was not fast enough, the brothel's owner beat him with a bamboo cane. His mother never intervened. The filthy whore just sat back and reveled in a drug induced comatose state.

She never acted motherly to Ignacio. To her, he was a bad mistake resulting from the pursuit of a little extra cash. Normally, she insisted on condoms during her work. For more money and a little bit more heroine, Mariya gladly let a john hump her bare back. She was sixteen when she conceived Ignacio. Only thirteen days past her seventeenth birthday was when she birthed her bastard son.

Ignacio grew up knowing the extreme forms of human ugliness. He watched his mother sell herself for five dollars a half hour. The rest of the time, his life was a series of endless beatings, rotten food, and lovelessness. His only escape from it all were the nuns who flocked to the sex parlors and bars in search of those who wanted to escape. Though they could not give him another place to live, the nuns did help him learn to read and write enough to pass the Navy's entrance exam. The nuns introduced him to Jesus Christ. They taught him Jesus came to Earth to save man from himself.

They taught Ignacio that Christ forgave all of their sins no matter how bad they were. This is what brought the new CPO out into the Washington downpour. Candles flickered about him and cast shadows on the wall making the church appear more haunting than forgiving. His hands clutched his rosary prayer beads. He ran through the fifty Hail Marys, Six Our Fathers, and the Glory Be prayers by rote. He knew the priest would not be pleased to hear his confession again. They never did. Most times, as soon as the priest heard his confession, they were repulsed and fear stricken. In their lifetimes, priests, especially the elders, believed they heard the worse man could inflict onto his fellow man. Medina's confessions proved their theories wrong. Father Nguyen was the exception to this rule.

Like himself, Nguyen immigrated to America. He escaped the killing fields of Cambodia. Like Medina, he grew up in the slums and slaved as a boy prostitute to help feed his large family. A group of missionary's nuns helped him find solace too. His escape came from entering the church wearing a white collar vice escaping by sea as Medina did.

Their similar pasts led Father Nguyen to convince the murderous confessor to confide in him only. They both experienced similar brutal and tragic childhoods. Both escaped but one had evil branded into his soul while the other truly embraced Christ's teachings.

Father Nguyen stood at the end of the church's aisles watching his most unwelcome parishioner. He silently mumbled prayers to the Almighty for strength, guidance, and that Medina would not again bring his tales of terror and torture into the holy confessional. It was a wasted prayer.

Nguyen learned quickly the only time he saw the penitent monster was shortly after he committed murder. The last time he appeared, Medina confessed to kidnapping and brutally torturing a black man in Seattle. His only crime was soliciting an Asian hooker. Medina took thirty minutes describing to the priest how he kept seeing his mother being thrust upon by some unknown tourist, sailor, or soldier. It did not matter the person he tortured never traveled to the Philippines nor knew his Mother.

When in a murderous frame of mind, Medina confessed he never saw the face of the person he was beating, cutting, burning, or choking. What he saw was his whore-mother's dignity stolen and with it, his own disappeared. It consumed every bit of his mind, body, and soul. His deadly ritual cleansed his mind and body to a more balanced state. Yet, his soul remained tortured until he arrived at the confessional.

Not a single priest ever granted him absolution. All that mattered was he was able to tell someone and relieve the pressures haunting his thoughts. Unluckily for the priests, they were bound to an oath of secrecy. Unless the priest wanted to renounce his vows and pledges he made to his Lord, the secret remained safe within the narrow confines of the confessional walls.

A priest the short Pilipino selected to confess his gruesome sins needed to be dedicated to his religion. A priest with a weak constitution and appalled by his gruesome tales might be tempted to give up his beliefs and turn him in. That is why he liked coming to Father Nguyen. This priest was more devout than the standard, run-of-the-mill clergyman.

He had confessed his sins to multiple priests wherever and whenever he killed. A wave of relief swept through his body when he did. It was somehow different with this Cambodian clergyman. Medina stood two inches taller than the Asian priest did yet it seemed the priest possessed an omniscient presence, which loomed over the villain's spirit. It weighed heavily upon Medina's mind. Nguyen's karma plagued his dreams. The holy man possessed strong spiritual power.

Chief Electricians Mate Medina focused his eyes on the dimly lit statue of the Virgin Mary. Only when he sensed the priest passing silently by to take his station in the confessional did he rise, cross himself, and move towards his only source of relief.

Medina pulled back the heavy crimson curtains and entered the dimly lit reconciliation chamber. Kneeling on the worn pad in front of him, the murderer heard the priest flick on the light indicating the confessional was occupied by a sinner exposing his soul to God.

A rectangular panel peeled back with a light swoosh.

"Yes, my son," came a voice from behind the confession-al's screen.

"Bless me Father, for I have sinned. It has been three weeks since my last confession."

"Three weeks is quite soon my son. I hoped never to see you again after our last talk. Your vile sinning is becoming more fre-quent," scolded the middle-aged priest.

Father Nguyen wanted to believe he was affecting the sadist kneeling in front of him. Why else would he return? Extreme caution was called for. If he went too far, the murderous demon would turn his hatred upon him. Worse yet, disappear. If he left, he would never be able to whittle away at the man's conscious as he had for the past few months. Father Nguyen devised a plan to convince this murderous abomination to end his evil. It was to make the man's conscious so distraught over his sins that sooner or later, he would confess his sins to the authorities or he would release the priest from his oath of silence.

A delicate game Nguyen played. At first, the man kept his identity a secret. Through his own investigation, he learned he was a sailor stationed on a naval ship in Everett. From there, he used his contacts to volunteer his time to the base's Catholic con-gregation. The base priest knew nothing of what was going on. He was just thankful a local clergyman wanted to help him serve his congregation.

Every opportunity, Nguyen made it his mission to coinci-dently meet the CPO on the base or out in town. Each time it happened, Nguyen wished the guilt rising in the man's face, when confronted by the only man who knew of his horrific deeds, would steer him to righteousness. He knew it played on the kill-er's mind to have the priest look him in the eyes and act as if nothing was wrong. The murderous sailor wanted a complacent audience. Nguyen refused to be that cooperative spectator.

The psychotic electrician continued with his confession. "Yes Father, I have committed another grievous and mortal sin. I seek the Lord's forgiveness through the Sacrament of Reconciliation."

"Tell me your sins my son."

"Father, I violated the Lord's fifth commandment again. I have committed two murders. The first was a man. The second was a woman. Neither ever harmed me in any way, but I felt compelled to serve God by ridding the world of two horrible defiled creatures. The man, I beat him with a shovel until his bones protruded out from his skin. Before he died, I made sure he knew of his sins. I sliced off his cock and shoved it deep into his bung-hole." Nguyen sat stunned and motionless in the confessional chair. Sweat beaded at his forehead. Tears trickled down his cheeks. He forced himself to remain calm though he wanted to vomit where he sat. "Go on my son," he said in the most reverend and caring voice he could muster.

"The woman, I really cared for. She was as beautiful as my mother was. Her skin was so soft. Her eyes shone brightly with life but I could not stop myself from killing her," whimpered the man.

Father Nguyen waited for this opening. He waited for the man to become vulnerable so he could chip away at his conscious.

"My son, if you really cared for this woman," emphasizing the phrase, "Why did you believe it necessary to murder her." Nguyen purposely used the word murder instead of kill to drive home the sin and crime the offender committed.

The sobs ended from the other side of the Priest's screen. "Father, she was nothing but another dirty whore who deserved to die, just like my mother. She did not do it for money though. She liked flaunting her young body in front of all of the other men she worked with. She was a dirty, dirty slut that needed to be punished."

"Why do you think you have to be the one who administers the punishment?"

"Because I am God's servant, Father. Just like you. God enlisted me to fight a war against people who spit in His righteous eye. It always seems like I fall into a deep trance when I sin. God's will possesses and controls me."

The man never used the word murder. That was why it was important Nguyen used it himself. Obviously, guilt riddled the murderous beast. Why else would he seek peace and solace from a priest? He only took a few courses in psychology during his theology studies and those mostly instructed him how to help a person get over the loss of a loved one or to help a couple save their marriage. Nguyen needed expert advice on how to dig deeper into this man's psyche.

The devil certainly possessed this man. Thinking he carried out the will of God did not come from above. It came from hell's fiery depths.

"Father, will you forgive me of my sins?" pleaded Medina through the barrier.

"No. I will not. You know I cannot do that until you truly repent your crimes. You know what you are doing is wrong. Why else would you be here?"

It was time to paint the real picture to this demon.

"The devil is working through you my son."

Nguyen knew he had to keep calling him son. He called many of his flock son or daughter because he saw himself as the male parent of a large family. In this monster's case, it was all the more important. He believed establishing a positive paternal bond vice the one his mother fermented in him long ago might help.

"The only way you can come back into the grace of God is coming out of the dark. You must deny Satan's power over you. Take responsibility for the horrendous crimes you committed." This part made the priest's stomach turn. He had to personally relate with the beast to gain his trust. He had to empathize with the creature before him. "You said the man you murdered was with a prostitute? Is that not what you said?"

"Yes, Father. He was stealing the woman's dignity and making her give up herself for money," the man rationalized.

"Yes, my son, he too was committing a sin. Was it a sin punishable by death? Why did you think you had the right to judge this man? Are you above God? Just like what you are seeking from me, only God has that authority. I want you to think about that my son. What about the man's or the young woman's family? Are they to go through life without their husband, father, sister, or daughter? Do you think the atrocities committed upon you during your life grants you license to commit murder upon others in this world?" When he first tried to sermonize to the murderer many months ago, the madman stormed out of the confessional. He was determined to whittle away at the man's soul. The black garbed padre knew he could only press ever so hard. It would have to do for now. He made a mental note to work on the base for the next few days. He wanted the killer looking him in the eye and feeling more shame and remorse, if that was at all possible. It was his only recourse until he thought of another, better plan.

The confessional's occupant stifled his sobbing and rose from the kneeler.

"Thank you, Father for hearing my confession. Even though you have not absolved me from my sins and assigned my penance, I will say one hundred of our Lord's Prayer, two hundred prayers to his Mother, and dedicate candles for the sinner's souls I freed from their debauchery." As if citing a few rote prayers would make a difference. Medina left the priest in the dimly lit closet, alone and frightened for the world.

The priest felt powerless. All he could do for the moment was switch off the confessional light. He sat silently in the dark shrouded space weeping and praying for guidance and salvation from this gruesome task.

When the murderer first came to him, Father Nguyen kept questioning God why he was selected to carry this awful burden. God answered by making him realize it was his cross to bear as a priest. Most priests dealt with adultery and other normal sins that people revealed to their priest. He recognized God chose him for this duty. It made him even more in love with his spiritual vocation. God was not only helping him shepherd a flock. He tasked him to ferret out satanic evil from the Earth. The only thing God did not give him was a recipe on how to accomplish the overwhelming task.

Father Nguyen understood God honored him with this challenge. In his studies, he learned of priests specializing in excising demons from the body. This was different. Here, God presented him a real demon to defeat. Not some hidden entity lurking deep in a person's shadow. The task proved daunting and a solution was damn near impossible. Nonetheless, he still prayed fervently to the Almighty for an answer. Eventually it would come. His faith remained strong.

CHAPTER FOUR

Sergeant Hendricks parked his Chevy Tahoe behind the bland white building in a space designated for police cars. He found the hardest part of investigating a homicide was the initial sight of the corpse. Knowing nothing about the person who was murdered made it feel so impersonal.

Experts advise detaching yourself from jobs like his. For Hendricks, learning who the person was, how they went through life, who their family was, or what they liked or disliked made it easier for him to cope. Being personable allowed him to take ownership of the case. Relating to the victim forced him to accept the mission. It drove his relentless hunt for the culprit.

Over his twenty years on the job, twelve as a homicide detective, he had solved thirty-two homicides cases. There was only one case committed that remained unsolved on the books and unresolved in his mind for eight years. This single case haunted him daily. What bugged him about it was the brutally involved and how the man clubbed to death did not have any enemies. He was a normal Joe, had a good family, and led a modest, if not a non-descript life. To this day, he could not talk with the man's family without feeling guilt for not measuring up to the task.

Hendricks scooped up a pink box off the passenger seat. He intended to give the tasty pastries he purchased from the tiny mom and pop shop down the street to the Colby boys who craved sweets when they worked overtime. The sugary delights fueled their enthusiasm. He recognized they had worked twenty-eight hours straight to finish the crime scene's analysis.

Hendricks liked how the brotherly team knew the importance of not letting the trail go cold. Each day lost without progress makes a murder investigation nearly impossible to solve. The killer may disappear. Important clues might be lost forever. Worse yet, he could be pulled off the case if it was taking too long. Once an investigation became stale, the evidence and investigatory notes were boxed and banished to cold case storage. From there, an investigation rarely reopened.

It was a rare sunny winter day in Island County, Washington. Sunbeams pierced the damp air and warmed the police officer as he walked the short distance to the building's entrance. He grew up in the rainy weather and it rarely bothered him anymore. The soothing sunshine made him feel optimistic. It was a good omen.

Israel and Ishmael huddled over a microscope. They did not notice Sergeant Hendricks enter through the laboratory doors. Ishmael first realized another human presence when the scent of a glazed donut reached his nostrils.

"Detective Hendricks, great...you brought breakfast!" exclaimed Ishmael. "You also arrived just in time. We have had a few breakthroughs regarding Amanda you'll be interested in."

"I'm glad you're thrilled to see me," the cop replied. "Who the hell is Amada?"

"Oh, right...I forgot there for a moment. Amanda is our murder victim. Israel and I have been calling her by her name ever since we found out from the Department of Defense who she was. They emailed her entire file thirty minutes ago. We would have told you sooner but we figured you were on your way here."

"That's fantastic!" said Hendricks. His mind began to churn. This was a most fantastic and fortunate turn of events. He did not expect her identity to be uncovered so quickly. Once a murder victim's persona was established, it made his job much simpler. Knowing her name opened many, many doors to explore.

"You said the Department of Defense, did you not?" he asked. "What else do you know about her? She served in the military? That explains her teeth. What service? When did she get out? Where did she come from?" The questions flowed from his grey matter.

With a huge bite of a cream filled chocolate donut stuffed in his mouth, Israel started answering the police officer's questions. He had not eaten in over twelve hours. The sugar rushed to his brain while saliva seeped out the corners of his mouth.

"Our victim is Amanda Jackson from Biloxi, Mississippi. She is twenty-four years old and she is in the navy. Er...I mean she was in the navy," reported the donut eating technician.

"There is more," Ishmael spoke up while he raided the donut box Hendricks supplied. "She is, correction, she *was* a sailor stationed right here in Everett aboard the aircraft carrier *USS ABRAHAM LINCOLN*. Amanda is a Quartermaster. The navy is sending a NCIS agent to get involved in the investigation. The navy had her listed as absent until we called.

"What the heck does a Navy quartermaster do and what else do you know?" inquired Detective Hendricks.

"Hey man, you're the detective. Remember, we're just scientists," laughed Israel. "We wanted to know too so we asked the Navy the same question. Their job abbreviates to QM. They are the sailors who specialize in navigating the ship. They prepare the ship's charts and courses needed to get from one part of the ocean to another. It sounds like a pretty cool gig. The added bonus is we deduced how she died."

Hendricks raised his eyes from the notepad he jotted his notes in.

"Amanda Jackson died horribly from asphyxiation. She was not choked or smothered to death. A bag was placed over her head. She died a slow death from oxygen starvation." Israel let that part sink in before he continued.

"Whatever was put over her head was tightly tied around her neck. With her arms and feet bound, we are betting she thrashed about a lot. The killer probably watched her suffocate. Bruises on her skin were not apparent when we first examined her in the woods. We witnessed the autopsy. The bruising under the outer skin became apparent under ultraviolet light."

"By suffocating her the way he did, Ms. Jackson could not have felt any pain. She sucked in the bag with desperation trying to get at the air. Eventually she passed out from breathing her own carbon dioxide, right?" asked Hendricks. "But, if she was awake, she would have been in complete terror for a couple of minutes until all of the oxygen was depleted."

Ishmael took over the reporting. "That is correct. Most likely, the ordeal terrified her but she did not die in pain. Whoever her killer is, he cared for her for whatever strange reason he had. He was not fixated on control. Undoubtedly, he had other motives for killing her. As murders go, her's was terrifying but relatively painless."

"Was there any evidence of sexual assault? Has the toxicology results returned from the lab? If she was drugged with an exotic narcotic we can locate her killer that way."

"This is the strange thing about this case too. You saw Amanda. Despite her being dead, don't think I'm weird; and a gorgeous woman, she was not raped. Normally, when a girl like her winds up murdered, 9.99999 times out of ten it involved sexual deviancy. Not this one. To answer your second question, unfortunately the toxicology results will not be ready for another two days."

Israel saw the disappointed look on Hendricks' face and chimed in. "We requested a complete analysis of Amanda's fluids."

"Okay, I am not disappointed in you guys. You know the faster I have any tidbit of information, the closer I come to nailing this perp to the wall," said Hendricks.

"There was one other curious aspect Amanda gave us. It may not be much of a clue but its evidence nonetheless," said Ishmael.

Hendricks sat down at the stainless steel lab desk to continue jotting notes from the duo's analysis. Raising his head signaled Ishmael to carry on.

"Amanda was bound to a chair with tape. We know she was sitting because blood pooled in the lower half of her forearms. Her arms were definitely parallel to the floor. Blood is susceptible to gravity just like any other fluid. It also collected in the fatty tissue of her butt. That is how we know she was sitting."

"How do you know she was confined using tape? Any way to trace it to its source?" came the questions from the officer who sat mimicking the manner in which his victim may have been positioned.

Israel picked up where Ishmael left off without missing a beat. Being twins made them think as one.

"Amanda had glue residue left on her wrists and ankles. However, there is skin not covered in the tacky substance, which is consistent with a person bound against a hard object. The parts of her skin that were flush against the chair arms and legs do not have any glue residue. We first assumed the killer used duct tape. Because of its material strength, glue adhesives, and cheap price it normally is the tape of choice for deranged maniacs. In this case, we found by comparing different tape compositions the tape used was industrial grade electrician's tape. It is tremendously strong. Examining the glue pattern makes the tape four inches wide."

Hendricks eyes sparkled to life again. This discovery could be the killer's first mistake. Using industrial strength tape supplied a small yet potentially significant clue.

Israel was right. If a criminal binds his victims with tape, the universal tape of choice is duct tape. It is easily purchased from any Target, Wal-Mart, or hundreds of other stores. Industrial grade electrical tape was a different story. The discovery was a genuine lead to the monster who suffocated Amanda Jackson.

"Is there any way to narrow down the tape?" asked Hendricks.

Ishmael spoke up. "I am glad you asked that. Doing so is our next step. We will access the FBI materials databases to investigate. The Bureau holds an extensive database analysis of tape and the types of glue used with each. With some luck, we will be able to narrow down what tape manufacturer used this type of glue. Then, we can hone in on the store where this type of tape was purchased. Localization beyond that would be difficult. That is your job. We extracted as much information as possible from the clues left on Amanda. I think we can rightly assume though, our killer is some type of contractor or someone who works in an industrial environment."

"Good work guys," beamed Hendricks. "What about the crime scene evidence you collected? What does that have to tell us about the bastard who killed Amanda?"

"Ahhh…" came the reply from Israel. "Our criminal is not that bright after all. He is smart but not smart enough to cover all of his tracks. It is my opinion that a rapid discovery of Amanda was not expected. We got lucky with Roosevelt the wonder dog. If it were not for that pooch, she would still be rotting in the forest for God knows how long. We figure Amanda was lying there in the woods for approximately twelve to twenty-four hours. The road leading to the dumping site was quite muddy. I was able to cast tire tracks from three separate and distinct vehicles. All three vehicles have a wide wheelbase, which means a truck, a van, or a SUV."

Hendricks felt the twins were approaching the end of their story. He knew when to let them keep going and not interfere with their train of thought.

"The best evidence the killer left was his shoe print. He wears a size nine. The impression's means he weighs approximately 140 to 170 pounds. The shoe length leads us to believe the killer is not that tall. Five foot nine, max." concluded the criminal scene investigator.

Sergeant Hendricks made final notes in his notebook, flipped the tablet closed, and stowed his pen back in his shirt pocket whence it came. The boys provided some good information. There was not a smoking gun; but it was a better start than he thought they would give him.

"You two should be extremely proud of the work you've accomplished," Hendricks preached as he gazed over Amanda's death pose photos posted on the lab's white board. "Get some sleep. Forward the information to the FBI profiling shop in Quantico. I have a feeling this is not the first time this creep has struck terror into someone's life. The faster we get on this pervert's scent, the faster we seek justice for Amanda's death. I am going to pay a visit to the NCIS office. I have some contacts there and I want them to give me access to Amanda's military file as quickly as possible. Okay? If they come to you, just refer them to me. None of your evidence goes anywhere except to the FBI."

Both scientists readily nodded their assent. They left the politics of the case to the police and district attorney's offices. Their job was to collect evidence, analyze it, and report it to the investigators. Otherwise, they kept their noses out of the investigation's politics. Intradepartmental jurisdiction squabbles were ugly. Observing from the sidelines was the safest place to be.

Hendricks shook Ishmael's and Israel's hands, patted them on the shoulder, and muttered more words of encouragement. He exited the analysis's lab with a great deal more than what he had when he arrived. The Pacific Northwest sun warmed his face again as he inhaled the cool Northwest air while processing everything he just saw and heard. The information was a real boon. He had nailed other murderers on far, far less information. He had a good start.

CHAPTER FIVE

Ensign Shea received his naval commission through the NROTC eight months ago. His first two months in the Navy were sitting on his behind in a classroom in Newport, Rhode Island learning the duties he was to perform when he reported onboard a naval man-of-war. He used another month taking leave recharging himself after four years of studying mechanical engineering at the University of Nebraska.

Adorned with shiny new ensign gold bars pinned to his shirt collar, thirty-two sailors stood at attention in front of him. He had no idea how to lead them. Ten of the sailors were his Father's age. Most obeyed him because he was an officer not because they respected him. It would take hard work and a bit of charisma for the young junior officer to earn their confidence and respect. That is why the Navy had Chief Petty Officers. When it came to the enlisted men, an officer's job was to be the liaison between them and the rest of the chain of command. Ensign Shea's purpose was learning how to conn the ship without colliding into another vessel. Not managing his division's workload.

Ensign Shea towered over his CPO. The difference in height did not make up the difference in stature. What mattered was the men and women in the Division listened to Chief Medina. The senior NCO would teach the rookie butter-bar how to lead his new Division.

Ensign Shea started the morning monitoring his division as the Chief read off the day's plan, the sailor's work assignments, and other miscellaneous details each sailor needed to know to function onboard. The Chief left the last item on the agenda for the young Ensign to cover. It seemed appropriate because it was word passed down directly from the Commanding Officer.

"This afternoon, all hands shall muster in the hanger bay for a memorial service for Petty Officer Jackson. The uniform for the service is Service Dress Blues. You will be on station and in ranks by 1315." Ensign Shea paused for the order to register with the sailors before he continued. "As you know, QM2 Jackson was discovered in the woods about fifty miles from here. NCIS is canvassing the entire ship and interviewing her shipmates. They are trying to find her murderer. Chief Medina will arrange the times for each of you to meet with the investigators. Remember, no detail is too small. Just let the sheriffs know what you know and do not know. Let them sort it out."

Chief Medina stared through the sailors while the young officer spoke. He found it humorous how the butter-bar used the same word the priest did, *Murderer*. Somehow, Ensign Shea did not have the same effect as the Cambodian clergyman. Her death was regrettable and unplanned. He typically did not kill so close to home. The urge to silence the throbbing pain in his head was too great. She was in the wrong place at the wrong time. He was in the right place at the right time.

It was dumb luck he met her coming out of a bar in Seattle. Her girlfriend who went to the nightclub with her left with a dude she had been trying to hook up with for two weeks. Her plans were to grab a cab and head for the hotel room she and her friend checked into earlier that night. When she bumped into the E-Division Chief outside the bar, she thought she found a way to save the twenty bucks for a cab. Twenty dollars is a lot of money for a young woman in the Navy. Every penny was budgeted. She believed she was safe.

Chief Medina had seen Petty Officer Jackson on the ship many, many times. She was the prettiest woman on the ship. Skin the color of milk chocolate brown and eyes that were a deep, tranquil green made her the desire of many young sailors. Her silky black hair, when not tied up per naval regulations, cascaded down to her shoulders framing her face. On Amanda's last night alive, she wore a tight, rich purple, silk tube dress, black heels, and carried a matching silver handbag.

Amanda recognized him immediately. He frequently worked on the bridge's electrical system. Without the air wing embarked, the ship's crew numbered almost 3000. It resembled a small town encased in a steel tube. If you stayed on board for over a year, you were acquainted with everyone.

The two sailors chatted briefly outside the nightclub in the damp air. Amanda asked where the Chief was going. "Home," he said. She asked if he could drop her off at her hotel. It was nearby. Only a few miles down the interstate she added.

Her beauty mesmerized Chief Medina. He eagerly wanted to offer her to his Lord as a sacrifice. The tight dressed hugged her hips. She excited his body; but his mind found her sex repulsive. The young, black tart beckoned men to gawk at her. She purposely made herself into an object lusted after. His mother did the same. The prettier she outfitted herself the more the customers paid for her. Amanda was no different from his prostitute mother.

Median quickly thought if anyone could connect him to her. Theirs was a chance meeting. Petty Officer Jackson trusted him. Median was a CPO from her ship and the Navy trained her to implicitly trust the chiefs and officers leading her. No one lingered outside the bar that could bear witness they saw the two sailors together. God provided this opportunity just for Medina to continue his task.

He readily agreed to drop her off at the hotel. Before he did, he wanted to stop for a hot chocolate. Amanda did not see any harm in that. A hot chocolate sounded great on a cold and damp night. What young woman would turn down a steaming cup of hot chocolate to take the edge off the cool Northern Pacific chill?

Amanda waited on the dark street while Medina returned with his Nissan Pathfinder. They drove silently in the Washington mist until the CPO steered his SUV into a convenience store parking lot. He returned with two steamy hot chocolates covered in whipped cream. Amanda eagerly accepted the beverage. The warm brew nourished her body's core. The odd thing about it, it also made her drowsy. Medina watched her intently. Her eyelids slowly closed and her head dropped to her firm breasts. Her hand lost control of the cup it held causing her drink to spill onto the truck's carpets. Medina sipped his hot chocolate and gazed at his new conquest. He ran his hand along the inside of her smooth thigh. Amanda was not wearing any panties. He spread her legs and gently petted her. She was an unbelievable catch. Medina stopped himself from fondling his new conquest further. There was too much danger where he was at to indulge in her. It was time to take her to his lair.

When she woke, she found herself not in the Chief's truck or her hotel room. Amanda was sitting in a brilliantly white painted room bare of furniture. The windows were not windows. Amanda recognized the outlines where the panes were supposed to be. Bricks painted the same color as the walls replaced the glass.

Chief Medina stood behind her when she first awoke. He loved seeing his female victims panic when the drugs wore off. They realized they were in a strange and dangerous place. They sensed their clothes had been removed and were entirely vulnerable. They always tried to rise from the chair but it was bolted to the sterile, white tiled floor. His victims struggled and struggled against the thick black electrical tape pinning their arms and legs. Some thrashed back and forth. Some screamed. Some realized the uselessness of struggling, accepted their fate, and softly sobbed, knowing they were going to die. At this stage, his previous sacrifices typically started begging not to be hurt, raped, tortured, or murdered. They had no idea he had already used them for part of what he wanted. While they slept, Medina laid them in his bed unconscious and naked. He removed his clothes and held their warm bodies close to his. His mouth would lower to their breasts and suckle their nipples. It transcended him back to his boyhood. More correctly, to a false childhood he wished were true.

Sucking and kissing their nipples took him to a safe and comfortable place. It replaced the abusive memories of a helpless, beaten child. Feeling the women's warmth radiating through his body expelled the horrible specters haunting his mind and he felt at peace. He felt love emanating from their bodies. He consumed every bit of it.

His clandestine activities only completed half of his sacrificial ritual. The pain in the lunatic's skull still throbbed no matter how long he lay next to the woman absorbing her karma. He never liked what he had to do next, but the ritual had to be completed. His God demanded a sacrifice. The thought of snuffing out another life weighed heavy on his mind. Going to confession sometimes helped him deal with the guilt associated with the taking of another's life. The pain in his brain and the thoughts implanted into his consciousness compelled him to complete the act as programmed.

Amanda reacted uniquely. Her responses were unexpected and unwelcome. She did not scream. She did not cry. She did not struggle to break free from her bonds. She gazed upon her bindings, understood her predicament, and realized she was trapped. Escape was a useless thought. Amanda remained calm. Her eyes darted back and forth and up and down scanning the room and assessing her situation.

"Why are you doing this, Chief?" she asked. An answer did not come. "Chief, I know you're there somewhere. Whatever you plan, it does not have to be this way. Do you want to have sex with me?"

"No, I do not want to hump you, you dirty little wench!" he screamed into her ear. "That is what women like you think men want. All of you think we just want to screw you. That is why you dress up in your tight clothes, paint your faces, and flaunt your stuff around. It is a beacon for us to come and throw money at you so you will let us screw you. You are all nothing but eff-ing whores!"

Panic engulfed Amanda before she could reply. A thick, clear plastic bag whipped over her head. She felt it tighten around her neck as the slack from a zip tie pulled tight sealed the bag around her neck. Terror overcame her ability to reason.

Medina enjoyed watching the life leaving his captives. He stepped in front of his victim. The calm left her body. Terror and fear screamed from Amanda Jackson's eyes. Her head shook vio-lently trying to cast off the bag suffocating her. Her chest heaved as she gasped for breath. She sucked part of the bag into her mouth trying to bite it open. All she had to do was tear open a tiny hole and the life sustaining air would rush into her strained lungs. Amanda's eyelids drooped. Her body became limp from consuming too much of her own vapor. The beautiful Amanda Jackson went from vibrant energy to a listless hunk of flesh in less than two minutes. Medina fell to his knees with his hands tightly clasped together in prayer.

"Almighty, I am sending you another dirty, rotten whore. Cast this wretched woman into hell with my mother. I will not shirk from the duties you have charged me to carry out," he mumbled. He knelt and prayed over her body until the same warmth he coveted earlier left her tender body forever. Medina remained stationary, in a trance for hours, praying over his sacrifice.

His eyes slowly opened knowing exactly what he had to do next. Amanda's murderer removed her bonds and the death bag. He deposited his torture instruments into a paper bag already filled with the regal, silky dress Amanda wore that evening. Later he would burn it all after he dumped her body deep in the forest.

Medina's daydream disappeared when he heard his name spoken. The murderer snapped back to reality.

"Chief, take charge of the Division. Make sure they are in formation by 1315 and ready for my inspection. We shall pay our respects to Petty Officer Jackson in a military fashion," ordered the green officer.

"Aye, aye, sir," replied the CPO who snapped the sailors to attention and dismissed them to commence their day's work. Medina felt good inside. Reflecting on how he ministered God's will made him complete. He relished in the thought that God's angels would blow trumpets and welcome him to nirvana for his the great deeds he did.

CHAPTER SIX

Rain splattered unnoticed on Hendricks' windshield. He no longer paid attention to the falling precipitation. Living in the Pacific Northwest, either you accepted the omni-present rain or you moved away.

He piloted his truck along Interstate 5 en-route to Seattle. He was meeting Detective Paul Raphael from the Seattle Homicide division. Before Paul was promoted, he and Sergeant Hendricks' partnered for three years. Every so often Raphael called him seeking advice from his old mentor.

A body recently discovered in the warehouse district five days ago baffled his ex-partner. Raphael provided a brief description when they spoke. The victim was an African-American male, thirty-nine years old, and married with three kids. His lifestyle was ordinary and boring. A criminal record was nonexistent. Savagely beaten to death made it a gruesome murder. It was so brutal that the only way they identified him was through a process of elimination. Fingerprint analysis was useless. Dental records did not help either. All of the man's teeth were broken, shattered, or missing. The only way they put a name to the body was by going through the missing person's reports and matching DNA with probable family members. They luckily popped positive on one test.

The victim was Samuel Williams, an accountant who lived and worked in Marysville. He worked for H&R Block and did not have any access to any funds to embezzle. His wife and friends said he was a model citizen. Williams was a church deacon and a coach to his youngest son's basketball team. Overall, Mr. Williams led a pretty dull and uneventful, nondescript, yet happy life. So, why would someone bash his head in and beat his body to a bloody pulp? Did his wife discover a secret love affair and hire a thug? Was he a closet gambler who owed money to the local muscle? Did he have a dark side no one ever discovered or suspected? This is why Detective Raphael wanted Hendricks' help. Hendricks had a knack for seeing the most irrelevant detail that everyone else overlooked. The man was a human bloodhound.

Detective Raphael sat facing the coffee shop's door. He no longer did it purposely. Being a cop, he learned over time how to select the best vantage point to protect himself wherever he was.

He thumbed through the Williams case crime scene photos for the hundredth time. It was the most brutal case he had ever handled. He wanted to nail the monster that did this to a man who, at first glance, had never harmed anyone. Williams simply wanted to raise a family and live out the middle class American dream.

Detective Raphael did not rule out a hate crime, but; it was highly unlikely. Racism was not as prevalent in the Pacific Northwest as it was in other parts of the country. Seattle built a reputation for being intolerant of bigotry and championing ethnic tolerance. A racist attack normally left the victim intact and the assailants would have left their calling cards. In this crime, humiliation tactics were evident. Beating a man to the point where almost every bone in his body was broken was the genesis of sheer unadulterated rage, not racism. Raphael easily characterized Williams's attacker as being mentally unstable and extremely dangerous.

Hendricks entered the coffee shop and scanned the dining room for his pupil. Sighting his protégé, he made his way to Raphael's table. On the way, he stopped a waitress and asked for coffee, two creams, and two sugars.

Paul stood up and shook Hendricks' hand. Hendricks gripped his hand and slid into a seat facing the window giving him a clear view to the restaurants' front door. He noticed Raphael positioned himself likewise. Good to know his old partner practiced what the veteran investigator taught him.

"Paul, it's been a long time since you've asked for my advice on a case. Something got you stumped?"

"Hey, Benjamin. Thanks for taking the time to come down. I know it is hard to drive through the traffic." Raphael sipped his coffee composing his thoughts to frame the case for his mentor.

"I got a hummer of a case. The victim, his name is…er…was… Samuel Williams, was beaten so badly you can barely make out that he is human. Whoever did it used a heavy, blunt instrument and went to town all over the dude's body. Somewhere along the line, the sick bastard sliced the dude's cock and balls off and stuffed them in his mouth and anus. Right now, we do not have any leads of why anyone would want to do this to him. Williams was an average working stiff and a good family man. He paid his bills on time. His wife did not suspect him of having an affair or practicing any other vices. His kids are all honor students. A genuine nine-to-five type family guy. Unless I am missing something, Mr. Williams was a straight arrow. He led a pretty dull and ordinary life. Because the murderer cut his penis off, my initial thoughts jumped towards a racially motivated crime but I ruled that option out. On the other hand, he might be involved in something funky and someone is sending a message. It would not be the first time. I know I am missing something right in front of me. I hoped you could look over the case file, forensics, and crime scene data and give me your opinion about what I overlooked."

"Not a problem. Do you have the files with you?"

Patting a folder lying on the table, "Right here Sarge."

"Okay, I'll take a look at what you got. Come back in a couple of hours and I'll let you know what I think."

"Roger that. Thanks. I know it is there. I have canvassed the data for the last three days trying to find the right thread to pull. It's invisible to me," shrugged the junior detective.

Raphael knew his ex-partner well. Hendricks needed time to study the evidence and to let it stew in his brain. If he could not find the missing link, then the case was en route to the cold case file fast.

The waitress delivered the coffee she had silently promised. She left the table with an order for a patty melt, fries, and a Coke. She liked the man at table number nine. He did not say much, but the fast approaching middle-aged woman was attracted to the strong silent type. It meant he would not play any games. A quick dash to the back room to splash on a bit of perfume might increase her chances of getting him to notice her.

Hendricks doctored his coffee to a pleasant tan and slightly sweetened his brew. The coffee was good at "The Diner," a local cop hangout. The food was tasty, plentiful, and, best of all, cheap. The owner loved being a cop shop. He never had any problems and business was always brisk.

Looking at another case was a much-needed distraction from Amanda Jackson's murder. Sometimes, it was best not to think about what you have been concentrating on for a while. Then, when you go back to it, you look at it fresh. You might notice the one detail that eluded you. Raphael felt the same way. The frustrating thing was the clue was always staring you right in the face the whole time. It was just too familiar.

He opened the folder and rapidly scanned the information front to back. The crime scene photos taken of the body captured his immediate attention. Raphael was right. Uncontrollable rage was definitely present. The man in the photo was saturated in his own blood. His legs and arms were more jelly than skin and bone. The right forearm folded back upon itself. Williams' spread legs made an upside down T with his torso. The man no longer had a face. It was a mash of pulp mixed with bone.

Located behind the crime scene were the medical examiner's photos taken after the victim's body was cleaned for examination. Without the blood hiding the body, the damage caused by the murderer was readily evident. Crescent shaped bruises covered the entire body.

Hendricks paused and looked outside to settle his stomach before he continued. The photos showed bone fragments puncturing the skin. Stalagmites grew from the inside out. His teeth and jaw were smashed back into his face. Jagged, sharp stumps were now his teeth. After the initial shock of looking at the two sets of photos, Hendricks went back over the bruises with a magnifying glass. It seemed like a Sherlock Holmes-ish tool to use when more modern and precise tools were available to use by the police. The glass was simple, portable, and it allowed him to study the wounds without others hovering over him clouding his thoughts. It helped Hendricks hypothesize about the kind of weapon used to beat the man to death. The coroner's report stated a blunt instrument caused the damage. It was an obvious conclusion to him. He needed to determine the murder weapon. The Colby twins could help to figure that detail out.

From the size of the bruises, he could tell it was a wide instrument. The criminal used some type of tool that could withstand the force of being slammed into something repeatedly. A sledgehammer, a spade, or a shovel was his best guess.

His patty melt sandwich arrived in front of him without him looking up. Hendricks was deep in thought but he raised his head to smile at the sweet smelling waitress. He could not help but notice the lacey bra covering a nice set of tits.

"Here ya go, hun," smiled the tow-headed server. "Anything else for ya," while she continued engaging the detective's eyes with her own.

"How about that Coke, ah…ah…" the detective said as he searched for her name tag, "Cheri?"

"One coke coming your way, hun." Men liked being called hun, sugar, baby, or sweetie. She intentionally did not bring his soda to give her an excuse to visit with the man some more.

Before he went back to his file, Hendricks made a mental note to chat with Cheri. She was cute. He would like to ask her out. There was not a wedding band on her hand. Anyways, he sensed she wanted the attention. Why else would she spray on fresh perfume and unbutton her blouse a bit more so she could expose her cleavage when she bent down to deliver his food. Sometimes it was good to be a professional investigator. Dates were okay. The problem was the relationship that came after. Most women want their men sharing their time exclusively with them. Not dealing with dead bodies in the small hours of the morning. It takes a strong woman to cope being a cop's girl. They are always in danger and the hours are too long. Many turned into alcoholics, gamblers, or become abusive. The pressure they lived under and the ugliness they witnessed tended to make even the strongest minds crack. That is why Hendricks had never married. He was absorbed in his job. Maybe someday he would settle down and meet someone to share his life with. Nevertheless, a couple of dates and a bit of fooling around in the bedroom never hurt anyone. After all, they were both adults.

Hendricks shook the thoughts of the big breasted, sweet smelling, blond waitress from his head and turned his attention back to the report. The cause of death was a no brainer. Blunt force trauma; the man was severely beaten to death. The coroner was unable to fix how the man eventually died. It could have been from a heart attack. It could have been from blood loss. He could have choked on his own tongue, teeth, or his own testicles stuffed into his mouth. Or, it could have been from the first good thump the man received on his skull. The body was so mangled that it made making a simple conclusion impossible. The inner organs were battered making it impossible to pinpoint what actually caused him to cease living. Rage, evil, and contempt filled the soul of whoever did it.

Hendricks was not an overly religious man. He believed people who had defects of the brain committed some murders.

However, the uglier murders involving torture or sadistic acts came from unadulterated evil. These days, with science providing the explanations for the unknown, man had forgotten the ever-present devil who works his will from the shadows. The excuse, "the devil made me do it," is a good explanation many murderers claim but impossible to prove in a court of law. Sure enough though, Lucifer was present and having a grand old time torturing weak souls.

Giving up on the coroner's report, Hendricks revisited the forensics report and crime scene photos again. The crime scene was difficult to process. Williams was cast aside in a habitual Seattle dumping ground. The photos showed abandoned cars, rusted shopping carts, bags and bags of rotting trash, a dead dog, and all other sorts of discarded city refuse.

The report went on to read that a homeless guy rooting through the debris for cans and bottles found the body. Discovered in the middle of the garbage heap, the man's blood showed up in the pictures as black goo. The report also stated the only evidence they found was twenty-seven different styles of tire tracks ranging from small compact cars, to trucks, SUVs, and motorcycles. It would take more than two weeks to isolate the tire types. Probably a waste of time he thought.

The crime scene team collected fifty-four different sets of footprints. One good thing about the area under the bridge, it had mud that did not dry too quickly nor was it exposed directly to the Seattle rain. It would take three weeks for a single technician to identify the foot sizes and narrow down the shoe types. Add another week if any of the footprints possessed an anomaly. The crime lab report included photos of the tire and foot casts made. Hendricks had to give the Seattle crime lab credit. What they lacked in real evidence they made up in volume. They made sure the crime scene was fully documented and photographed. Crime tape or no crime tape, areas like this would be covered in another layer of trash and junk within two days. If they ever did catch his killer, they had to be able to recreate the scene and extract information from what they collected. What better way to do so than using photographic collection processes.

Striking out, Hendricks continued to flip through the photos. He started to go through the photos capturing the crime scene's overall circumference. A black speck in the corner of a photo containing the concrete underbelly of a bridge captured his attention. The detective reached for his magnifying glass and focused on the fuzzy object. He raised his eyes from the photo. Looking through the glass for long periods made him tired. He reexamined the photo to make sure he saw what he thought he saw. There it was, a Seattle Department of Transportation highway video camera monitoring the traffic traveling under the bridge. He knew they had to keep a week's worth of data in the event an accident investigation popped up. With luck, the tapes just might show something of use. It was a long shot, but it was somewhere to start. Hopefully, the forensics lab's technical division could extract something from the video. That is, as long as the camera worked and S-DOT followed their own protocol. They had to work fast to get the raw video.

Sergeant Hendricks had one more page of the forensics report to review. He would then be able to go back and concentrate on Amanda Jackson's case. Doing this was a good diversion. He did not believe the report's last page would yield anything of significance. It rarely did. He browsed the toxicology report of the samples the coroner forwarded to the crime lab for processing. It proved Williams did not have any alcohol or drugs in his system. It was the last sentence that caught his attention.

"A sticky substance was found on the victim's left ankle and calf muscle. The residue was analyzed. It was determined to be consistent with adhesives used with industrial strength tapes. The tape type is unknown. It will take approximately two weeks to research and determine the types of tape this glue was applied to. End of report."

Ten pots of coffee could not have opened his eyes wider. Hendricks re-read the second to last sentence of the report. He read the sentence three more times, making sure he read what he thought he had found. Two murders within a week involving a victim being taped were way too much of a coincidence. The killings had to be linked. He needed to get the tape evidence to the twins immediately. His mind raced as he laid out his game plan to combine the evidence of both cases. Not overly religious, a fleeting thought entered his mind that God provided just enough of a clue for him to lure his optimism. What were the odds his criminologist protégée wound up with a case possessing a crucial link allowing him to solve both Amanda's and Mr. Williams's slayings. Practically impossible.

Having Paul as a partner again, especially with the city resources he brought to the table, made him relax a bit. Paul would be eager to team up again. They made a strong pair fighting crime and taking ruthless men and women out of circulation. Hendricks would enlist Paul's help in getting the glue evidence and all of the tire and shoe imprints to the twins. They wouldn't have any problem transferring the evidence to their custody. The real key was getting their hands on the video from the highway department.

"You're smiling, hun," a voice over Hendricks shoulder stated. It brought Hendricks back to the real world. A grin ran across his unshaven face. Cheri, the middle-aged waitress perked up thinking the smile was aimed at her. Before he could say anything, the blond waitress floated the tab on the table with a note with her phone number scrawled on it. She desperately wanted company. She longed for the type of fun only a man could give a woman. Who cares if she was being forward? She liked him and she wanted him to know it.

"Oh, sorry," he said. "I just discovered one of the biggest breaks I will ever have in my career."

Seizing the happy moment, Cheri let herself flirt some more by sitting down at the table with her new crush. Overdoing it just a bit, she wanted to sound excited for him. "That is awesome sugar, whatcha find?" asked the bodacious blond.

"I hate to tell you this Cheri, but I cannot tell you." Noticing her balloon deflating a bit, he charged on. "But, I can tell you I think you have a great smile and I would love to take you out to dinner. Are you free this week?"

"That sounds wonderful," the overjoyed woman replied.

"Great! How about the night after tomorrow? We can go down to the harbor and have some yummy clam chowder in a bread bowl and a few beers. Sounds good?"

Her conquest complete, Cheri stood up making sure her cleavage sweetened the pot. "That sounds like a lot of fun," she said as she scribbled her address on the paper with her number on it.

Unable to resist looking at her exposed cleavage, Hendricks looked on as she wrote. Her eyes sparkled as she looked up knowing he was checking out her goods. He pocketed the paper and felt warmth in his heart and stiffness in his pants as Cheri sauntered away. Gazing out the window, Raphael was parking his car. The two hours he spent on the case and flirting with Cheri flew by. Excitement surged back into his body as he watched Paul cross the parking lot. He had found a real clue. Now they had to exploit it.

"Ah-ha, I knew if I let you look at the case you'd find something," Paul exclaimed when he looked at Hendricks. After you have worked closely with someone every day of the week for a few years, you get to know the person, his expressions, and many times, his thoughts.

"We got some work to do Paul."

Paul was confused. Why did Hendricks say we? Sitting down, he patiently waited for the answer. It took ten minutes to explain. Sergeant Raphael's shoulders flexed as the links were unfolded.

He listened intently and agreed with his mentor's investigative plan. There was only a single item bothering him.

"There are a lot of coincidences with the cases. I am not going to get too optimistic, just like you, until we see the evidence comparison. There are too many 'ifs' with this to begin with. If there is some common evidence, we have to figure out the link and the common denominator," opined Raphael.

Nodding his head in agreement, "You are absolutely correct young Jedi. The only things I see in common are both victims are black and the tape residue. I do not think they had anything going on together but we cannot rule that out until we start delving into their personal lives. We got some serious police work ahead of us. Let's get started before the trail runs cold."

Both knew there was nothing else to say. All there was to do was to start putting the puzzle together from what they both had. Hendricks rose from his seat, pulled a twenty out of his pocket, and laid it under his bill. The food only cost eight bucks but he did not want Cheri thinking he was cheap before his first date. For some reason he liked her more than most of the women he dated. She seemed genuine. Time would tell. He thought the same thought about a few women he fell in love with only to find out later they were completely incompatible. A couple of the women turned out to be real devils in tight blouses. There was not any need to start thinking like that. All they wanted was some adult company to keep away the lonely nights.

Hendricks and Raphael made their way to the door. Hendricks made sure Cheri was watching him before he waved goodbye as he left the diner. Raphael noticed the smile he gave her. Good for him. He needed something warm, soft, and curvy to help ease the harshness he saw every day. Once outside, the two detectives parted ways knowing what each had to do. They would communicate tomorrow or the next day to cover what each learned from their inquiries. All they could do now was to sift through the evidence and cull the clues from the ghost trails.

CHAPTER SEVEN

The Colby boys were methodical if not anal about their work. The detective working the Amanda Jackson case called yesterday to tell them to analyze more evidence relating to her death. What they expected were her personal affects, which was standard protocol. What they received was surprising but intriguing. Hendricks added a new twist to the story.

The Navy did not grant them access to the aircraft carrier she worked on; thus, barring them from collecting evidence on site. It was a political thing. Their bosses had to submit official requests through the District Attorney's office that had to submit official requests to the Department of Defense who had to submit official requests to the Secretary of the Navy. The process was laborious and painfully bureaucratic. If evidence sat too long it had a way of disappearing or becoming stale. They did learn that as soon as the girl's military superiors found out about her death, they secured all of her possessions and workspaces.

The navy left it up to the Naval Criminal Investigation Service, NCIS in navaleese, to process her affects. That was not what they received. Israel and Ishmael were shocked to see boxes containing evidence from a recent Seattle murder of a middle-aged black man.

A quick call to Hendricks shed light on the situation. The detective was surprised the evidence made it to their lab so quickly. That is the benefit of having his old partner as the lead detective on the case. Hendricks told the young scientists his glue theory. He wanted them to process the data and compare it to the glue residue discovered on Amanda Jackson.

Both men quickly agreed that the theory had merit. Two murders occurring closely in time to each other with both victims bound with tape was too much of a coincidence.

Being methodical by nature, Israel and Ishmael started their analysis first by sorting the evidence on long, silver surgical steel tables laid parallel to one another. With the material spread out, displayed, and ready for comparison, the forensic scientists scanned it for tell tale signs of something interesting. It did not take long to decide what needed in depth processing. Three items were common between the two murders.

Israel concentrated his examination on the glue analysis, the tire treads found at both scenes, and the footprints. Meanwhile, as Israel did the slow, tedious processing of the crime scene evidence, Nathanial loaded the Seattle Department of Transportation traffic recordings into his computer's memory. Lady Luck smiled upon them again. S-DOT's traffic monitoring system recorded an entire week's worth of traffic which was automatically saved as a digital file. The real question was whether the camera captured the area under the bridge where Mr. Williams was. The second question posed was, did the camera possess enough fidelity to record the events taking place? He would see shortly.

Ishmael's lab possessed digital matrix-algorithmic based analysis software. It took him a year hurdling bureaucratic obstacles to obtain the funding to buy the software. He persevered and pestered until he achieved his goal. Here was the chance they needed to prove the wait and cost were well worth it.

The spy satellite software came from the National Security Agency. Before the 9-11 attacks against the World Trade Towers and the Pentagon, the second borne Colby twin never dreamed of approaching the NSA for their capabilities. The 9-11 Commission recommended to the president to break down the barriers preventing federal, state, and local law enforcement agencies from effectively working together. He readily agreed. The firewalls and stovepipes tumbled down.

The various national law enforcement and intelligence agencies initiated programs collaborating and synchronizing their efforts. The goal was to root out potential terrorist cells and networks. It did that successfully, but it also had great side benefits in solving domestic crimes. Access to military and federal databases, previously deemed untouchable, magically opened up a completely new aspect to solving domestic crimes and taking bad people off the streets. Besides being able to tap into the federal government's treasure trove of intelligence assets, the next best asset was the fed's inter-state crime network. Now, any state could search the other's crime files for crime patterns.

The Colby's used the resources to catch a rapist who committed crimes in three different states. His crime spree spanned three years. He was able to get away with it because one state's law enforcement agency did not know the same types of rapes were occurring across the borders in their neighboring states. The process took time though. The database was immense. It had a strong computer search engine built into it and an entire set of servers dedicated to the process. Google would be impressed by the computing power the federal government had. It did have an Achilles' heel. It did not have enough bandwidth to support all of America's fifty states and territories simultaneously.

Ishmael worked out the search criteria. Without a priority clearance, the database search could take as many days as the week was long. Ishmael started the process three days ago. He would have to update it to include Samuel Williams. It would make the process a bit longer.

The killings were too methodical and too well thought out. The crime scenes were either too clean or exposed to numerous contaminates. He surmised they were dealing with a person who knew how to clean up after himself. Israel agreed with Ishmael's assessment. The killer they sought was an expert. He had done it many times before. Their job was to find out where, when, and how many murders he did commit. They just needed to communicate that to Sergeant Hendricks and the new cop on the team, Raphael.

Ishmael started converting the traffic camera's recordings to a format readable by the NSA software. It would not take too long since the traffic camera did not use any type of compression format. It was a simple digital recording of cars speeding by.

Traffic monitoring during the day occurred from a remote station. At night, it really did not matter since rush hour was long over and knowledge of traffic problems was not a major concern. Nonetheless, it recorded the traffic twenty-four hours a day, seven days a week, three hundred and sixty five days a year.

Three mouse button clicks converted the files with ease. Another click searched the files for the times in question. According to the homicide file, Williams's body turned up on a Tuesday. The Seattle coroner approximated the man's time of death somewhere between Saturday night and early Sunday morning.

Normally, Ishmael enjoyed taking risks. He sought pleasure extreme skiing, doing tricks on his snowboard, challenging Washington's mountains with his mountain bike, or climbing Mount Rainier. When it came to work though, he erred on the side of caution.

Establishing time of death was not an exact science. He commanded the computer to search for files starting Thursday afternoon to the Wednesday after the body was found. Many times, however cliché, a killer does return to the scene of the crime. They are compelled to return by their morbid blood thirst. The computer displayed its results twelve minutes later. The central processor unit identified ninety-six hours of recorded data. It would take almost just as long for Ishmael to review the files and to exclude the ones he did not desire to look at. The next step was cumbersome. Manually examining each file for photographic evidence of the killer would take time. This was the essence of his job… patience and perseverance.

Evidentiary examination took a while, but; the slow process did work. Eyewitness testimony and confessions were not always enough to convict a criminal. You had to back it up with hard evidence putting the criminal at the crime scene without a shadow of a doubt. Piecing the puzzle together to provide the necessary information was what made the job fun. He loved a good riddle. e HHe In the meantime, waiting patiently for the computers to complete the searches, he wanted to spend a little time talking with an Interpol agent in London he met three months ago.

Ever since the European Union formed, Europe's national borders became just as porous as the borders between the States. Interpol was well known and internationally respected when it came to tracking crimes across the national borders. Their police agencies regularly worked together. He never knew when he would need to use their databases. His motto was to always be prepared and one-step ahead of the criminals. It was time to expand his investigative horizons.

Israel busied himself in other aspects of the puzzle. Being as meticulous as his brother, he prioritized his efforts. The easiest task started with analyzing the glue found on both victims. Blood, dirt, and grime from the bridge site contaminated most of the residue found on Mr. Williams. His task involved sifting through it all and identifying a satisfactory sample for comparison. He also had to compare the tire and foot print photos and the moldings he collected from Amanda Jackson's dumpsite against those of the William's dumpsite.

The sheer number of imprints taken at the scenes made the process cumbersome and difficult but not impossible. Akin to his brother, all he needed was time. He looked for two items linking the cases. The size nine boot and the tire tracks matching those he collected in the woods. The tire tracks left at Amanda's scene matched to Goodyear tires. Nothing was special about the tires themselves. Thousands of trucks and vans in the North America drove on the same tire style. However, having the same tires at two different scenes narrowed his focus.

Israel and his brother grew up and were educated in the computer processing generation. He scanned all of the photographs and molds the Seattle crime scene units took from the Williams scene and started a comparison against Amanda's dump site prints. The slow process was working the scanner. After he had the tracks scanned, his parallel processing computers shouldered the grunt work. With everything entered into the computer it was downhill from there. He estimated it would take less than an hour to determine if any tracks were similar. His computer programs made short work of the comparisons and filtering.

The young men did not depend on luck. Their art was investigative science and they excelled at it. Their efforts built cases so the long arm of law could crash down upon the killer's ears, snatch him up, and incarcerate his butt so the criminal psychologists could have an interesting yet mad subject to study for the next forty years. The brothers went about their business methodically. They only took breaks for food, sleep, and a bit of exercise riding their bikes around the island. The bike rides refreshed their thoughts and let their cunning brains work on the massive amounts of data they consumed. Hendricks would be pleased with their efforts.

CHAPTER EIGHT

Father Nguyen researched his dilemma amongst the church canons. His vows gave him little latitude to work in. Unless the murderer voluntarily surrendered himself to the police, Nguyen could not provide any information regarding the confessional conversations between him and the murderer. He was determined to find a clergical loophole.

The Arch Dioceses leader, Bishop Lee, the only Chinese-American bishop in the United States, gave him scant yet sage advice. Just like Christ speaking to his flock, he did not come right out and give him a direct path to follow. Lee told him to search his inner soul for the answer. Lee recommended Nguyen take a break from his parish. "Get away from the day-to-day routine," the Bishop advised. "God will hear your prayers and lead you to the solution. Be patient."

Following his mentor's suggestions, Father Nguyen hiked deep into the Olympia Mountains in pursuit of his answer. To him, walking in the woods and sitting by a cool brook with his feet immersed cleared his thoughts from all distractions. As Christ made a pilgrimage to the desert, he made his own to ponder his fate and the repercussions of his actions or inactions. He concluded doing nothing would haunt him for the rest of his life. Besides being the spiritual leader for his parishioners, his first duty was to confront and combat evil. God laid down for him this test.

Nguyen concluded that whatever he did it was fraught with grave danger. So be it. If he had to give his life up to stop the madman from killing more of God's children, he would make that sacrifice. If Christ could accept persecution and the agony of being nailed to a cross, he could follow his example by confronting evil with just as much zeal. No matter what the cost or danger. He struggled with images of a demon capturing innocent souls and reaping his own form of perverted hatred upon them. Sheer terror filled his soul when he imagined the scene. He trusted in God to provide him answers. All he had to do was pray, meditate, and wait for the light.

Thoughts and ideas flooded his mind. His first option would be to ignore his vows and go directly to the authorities. It was not viable. That thought smacked of the devil tempting him to the dark side by offering the path of least resistance. It was easy but it violated the promises he made to God and to his fellow man.

He loved being a priest and he loved his religion. There had to be another way. Father Nguyen thumbed his Rosary Beads with the sun warming his back. He bent over in meditation appealing to the Almighty for guidance. He could continue to talk and reason with the murderer. No, perpetual conversation would not get him anywhere either.

The Cambodian Padre demanded stronger action from himself. Pacific confrontation was the only way. Violence was out of question. Whatever he did, he had to mimic Christ. Jesus's love would provide the strength he needed.

A drop of water suddenly struck the Priest on his face disturbing his thoughts. Strange he pondered. There was not a cloud in the sky but it seemed a drop of rain struck him. In the corner of his eye, he witnessed a trout leap from the water, gobble a brown fly, and silently disappear back into the stream. The serene image burned into his mind.

The enormity of what he just witnessed crashed into him swiftly filling his soul with jubilation. Nguyen realized what had just happened. God descended to the Earth and answered his prayers.

The fish was more than a scaly, hungry bug eater. It was a vision sent from above. A true and holy sign from his Lord. Christ fed thousands with forty fish and forty loaves. Now, mysteriously, he fed the clergyman's quest through a lone brook trout. The fish did not lead to his epiphany. The water droplet striking him in the face opened his thoughts.

His path was as clear as the water gurgling at his feet. Bishop Lee's wisdom was correct. He prayed for God's guidance and it came. The 'fish tear' helped him realize his course.

The murderous demon lived and worked on the water. That was where Nguyen had to go. The demon's den became his target. He had to get aboard the sailor's ship, somehow. How, he did not know. Onboard the ship is where he needed to stalk and confront his unholy prey. If the demon wanted to violate the house of God, then he would reverse the equation. Nguyen decided to haunt the demon's house. He had to go to the source of the murderer's strength.

Spiritually uplifted, the black clad Reverend stood, raised his hands to the sky, and gave thanks for the divine intervention. On the trek home through the forest, Father Nguyen prayed for resolve and strength. It would not be an easy battle and he needed all of God's power to circumvent Satan's handy work. The four-hour hike home gave him more time to strategize his coming moves.

The Everett Naval Station Chaplain always asked for community assistance onboard the ships. When an aircraft carrier was in port, there were not enough religious personnel to help all of the problems that come along with the flattop. Most of the military's chaplains volunteered to go overseas. Their presence on the front line gave tired and scared soldiers, marines, aviators, and sailors the opportunity to practice their faith. The cliché that there were no atheists in foxholes was true. Soldiers and sailors waging war on terror needed spiritual help the most. Not knowing who was friend or who was foe weighed the American warriors down with stress. It was important they had a way to manage and cope with their fear. Putting that fear into God's hands was the Chaplain's job. Providing for those forward deployed left the state side force lacking spiritual guidance. It would have to come from the local communities. That lack of reverently mentoring was Father Nguyen's foot into the murderer's lair. One phone call gave him complete access to the base. Volunteering to help on the ship gave him unfettered access to the demon. Once he got there, he had no idea what he would do. That would take a bit more thought. His faith in prayer and God never let him down yet. God's aqua-messenger proved that. All he had to do was to clear away the noise in his head, listen, and wait for God's message.

CHAPTER NINE

Hendricks and Raphael met for a hearty Mexican breakfast to kick the day off right. Forbidden during mealtime was discussion of either case. Hendricks insisted upon this simple rule when Raphael came to him as a rookie detective. The only way they preserved their sanity was detaching themselves periodically from their cases. It did not mean their compassion levels were low. It meant they were human and needed a break. Agreeing not to speak about the cases while they ate afforded them a respite from the cruel and depraved shadow world they lived in.

Hendricks' rule was important for a plethora of reasons. If detective work was the only thing they did, police officers burned out quickly. The job consumed those who did not heed the warning signs. Both men witnessed many of their friends turn into alcoholics, gamblers, abusers, or became bitter and mean from all of the hate they experienced. Some even transgressed to the other side and became criminals. Arresting your fellow officer was the hardest thing any cop had to do.

Another reason boiled down to their own safety. Danger lurked around every corner for the peace officer professional. Rare though it was for a cop to pull and use his weapon, being prepared to do so was in the forefront of their minds. When the time came to shoot their weapons, a cop wanted to feel his six was covered. He can only do the job by trusting his fellow cops. Learning the likes and dislikes of their partners and becoming friends was vitally important to their sanity and safety. Not speaking about cop stuff over lunch helped them develop that bond.

Fried chorizo sausage mixed in their scrambled eggs, bacon, tortillas, and strong coffee was their fare. Being pseudo partners again, they unceremoniously fell into their past rituals. Sports were the topics du jour.

The Seattle Mariners had a chance to win the wild card race for the American League baseball playoffs. Football was thrown around too. The Seahawks first game was Sunday. They both agreed the ‹Hawks would trounce Tampa Bay.

The subject of women always came up too. Raphael described his recent vacation to Hawaii he took with his wife and kids. They visited the island of Kauai for ten days. His eldest son, Pedro, learned to surf. He actually fell more than he rode the waves. It did not matter. The boy gained more self-confidence in those ten days than he had in a year. His daughter, Lucia, spent most of her time taking hula dance lessons. His wife, Rose, spoiled her with Hawaiian dresses and braided her hair with fragrant plumeria flowers. He did not share with his ex-partner the moonlight love making Rose and he shared on the soft sand whilst waves crashed ashore in the background. It was a great vacation.

Hendricks talked about his third date with the waitress from the diner. Cheri is a lot of fun he said. She did not push, act pretentious, or expect a whole lot. She went with the flow and was carefree. It felt good to date a woman like that. They had slept together that night too. It was passionate yet clumsy. Neither knew each other well enough to make it enjoyable. What they lacked in experience of each other, they made up for in lust.

The conversation ended on whether or not Hendricks would continue to see Cheri. He definitely would. It was a good feeling to let loose and not worry about all of the crap he saw on the job. A sense of normalcy swept over him when he and Cheri spent time together. Maybe it was because she was around cops so much at the cop dinner. She knew how to get them to lower their guard. Whatever it was, he just knew he liked her a lot.

After breakfast and the light conversation, the two policemen drove to the ferry station, paid their fare, and parked in the line waiting to board the next ferry boat to Whidbey Island. It was the one wrong about the Island County government. The county offices, including the Crime Scene Unit offices, were located on Whidbey Island. They did admit they enjoyed taking the ferry across the Puget Sound. Rain or shine, the forty-five minute trip was relaxing and scenic.

Predominately working cases in Seattle, Raphael rarely took the ferry except for fun with his family. The scenery was breathtaking. Seeing the boat cut through the crisp waters and, if you were lucky, watching majestic Orca killer whales splash around Puget Sound turned the ride into a National Geographic show.

The twins called the detectives yesterday to arrange the meeting. They completed their analysis and were ready to present their findings. The Colby brothers wanted the cops to travel to their lab to discuss their findings. They hinted they had good news. The two never let the cat out of the bag unless it was on their own terms. Calling them to their scientific sanctuary made it a big deal. The criminal scientists must have found evidence proving to be extremely helpful.

The green and white striped ferry slowed its engine to moor to the auto loading ramp. Men stationed on the pier quickly fastened the three inch mooring lines cast over from men on the ferry to heavy cast iron bollards on the pier.

The boat was made fast and lowered its ramp in less than five minutes. Cars filed from the hull two at a time. It was a smooth operation. The faster passengers disembarked the better. The ship's captain had a tight schedule to keep. Luckily, Detectives Hendricks and Raphael were on the outer-tiered rows of the boat and were first to be offloaded.

The drive up the center of the island to the CSI building was a quick affair. Driving in silence, each officer lost themselves in their respective thoughts. Douglas firs lined the highway casting the road into an evergreen channel. Hendricks activated his left turn signal and entered the parking lot. No matter how much they tried to maintain their calm, the energy flowed from the anticipation each police officer felt.

The Colby brothers awaited their arrival in a conference room. It was more a sterile surgical operating room than a place to hold meetings. The walls were brilliantly white. White, glossy tile encompassed the walls from floor to ceiling.

Four large flat panel screens hung from a windowless wall. Israel gestured for the detectives to sit behind a long white marble table. Unlike other conference rooms used in business pursuits, the lab's table helped to fight crime. The white walls shed more light upon evidence they wanted to examine when it was unloaded on the marble table. The hard, smooth, and lightly colored marble allowed the CSI crew to notice the tiniest piece of fiber, hair, dirt, or whatever. Miniature pieces of evidence contrasted well against the light marble.

The lights configured overhead shone white light, bright or soft and at different intensities, ultra-violet light or infrared light. Natural light was not wanted.

Up against a sidewall was a desk where two Macintosh workstations sat. The Mac was the computer of choice in the graphic analysis industry.

Ishmael Colby punched some hot keys on the keyboard and clicked the computer's mouse button twice. Data immediately flashed onto the oversized screens. Israel began their presentation.

"Hello detectives. Shall we begin?" the young analyst asked.

Hendricks and Raphael understood what was happening. The Colbys did not go to this much trouble if they had not found substantial or significantly relevant evidence. They were about to present their scientific conclusions as if they were defending a doctoral degree dissertation or testifying in court. Professionalism was the name of the game.

"After careful examination of the evidence from the Amanda Jackson murder and the Samuel Williams slaying, Investigator Colby," motioning his left hand towards his brother, Israel, "and

I have developed significant conclusions we believe you will find extremely helpful in your investigations."

The detectives knew not to interrupt with any questions until the presentation was complete. However, both instinctively opened their notebooks to jot down questions each wanted to ask when they reached the end.

Ishmael took over the speech. "Please focus your attention to the left and right top screens where we will start describing the forensic analysis we performed."

Ishmael struck a key on the computer keyboard. A series of tire mold photos appeared.

"The molds on the left are Goodyear tire treads found where Miss Jackson was deposited in the Camano Island forest," pointed Colby with a brilliant red laser dot. "The impressions on the right are the tire impressions collected where Samuel Williams was found. The Goodyear tire is quite common, and as we told you before, it is the leading sales tire for trucks, vans, and sport utility vehicles in the United States. However, we concluded the tires came from the same vehicle. This is based on tread wear and unique cuts we discovered on the tires imprints." Ishmael went on and pointed out six different unique identifiers linking the two tire sets together. Hendricks and Raphael scribbled more questions in their tablets.

It was Israel's turn to speak again. "On to the next set of evidence," he began as images appeared on the lower two screens. "The graphs you are observing depict a chemical analysis of the glue left on each victim's body. As you can see, the results are eighty seven percent conclusive." Anticipating their questions before the cops could express them, Israel answered their silent queries.

"The glue is from an industrial strength electrical tape used to seal extremely high voltage electrical wiring. It is mainly used at electrical generation plants." Pausing for affect, the young man continued his discussion. "We compared twenty different industrial grade electrical tapes and the adhesives used on the tapes. We discovered an interesting anomaly amongst the two samples and the tapes we tested."

The detective's eyes shifted from the computer screens and focused on Israel Colby.

"The anomaly we discovered is salt. Specifically, ocean salt. The tape used on the victims has been exposed heavily to the marine environment."

"Please focus your attention back to the screens," Ishmael said. A video clip started playing on all four screens. The cops had to admit, the Colby brothers knew how to make their science dramatic and gripping. It was like a novel. They slowly built their story, adding more and more drama as it went along. Their testimonies in court always proved credible for this very same reason.

What the investigators witnessed was a series of vehicles pulling into the area under the bridge where Samuel Williams' bloody and unrecognizable body lie. There were twenty-two clips in all. Hendricks and Raphael did not have to be told where the images came from. The vantage point came from the traffic cameras monitoring the highway's congestion.

"It was amazing how many cars and trucks frequented the underneath of the bridge where Mr. Williams was dumped," commented Ishmael. "Most of the activities captured under the bridge by the traffic cam were losers getting ten dollar blow jobs from crack whores, junkies buying drugs, or people dumping their junk. The vehicles you see are a select subset because we narrowed our search based upon the Goodyear model tire we were looking for. Unfortunately, the cameras field of view and fidelity is poor. The cameras used to monitor traffic flow only need to watch traffic not focus on license plates or the drivers in their cars. Thus, we couldn't make out any license plate numbers or other descriptive data," said Ishmael.

"But," interjected Israel who was now showing signs of excitement, "We have a vehicle list documenting possible auto types that may have carried Samuel below the bridge. It's definitely a good start to catching the killer."

On display were sixty-two vans, sports utility vehicles, and pick-up trucks. Just as Ishmael stated, you could not get a visual on the drivers, license plates, or any other identifying marks. Worse, the place where Williams was cast aside was out of the camera's range. As Israel stated, they now had a guess at the killer's mode of transportation. It would make connecting the mystery's dots easier when Hendricks and Raphael compiled their suspect list.

Ishmael stopped the films from playing. The twins looked at each and nodded simultaneously. Israel flicked a switch on the wall. A screen unfolded from the ceiling. Once it settled into position, a projector displayed a United States map.

Small red circles were scattered about the nation, especially along the Atlantic and Pacific coasts. There were circles in Rhode Island, New York, Virginia, Florida, Texas, Illinois, Michigan, California, South Dakota, Wyoming, New Mexico, Tennessee, and Idaho. The list did not stop there. Some states had more than one. California and New York had sixteen and nine circles respectively. Over two hundred of the little blood red dots covered the map.

"Sergeant Hendricks and Sergeant Raphael," hailed Israel. He stated their names for dramatic affect but it was unneeded. The detective's full attention was riveted to the map.

Israel announced, "Each circle is a murder. Each dot represents a gravesite of a brutally beaten man or a suffocated and naked young woman. All of the circles are active unsolved homicides. The oldest is sixteen years old."

The cops sat stunned. The Colby's analysis yielded not only a link between two murders. It unearthed a serial killer flying under the radar screen for at least sixteen years. Their tenacity uncovered a link to hundreds of unsolved slayings and a serial killer.

Inset to the map was a legend with the victim's names and the dates their bodies were discovered. Hendricks seized upon an oddity amongst the numbers displayed. He could no longer sit back and calmly take notes. There were gaps in the crimes numerology. There was no doubt they were dealing with a serial killer. A transient one made matters worse. The weird fact was the range of dates. At times, there were numerous murders committed during a certain timeframe. Then, 'whoosh', the murders stopped for several months or years. Hendricks' first impression led him to believe they would be searching for a professional criminal who was in and out of prison. The explanation seemed plausible.

Raphael spoke first. "Holy shit! If those murders were committed by the same psychopath, we will need some more help," he said with a stunned expression. "This guy has been operating undetected for sixteen plus years."

The Colbys created the affect they desired. The two police officers were stunned at what the crime scene analysts discovered. When Ishmael's countrywide data base search revealed its ugly news, at first, he nearly blew a gasket. However, his professionalism as a scientist took back control. He regained his composure quickly and started to analyze the data he unearthed. Before he could tell anyone, he had to make sure the data was accurate. He spent days and nights pouring over the details of each crime. The facts stood by themselves. Most of the crimes were committed against female prostitutes and men who did not have any enemies callous enough to kill them. Spread out across the country, randomly occurring, and over a great swath, no one connected the dots until now. He knew it would end up as the most significant multiple homicide case in the decade. If not the century.

All of the women were young, pretty, and found naked without any signs of rape or torture. Each woman was deposited in a tranquil, peaceful setting. One woman was found lying under an oak tree next to a lake. Another was discovered amongst a nursery's flower field. It seemed the victim's final resting places were choreographed to be serene and peaceful.

The real resemblance was the manner in which they died. All died from asphyxiation. More-or-less peaceful deaths as murders go. Nevertheless, it was still murder. There were too many similarities. They had to conclude the same perpetrator committed the murders.

On the other hand, when he researched how the men died, it made him stop and refocus his energy once again. What he discovered was horrendously disturbing.

On the laboratory walls, he pasted all of the crime scene photos from each murder he uncovered. The gruesome scenes looked right back at him like the victim's were pleading with him to unveil their killer and to seek retribution. Unbridled rage was the way to describe how each man suffered under the nut job's merciless hands. Jagged, splintered bones thrust through the victim's skin. Eyeballs lay out of their sockets by the arteries and veins. Heads were crushed like rotten pumpkins. The pictures showed nothing but blood, misery, pain, suffering, and profound cruelty.

The last link making Ishmael decide the same man committed the crimes was the duality of the murders. Each crime levied against a woman and a crime made against a man in the same area always occurred within two or three days of each other. The killer exercised some form of sadistic homicidal therapy. He needed to kill a beautiful woman and a man to satisfy his violent lust.

Silence engulfed the laboratory. The detective's brains churned with the new information. They would have to sift through all of the evidence to comprehend what the twins uncovered.

One thing was certain. This was no longer going to be a small mutually collaborative homicide case between two Washington jurisdictions. The sheer volume of the crimes committed in a single state demanded a task force. The murderer's longevity, extreme psychopathic nature, and murders being committed across the state lines demanded a single recourse. It was time to call the feds.

Hendricks and Raphael needed the major resources only the federal government could muster. The Federal Bureau of Investigation and its vast pool of expertise were required. The murderer was on a sixteen-year rampage with no signs of ever stopping. The detectives knew they needed the resources the FBI's criminal profiling division, its vast connections into other law enforcement agencies, and its communications systems. This was going to turn out to be one hell of a manhunt. No doubt, their perpetrator would quickly ascend to the top of the country's most wanted list.

Hendricks' stood, walked to the coffee pot and poured himself a cup of Starbucks the Colbys brewed before the meeting. He deliberately kept silent to capture his swirling thoughts. Raphael remained at the conference table studying the map and the data. With a case of this magnitude, Paul would reserve his questions until Hendricks' finished his. He ceded to his partner's experience and wisdom.

Swirling the sugar and cream into the black brew, Hendricks walked in front of the projector screen. Sipping the hot liquid, he pondered the map cast on the screen. For ten minutes, he stood gazing at the tiny circles. His eyes darted back and forth while his crime-solving mind channeled and categorized his thoughts. Drinking the last sip of the coffee, his first words were for Israel Colby. "Did you say the residue found on the electrical tape had sea salt on it?"

Glancing at his notes though he did not need to, Israel replied, "Yes, the sodium found embedded in the tape's glue is consistent with salt found only in the ocean. Normal table salt or other rock salt has a different chemical crystalline construction." Pausing to review an item in his notes, he continued with his answer. "I also compared the sample to our waters here in Washington. The samples were remarkably similar in nature. The concentrations were not what we find here in Washingtonian shore waters; however, it is Pacific Ocean salt nevertheless."

Hendricks' mind latched onto an important observation. The circles concentrated on the East and West coasts of the United States. The left and right coasts were the maniac's primary hunting grounds. Whoever it was, the murderer connected somehow to the sea. Something took him across the country often. It was his one and only mistake. He covered his tracks well; but, over time, and with the help of modern technology, he finally surfaced. He escaped notice for sixteen years. Now, they had a scent. The predator was becoming prey.

Turning slowly left to face his peers who sat silently waiting to hear his thoughts, "This psychopath is somehow involved in the maritime industry. The electrical tape with the ocean salt is his tell. Other killers use everyday duct tape, rope, zip ties, or even wire. This moron uses what he knows is strong and can't be broken. We are looking for a person who works on ships. I bet you dollars to donuts he is an electrician in a shipyard. His hunting ground is now the Pacific Northwest." His audience remained still and silent. They knew he had just begun his hypothesis.

"Based on what the Colby boys discovered, we can start narrowing our search to that realm. I know it is huge now, but we have our first puzzle pieces." His eyes focused on the Pacific Northwest shoreline. Seattle was one of the busiest ports in the US. There were hundreds of possibilities where the suspect could be. The surrounding area thrived from the marine business. It employed thousands of people. Then there was Tacoma, Olympia, Bremerton, and countless other smaller ports the killer could be. It was the proverbial needle in a haystack. However, it was a start. A good start.

Raphael knew Detective Benjamin Hendricks finished speaking. They possessed an extremely significant part of the puzzle now. They had their corner on which to build the rest of their investigation.

"I agree," simply stated Raphael. "With a case this size and what Israel and Ishmael reported, we have enough to bring in the

Feds. They can profile this sicko. The FBI psychologists possess a superb reputation when it comes to getting inside a psycho's head. We give them the data you two dug up and we'll have our first composite of this nut job in two days time. Then the field will narrow quickly." Raphael said closing his notebook.

In the next few hours, there were tons of phone calls to made, a ream of reports to file, and a task force to assemble. Stewing on the information for a few hours would be healthy. The two detective's minds needed to filter what they heard, collate it, and rationally develop a game plan to catch a predator on the loose for over a decade and a half.

The team shook hands. Discussion ensued on how the information was to be sent to the cop's offices. The Colby brothers did not miss a beat. They already had the data burned to compact disks. Each detective received a CD. Knowing Hendricks was old school, Israel presented him three brown legal folders with paper copies of everything they found knowing the wise police constable preferred hard copies.

The sun was high in the sky as Raphael and Hendricks opened the building's solid steel doors. Its rays shined down upon them warming their souls despite the ghastly news they just received. No longer were they looking for someone bent on a bit of stray warped revenge. The two cops were stalking a sophisticated monster.

CHAPTER TEN

For his work onboard the *USS ILORETA*, Agent Sherman received a promotion and a medal presented to him by the United States Attorney General behind closed doors guarded by a security force sworn to secrecy. The promotion came with a transfer offer taking him away from undercover duty to a post as the senior field agent of the Miami field office. The promotion meant more money which no one who worked for the United States government ever turned down. The wages the FBI paid their superstars were the same for those who sat behind a desk and punched numbers into a database. It was not a fair system. People became FBI field agents not for the money but to quench a thirst inside them. They lived for the challenge of the pursuit.

The medal rewarded his ego. It was a cheap collection of brass and colored ribbon. A mass produced piece of parchment extolling the barest of virtues about the real mission came along with the medal. Since his mission was covert, only a select few and well trusted individuals in the Bureau knew what the citation really meant.

Being an undercover agent prevented his merits from being proclaimed or publicized like normal nine-to-five FBI agent's exploits were. His name never appeared in any newspapers or within the Department's internal newsletter. He would not receive any recognition from his peers or any pats on the backs except from the five people who attended his sequestered ceremony. The medal would collect dust in a cabinet in a sparsely furnished two bedroom apartment where he stored the other awards he had received during his FBI tenure. His apartment was more storage facility than home. Such was the life of an undercover FBI agent. His job depended on his ability to blend in. He became part of the crime scene waiting for the optimum moment to pounce on his criminal prey. He did think heavily about the offer of being a major city's senior field agent. It meant sitting on his butt shackled to a desk. Babysitting other agents was not his cup of tea. He could not do that. He was only thirty-six years old and needed to be in the field doing what he did best. Sherman did not understand why people were drawn to such isolated and stressful jobs. All he understood was he was good at infiltrating a criminal organization, sniffing out the evidence, and, when the timing was right, summoning the cavalry to secure the bust. There were a few others like him too. His kind was a special breed. Flying under the radar screen, unbeknownst to their brother peace officers yet envied for their courage and discipline. The life was also very lonely. Fleeting relationships with women without any lasting relationships and only a snippet of friendship left a gaping hole in his heart.

Three weeks after the drug bust, he received a call from his handler calling him back to duty from vacation. Agent Almestad was a superb handler. He only contacted him when it was necessary. Handling an undercover agent took finesse and kid gloves. The rules handler's lived by included minimal contact, fast reaction, and steadfast devotion to keeping the agent's identity a closely guarded secret. Almestad instructed Sherman to pack his bags for a couple of weeks and report immediately to FBI headquarters in Quantico, Virginia. He would report to Dr. Ohms who worked in the behavioral science group.

Sherman had heard Ohms's name before. He was an intelligent and highly respected psychologist who headed the FBI's specialized detachment developing criminal profiles on serial killers, rapists, terrorists, and other assorted lunatics. Curiosity ate at Sherman. His undercover work mainly dealt with drug dealers, the slave trade, illegal weapon shipments, or terrorist infiltrations. Why would Almestad send him to Quantico to see the FBI's eggheads?

His plane landed at Dulles International Airport. It was a good flight from San Diego. The pilot took advantage of a tail wind and anticipated arriving twenty minutes early. Always a good thing. Being six foot two and stuck in coach made it an uncomfortably long ride. Although in great physical condition, having an old woman sitting in front of him fidgeting in her seat and pressing her seatback against his knees made the journey longer. He looked forward to the three-hour drive to Quantico. It afforded him time to think on how he was going to assimilate with Dr. Ohm's team. If he was to work on some case with the behavioral science group, he knew they would attempt to classify his personality as soon as he arrived. If they succeeded, then they would try to manipulate his thoughts and reactions. It was not their fault. The behavioral science teams were renowned for their work. Classifying every person they dealt with was second nature for them. They did it without thought. What Sherman wanted was to get into their minds. To pull out the real information he needed to do his job. That is what he did best. He looked for an opening and extracted as much information he needed to capture his prey.

Just as the pilot predicted, the plane landed twenty minutes early. Deplaning took ten. Despite Sherman's annoyance at the old woman sitting in front of him, he helped her retrieve her carry-on luggage from the overhead compartment. It made her day. She appreciated the help and attention from a handsome, young man with manners.

Thankfully, picking up the rental car was a snap. Traffic in DC was a different story. He had to head south and the best route was using the Washington beltway. Traffic snarled and inched along. He calculated his short three-hour transit to Quantico would take at least four and half to five hours. Meeting Dr. Ohms today was impossible. It would wait until tomorrow morning. That was best. He wanted to be fresh when he met the behavioral scientist. A hot shower, a hot meal, and a cold beer would recharge his batteries.

The following morning, Dr. Ohms met Sherman at the building's reception desk. Sherman expected a much older man. What he found was a physically fit man standing five foot eleven inches tall. The slight bulge located on his left hip told Sherman the good doctor packed heat. He obviously shot left-handed and carried a standard issue nine-millimeter semi-automatic pistol. Apparently, the doctor took serious his role as FBI agent as well as his role as scientist.

Sherman knew the doctor was assessing him and developing his first impressions about the agent the Bureau assigned to his team. Sherman reciprocated. He sized up Ohm's based on his own field experience, training, and intuition. Dr. Ohms's persona assessment was developed from what he learned in books about the human psyche and from years delving deeply into the subconscious of the criminal mind.

Dr. Jeffery Ohms's observations were correct no matter how hard Sherman attempted to conceal his inner self. Ohms sized Sherman to be a Type 'A' personality with a touch of Attention Deficit Syndrome. He surmised the agent was in superb physical condition with a mind as chiseled as his body. If the FBI did one good thing, they knew how to task the appropriate people for a tough case needing immediate resolution. He had worked with many agents over the years giving them advice on how a criminal worked, what a crook's motives were, what targets he stalked, what his child life was like, and who he was really striking out against. Characterizing FBI undercover agents was almost as complicated. They tended to march to a different drummer than the rest of humanity.

Unlike what people saw on TV or read in books, a real life psychopath committed crimes of such viciousness even the most imaginative screenwriter could not dream the stuff up. Fiction writers never fully imagined these. When a person went mad, their minds functioned to feed their manic desires. They ruthlessly hunted their prey. The results often sickened the most seasoned and battle hardened officers who discovered the aftermath.

The worst type of criminal, by far, was the child predator. Hollywood and novelists shied away from stories where kids were the target of molesters. Child predator stories did not sell. People read books or went to the movies to escape reality. Seeing a human animal stalking a child was not what people wanted to see on the big screen. Ohms despised investigating child predator cases. Being a father of three boys made his detachment from the cases difficult. He and his team spent hours, days, weeks, and even months with a psychologist afterwards attempting to drive out the images burned onto their retinas after they discovered children brutally beaten, raped, tortured, maimed, or enslaved. When a child predator case was assigned for him to solve, he brought his "A" team to bear. He wanted to solve the case quickly to protect not only the innocent children from predation but also the countless other people involved as well. Criminal mischief rippled and damaged many innocent and unsuspecting lives over a wide spectrum.

This new case was very similar. The case file review and interviews with the Washington cops and crime scene investigators took him five days. They were dealing with an extremely dangerous and evil individual who had no intentions of stopping. On the contrary, the monster they were stalking was committing more and more murders as time flowed by. As it typically happened, the criminal started out slow. He was clumsy at first but he made superb efforts cleansing his tracks for no one to suspect.

During his first year, the killer stalked the East Coast. He killed four people. The murders came in pairs involving a man and woman each time. The men suffered the worst from torture and severe beatings. They were dumped without regard to any form of human civility. It demonstrated the killer's desire to manifest excise rage buried deep within his core. On the other hand, both women were young and pretty. Each was outgoing. Each attracted a lot of attention from the opposite sex.

Ohms plotted to attack the crime from two ends in parallel. Half of his team researched the lifestyles of the victims while the other half analyzed the problem from the beginning. It presented a clearer picture of the murderer. The parallel study exposed traits the murderer desired in victims and how his targeting technique matured over the years.

The case would be the most daunting of his career. Because the murders went undetected for greater than sixteen years, there was a lot of ground to cover in a very short amount of time. Empowering him with a limitless checkbook, resources were not a problem. What he wanted was a stellar team of the best agents the FBI could put together. Thus, the reason Sherman was assigned.

Sherman's undercover experience and his knowledge of the mariner's trade brought tremendous insight to the case. Once a suspect was targeted, it was Agent Sherman's task to target the criminal for arrest and prosecution. They were dealing with a ruthless maniac capable of committing vile and cold-blooded murders. That made him even more dangerous.

The police needed agents in the field who matched their query's cunning and were capable of protecting themselves. Sherman was that man.

The information the Seattle PD provided proved a good place to start. Ohms was tempted to offer the Colbys positions within the FBI crime scene analysis department. The two scientists were far superior compared to most state CSI technicians. Their presence in the FBI lab would make a fine addition to his talented and overworked staff.

The tape analysis was the keystone behind the investigation. They had a general location of the killer's present hunting ground. The killer knew the lay of the land. He lived or worked in the Pacific Northwest before. Dumping Amanda Jackson's body in the middle of a forest on an island was not a random act committed by someone unfamiliar with the area's topology. To behavioral scientists, it meant he planned the murders with little remorse and knew exactly where to dispose their bodies without fear of discovery. However, in this case, he did not account for the random act of a dog owner taking a hike with his dog in the forest. This happenstance gave the team a red-hot scent to track. The team called it a major breakthrough. Dr. Ohms called it luck. He struggled with the sheer quantities of murders committed.

The murderer killed in various locations. Some were in Virginia. Some were in Texas. Bodies turned up in Florida, California, Washington, Rhode Island, Michigan, Virginia, Texas, and the Carolinas. Most of the victims were found near the coasts. It lent credence to their hypothesis that the criminal worked in the maritime trade. Other murders fitting the same pattern were discovered in Tennessee, Illinois, Michigan, Idaho, Kentucky, Nevada, Utah, Montana, South Dakota, Wyoming, and New Mexico. Most were killed near the ocean but sporadic double murders were committed in the country's interior. This anomaly baffled Dr. Ohms.

He hypothesized the killer was a gypsy. The killer shifted coasts for some reason. When he did, he traveled through the inner states killing as he went along quenching his evil passion. What puzzled and gnawed at Ohms was what type of job gave the maniac the kind of freedom to roam about the country committing atrocious murders without anyone noticing. There were only a few possibilities. A truck driver was one. Being independently wealthy was another. It baffled the scientist-agent.

Another incongruence troubled Ohms. Sometimes, two or three murders were committed within three to five month periods. For some unexplainable reason, the killings ceased for two, three, or six months at a time. There was even a period when the murders stopped for two years. What happened during that two-year sabbatical? Was the killer in prison? Did he find another method to channel his anger? Did he marry and became content with life? Did he move out of the country? Hundreds of question peppered his brain. All he could do was to write them down to sort out later. It was the investigation's brainstorming state. The details would fill in overtime with hard investigatory work.

The last disturbing thought Dr. Ohms pondered was the amount of murders committed. Over the sixteen year span, the Colby's identified three hundred and forty eight known cases fitting the modus operandi. That averaged to roughly two murders per month.

Statistically, the victims discovered and attributable to a serial killer were typically a small subset of the total he committed. How many people did this maniac really kill? They were dealing with a well-oiled killing machine. Only by capture would they be able to discover the true magnitude of his madness.

The case required strict security. If information leaked to the newspapers or the television networks, the killer would dive underground and be lost forever. Somewhere along the line, someone involved in the investigation would leak information to the press. This fact added additional urgency to cracking the case. Greed and the desire to be famous always outweighed the need for secrecy when a human-in-the-loop was involved. Precautions were in place to prevent a leak, but the longer the case went on, the probability someone would speak to a reporter increased exponentially.

"Welcome back to Quantico Agent Sherman," Dr. Ohms warmly said. "Follow me and I will explain the purpose behind your summons. Based upon your superior's recommendations and my review of your record, I believe you are just the agent we need to handle the field work required to solve the biggest case in your career," continued the Doctor as they entered the elevator and ascended to the sixteenth floor.

Sherman remained silent for the moment except to remark it felt good to return to Quantico after fourteen years where he received his initial FBI recruit training at Quantico.

Agent Sherman played a tight poker game. He wanted more information about the case and those involved before he became too friendly. The game was all about trust.

Arriving at the FBI's Behavioral Science departmental offices, Dr. Ohms held the door open for Agent Sherman and led him to his office. A retina scan and keypad entry was required to enter. Cameras monitored the hallways and entryways. An armed guard monitored every move. Whatever resided behind the doors demanded extremely tight security protocols. This intrigued Sherman even further.

Ohms entered the door first, walked through a room filled with computers, data storage containers, printers, and equipment storage bins. He proceeded through an automatic door that swished aside revealing a basketball court sized multi-tiered command center.

On the lower tier, tables and chairs were strategically located in a horseshoe configuration allowing for group discussion and easy viewing of large screen displays. The upper tier teemed with agents' busy posting information onto white boards, sitting at desks talking on telephones, or working at computer workstations. Some worked in small groups of two or three at conference tables. Others worked alone. Nonetheless, it was obvious all concentrated upon their individual tasks. It was a beehive of investigatory action.

Sherman instantly recognized it as a task force. His internal questions were, "Why is the task force assembled? What did they need him for?" There was not a need to ask them outright. They wanted his expertise for something and bringing him into the eye of the storm meant he would receive his answers soon enough.

His eyes surveyed the fifty white boards. Each board represented a state. On each were maps with green and red circles.

Arrows originated from pictures pointed to the circles. Each photo set was divided. On the left were candid pictures of people captured in real life. The right contained pictures of their bodies after being murdered. Green arrows represented women. Red arrows represented the men.

Sherman began to see the picture. The case revolved around some type of massive gang or mob war the Feds were trying to piece together. On the other hand, and highly unlikely, the case involved murders. There were too many circles and too many locations. No single killer could possibly kill so many people and in so many places. It would be next to impossible to go undetected.

Doctor Ohms beckoned Sherman to follow. Walking through the task force area, the FBI team paused and cast their eyes upon the new stranger in their midst. Sizing him up, he or she instinctively recognized him as another agent. They did not recognize him. He came from outside the Quantico walls. The people in this room were all specialists at this type of investigation. They knew all of the personalities able to lend their expertise to the project. The unknown agent following their leader was not one of them. Consummate professionals, they knew it would be explained to them in due time. They trusted Dr. Ohms's judgment immensely. The same task force team worked for Dr. Ohms on cases in the past. They respected his vast intellect and his ability to lead. A good leader knew how and when to communicate to his team. Dr. Ohms did it best. He was able to identify an agent's strengths and weaknesses. He then used the information to determine how the agent would be best fit into the investigation. Moreover, he shared his knowledge with the entire team. There was no political infighting when you worked on his task forces. You were kept up-to-date. You were asked for your expert opinion. You were asked to perform the way you were trained. A simple formula for success. Most of all, he asked for their loyalty. Their goals were to capture the most notorious criminals known to modern man. Therefore, if he thought it necessary to bring in an outsider, he had good reason to do so. The task force dismissed the agent from their minds and went back to work.

Ohm's motioned to the chair placed in front of his desk. He rounded his desk, poured two glasses of ice water from a clear picture, handed one to Sherman, and wordlessly lowered himself into his chair. He continued to analyze Sherman since the two met. Ohms developed a basic understanding of Sherman's motivation, character, and personality from studying his service record. He admitted to himself that he was not dealing with an average FBI agent.

Similar to the behavioral sciences group, undercover agents possessed unique traits not found amongst other agents. They possessed an innate drive to succeed. They demonstrated a more than normal sense of right and wrong. They did not do their job for the money because if they did the FBI could not afford them. Living in a shadow world, the agents suppressed all of their personal traits to assume a personality foreign to them. In his opinion, undercover agents were twenty-five percent thrill seekers, twenty-five percent Sir Lancelot, twenty-five percent chameleons, and twenty-five percent actors. Combining all four traits made an extremely effective agent. They were able to withstand insurmountable pressures while maintaining their sanity. Their breed was rare amongst the human race.

An agent remained undercover for five to seven years. After that, the agent would either become one of the bad guys or need a great deal of therapy to help the chameleon adjust to a normal life again. Sherman was an anomaly. Even after eight years working underground, he did not display any tell tale signs of stress or fatigue typically haunting undercover agents. Sherman's superiors stated he was uniquely adept at his assignments. Being underground was his destiny. It was what made him. They believed the FBI field agent was fighting battles he truly believed in and had the dedication of a thirty-year career man. People wondered how a person could spend so many years confined to the small spaces of a submarine. Only certain personalities withstood the isolation and confinement. But, unlike Sherman, they had fellow sailors as friends who experienced the same rigors. Thus, they had a ready-made support system. However, the undercover agent did not have that luxury. His guard was constantly on alert. He had to become his false identify. The slightest slip would reveal his true purpose and identity which normally meant death if he was discovered. Criminals were notoriously paranoid and rightfully so. The criminal deliberately broke the law. Most were not smart nor possessed the faculties to root out an informer. Over time, they developed trust in a person if their goals met his goals. The challenge to this theory was organized crime. In the mob, you had to know someone who knew someone who knew you as a child and was connected genetically. That's what made them effective. Treachery was dealt with quickly and with brutality. Their message ran up and down their organization warning if you were a rat, you were going to be eliminated just as a rat would be. Complete extermination. Organized criminals spared no mercy or remorse when they attacked an informer's family either. The messages sent were received loud and clear. If you turned on your fellow criminals, not only would you pay the price but everyone close to you suffered as well. The method was brutally effective.

"Agent Sherman, your reputation precedes you." We have a case requiring your most unique talents of going deep into the general population, blending in, and rooting out a criminal."

Sherman sipped his water, nodded, and waited for Ohms to continue. He knew Dr. Ohms was just warming up.

Agent Sherman was a thinker and in full control his emotions noticed Ohms. Most men shifted their body in their seat or leaned forward awaiting the explanation for the summons. Not Sherman. He sat with his hands neatly folded in his lap and waited patiently as a tiger waits in the tall grass for a gazelle that mistakenly grazes into the predator's kill zone.

"As you obviously observed, we have established a task force to catch a criminal. This criminal we are hunting is not your run of mill drug dealer, gun runner, mob guy, or anything else you may have come across in your career. At this point, you really will not have a great deal to do except to study the man, to learn his behavior, and to assist the team wherever needed," said Ohms. "Your unique undercover talents will be useful in the end game, whenever that might be. However, for you to know what to do and when to do it, it is important that you fully understand whom you are dealing with and what he is capable of doing. For a lack of a better analogy, you are like the knight in a chess game. We will put you on the board to use your specific talents to corner the king so the rest of the pieces can close in to make him fall."

Sherman reflected upon Ohms's statements. He was an avid chess player but he never developed that analogy. He liked it. It characterized his duties to the tee. Ohms no doubt played chess. He would like to sit down and play him. Sherman bet it would end in a draw.

Finally Sherman spoke. "Yes sir, I have no problem with that. Being called in by the renowned FBI Behavioral Science Division is a prestigious honor very few FBI agents receive. I am looking forward to working with your team and I will do everything I can to help."

The young doctor sensing sincerity gazed over his glasses at the crafty agent.

"What I am about to tell you, goes no further than the task force walls. The utmost security must be maintained. We will not involve the press because it will spoil our hard work and drive the target underground and lost forever. We will bring the news peddlers in when we need to excite the bastard and make him loose his cool. Until then, let me tell you what we are dealing with. Your prey is a brutal killer who has been on the loose for no less than sixteen years. We don't know even know who he is…yet," stated the task force leader. "My division was called five days ago for assistance from the Seattle Police Department. The criminal we are looking for has been on a nationwide killing binge for over a decade and a half. Probably more."

Ohms handed Sherman a file full of victim's photos. He wanted to gauge his reaction while his mind was busy taking in the details of the conversation. An old ploy. It was a simple method used to assess a man's persona. While focusing on something else, the subject under scrutiny inadvertently showed Ohms how their mind processed information. Surprisingly, Sherman took the file and placed it on the seat next to him. He did not bother to open it to view the contents. There was ample enough time for that later.

"Continue sir. Tell me what you and your team gathered so far," coolly remarked Sherman. He knew what Doctor Ohms was doing. Typical. He was surprised the most profound behavioral scientist in the American national government would basically insult his intelligence with his cheap psychological ploys. These scientists always study the bad men and never the men who actually caught them. Law enforcement agencies covet their undercover men. They put a fog of mystery around their jobs when it was actually quite easy. All you had to do was assimilate to become the person you were trying to portray. Hollywood actors whined it was the toughest job they ever had because all of their emotions, all of their body language, and all of their soul had to be converted into the part. Besides graduating top of his class from University of Southern California with a BS in criminal justice, Sherman still took his education seriously. Just like his peer sitting in front of him, he liked to study human behavior. He read the same books Ohms did but he went even further. His true research came from being on the street amongst the people. He hunted predators on their turf. And, the only way to win was to think and behave like the predator.

"Besides your normal duties, I called for you because of your maritime specialization. What we know about the predator makes us believe he is involved in marine repair. The most significant clue some Seattle criminologists unearthed was a residue found on the victim's bodies. The Seattle victims were both bound using an industrial electrical tape. The sticky residue contained traces of sea salt. The rest of the murders we linked together from his modis operandi. The majority were discovered along the west and east coasts. Some were committed inland. These were the exceptions to the rule. Based on our analysis, we believe the killer is a merchant marine, a shipyard worker, or something of the sort. He travels frequently. He could even be in the Navy for all we know at this point. All of the killings were near some type of seaport or large ship repair industrial area. That narrows the field down but it is not enough," Ohms said as he paused to sip his water and allow the information to sink into Sherman's conscious.

"Since the last victims were found in Seattle, logically, it is the best place to concentrate our efforts. If he continues with his murderous habits, he is most likely to strike again within two months."

Now Sherman understood why he was assigned. What did he know about Seattle and its marine industry? Not much he thought. Seattle was a major west coast port. It handled thousands upon thousands of imports and exports every day. Seattle was the biggest port located in the Pacific Northwest. There was also Tacoma, Fife, Everett, and the list kept getting bigger as it was developed. Not to mention Canadian ports which were less than a two hour drive away. Much of the state of Washington owed its livelihood to sea commerce. However, there was an upside to it. They had the killer's location narrowed down. Listening to Ohms describe the murders and the locations, if they had to search nationwide, the task would be almost impossible. He felt sorry for the latest victims as he always did when innocent people were killed for being in the wrong place at the wrong time. But, their murders were relatively fresh. That meant there was no doubt in his mind their deaths would be the catalyst behind capturing their killer.

For the first time since Dr. Ohms started his explanation, Sherman expressed his thoughts. "It is evident why you want me on this case. Based on my maritime background, I will know how to get close to the murderer. This file of photos is quite a Butcher's Bill. When the time is ripe for me to start getting close to the perpetrator, I will need to know everything about him. What has your team come up with so far?" questioned Sherman.

Leaning forward towards his desk and peering over his eyeglasses at Sherman, Ohms stated, "Ah...that is a great question for you to ask my friend. Granted we have been on his trail for a whopping five days, we reviewed the data and formed a preliminary profile."

Sherman refolded his hands and rested them in his lap. He knew he would be hunting a ruthless sociopath. So, to capture him he needed to understand what drove the maniac. How he thought. What benefits he received from murdering his victims. This is what Ohms's team was designed for. They recruited the best psychological talent in the country. When they studied their target, their predictions typically hit the mark.

"First, before I begin, you have to explain something to me. You just made a remark about the photos as being quite a ‹Butcher's Bill'. I have never heard the term coined before. Please explain it to me." He was a man who readily admitted when he did not know something. That made him a good leader. Many a great man could not admit they were wrong or did not know something. Not being able to do so, detracted from a person's ability to solve a problem. Especially in his line of work. There was too much at stake for his team to get hung up on their egos. Ohms recognized his boundaries.

The question surprised Sherman. He did not realize he used a navy term to describe the killer's murderous tally. It was easy enough to explain.

Sherman explained, "The phrase 'Butcher's Bill' is quite old. It originates from the United Kingdom's naval history. In the days of sail, when the British Royal Navy ruled the seas with wooden ships and iron men, the combat they encountered was the bloodiest and most ruthless that ever took place in war.

Gunnery science had yet to perfect the rifled or spiraled barrel. All cannons were loaded from the front with either a single shot cannon ball designed to penetrate the wooden hull of a ship, canister rounds invented to kill and maim, or chains attached to two balls used to slice through masts and rigging. The range these horrible weapons were fired from was murderously close. Once the ships finished bombarding each other, the vessels grappled in hand-to-hand combat. Rude and crude weapons like cutlasses, hand pikes, axes, pistols, and hand grenades were used to hack, spear, impale, and decimate the weaker adversaries. As you can imagine, the fighting was barbaric and bloody. Sailors fought at sea; thus, they had no avenue of retreat once engaged in mortal combat. Blood flowed freely through the scuppers. Men lost arms, legs, eyes, and such. You get the picture. Medical science back then was crude too. Infection from wounds killed just as many men as a battle did. Sometimes more. When the fight was finished, the ship's captain would be presented the Butcher's Bill from the man-of-war's surgeon. It officially documented for His Majesty's Royal Navy the injuries sustained and the inevitable deaths encountered during the battle. The hand-to-hand combat was akin to a butcher slicing through meat. Thus, the Captain paid the butcher with men's lives.

When out to sea sailors on a man-of-war did more than fight. Many were carpenters, blacksmiths, sail makers, and such. Moreover, the officers were schooled in celestial navigation on the high seas. So, if the Butcher's Bill was severe and held on its list sailors who skills were critical to fight and sail the ship, the Butcher's Bill depth could severely hamper a Captain's fighting and sailing effectiveness."

"That is one hell of a definition. In this case, I have to agree with you. It is one hell of a ‹Butcher's Bill'. Now that you satisfied my curiosity, let me tell you what we have deduced so far. Our review of the ‹Butcher's Bill' demonstrates that all the murders were committed by a killer who wants to maintain his invisibility."

"Our experience shows that the first murders a serial killer commits are sometimes clumsy and full of expression. When it comes to Butcher Bill's crimes, they are all remarkably alike. That tells us he has killed a lot more than we have discovered," said Doctor Ohms.

Sherman noticed that the killer now had a name, *Butcher Bill*. Later, when novelists researched the murderer as he sat on death row, they would wonder how his moniker was coined. It is not like he chopped up his victims or dined on them like Jeffery Dahmer did. They would have to dig deep to come up with their answer.

Ohms continued his theorizing. "He is thorough. He knows how to sanitize a crime scene. That fact tells us he has studied crime scene analysis and has had a lot of practice. In addition, the crimes linked to him make us believe his killing rampage spans longer than sixteen years. He had to have a period for learning and developing his style. The methods he kills his female and male victims by speak volumes about his thoughts. Regarding the women, he exercises death upon a person whom he loved but despised at the same time. No doubt it was a special woman in his life. Possibly his mother or a wife. When he kills women, he commits the act gently through suffocation. Then, when he dumps their bodies, they are always found naked and lying in a peaceful pose vice being dumped haphazardly as the male victims were."

"When it comes to the men we witness a dichotomy. We see unbridled rage. He pummels the men with blunt, crude instruments. Shovels, hammers, pipes, ex cetera are his weapons of choice. Victim disposal was akin to him taking out the trash. He simply dumps them where they will not be found for a long time. The chosen sites are convenient yet hidden. The facts lead us to believe he is taking out long seated aggression on a male figure or figures that interfered with a relationship with the female figure in his life. He seeks revenge. It is hard to tell if he gains any sexual satisfaction from slaying the men. We believe he does not. Sexual gratification from the killings is all about control and anger. He's settling a score."

"You said that his methods were refined regarding the cases we do know, is there anything else the data tells you?" asked Sherman.

"You bet," replied Ohms. "It means there are more murders out there that we do not have a clue about. One hypothesis is his training ground existed not in the United States but overseas where the police are not as well organized. The murderer travels from one site to another on a more-or-less frequent basis. For example, every two to three years, he changes geographical location. Who is to say that he is not an immigrant from where his first crimes were committed? This is the thread we need to tug more on. Another FBI team is requesting support from international law enforcement agencies to find out if the pattern fits any of their unsolved crimes. The trouble with this is many third world countries do not maintain crime databases like developed nations do. If he killed in Europe, we could get a match. If he came from Asia, South America, or the Middle East, then this line of inquiry could be dead in the water."

Ohms shuffled his papers together signaling that he was almost done and the conversation was coming to a close.

"As I said before, based on the small amount of information we processed so far, I believe we are looking for a man in his late thirties to early fifties. He is educated and extremely bright. On the outside, he appears as an average Joe. No one around him would suspect otherwise. He lives alone and is a bit antisocial. He possesses a personality that allows him to get close to women quickly. They drop their guard because he establishes trust and confidence quickly. A man like that has charisma and knows how to interact well with others. On the other hand, his friends and coworkers will probably think that he is a loner because he never engages in any activities with his peers outside of his work or the normal sphere. We know the real reason behind this because he is stalking his next victim that consumes his time. That in a nutshell is the animal you will hunt. I know it is not much to go on. With you and my team helping the Seattle Police, we can narrow the geographical scope and send you on your mission soon. Do you have any more questions?"

"No sir. You have explained the case thoroughly. I appreciate your candor and trust you have regarding my abilities. We will catch this twisted son-of-bitch. Let's turn-two," replied Sherman.

Rising from his desk chair and offering Sherman his hand to shake, Ohms said, "Good. You will have the office next to mine. I want to hear your thoughts on everything you see. No matter how minor. You would not believe how many cases we have solved going off of some idea or hunch."

As Sherman walked out the door, Dr. Ohms made a mental note to find out what the heck "turn-two" meant. It must be another sailor's term. His curiosity would drive him to learn what it meant. He realized he was out of his depth in knowledge of military or marine dialect. Plus, Sherman's confidence and intelligence intrigued him. He spent years studying the criminal brain. It never occurred to him that he should focus his attention on the good guys. Another mental note made and possibly a good topic for his next book.

CHAPTER ELEVEN

Agent Sherman dove into the case files. What he discovered was unrelenting horror, severe pain, and unbridled hatred. There was only one description fitting the murderer they pursued: evil.

The more he studied the police reports, forensic evidence, and hundreds of photos that captured every gruesome detail, the more convinced he was that 'Bill' possessed extraordinary criminal skills. Sherman wanted to become in tune with 'Bill's' desires, needs, personality or personalities, and his thought process.

Although Ohms coined the killer's handle, *Butcher Bill*, the team did not use it when they hashed over the infinite details in search of the elusive case-breaking clue. In reality, Ohm's moniker for the killer received token homage during the daily official briefings. Otherwise, when the taskforce concentrated on the tedious work of sifting through endless notes for trace evidence, they referred to the killer simply as Bill. The team saw the irony in the name they chose. It was such a generic name for a man likely to go down in history as the worst homicidal maniac in American criminal annals.

The task force worked the case on a twenty-four hour basis. The Bureau granted Ohms full authority to enlist any resource he deemed appropriate. He did not take that authority lightly. He summoned crack agents from the National Security Agency, the Central Intelligence Agency, the Department of Homeland Defense, and various experts from other federal and local law enforcement agencies. Other renowned psychologists around the country completed work off site. No single person or group besides the core task force was allowed to review the entire case. Instead, the experts brought their individual competencies to analyze bits of the case. That way, operational security was maintained.

Ten days after his office took over; the task force grew from a paltry fifteen FBI agents to well over two hundred. The small knit of agents turned into Ohms's private army. The Command Center was too small for the entire team to use. Enough desk space, computers, or telephones were not available. Therefore, he ordered the building's audio-visual auditorium taken over. Desks, chairs, phones, computers, printers, faxes, white boards, cork-boards, coffee machines, and even a refrigerator littered the room. A constant hum churned from the conversations, ringing tele-phones, keyboard tapping, and the low-level frequencies buzzing from the electronic equipment. Guards maintained vigil at the elevator doors and the entrances of the Command Center and theater. Their job was to keep lookie-lous out and to make sure no one carried any material away from the investigation. Cameras and cell phones were strictly forbidden.

The Command Center hummed with activity. Inside, the task-force core team labored to put the pieces of the puzzle together. The group was still composed of the original handpicked FBI agents, Sherman, and Ohms's Deputy, Ms. Catherine Amecii.

Handpicked by Ohms to run the operation's day-to-day details, Agent Amecii ruled with an iron fist. Educated in crimi-nal psychology from Stanford, possessing a Masters Degree in Urban Cultural Anthropology from Yale, and a graduate from the FBI field agent training at Quantico, Virginia, Ms. Amecii was a heavy thinker. Her two degrees complimented each other. Her Psychology degree gave her a solid foundation regard-ing why people do the things they do. The human psyche was remarkably unpredictable. Her Urban Anthropology degree let her dig into the social environment that shapes people. All of this coupled with her FBI training made her a potent agent. Unlike Sherman who earned his reputation by busting criminals in the field, Amecii did the research that provided the field agents the information where to look and how to handle the criminal once found.

Her reputation preceded her outside the FBI compound. When the Iraqi occupation turned sour, the US Army requested her assistance to determine the best method to wage a successful psychological warfare campaign against the insurgents and their hold over the indigent local communities. To her it was not a difficult task. All it took was a fresh look and a firm appreciation for how people thought. She brought that perspective to the table. Her solution empowered the people, especially the women. The Middle Eastern family is traditional and known for its strong family ties. Her theory was if you show the women their family's well being was truly at stake while simultaneously improving their living standards, improvement in the social climate was the logical outcome. The Army bought her theory. They opened hundreds of medical clinics, educational centers, playgrounds, daycare centers, and made sure the husbands got jobs. The only catch was they had to provide security to make sure the pilot programs took off and the communities embraced the concept. Once the community vested their interest into the programs, peace dividends sprouted. The communities desired to defend their hard work. Her last bit of advice to the Army included a caveat. Only long-term dedication to the programs would make them succeed. That meant the majority of the soldiers who oversaw the program and provided protection were there for the long haul. The Army bought into that concept too with an added touch. Where the programs were established, military volunteers did it. People who volunteered did so because they wanted to effect positive change. The program worked astonishingly well. During the first four months, as expected, most families were skeptical. However, there were risk takers amongst the community. Trust was established and continues today. For the most part, the Army started pulling their troops out after a couple of years work. They turned all security over to local police. The policemen turned out to be the husbands and fathers of the wives and children in the programs.

Regardless of her past accomplishments, the Butcher Bill task force assigned her the call sign Napoléonanna. She drove her troops to exhaustion just as Napoleon had with his armies. The difference between the two is the task force did it willingly. They knew the stakes and they trusted her judgment. Battling the clock was their concern. The quicker and more thorough they performed their duties, the faster they could send Bill to the long, cold, sterile table for a death cocktail to circulate through his body.

Her team respected her. Plus, they liked her. True, she could be a firebrand but that only happened when the situation dictated that type of leadership style. Typically she led through the power of suggestion and steering her co-agents in the right direction. She had a knack for identifying an issue quickly. Though she already knew the best avenue to take, Catherine took the extra couple of minutes to help her teammates reach the same conclusion by themselves. Personally, she utterly despised having to use the rod versus the carrot. Situations dictated where a bit of arm twisting was needed. Nevertheless, she rarely resorted to a coercive leadership style. She had seen too many investigations flail and falter because a lead agent threw around his positional authority. That type of leadership wore welcomes out quickly and broke an investigation just as fast. Nonetheless, people enjoyed working for her. Making a hard decision and making it timely appealed to her subordinates. It meant they could do their jobs without waiting for any politics to settle. Her superiors liked that too. True, in the past, she made some wrong decisions. Those were chalked up to inexperience and no one ever died from them. Her most telling trait made up for the mistakes. She learned and admitted her fault.

Sherman instantly liked her and it was not just the long legs, apple bottom ass, Tahoe blue eyes, and auburn hair that captured his attention. He knew appearance was fleeting. Someone beautiful could become just as equally ugly if their mind curdled. In Amecii, he liked the way she thought. Most times, it was completely logical. Other times, he admired her ability to think outside of the box.

Her core investigative team quickly developed a composite picture of the case. 'Bill' was not prejudicial when it came to skin color. The entire group of men and women Bill slaughtered were ethnically diverse and random. He never focused on any single race. On one killing spree in Virginia, he murdered twelve people, six women and six men. It was like that. More-times-than-not, he killed in pairs. The victims included four Caucasians, three Asians, two African-Americans, two of Hispanic heritage, and a single Native American. What interested Sherman was all of the women were young. All of them between nineteen and thirty-five. All were attractive and sexually active. An oddity surfaced when they compared the women's ages to the male victims.

Bill did not discriminate by age with the men. His male victim's ages ranged from twenty to fifty-six years old. Most were average and nondescript. None were traced back to any of the dead women. He did not stalk prostitutes or drug addicts. He wanted beautiful, clean, fresh women to taunt and to conjure evil upon. The team focused upon the duality of the murders. Bill killed in pairs. Doing so quenched his anger and rage. As of yet, they could not determine who he killed first. That was a grunt project farmed out to a forensic scientist brought into to analyze the times the victims were found. If there was an apparent appreciable difference, they might be able to determine who died first. Everyone on the team believed it was the woman who met her doom first at Bill's sick hand. It stood to reason. Making assumptions was normally not a good game plan. They needed facts but the evidence was still too lean. Crunching numbers was laborious yet necessary to refine the picture.

Bill was a male taking vengeance yet paying homage to some female figure in his life. Despite murdering the woman, he always disposed of them with pseudo-respect. The psychological profile in development theorized the male victims were brutally beaten because Bill transferred his own killing of the women to the male victim. In essence, the male victim did something to the female victim to cause her to die. He knew he murdered the women, but it was what the male figure in his mind did that caused him to believe the men were at fault.

Sherman studied the wall where the murdered victim's photos hung. The boards were organized alphabetically by state. Atop each victim's death photos, were numerous real life snapshots that captured a small glimpse into the dead person's life. The team posted these to make sure they did not forget that Bill was snuffing out innocent real people to curb his sick destructive passion.

Capital cases like these forced the investigators to detach themselves completely from the victims. But, removing all resemblance of humanity from the case was counterproductive. People needed to know why they worked eighteen hours a day or missed their kid's school plays, birthdays, or anniversaries. Somewhere in Washington preyed a monster. Quick capture mandated self-sacrifice. The hard part about it was the investigators could not share any information with their loved ones. Stressors on marriages and relationships would eventually result. If the strain went too long, infidelity, separations, and divorces occurred frequently. Bill's affect far outstretched his murdering madness.

"Quite a gruesome memorial we have here is it not?" spoke Catherine handing Agent Sherman a steaming cup of coffee in a heavy white mug.

He did not hear her approach. Sherman's attention was focused entirely on Bill's handy work. Seldom did he let someone get close to him without his attuned senses picking up their presence. Now that he was withdrawn from his concentration, he felt a magnetic attraction toward his new boss. Turning towards

Catherine his eyes did not focus on a stern battle-axe who was all business, but a young, feminine, and sensitive woman standing in front of him. Her scent taunted his heart as it wafted its way through his nostrils to his nervous system. Not many women ever managed to have this affect upon him. It caught Sherman off guard. It was not just her beauty that he desired. Ms. Amecii captured his attention in some other fashion. He liked the way she thought.

He turned and outstretched his hand to receive the coffee vessel. A warm smile crossed his lips. "Thanks, a good cup of coffee right now hits the spot," he softly spoke. Standing shoulder to shoulder, the pair focused on the wall. Sherman started the conversation.

"We need to bring the wall with all of the murder sights over here. I believe we have a pattern here that might narrow the search," he suggested.

Before Sherman said another word, Amecii walked to the board containing the murder map. It was posted on a board with wheels attached for easy portability that she rolled near the photo board. "There you go, let's hear your theory," she said.

That was something Sherman liked about her and had observed over the past few weeks. Most leaders ordered a team member to do what she just did. Instead of wasting time, she did it herself. She took initiative and knew when it was easier to do a task herself.

"I have been going back and forth to the map and to the photos. Do you see a pattern of any kind?" he inquired.

"The research shows Bill commits the murders near the coastline the majority of the time and typically close to an area with a maritime industry," Catherine replied. "What we do not understand is his inland killing grounds pattern. The best theory we have so far is he is transferring or shuttling between coasts for work. If you look at the map, Bill covers a large swatch of ground. He is lily padding from one killing zone to the next."

"That is exactly the piece I have been trying to work out and I believe I have."

Catherine turned her body towards Sherman. Her superiors gave her the low-down about the agent in front of her. Highly intelligent, thinks on his feet, and able to adapt to any situation, he was a star undercover agent. Placing her hand on his shoulder, she stared into his eyes, cocked her head, and waited with primal anticipation to hear what he would say. She felt the magnetic attraction as much as Sherman did.

Her touch sent a pleasantly electrifying jolt down his spine. He never felt that type of energy from a woman before. Clearing the momentary fog caused by her tenderness, he rapidly suppressed his urges and spoke his thoughts.

"Sometimes, you simply need to look at what is right in front of your eyes. Boxes of evidence and tons of scientific clues are helpful but you need to know how to put the pieces together. I know I am preaching to the choir. Look at the killing radius in each state. Typically, it does not go beyond fifty to sixty miles. Meaning, he traveled to where he stalked his prey; however, there exists an epicenter for each series of murders. Looking at each point, we can estimate where his den lies and where he needs to find employment. As you said, each is concentrated near a body of water which in-turn can be linked to a maritime industry."

Amecii knew better than to interrupt. Agent Sherman's brain was turning fast, and she anxiously waited to hear his theory and conclusions.

"I believe the key is looking for the common denominator. As you said, the murder sites are near maritime industries. The real question becomes how you explain the inland murders. I think I know. Naval Bases are Bill's epicenter. I bet he's a squid."

"Go on," Catherine politely uttered.

"All of the dump sites are located near a Navy base. If you look at the inland sites, those too are near Navy bases. Most people believe the Navy only possesses property on the coasts. It makes perfect sense. Navy, oceans, and coastlines naturally equal where the Navy would work. The thing the typical layman or even experienced investigators don't realize is the Navy owns as much real estate inland or along the Great Lakes as they do on the coastlines." Touching the map, Sherman started pointing at different locations. "Here," he stated while he selected the state of Idaho. "Here in Idaho is the training facility for all nuclear engineers trained to operate submarine and aircraft carrier nuclear reactors." Moving his hand to Michigan, Sherman kept up his discourse. "Michigan is home to the Navy's recruit training command. Every sailor goes to the Great Lakes Recruit Center for boot camp. There are eighteen murders committed there. Six were committed in 1991 with the other twelve committed in 2000. Then, Bill shifts back to the west coast to three hunting grounds, San Diego, San Francisco, and Seattle. Two hundred and thirty-one murders over a span of ten years were committed near those locales."

"Oh my God," were the only words escaping from Catherine's pouty mouth. Sherman extracted a huge clue her team overlooked despite pouring over the data for hundreds of hours. Ohms definitely knew how to pick his team. A set of fresh eyes with different experiences and background allowed the information to be analyzed using a different mindset. Talk about thinking outside the box.

"Oh my God," Catherine repeated. "What you're saying to me is we are looking for a sailor in the Navy. It stands to reason. Butcher Bill's latest victims were found in Washington. There are Naval Bases less than an hour's drive from where he left the two victims recently discovered."

She catches on quick thought Sherman. "You're on the right track," he said. "Within a sixty mile radius from where Amanda Jackson and Samuel Williams were discovered are the Everett Naval Station, Whidbey Island Naval Station, Puget Sound Naval Shipyard, Keyport Submarine Base, and other smaller units."

"Any idea where we should start looking?" Amecii inquired. She wanted to draw out as much of Sherman's thoughts as possible. His theory was entirely plausible but she wanted to hear more. She knew his theory contained more postulations.

"The evidence shows the victims bound with industrial grade electrical tape. If you couple that evidence with the murders in Idaho, and the fact there are aircraft carriers, ships, and submarines located at those naval bases, we can narrow the scope of the investigation. I think we are looking for a naval electrician. I am betting he is at least a Petty Officer First Class, Chief Petty Officer, a Mustang Officer, or a Chief Warrant Officer. He has to be one of those ranks. His killings have spanned over sixteen years. Assuming he was in the Navy when he started, after sixteen years he probably holds a senior rank. That would explain why so many murders were committed at various locations. The murderer was either stationed in the vicinity; traveled there to work, or to attend training. Doing so allowed him to fly under the radar committing the murders and leaving his deadly trail behind baffling the cops; thus, making their cases unsolvable."

"What makes you so sure he's an electrician? That is a pretty big leap," She knew he was right, but; she wanted to hear his reasoning.

"There are two key elements making me believe this. The first is his using the tape to bind the victims. If the analysis is correct, I bet Bill used high voltage electrician's tape. The next fact is where he killed people. There are murders at many different sites across America. However, the murders in Idaho make me believe he is an Electrician's Mate. There is a Naval Base in Idaho; home to the Navy's nuclear power reactor training facility. The Navy trains all of nuclear qualified electricians at the school who work onboard nuclear powered aircraft carriers and submarines. So, we can concentrate on the subs and bird farms stationed in Washington."

Catherine's face flushed red with excitement. "That makes perfect sense. We have some more homework to do Andrew.

Finding out what aircraft carriers and submarines were in-port when Amanda Jackson's body was discovered should narrow the field down even more. We'll assemble the team and brief them. You get the team together and meet in the conference hall in fifteen minutes to explain your theory while I find Dr. Ohms."

It was the first time she had called him by his first name. For some strange reason, he liked receiving her approval. Normally he took other agent's opinions with a grain of salt. Especially those who were not field officers. Not hers though. He wanted her to notice his intelligence and expertise. Sherman was romantically falling for Agent Amecii.

"Roger that Catherine." It was the first time he used her first name since they were introduced. Both agents were excited. Without realizing it, they looked at each other, closed the gap between them and hugged. To an onlooker they might have mistaken the embrace for a mere congratulatory expression for discovering the key unlocking another portion of the case. However, to Amecii and Sherman it was more than that. The natural magnetism shared between them was unleashed. Just as suddenly, as they clutched each other they realized what swept over them had to be rebottled. Involved in the most secret manhunt either had ever been in could not be jeopardized by their lustful fleeting emotions. Letting romantic thoughts to cloud their minds was unacceptable. The thoughts and feelings tickling their inner senses had to be extinguished.

Catherine offered an awkward smile. Sherman stood rigid trying to suppress the stirring he felt rising in his pants.

Catherine spoke first. "Um…I better go talk to Dr. Ohms about your observations," she said shyly as she turned on her heels to leave.

"I won't say I didn't enjoy it Ms. Amecii. Best we keep that type of stuff isolated. Do you agree?"

Catherine's skin turned the shade of her Auburn hair. She knew what he said was right but it did not help with the rejection she was experiencing. After all, she was a sensitive woman hiding behind a cool exterior.

"Yes, Agent Sherman. Let's not do that again," she said knowing it wasn't what she really wanted to say. Something about Sherman captured her. It was not a single thing that created her attraction to him. All she knew was she felt whole when he held her in his arms. It was a new sensation for her. She dated a few men who interested her greatly but they never had that type of affect on her.

Sherman smiled knowing she was lying as much as he was. There was nothing he could do about it except watch her turn and saunter away. He watched her soft red hair bounce lively about her shoulders. He had to get her out of his mind fast or he will never be able to function around her. The agent turned and refocused his attention on the crime scene board. The innocent people slaughtered by Butcher Bill demanded his utmost. His chance at love demanded patience and emotional suppression.

CHAPTER TWELVE

Arranging his access to the naval base proved easier than Father Nguyen expected. Just as he suspected, the base Chaplain's office eagerly accepted his offer to help them handle the military community's spiritual and counseling needs. Having an aircraft carrier in port created challenges for the many organizations tasked to provide support for a ship. Totaling more than twenty five hundred crewmembers, the USS ABRAHAM LINCOLN was a small town instead of just a ship. As with any small town it came with its share of problems. The local religious program office had a finite set of resources. The armed services supported their programs with zest; however, when budgets became tight, the military bought bombs first, religion second.

A ship recently returning from an overseas deployment brought back a hornet's nest of personal problems too. If the Navy learned anything, when they had a ship returning home from a six month deployment, divorces were common. LINCOLN's return was no different. Many sailors returning home received warm welcomes from their families. Many did not. What they returned to were cheating spouses, eviction notices because the rent had been gambled away, or a home cleared of furniture with a note saying the Navy life wasn't for them anymore. Problems like these taxed the professional counselors and clergy who tried to assist the sailors coping with life's unfortunate dilemmas. That made Father Nguyen's offer to help most attractive. It was a win-win situation for Father Nguyen. He could offer as much assistance to people who really needed it while simultaneously closing the gap between him and the murderous sailor haunting his confessional.

He did not possess any particular plan on how best to deal with the situation. The Cambodian clergyman trusted his Lord to guide his hand and actions. His prayers were answered once when he took refuge in the woods seeking God's wisdom. Now, he had to figure out how to negotiate the trail the Almighty wanted him to travel upon. His first task was making his presence felt. The demon he sought to destroy needed to recognize God was present and taking action against the devil's despicable disciple. Getting assigned onboard the ship presented the first challenge, but; not overly difficult.

Lieutenant Commander Henry rendezvoused with Nguyen at a diner outside the naval base's main gate. He explained the current spiritual climate. Three Navy Chaplains provided the spiritual support to the *USS ABRAHAM LINCOLN*. Henry, a Protestant chaplain by faith, led the three in their duties aboard ship. Besides him, a Born-Again Christian minister and a Catholic Priest made up the religious threesome. All looked forward to meeting Father Nguyen and gladly anticipated his support. They were dedicated men but there was only twenty-four hours in a day. Most of it was chewed up by the ship's daily routine. In addition, the three Padres learned the *LINCOLN* would not have a long break. Given three months to repair her broken equipment, to refill her supplies, and having the ship's nuclear reactors inspected, the aircraft carrier sailors had limited time to enjoy life ashore again. The *LINCOLN* was returning to the Arabian Gulf to support the never ending operations in the ever tumultuous Middle East. The clergymen's spiritual work was just as compressed. The clergymen did their best to help sailors cope. Learning the ship was headed back to sea with such short notice complicated matters. Father Nguyen's offer to assist was received with sighs of relief and a sign that God had answered their prayers.

The meeting at the diner proceeded well. Lieutenant Commander Henry told the civilian priest how to obtain a pass for his car, get an identification card allowing him access to the base and ship, and gave him a crash course on military protocol. Henry taught him how to distinguish an officer from the senior and junior enlisted personnel. He explained the ship's chain of command, how to request permission to board and leave the ship, and how to find his way around the massive hundred thousand ton ship.

Nguyen was onboard for two weeks and finally understood how to use frame and deck numbers to know his exact location within the structure's maze of offices, berthing areas, and equipment compartments. Besides his ultimate goal to stop the murderous sailor, Nguyen enjoyed what he was doing. Each morning he arrived before sunrise and accompanied the sailors responsible for raising the ship's flag. It was a simple ceremony. Two sailors and a junior officer marched the flag to the stern, attached it the halyard on the flagstaff, and dutifully waited for a broadcasted whistle signal. As soon as they heard the whistle blare, they smartly raised the ship's colors. Seeing the flag unfurl and snap in the wind made the priest's heart warm.

Every time he walked across the ship's brow requesting permission from the Officer of the Deck to board the mighty warship he felt a sense of being part of something life changing and awe inspiring. He dived deep into the assignments Lieutenant Commander Henry asked him to work on. Nguyen met with individual sailors feeling homesick, over stressed from their high operational tempo, or with young married couples learning how to cope with the rigorous demands placed on sailors going to war. For him, it was rewarding. Here were people who truly needed his guidance. It was far more rewarding than dealing with the everyday and common issues he normally dealt with in his own parish. Nguyen seriously pondered joining the military's Chaplain Corp after his quest was resolved. Lieutenant Commander Henry discussed the option often. It would not be hard to do. The Navy was shorthanded and the process to bring in new clergyman into the fold was recently streamlined.

ABRAHAM LINCOLN's Quarterdeck is the focal point for the crew, repair contractors, and any visitors entering the ship. Led by a junior officer or senior petty officer, a small team of sailors supervised the station. Anyone coming onboard presented their credentials for inspection and were either allowed to enter the ship or turned away. A bank of phones, alarm control stations, radios, and computers allowed the small four man party to control the ship's in port heartbeat.

This was where Father Nguyen decided to first make his presence apparent to the demon he sought to battle. Every day in the last two weeks, Father Nguyen assigned himself to the quarterdeck when crewmembers came aboard to start their work. Unlike the crew who wore blue shirts, dungaree pants and black work boots, he wore his black suit and white collar. Once a person checked in with the Quarterdeck watch, he eagerly greeted each with a cheery good morning and a smile. Sometimes he chatted with a sailor for a few minutes about the weather, sports or whatever. He quickly became a welcomed addition to his adopted marine parish.

Captain Bach, the carrier's Commanding Officer, appreciated his clergyman's approach. One morning Bach asked him to his cabin for coffee after seeing Father Nguyen religiously stationing himself at the Quarterdeck every morning. He told Nguyen that making himself visible to the crew sent a passive signal to them that he genuinely cared. Captain Bach believed it was good for the ship and his crew who typically take a long time to fork over their trust and respect. Father Nguyen took the conversation to the next level. Not knowing every minute of the Captain's time was scheduled for training, meetings, briefings, inspections, and operational planning, Nguyen suggested to Captain Bach he join him at the quarterdeck each morning. It would be good for morale if his sailors saw him there too welcoming them back aboard their ship. Lieutenant Commander Henry and the other two chaplains who accompanied Nguyen to share coffee with the CO tried to intercede. To their great surprise, Bach quickly accepted Father Nguyen's suggestion. He believed it was a capital idea. His crew should have access to their CO. The next morning from six to seven, Father Nguyen happily stood next to Captain Bach welcoming his crew back aboard. At first, many crew members were intimidated with their Captain stationed on the Quarterdeck. Typically, the only time they ever saw the old man was if they were in trouble or when he was giving the ship a briefing at an all hands meeting. The ship buzzed with approving gossip of the CO's new morning routine. The vessel's senior enlisted leader, the Command Master Chief, was pummeled with emails testifying to the crew's approval. Morale took a turn for the better even though another backbreaking deployment loomed just over the horizon.

Father Nguyen did not lose sight of his ultimate goal. The real reason he stationed himself at the quarterdeck to greet the sailors was to ensure one sailor in particular knew he was there. Their first encounter and every one after that filled the priest's heart and soul with insurmountable fear, loathing, and dread. He dug deep into his soul to render a smile and a comforting word for Chief Petty Officer Medina every time they met. Father Nguyen quickly asked the Lord for strength and guidance when he saw the murderous demon approach his station. Shock overcame Medina the first time he eyed the black clad figure posted at the quarterdeck shaking hands and making small talk with crew members as they came aboard.

Nguyen knew the demon would try to avoid him. He dispatched himself quickly from the sailor he was talking to and made sure he was in line with the Chief's path as he came aboard. He simply said "Good Morning Chief," to the evil mariner. All he received in return was a wicked glare from the unholy spirit's eyes. The murderer quickly brushed past him as Father Nguyen followed him with his eyes until he reached a point where the sailor disappeared into the ship's labyrinth. He accomplished his mission. The Priest desired to make his presence known to the wayward soul whose only purpose was to leave destruction, pain, and terror in his wake. Father Nguyen maintained his composure as the ship's crew filed past him for their morning greeting despite his heart thumping in his chest. His palms perspired, sweat dripped from his brow. How could he beat the monster? Fear gripped his every thought. God placed such an enormous task in front of him. Nothing prepared him for the cross he was given to carry. What would he do now that the creature knew he was in his den, in his haven, in his comfort zone? Would the insane man continue his dastardly deeds knowing he was being watched? The Priest hoped not but sensed it was a false hope. His next step was unbeknownst to him. His presence alone might prevent the destruction to continue. Nguyen knew he could not rely upon that. Knowing the priest was taking an active role vice allowing him to abuse the confessional might change the status quo. Time would tell was the only answer the pastor came up with.

CHAPTER THIRTEEN

"That meddling priest," angrily mumbled Medina. It was not significant the priest was there. He understood the padre's vows prevented him from doing much more than saying good morning to him. His secret remained safely contained within the confessional walls from the rigid standards established for hundreds of years designed to protect the sacrament from abuse.

Pain throbbed in Medina's temple. "My need to curb the anger is becoming more and more frequent," he whispered to himself as he changed his work uniform for blue jeans, a white sweater, and a brown leather jacket.

His tool bag lay on his bed. It contained a flashlight, electrical tape, surgical and leather gloves, a buck knife sharpened to a razor's edge, plastic garbage bags, a lighter, matches, and a plastic baggie holding red and blue colored pills. Medina readied himself for his next abduction. Adrenalin coursed through his body. He followed his new sacrifice for weeks. The time to strike has arrived.

He memorized her patterns and schedule. He knew where she would be and at what time. Charlotte Channels studied mathematics at the University of Washington. She hailed from South Carolina and arrived in Seattle four months ago. She wanted to attend a West Coast school to broaden her life experiences and to escape the hum-drum existence of Weston, South Carolina. The town did not offer much to stay. Living somewhere with more than one traffic light appealed to Charlotte. She came to Washington to learn about herself as well as to study math. Medina knew this because Charlotte told him this over coffee at the Barnes and Nobles bookstore.

He first spied her long blond hair, pouty lips, and slim figure, while he browsed for a new book to pass the time onboard the ship when he had duty. From a safe distance he watched her as she selected a book, paid the cashier, and then headed to the adjacent Starbucks for a latte. He did the same while maintaining a watchful eye on her every move. Luckily, she sat down at a nearby table, cracked open the pages to her new text, and sipped her coffee while reading the beginning pages of the "De Vinci Code." The Starbucks tables were filled with customers. A seat remained open at Charlotte's table. It provided the opportunity to engage his prey. He softly approached, laid his books on the table, and politely asked if they could share the table. Charlotte looked up from behind her book, saw he did not pose a danger, smiled, and motioned to the chair. People did that at the bookstore's Starbucks. People liked to read their new books while relaxing with a scone and cup of java.

Ten minutes later Medina and Charlotte were deep in conversation. He learned all he needed to know in the short discourse. It amazed him how open people are with their life stories to complete strangers. He told her he was a sailor in the Navy. The statement made the conversation go even easier. Most folks were programmed to believe the military were guardians. It was akin to talking to a police officer or fireman. They immediately lowered their guard. They felt secure in their prescience. It made his quest ever so much easier. The conversation petered out quickly. It did not matter. He closed his book, smiled at Ms. Charlotte Channels from South Carolina who studied mathematics at U-Dub, who had no family or close friends established in the area, said good bye, and strolled out of the shop. She was perfect. He patiently waited in his van until she emerged with her coffee in her left hand and her books and purse in the right. Charlotte unlocked her Chevy Malibu not knowing she was being stalked from afar. Medina tracked her for the next three hours. She made a stop at the local Safeway, filled her gas tank at a Chevron, and picked up a movie from the movie kiosk. Finally, she arrived at her apartment complex. She parked in a covered parking lot, gathered her purchases, and made her way to her second floor one-bedroom apartment. Sensing her errands were finished, Medina tired of his surveillance. Now he knew where she lived. Everything else after that was business as usual.

He took a few days leave from work to follow her during the day. It was January and the university term had just started. She left her apartment for school every day around seven thirty in the morning. A stop at a Bally's Health Club four miles from her home ended her school day. Instead of showering at the gym, his target traveled home, showered, ate dinner, and returned to the school's library. She typically studied alone. Sometimes two or three fellow students joined to work out calculus problems.

Medina hoped she was not involved in a study group tonight. The library closed promptly at eleven o'clock. From there, she walked to her car and drove home. He cased the parking lot and the surrounding buildings. Security cameras did not cover the student parking areas. That was a stupid decision whoever the chief of security was. A campus security car made its rounds at ten fifteen and again at twelve fifteen. That was his window of opportunity. Thankfully, Charlotte was committed to her studies. At eleven o'clock in the evening, the library's parking lot would be virtually empty. Medina planned to park his van extremely close to her car and as she started to reach for her door handle he would thrust open the vans door, drag her inside, tie her hands and legs, and tape her mouth shut. It helped that he had sound proofed the van's cargo area. She could scream as much as she wanted. Once she was in the hold and the door shut behind her no sound would ever escape its walls. Her cries, like many before her, would go unanswered. Medina estimated he could snatch, bundle, and transport his captive to his house in three hours. He just needed to make sure no one saw him snatching her. Capturing her and pulling her inside the van would take less than a minute. When he kidnapped his prey, it was as fast as a moray eel striking out against a luckless fish. Wham…and it was done. With men, he normally knocked them out with a strike to the neck. Women were much easier to subdue. They were light and not as strong. They flailed a lot, but a punch to their abdomen normally stunned them. Tying them up and gagging them became easier.

Medina gathered his tool bag, left his stateroom, and made his way through the ship's passageways towards the quarterdeck. The priest would not be there at this time of night. His sailors told him the priest only hung out at the quarterdeck for an hour in the morning. Most of the ship's crew had hit the beach already. Evening chow was being served. He liked leaving while the duty crew assembled on the mess decks to eat supper. The fewer people he encountered the better. He had a schedule to keep. Best not to take any chances he thought.

He slept on board the ship most nights. No one knew he kept a private residence in town. He bought it right before the *LINCOLN* left on its last deployment. It lay vacant while he was gone. He selected his execution sites carefully. Normally, the home was isolated and away from other houses. He never took the risk of some neighborhood kid stumbling onto his activities by accident. Stationed in Washington made it easier. Real estate was much cheaper than it was in San Diego. Coupled with the slumping market and cheaper prices, Medina bought a home situated on three acres and surrounded by pine trees. His nearest neighbor lived four hundred yards away. Renovations started before the ink on the mortgage papers dried. He quickly constructed his playroom. Like his van, the sacrificial chamber was utterly sound and light proof. He built a room inside a room. It was the perfect sacrificial chamber to excise his pain.

Medina's palms perspired with anticipation. He needed to do this. He hated kidnapping and murdering, but he had no other alternative. When he began his murderous path over eighteen years ago, he found peace in his soul after he smothered a Filipino whore. She looked very much like his mother. She was kind too despite the filthy woman prostituting herself. The first time was clumsy and amateurish. He killed her on a whim after he had done her for ten dollars. She certainly screwed well and knew how to please a man. It drove him insane with rage when he was paying her. He envisioned his mother doing the same thing repeatedly. The whoring had to stop. He reached out, grabbed the prostitute, and threw her back down on the bed. She believed he wanted a second throw until he jumped on top of her and pressed the pillow down hard over her face. Her arms and legs flailed madly trying to beat off her murderer. She tried bucking him off with her hips. She tried rolling side to side but her cus-tomer turned assailant kept sapping the strength from her body by pushing the pillow down harder and harder. It took Medina less than a minute to murder her. He rose from her and started to panic after he regained his composure. What he thought lasted hours actually only took a couple of minutes. *What to do now?* He calculated how to remove her body from the small apart-ment without being seen and how to dispose of the body with-out leaving any evidence. Covering his tracks proved easier than expected. He waited until very early the next morning. The time was a hiatus between the time the bars and brothels shut down and when the morning merchants opened for business. The Filipino slut weighed less than a hundred and ten pounds and was not very tall. He remembered how he stuffed her into a large box, taped it shut, and wheeled her to his truck with a loading dolly. Driving her twenty miles outside of town, he stripped and burned her clothes and washed her body with fresh water from a nearby stream. He did not mean to kill her. Remorse and shame haunted him. She was a nice girl. He could not just dump her like garbage. God would not forgive him for that. Medina remem-bered seeing a serene park just outside of town. There he made a bed of palm fronds. He laid her gently under palm trees swaying back and forth in the light morning breezes. The archipelago's animals and insects would quickly dispose of the evidence.

Medina did not plan to commit the murder. It happened so fast. All he could think of when he pushed the pillow down on her head was seeing his Mother humping a collage of men. While he smothered the Filipino whore, he imagined his mother lying underneath his body dying a horrible death. He killed her for starving him of her motherly love. He killed her for the abuse she inflicted upon his young innocent soul. He killed her for robbing him of his boyhood. In his mind, it was more an act of chivalry than homicide that brought a macabre sense of relief to him.

The second time he killed occurred two weeks after he murdered his first victim. In a Thai bar he watched a European spending money on women, booze, drugs, and food. The party went on for more than three hours until most of the patrons were too stoned or drunk to stand. The European woke from a drug induced stupor long enough to find one of the party's prostitutes rummaging through his pockets for money. The guy grabbed the whoring thief by the hair and began wailing on her. He pummeled her with punches to her face and body. She collapsed in a bloody and bruised lump to the grimy floor. He did not stop there. The beating became more furious and with more ferocity. The girl lay in a heap at his feet dripping blood and whimpering for him to cease. No one stopped him or attempted to help the young, beaten woman. They understood the local unwritten code. He had a right to beat her for her treachery. The harlots lived by an unwritten code. They had sex for money. They did not steal it. If their brothel received a reputation for robbing its customers, they would be out a job. It was a brutal business but effective. Medina understood the code. He lived his entire boyhood under those rules. He had seen his mother beaten many times before. She abused everything. Drugs, booze, and even, her only son. When her pimp did not want to beat her anymore, he turned on her innocent child and she did not do a thing to stop it. It all changed that horrible night. The drunk who wailed on the whore as if he had a right to cause her pain found that the prostitutes had a guardian angel.

Medina followed him to his hotel, forced his way into his room, and pummeled him to death him with a tire iron. The hotel was cheap and no one saw him enter. He left the body where it lay. His ship weighed anchor at dawn. The police could not connect him to the body. They most likely would think the whore's pimp came and executed him for damaging his property.

Those two murders freed Medina and opened an entirely new world to him. Feeling remorse or shame never occurred to him. He felt more alive than at any point in his young life. Frustration and painful emotions captive inside him vaporized from his soul. He knew he committed mortal sins but did not care. Killing the whore and drunk made life refreshing for the first time in his life.

Seventeen years later, committing the murders became part of his spirit. Excising his pain through killing was an evil habit. It was a part of him now and he could not stop if he wanted. To Medina, making the human sacrifices became routine and rational. Some small part in his brain knew the murdering of innocent people was wrong and against God's will. However, the murderous addiction consumed him and prevented him from shutting the door to his evil ministrations. Confession helped squelch the guilty feelings. Absolution eluded him. He understood why. Being able to tell someone about his horrible deeds helped to lessen the guilt, especially if that someone was sworn to God to remain silent.

Medina drove his car to a nearby parking garage where his white utility van awaited him. Whenever he stalked his prey or captured them, he used his nondescript van. He took the precautions ever since 1996 when a policeman showed up at the ship asking him some questions of why his car was seen so frequently near an elementary school where a teacher came up missing. It was the closest the police ever came to capturing him. From that point forward, he meticulously prepared his every move beforehand and left nothing to chance. The vans windows were tinted. Painted white and left dirty, most people assumed it was a work van belonging to a plumber, mason, or carpenter. In any city, there were hundreds if not thousands of vans like his. The vehicle would be hard to trace.

His calculations proved correct. The drive took less than two hours to make. He arrived at the university precisely at 8:26 pm. Sure enough; Charlotte Channels was a slave to her routine. And why not? She did not fear anything or anyone. She made no enemies who desired her harm since arriving in Washington. Charlotte remained a corporative victim. She parked her car away from other cars. Worrying it might get bumped or scratched if she parked closer to the library. The new Chevy was a gift from her parents. Campus security regularly patrolled the well-lit grounds. Charlotte felt safe.

As planned, and as it worked so successfully in the past, he parked the van with the right wheels over the parking slot's white lines. The cargo van doors lined up opposite to the driver side door. He never exited the van. If there were any security cameras that he missed during his reconnoiter, the cameras would never capture his face. The license plates smeared with dirt made it near impossible to make out the numbers and letters stamped into the metal. Waiting and being patient was what he had to do now. He slid his seat all the way back and opened a brown paper bag holding a submarine sandwich loaded with salami, Italian ham, pepperoni, and pepper jack cheese. Driving made him hungry. Enough light entered the van to read the newest issue of *Reader's Digest*.

The dashboard digital clock slowly counted the time away. Right around ten o'clock, students trickled out from the library after their night's study. Charlotte appeared roughly forty minutes later. She was early Medina thought. The blond co-ed typically stayed until closing. Medina slowly crawled to the back of the van while watching her progress through the parking lot. The lot remained deserted. Charlotte carried a purse in her left hand and a book bag in her right. It rained earlier causing the temperature to dip below forty degrees. Steam escaped from her mouth enveloping her face with every exhale. The parking lot light rays shot through the steam and caused a refractive halo to surround her head. Medina knew the lighted shadow about Charlotte's tired face could be explained away by physics but he pondered for a second and then dismissed the idea that it was an omen he should heed. She walked with her head slightly bent while she pondered upon a story she had read for her English Literature class.

Medina tugged a black ski mask over his head, donned the leather gloves, and peered out the window monitoring her progress through the parking lot. He had to time opening the door at just the right moment. His surveillance on Charlotte over the past few weeks made him believe she would open the passenger side door first and deposit her books and purse inside. Then, she would walk around the back of the car looking inside to ensure there weren't any uninvited guests ready to ambush her. Her Daddy taught her well. People were creatures of habit though. It made them predictable and easy prey.

Twenty feet away Charlotte pressed the key fob button unlocking her car. The murderer lurking in the van heard her open and close the passenger door just as she usually did. "One-Mississippi, two-Mississippi, three-Mississippi," he counted. On three-Mississippi, he whipped open the sliding door which crashed into the stops. Charlotte turned, astonished and confused. She started to scream but the black masked attacker grabbed her around the shoulders, violently pulled her into the van, and struck her aside her head. Stars danced in her mind. Charlotte tried to scream but nothing escaped. Tape prevented her mouth from opening. Terror ripped through her mind realizing she was being abducted. Her hands and feet were pinned, tied, and attached to rings on the floor. A hood draped over her head extinguished the world from view. Tears flooded down her cheeks as she shook from fright when she heard the door slam shut and an engine starting.

It was Thursday night. Medina had Friday, Saturday, and Sunday to perform his sacrifice. He took leave for the weekend and told people he was heading to Canada. It was only a short five-hour drive north. Driving five miles per hour over the speed limit, the drive took a little over two hours. Not much traffic existed on the northbound I-5 interstate at eleven o'clock on a wet and dreary night. When he exited the highway and steered the van onto the single lane road leading to his house, he passed a single car from the opposite direction. Approaching his house, the garage opened and closed remotely. After a quick once over inside his house to make sure nothing was disturbed, he pulled his mask back on. Whimpering filtered from under the hood when he opened the back of the van. All the women did that. Some men did it too. He ignored the sobbing, cut the plastic wire tie restraints pinning her to the van, and dragged her out of the van. Charlotte thrashed and kicked as hard as she could but it was a useless exercise. Her attacker struck her in the stomach knocking the wind from her diaphragm and lungs. Medina grabbed her wrists and raised them so he could fireman carry her into the house. It was always so easy. Charlotte weighed less than a hundred and twenty pounds. He carried her into a room furnished with a queen-sized mattress, an overhead lamp bolted to the ceiling, and a toilet without a seat attached to the far wall. The floor was hardwood, polished, and rug less. A globed security camera watched the room from twelve feet above. None of his victims ever reached it. He watched them try and try again to tear it down. They never succeeded.

Medina laid Charlotte back on the bed and used the buck knife to cut away the tape holding her hands immobile. He did the same thing every time he kidnapped a woman. In a little while, she would recover from her fright, cry for two or three hours, without taking the bag off her head. Braver and more resolute women shed the bag as soon as they could. Most believed it was a kind of security blanket. If they did not see their attacker, they could not identify them. It kept the false hope that they might not be murdered. Eventually, they all removed the hood. Typically, the crying and sobbing started again. He let them sink deep into depression for about twelve hours. Then, he would slide a tray of food through a slot in the wall. His victims never touched the food. However, they normally sucked down the bottle of spring water he provided. What they did not realize was the water was tainted with the date rape drugs. Within an hour, they were sleeping.

Charlotte was braver than most. When she regained her spirit and stopped crying uncontrollably, she realized her hands were free. She whipped the hood off and scanned the room. Her face, neck, and stomach viciously ached. She sat up and scurried into the corner furthest from the door. Her eyes darted back and forth looking for something useful to help her. A phone, a weapon, a window…anything to help her escape. There was nothing. It was a desolate room except for the mattress and toilet. It did not look like a cell, but; it was nonetheless. Her bladder ached to release its liquid contents. She determined not to use the toilet. Charlotte knew her every move was under surveillance. She would not give him the satisfaction. She thought he was some sort of freak that got off by watching girls squat and piss.

Time passed slowly. Charlotte felt every second slip by and with it any hope of rescue. The urge to use the toilet overcame her. Best to die with dignity then to piss her pants she thought. She did her business quickly while shielding her genitalia with her clothes. Her senses returned to quasi-normal. Scanning the room, she realized she was dealing with a seasoned psychopath. Nothing in the room could be used for a weapon. Even the toilet flushed using a laser motion sensor. Depression set in again.

Dragging the mattress back to her safe corner, she sat down, drew her knees into her chest, wrapped her arms around her legs, and awaited her eventual doom.

Medina watched every move. Every victim he kidnapped commented about him having a fixation on watching people use the toilet. To him, it was a repulsive sight. It was like watching a dog on a leash taking a crap and looking up at his master, who waited with a pooper-scooper and baggie in hand. You knew the dog suffered the humiliation of being watched when it crapped. It was the most vulnerable point in a dog's day.

Fourteen hours passed. Medina watched Charlotte panic and pound on the door to let her out. He watched her break down, weep, and call for her daddy. He watched her retreat to the corner countless times and stare into nothingness, consumed in her own thoughts and visions about what would happen to her. Most of all, Charlotte expended a lot of energy shouting at her captor, calling him a sick pervert, telling him he had a small dick, and what he was doing was because no woman would ever want to bone him. She even challenged him to a fair fight. Charlotte promised to kick his teeth in and stomp on his head until he bled from his eyeballs.

She was a fiery wench, he thought as he prepared her meal. The meal was simple. His captives rarely ate what he gave them. They believed poison laced the food. They did gulp down the water he provided. Almost an entire day without having water made the human body hunger with thirst. Just because the water bottle seal was not broken, it didn't mean it wasn't tampered with. His captives never bothered to think of that. They wanted to quench their thirst.

Long ago, he purchased a bottling machine. It was a crude contraption but he only needed it for putting a fresh seal on the water bottles. Before he resealed the water bottle, he crushed the date rape pills and dissolved the powder in the water. He put enough narcotic in the water so it would knock out his prisoner for at least four hours. Always enough time to do what he wanted with them without them knowing it.

He carried the tray with ham and cheese sandwiches, potato salad, a kosher pickle, and the bottled water to the door. He placed it on the floor, slid a panel aside, and pushed the tray into the room. The noise made by the sliding panel reawakened Charlotte's fear. Her eyes widened and her chest pumped up and down from her fright. Some of Medina's victims tried to curl up and make them self as small as possible in the corner. Others stood ready to fight their tormentor. They rationalized it was better to go down fighting instead of sitting there waiting for their slaughter. Some even ran at the door and reached out of the small slit hoping to grab their assailant. It never worked. Medina would kick their arms back and slam the sliding door home. Leaving bruises upon the body was against his rules. He took painstakingly measures to ensure his female victims were not physically marked during his homicidal rituals.

Charlotte stared at the food. The aroma from the pickle wafted through the small sterile cell. The ham sat on rye bread and beckoned her stomach. It growled from hunger. She went to the door, picked up the tray and retreated to the corner farthest from the door. Charlotte instantly decided to eat the meal. Maintaining her strength for the impending fight influenced her decision. The sandwich disappeared swiftly. The maniac did not provide any utensils. Using her fingers Charlotte scooped the potato salad into her mouth. Thirst overcame her. Whipping the cap from the bottle, she chugged its contents relieving her parched throat and lips.

Iggy Medina watched every move. Nine times out of ten, his past sacrifices ignored the food. The strong in mind and body ate knowing their body required the nourishment to provide strength against whatever lies behind the sterile white door. They didn't realize the real threat came from drinking the water. Seeing water when thirst is overpowering the body stimulates human adrenaline and fires brain receptors steering the body to drink. The mind kicks into overdrive wanting to stay alive and the first thing it needs is water. People stranded in lifeboats at sea went through the same reaction. If they were isolated enough and didn't having any fresh water aboard their life raft they soon hallucinated the ocean was okay to drink. They soon discovered drinking the salty ocean water was a poor decision. The salt dehydrated them more and their mind started on a journey towards madness.

Charlotte picked up the tray and examined it for use as a potential weapon. It was too light. Not even a simple knife could be manufactured from it. She tossed it aside. Her eyelids grew heavier and heavier. Sleep was out of the question. Maybe it was a bad dream she was having, she thought. Going to sleep in her dream will let her wake up in her own bed with a fresh new day ahead of her. Unwillingly, Charlotte slumped onto the clean new mattress. The room blurred from her vision until darkness only remained.

Medina watched Charlotte slip into unconsciousness. His blood pressure rose as it pulsated through his body with anticipation. The drugs would keep Charlotte knocked out for four to five hours. It was more than enough time for him to explore her body without any interference. He rolled back the bolt locking her cell. Picking her limp body from the mattress, he carried her through the house to his bedroom where a bed stood with a clean white cotton sheet. Towering over her as she softly breathed in her drug-induced slumber, Iggy Medina slowly removed her clothing. His member stiffened and throbbed against his pants. Kneading it with his right hand, his left hand unbuttoned her pink sweater, exposing her breasts. His breathing became excited as he removed her pants, bra, panties, and socks. He admired her soft, firm body. Needing to feel her heat Medina rapidly stripped his clothes off and shimmied up besides Charlotte. He pressed hard against her thigh while he reached his arm over and drew Charlotte into his embrace. It was not his thing to rape her. All he wanted was to hold her soft body next to his. He desired to commune with her soul, to be warmed by her essence. His left hand stroked her hair while his right explored her body. He caressed her breasts, petted her inner thighs, rubbed his feet against hers, and held her body tight into his.

Charlotte breathed down the demon's chest, oblivious to his motions. He rolled her over to touch her bottom and trace the spine in her back. His other hand rubbed and rubbed his manhood. The feeling exhilarated him. Emotions filled his mind and throbbed through his penis. It felt so good to hold her in his arms, to touch her and not being rejected for it. His hand pumped faster and faster. The milky white fluid came fast and hot, splattering onto Charlotte. Medina embraced her harder, rubbing the goo into her skin. He closed his eyes and fell asleep with his captive locked in his arms.

An alarm awakened Iggy from his slumber. Charlotte remained next to him. Her golden locks spread out on the bed; her knee was cocked over the other while she slept. Still under the influence of the drugs, Medina estimated she would stay asleep for another couple of hours. More than enough time to prepare her. But first he needed to wash her scent and his dried semen from his body. His shower lasted only a few minutes. Years of being in the Navy taught him to wash quickly because fresh water at sea was a precious commodity requiring vigilant conservation. The more seasoned sailors policed the younger sailors to conserve water. It sucked to be on water hours. Sailors learned to wash efficiently and quickly with the least amount possible. After a short while it became habit even when they were home and hooked to a well destined not to dry up for many years to come.

He dressed himself simply in a pair of blue jeans and a gray t-shirt. He had work to do. Medina returned to the bedroom where Charlotte lay passed out and unawares. Her blond hair reflected the light and made it shine. The cool air in the bedroom made her pink nipples hard. He could see the crease of her vagina as he stood gazing at her. Gone were the soft feelings he experienced while he lay next to her and jerked his cock off onto her flesh. He already sucked the warmth from her soul. His eyes glowed with hatred. The woman in front of him instantly became the object of his vengeance. Charlotte's face disappeared. What took its place was an image of his mother lying naked and sweaty after she serviced her latest customer. Almeda was his mother's name and after she screwed a man she shouted for Iggy to bring her vodka and cranberry juice, a wet towel, and a cigarette. The woman had neither shame nor pride. Her young bastard was more servant than son. Knowing no other life, Iggy did what he was told to do. He learned the hard way from his Mother's pimp what would happen if he disobeyed. The last time brought an iron bar struck against his calf muscles. Iggy no longer needed to be shouted at to bring her drink or smokes. His queue was the John walking down the stairs buckling his pants to get a beer at the bar.

He would enter the room and present his whore-mother the cocktail that she gulped down in a single swallow. The wet towel came next which she used to give herself a whore bath. Last was the cigarette he lit after she sponged herself down. It did not matter he was her son. Almeda Medina would sit on the bed with her legs open for him to see all of her when she began the chore of wiping the sperm, sweat, and spit from her skin. It no longer bothered Iggy that his mother displayed her wares to her son as if he were just another customer. He soon became immune to the sight. Just as some children learned their routine of waking up and going to school, Iggy's life routine involved helping his mother clean up after her work sessions. His mother never thought this steady stream of benign torture warped his young mind forever.

Charlotte no longer lay on the bed in front of him. His mother, Almeda Medina did. He no longer had to endure the contempt she felt for him or the brutal beatings waged against him by the bar owner or patrons. They would pay and pay dearly for their slow torture.

Medina reached down and clutched Charlotte, threw her over his shoulder, and returned to the sterile cell. He stood the mattress on end against the wall after placing Charlotte into a high back white painted chair. Moving quickly with practiced efficiency, he bound her hands and legs to the chair. Wrapping a leather belt around her chest, he tightened the strap until her boobs compressed into her chest. Confident he immobilized Charlotte; Medina left her sleeping and bound in the chair. His instruments of death were simple. Wanting to make sure his victim knew whom her tormentor was; he uncapped a tube of smelling salts and waved it in front of her face. Groggily, Charlotte came back to life. It took a moment for her to realize she remained a captive. A few more seconds past until she realized her nakedness and helplessness. Tears rushed from her eyes as she whimpered and prayed for mercy. Whimpering was all she could do. The leather strap constricted her breathing. Not knowing she was watched, Charlotte struggled against the bonds. She rocked back and forth and tried to pull up against the industrial strength tape. Her whimpering turned to violent outbursts.

"You yellow, weak coward. You're a deranged animal. You coward!" she shouted. "What's wrong with you? You can't get a girl by yourself so you have to steal me to get your rocks off. Show yourself if you're man enough! "

"Shut your mouth you filthy slut!" shouted Medina from behind Charlotte. Her eyes widened searching for her tormentor. Her eyes displayed surprise when she focused on her capturer.

"I know you!" she exclaimed. "You're the guy who sat down with me at the bookstore. What the hell are you doing and what did I ever do to you?"

"What did you do to me? What did you do to me? How can you ask that question you filthy wench? You know what you have done. All you nasty cheap whores do the same thing. You screw anything that has a pulse. All you do is want, want, want, take, take, and take" he shouted back. "You never love what you have. You always want more."

"What are you talking about, you crazy sick bastard? I'm not a whore. I'm a student. I don't even have a boyfriend. Let me go... *please*," she pleaded.

"Enough, Almeda," said Medina slipping a plastic bag over Charlotte's head. He made it fast and immovable with a quick zip of the plastic tie. Charlotte's breathing quickened. She did not care who Almeda was. She just wanted the death-bag off her head. The bag became cloudy from the moist air she exhaled into the bag. Charlotte's movements turned sluggish breathing in her carbon dioxide. Medina watched her struggle for the ten minutes it took her to die. He watched her suck her death bag into her mouth as she vainly struggled for life.

A penetrating wave of release left Medina's body. It was not a physical discharge. Ignacio felt his soul, evil as it was, renew from the euphoric adrenaline rush. The air he breathed seemed fresher. He found new strength from Charlotte's warm corpse. Her last dying breath was his rebirth. A heavy weight lifted from inside his inner being. For the next two hours, Ignacio knelt in front of the lifeless body imploring God to accept his sacrifice. The stink from Charlotte releasing her bowels after she died did not phase Medina. Nor did he acknowledge her lifeless, blank eyes staring into the ceiling overhead. She was no more than an offering to his retarded religious beliefs. Her existence was insignificant.

Medina awoke from his trance and commenced his last rite. He sliced through the dead woman's bonds with a razor sharp hunting knife. He unfastened the strap holding her upright in the chair. Stripping away the tape from her skin would normally pain a living person but Charlotte maintained her deathly stare. Pain no longer mattered to her.

Medina lifted her limp body from the chair and placed her onto a hospital gurney he retrieved from the outer room. Its stainless steel metal reflected gruesome shadows as he wheeled it into a bathroom with an oversized tub. He lowered Charlotte into the water, turned and headed back to the cell while lightly humming Amazing Grace. She would soak in the water for a while to let any residue, sweat, his semen, or any other telltale evidence dissolve from her body. What Medina was doing was as normal to him as brushing his teeth in the morning. As the dead Charlotte waited for him in the tub waiting for eventual disposal, he started cleaning the cell with bleach and scalding hot water. Not a single trace of his sacrifice would be left when he finished. He gathered her clothes, purse, books, backpack, and the sheets from the bed. He started a fire in the outdoor fireplace. Dousing the material with gasoline accelerated the obliteration of Charlotte's presence in his evil den. All evidence vanished in the blue flames. The hardest thing to destroy was her cell phone. It did not burn. In the fire, the phone would just turn into a crumpled molten mess. It had to be completely destroyed to ensure it could not be traced back to her. He removed the battery, held the phone with a pair of pliers and used a blowtorch against the phone's inner components. No one would be able to reconstruct the phone or the memory stored inside once he was finished. It took less than forty-five minutes to complete his macabre routine. It was a rote exercise for him to accomplish after so many years of practice. Dropping the charred cell phone in a thick plastic bag, he scooped the ashes from the fire into the bag. Every precaution to remove any trace evidence was thought of. He had been stalking and sacrificing his victims for eighteen years and still no one pounded on his door to arrest him. He chalked it up to his thoroughness of covering his tracks. When he first started killing, he learned quickly how best to dispose of a body and any trace evidence. It was actually quite easy. With a little research at the public library, he learned what criminal investigators looked for. It took a little extra time to do it right and to be thorough.

Confident he eliminated all evidence of his wicked deeds, the Chief Petty Officer returned to Charlotte. Spreading a large black plastic drop cloth on the floor in front of the tub he donned rubber gloves, a white disposable sanitation suit, blue surgical shoe covers, a hair net, and a face mask. He taped the gap made between his shoe covers and rubber gloves. The hair net was held tight with a strong hair band. From this point forward he would not allow any of himself to touch Charlotte until she was sufficiently scrubbed, washed, dried and encased in the plastic sheeting.

Charlotte's hair floated around her angelic face as he scrubbed her body with a soft brush. A soft horsehide brush did the best job of washing his victims. The brush performed well enough to remove any dirt but it did not scratch the body. His goal was to not leave any marks or residue for investigators to analyze. The hardest thing to wash was her hair. He used a shampoo designed for pets that killed bacteria but did not damage the hair or leave an odor. His chore completed, he drained the tub and rinsed her body with a hand held shower. Removing her cleansed corpse from the bathtub always proved tricky. Medina had to position himself just right so he could lift her from the tub and lower her gently onto the waiting black plastic sheeting. He positioned his arms under her thighs and shoulders, stooped down and effortlessly rose. He gently lowered her onto the plastic sheet and rolled her up burrito style. The heavy electric tape came in handy to hold the seams in place. His work was almost done. All that was left was carrying his victim into the van, cleaning the bathroom, drive the six hours to the site he chose to lay her to rest, burn the sanitation clothing, dispose of the ashes and cell phone, and scour the van. His ritual would take another fourteen hours to complete. Before he finished his duty, he decided to eat a sandwich, watch his favorite TV show, *CSI,* and take a nap. The short break recharged him to finish his dastardly deeds.

CHAPTER FOURTEEN

Ishmael's perseverance paid off. The Department of Homeland Security's new computer search engine accessed all state and federal criminal databases, intelligence files, military and immigration records, and tax returns. All thanks to the Patriot Act. The Patriot Act and the 9/11 Commission's recommendations forced the government's agencies to work together. Unbeknownst to Ishmael when he started his research with DHS, it also gave him access to a few foreign criminal databases as well.

The American database search yielded a wealth of information and took less than three weeks to complete. The data received was rapidly forwarded to the FBI task force for action and investigation. The foreign database searches took much longer. Reams of paper were filled out and faxed to the DHS agent who screened such requests. Having an FBI task force pulling the strings streamlined and expedited the process but it still felt like watching grass grow.

The hang-ups came when they approached the foreign gate-keepers in charge of approving or denying their requests for information. In this case, the FBI Director made his requests personally to his law enforcement counterparts in Great Britain, France, Italy, Spain, Greece, Turkey, Singapore, Philippines, Thailand, Saudi Arabia, Bahrain, Australia, and Israel. France and Saudi Arabia immediately disapproved the Director's request. They rationalized it had nothing to do with the Global War on Terrorism. In order to narrow the search, Ishmael narrowed the request to search for young women murdered, discovered naked, and dumped near the ocean with no apparent signs of rape or abuse. He wanted additional files documenting brutal murders of men at or about the same periods when the murdered women were discovered. He started with a narrow scope first. If nothing was found, then he would expand the net. Ishmael supposed that if the killer worked abroad he would have used the same modus operandi as what was discovered in America. He hoped his advanced search would identify potential Bill victims based upon his pattern. If the results came back negative, he would broaden his search. The task would become exponentially more difficult. Best to rely on a bit of luck he thought to himself when he filled out the initial ton of paperwork.

Some readily approved the request. A favor of this magnitude would be stored away for repayment later down the road. Nothing valuable came back except from Thailand and Greece. In Thailand, four unsolved murders fitting the investigator's query were reported. Each involved young women suffocated and men brutally bludgeoned to death. The Thai killings occurred during two separate periods spread apart by two months. The documents Ishmael received described the women's deaths by probable affixation. The male deaths resulted from severe beatings.

Both female Thai victims were prostitutes. A death of a Thailand prostitute was nothing new and the cases were quickly shut. They were not missed by anyone important so their initial disappearances were chocked up to the theory that they either found another bar in another city to work at, they went back to where they came from, or they found someone else to take care of them. The police reports were devoid of information. The Thai police had better things to do with their time then investigate a whore's murder. But, the files did have some information proving useful in the hunt for Bill. The women were strangled or suffocated. Neither victim showed signs of beatings or being killed with weapons.

The first file Ishmael examined contained three photos depicting a young Asian woman discovered in a secluded portion of a Phuket beach. The pictures showed a smallish woman with black hair and a pasty complexion. Exposure to the elements for three or four days before discovery made her appearance ashen. Luckily, no large animals feasted on her remains. If the Thai police report was correct, her body was not moved when it was discovered and photographed. She was naked from head to toe and her body lay in a supine position with her legs together. Her hair was relatively neat and combed. Her skin and teeth revealed her age was somewhere between sixteen and twenty-five.

The second woman's file was similar to the first. It too contained three pictures. The first was a close up shot of her body laying in its death pose. The second picture showed the body and the immediate vicinity around her. The third was taken from an opposite prospective capturing the rest of the surrounding area. If the police report did not identify the two girls as not being family, Ishmael could have sworn they might have been sisters or cousins. Just like the first file, the girl was a prostitute who worked the bars frequented by foreign tourists on the prowl for cheap and exotic sex. Her disappearance did not raise any heartache except to her pimp. He cared more about how much money he lost from her not sucking sex-tourist cock.

Her body was discovered in a pineapple field about an hour outside of town. Rats and other critters had feasted on her naked body. The photos showed a young pretty Asian female with bite marks all over her torso, legs, arms, and face. Ishmael put the file away for an hour or so after he first looked at the photos. Reading about a murder and seeing the photos of the victims is entirely two different subjects. Seeing how the young lives were snuffed out without anyone caring and being disposed of like trash at the curbside affected Ishmael's consciousness. He forced himself to remember that deaths like these were the reason he and Israel found themselves in the lab every day. He and his brother possessed special talents for rooting out evidence where seemingly none existed. It was their way of contributing to bringing a loathsome human being to justice. The bastard had to eventually answer for his crimes. Neither Ishmael nor Israel held any illusions that some humans sought pleasure in hurting each other. All they could do was practice their well-honed skills to take one sadistic animal out of circulation at a time. It was a small contribution but they believed it was well worth their time and effort.

Ishmael theorized why Bill committed the crimes against the women from the manner he left them. The second body was partially decomposed and gnawed upon, the position she was placed in showed similarities between the multiple victims found in America. Each victim was naked, clean, strangled or suffocated, and laid to rest in an area that was quiet and peaceful. The real difference between the Thai victims and the American victims were how their arms were arranged. The American female victims had their arms draped to their sides or folded neatly upon their stomachs. The Thai victim's arms and hands were clasped together over their breasts. The scene looked like they were praying. The scant reports revealed nothing further.

The male murders were much the same. Both were found a few days after the female victims were discovered. One male was from Indonesia. The other immigrated to Thailand from Sri Lanka. They traveled to Thailand for work and neither had any family in the country. The nature their killer chose them led credence to the theory they were selected because of their indigenous status and would not be immediately missed. Just like the women, the killer studied those he decided to kill and if they would be missed. Their murders were not random violent acts. Their killer probably befriended them at first to learn their backgrounds. Luring them to their deaths came later.

The same story unfolded in the Thai police reports as it was told in the American reports. The men died gruesome and painful deaths. The bodies were warped beyond recognition after being repeatedly pummeled with a blunt object. One man was discovered lying in the back of an abandoned truck on the outskirts of Phuket. His body was infested with maggots. Flies and other insects feasted on his blood, organs, and flesh. Every finger was smashed to a pulp, his cheekbones were caved in, and his arms and legs were riddled with jagged broken bones protruding from his skin.

The second male murder victim's pictures told the same tale. Unlike his dead predecessor, the Sri Lankan male turned up in a cheap motel. The name under the registry proved false and just like all the rest of the turn-a-trick Thai hotels, security was not on the top of their priority list. The police report stated the room was rented to an Abdul Jamar. It was a common enough name. The hotel's maids found him when they went to clean the room. They never bothered with the room for the previous two days because a do-not-disturb sign hung from the door's handle. The maids learned early in their employment to respect that sign. They did not care to know what went on behind those closed doors. Child, both male and female, prostitution was illegal but not rigorously enforced. Drugs and booze were in ample supply. The patrons using all three fueled the maid's paychecks. All they had to do was to clean up the messes. What went on between the time they checked in and when they checked out was not their affair.

In this case, Ishmael believed the killer did not have enough time to dispose of the body. He coupled it with the theory that Bill was a transient psychopath. Those two assumptions led him to deduce from the working psychological profile that the murderer could leave the body where it was without being discovered in time to prevent his capture. Jamal's death fit Bill's pattern. The murder occurred five days after the second Thai prostitute was killed. The Arabian black male's entire body showed signs of blunt, traumatic trauma. The pictures showed Butcher Bill's prey covered and lying in pools of his dried blood. The blood no longer possessed its reddish hue. It had turned a grim black when it dried. Bits of teeth and skull fragments lay scattered about the floor. Blood splatters covered an entire wall in the seedy motel room. Ishmael knew these were caused by striking the body with the murder weapon. The photos captured lifeless eyes with terror etched into the flesh.

The third file Ishmael gazed over covered the same ground as the first two Thai files. The only difference between the Asian murders and the Hellenic police file were the dates and locations. Two unsolved murders of a female Italian student, who was in Greece studying philosophy in Athens, and a male German tourist hiking his way through Europe were reported in June 1997. The Greeks were much more thorough in their police work.

This time the killer selected a twenty two year old Caucasian female. Her body was discovered in an olive vineyard forty miles north of Athens. The only difference between her and the Thai prostitutes were how the hands were arranged. Her hands were laid upon her stomach with her fingers interlaced. This was unlike the Thai girls whose hands were folded palm-to-palm, fingertip-to-fingertip in a praying fashion.

The German backpacker was disfigured from tremendous torture and dumped under a bridge. The German Police autopsy recorded multiple bruises upon his body. The record stated the likely cause was being whipped to death with a chain.

Another fact Ishmael noted as different from the pattern was how the killer concentrated his barbaric mutilation to the genital area. The autopsy reported his thighs, testicles, penis, and lower abdomen areas were repeatedly struck causing massive internal bleeding. The internal bleeding caused severe shock which eventually forced the heart to stop beating. The man suffered a tremendous amount of pain before his body simply gave out against the tumultuous assault.

Armed with the new information, Ishmael discussed the matter with his brother. They agreed it was too important to email their results. Instead, he contacted Detectives Hendricks and Raphael about the newly discovered evidence. They all agreed the material should be presented to the FBI task force in person. Hendricks scheduled the meeting for Ishmael and himself while Israel and Raphael continued the investigation in the Pacific Northwest.

The trip offered them their first opportunity to meet the lead FBI investigator assigned to profiling the criminal. Both Ishmael and Hendricks were scheduled to meet with the FBI's Deputy Director of Operations, Mr. Roger Morrison, Dr. Ohms, and two task force members at nine o'clock in the morning. The FBI team was extremely excited to hear of their new discoveries. The profilers were starting to piece together the puzzle. The more pieces they had, the easier it was to home in on their target. The task force planned on shifting the operations center to the field to focus on the Seattle area. Their analysts showed the killer being territorial within a two hundred mile distance from his base. He shifted his killing zone every eighteen to twenty four months. With two relatively fresh corpses, they would never have a better opportunity to capture him.

Hendricks prearranged to meet Ishmael at eight thirty in the FBI headquarters' lobby. Ishmael looked at his watch for the fourth time in two minutes. Time dragged on when anxious and enthusiastic. He knew the info he carried in his backpack would bring more guns to bear on their enemy. His enthusiasm did not reside solely on the case. He was enthralled to be in headquarters of the world's most powerful criminal investigative organization. Plus, he was about to meet some of the most brilliant minds in criminal psychology. And it all started with Ishmael and Israel performing their magic on the scant evidence they initially collected. It was a criminal analysis's wet dream. Israel and Ishmael were smack in the center of the biggest manhunt since the hunt for John Wilkes Booth or Osama bin Laden. From what Hendricks told him and his brother, the FBI was pulling out all of the stops on catching Bill. The murderer flew under their radar scope for far too long and he had to be stopped and stopped quickly. Now, he was about to brief them on more valuable material. Ishmael checked his watch again. An agonizingly slow thirty-eight seconds had ticked by.

His gaze remained focused on the entry doors and the security stations. Everyone entering the building as a visitor had to process through the main entrance, pass through the metal detectors, and succumb to inspection from the rent-a-cops. Ishmael reached for his cell phone to call Hendricks to make sure he had the correct meeting time. He abruptly ended the call when he spotted the middle-aged detective enter the building and proceed though the security checkpoint. His holstered pistol set off the metal detector beep but the guards waved him through anyway. His law enforcement credentials checked out.

Ishmael rose from the mahogany colored bench, collected his precious cargo, and strolled towards Hendricks. The two shook hands and headed towards the west wing elevators. The meeting started in twenty minutes. They reached the office where the briefings were being held, checked in with the secretary who escorted them to a conference room with a large expanse of windows looking out upon the Washington streets. The Washington Monument stood erect and shined white from the sun hitting its sides. Flags encircling the obelisk fluttered in the wind. It was a beautiful mild spring day. The Washington cherry blossom trees exploded with brilliance from their pinkish flowers. People wore light jackets as they leisurely walked to their destination with the spring sun cascading upon their pale winter skin. It was a long, cold, bitter winter in the Capitol. The warm spring day released them from their wintery bonds and exchanged it for springtime cheerfulness.

Waiting anxiously, two gentlemen and a woman entered the conference room. The first man was dressed in a pale blue suit and the other wore jeans and a sweater. The auburn-haired woman dressed smartly in a purple dress suit. Introductions were hastily made between Hendricks, Colby, Ohms, Sherman, and Amecii. Neither Hendricks nor Ishmael needed to be told who Ohms

was. They deduced from his command presence and the defer-
ence the other two gave him that he was the lead criminal profiler
and task force leader. Dr. Ohms introduced Agent Amecii as his
deputy and Agent Sherman as the chief field agent. Any action
by the FBI team when they arrived in Seattle would be led by
those two.

The secretary who initially escorted them in carried coffee and
pastries into the conference room. Another secretary arranged
the computer and briefing screens. Ishmael's power point slide
presentation appeared on the large conference room's projection
screen. Ohms quickly dialed a phone number, paging whoever
was on the other end they were ready to begin. Five minutes later,
FBI Deputy Director Matthew Bartholomew entered the conference room, poured himself a cup of coffee, plucked a cheese
Danish from the tray, and sat at the conference room table's
head chair.

"Ladies and Gentlemen," began Bartholomew in a soft voice,
you know why we are here. I am glad to finally meet the folks
who uncovered Butcher Bill." Pausing to sip his coffee he continued, "From Dr. Ohms's briefs, the Director and the Attorney
General realize we are hunting the most heinous murderer to
ever roam United States soil. The sooner we get our guys paired
up with their Washington counterparts, the sooner we can send
this guy to the table where a needle will send him straight to hell.
I understand you collected more valuable information to show
us. Mr. Colby, the floor is yours," stated America's second most
powerful policeman sitting erect and attentive.

Ishmael rose from his chair to speak. None of the attendees
asked any questions while he spoke. Their attention focused on
the information he brought to share. Their criminal investigative
minds raced to assimilate the new information Ishmael plowed
through. He finished his speech by saying it appeared the murderer altered his original pattern a bit when he disposed of the
corpses. He believed the killer sacrificed the women for some

spiritual and religious reason. An exorcism of sorts. Colby reached this conclusion from the manner the Asian victim's hands were clasped together in a praying fashion. Ishmael bolstered his argument by comparing photos taken eighteen years ago to the recent murders. Why he stopped posing his victims in a religious fashion, he could not speculate upon. He would reserve that right for Dr. Ohms and his behavioral science team.

Catherine Amecii spoke first. "This is incredible evidence you brought before us Mr. Colby. I echo the Deputy Director's words regarding the superb work you, your brother, and the Seattle PD did to surface Butcher Bill," she commended. "I agree with you about how the victims were sacrifices. However, the most significant information you brought us are when and where the murders were committed."

Catherine knew it was her turn to share information with her Seattle teammates. "As you are aware, we've developed a limited profile about Butcher Bill. In a nutshell, Butcher Bill is Caucasian or Asian. He is between thirty-five to forty-five years old. He is an athletically built transient male working in the shipbuilding or marine repair business. He is not married nor does he have any close relationships. He never has and never will. Agent Sherman culled through the past murders and developed this theory. Your information solidifies this hypothesis."

Catherine motioned to a wall where a United States map was posted. The map contained green and red circles where male and female victims were discovered. Blue dots with concentric circles enveloping them were added. "The red dots represent murdered women. The green are the murdered men. The blue dots are new which symbolize Navy bases. The circles drawn around the blue dots equal a two hundred mile radius from the respective Navy facility. We have done the math; over ninety-four percent of the murders were committed inside one of the blue circles. Gentlemen, we have concluded we are looking for a sailor in the United States Navy," said Special Agent Amecii.

Deputy Director Bartholomew liked what he was hearing. The briefing just migrated from an informational meeting into a working group. Evidence was shared and bright minds were jumping on it to solve the crime. He sat silent and listened as Hendricks chimed into the conversation.

"That theory explains why Bill broke his patterns in the United States. He did not stop killing because of some weird personal reason. The murders stopped in America because he was out of the country. When we retrieve information from the Navy regarding what sailors were stationed at those places, I bet Bill was deployed on a ship that stopped in Thailand and Greece for R&R. All of the pieces fit." The sage detective continued. "There is an aircraft carrier and three destroyers stationed at the Everett Naval Station. There are submarines at the Keyport Sub base. Plus, in Bremerton, there is the Puget Sound Naval Shipyard. The shipyard alone employs over ten thousand people and a lot of them are sailors."

"Colby brought us the link we were looking for ladies and gentlemen," announced Doctor Ohms. We have finally narrowed the focus of this investigation. I want Catherine to work with the Colby twins to track down the information about Bill from the Navy. Hopefully, the wheels of justice will turn rapidly on this. We can count on Deputy Director Bartholomew to cut through the red tape. If all goes well we should have a list of names within a week." Focusing on Hendricks and Sherman, Ohms barked more orders. "You two will travel to the west coast. Detective Hendricks, if you would, please help Agent Sherman learn the lay of the land in Washington. Take him for tours of the naval bases or whatever he needs to acclimate himself. How is your relationship with the Naval Criminal Investigative Service?" asked Ohms.

"We won't have any problems with the NCIS. They are as eager as us to track down Amanda Jackson's killer. They are cooperative and welcome the opportunity to assist. We may have to fill them in on what we know though," said Hendricks.

Bartholomew joined the conversation. "Do not worry about the Navy folks" said the Deputy Director. "I will speak with the Chief of Naval Operations today. We will have all of the assistance we need. However, I want to keep the investigation limited to the task force assigned. We are narrowing the field. Having this unravel because too many people are knowledgeable is a disaster waiting to happen. The task force will have unfettered access to any naval site we need in Washington. The CNO will take care of that. The net is about to be cast ladies and gentlemen, we don't want the fish escaping because we could not keep it taut. "The task force and Seattle Police Department have a lot of work to do. Good luck and good hunting."

Nothing further needed to be said. The task force had a path forward. Their marching orders were given and received with zeal. More slow and tedious investigative work remained on the horizon. However, the winds blew in favor of the FBI Task Force. Butcher Bill's identity would be uncovered soon.

CHAPTER FIFTEEN

Father Nguyen readied himself for the conversation with Chief Medina. He noticed the demon enter his church an hour before the evening mass started. As always, confession was offered prior to the service for those desiring relief from their sins. He was not scheduled to man the confessional this evening but he quickly volunteered to take over the presiding priest's duties. Father Gonzalez, a visiting priest from Mexico, gladly accepted his offer. The Hispanic Padre grew up playing baseball in Mexico City. He even had a shot to play minor league ball for the New York Yankees Triple-A farm team in Scranton until he heard his calling to the priesthood. He never regretted the decision to don the holy garments and dedicate his life to God instead of Yankee pin stripes to chase a ball around the baseball diamond. But, priest or no priest, his love for baseball remained a passion. When Father Nguyen suggested they trade nights to say mass, he jumped at the chance. The Seattle Mariners were playing at Safeco Field against the New York Yankees. He normally rooted for the Mariners since they were the home team. His favorite player, the Japanese transplant, Ichiro Suzuki, was on a sixteen game hitting streak ever since the Mariners traded him to New York. He would get to watch the ex-Mariners star attempt to extend his streak. Plus, he would watch his childhood favorite baseball team, the Yankees, play too. God surely worked in mysterious ways. He directly attributed Father Nguyen's kind offer as a message from his Lord. God understood he sacrificed a potentially brilliant baseball career for the black suit and white collar. This was his way of paying him back. He blessed Father Nguyen and dashed out of the church passing the evil presence sitting in the pews ten rows back from the alter. He had just enough time to grab his Mariners ball cap and catch the train bound for the stadium. If the trains were on time he might arrive for the opening pitch.

Father Nguyen smiled as he watched his friend and fellow clergyman exit the church with haste. He appreciated the passion Father Gonzalez exercised as a priest. But, he recognized his comrade's love for baseball. Gonzalez endlessly chattered about the sport. When his nose was not buried in some biblical text, he devoured the Seattle Times sports section. The Jesus-baseball groupie could recite every Seattle Mariner player's current and career batting averages, on-base percentages, and countless other baseball stats. Seeing his friend finding happiness and peace watching baseball warmed his weather beaten heart.

Nguyen readied himself for his own game. The first pitch would be thrown as soon as he entered the confessional box. He had to remain calm and in control of his faculties. Playing a dangerous game, he tread on dangerous ground. This would be the first time since he started volunteering onboard the aircraft carrier that he and the wicked mariner met alone. Medina showing up for mass meant only one thing. The demon wanted to confess another murderous sin. He realized many weeks ago this day would dawn.

He sat upon the blue velvet-cushioned chair inside the confessional booth. His watch read six o'clock. Mass started promptly at seven. The parishioners had fifty minutes to divulge their sins. Being a Tuesday evening, the church did not have many attendees for the evening service yet. Those present were mostly the elderly taking comfort in receiving daily communion in preparation of their fast approaching demise. They knew their days were numbered. Attending mass helped them cope with the pains old age blanketed them with. Going to church helped their health as well. Many walked to the cathedral. Many found it a good spot to meet with friends for coffee and pie afterwards. Their confessions interested the priest. When they entered the confessional, the aged did not confess recent sins. Their confessions could fill novels. The sins confessed were memories of sins committed years ago. Their specters haunted their consciousness. The stories interested the Cambodian clergyman. He understood his elderly patrons. They wanted to get something off their chest to reconcile wrongs committed decades ago in their youth. The penance Father Nguyen doled out was always the same. He told the parishioner it was not he who they should be confessing to. They needed to seek out the person the sin was committed against and to apologize for their behavior. No matter how hard it was to do, it was the only way they could expunge it from their memory. Of course, he granted absolution and forgave them. Most heeded his advice and returned with stories regarding the pleasant and sometimes not so pleasant outcome of their penance.

Another clique attending the daily evening ritual was the adroitly pious. They were enamored by the glory filling their hearts from Christ's teachings. Going to church each day was as habitual to them as brushing their teeth before going to bed. Attendance was mandatory to them. Nguyen labeled these people "God's Groupies." Some truly understood the Bible could not be taken literally. The good book needed careful interpretation. However, most of God's Groupies were more fearful of the Lord then they were enlightened by his messages. Their apprehension for missing mass or committing minor sins drove them to constantly worry about damnation to hell. The Groupies knew they wanted God in their lives. Their confessions were rather boring and mundane. No matter how minor the sin, a Groupie agonized on how their saying the word 'fuck' or thinking about their neighbor's tits would cause them to be stricken to fire and brimstone instead of enjoying the utopia of heaven. Father Nguyen exercised compassionate patience with Groupies. Their penance was to research a passage in the bible and compare it to the Vatican's interpretation. The second part of their atonement required them to practice the lesson and report back to the priest the results the next time they went to confession.

The confessions he enjoyed listening to the most were told by children. If a child attended the weekday mass they were brought by their parents for them to learn a lesson about some transgression they committed. The priest listened patiently to their jumbled rationalizations of why they stole a comic book or told their parents they hated them for not buying them the newest video game. This presented the priest an opportunity to influence them in their formative years. The traditional approach called for extolling the Ten Commandments. "Thou shall not steal," or "Thou shall not covet thy neighbor's goods," were the tenants needed to be driven home. Father Nguyen approached the situation from a different tack. Yes, he paid homage to Moses' tablets to make sure the child knew of their existence. His method took the biblical message a step deeper. He engaged the child in conversation much like Jesus Christ did. Unless the child realized their own error from the righteous path, then the confessional was only a rote exercise in futility. The child had to recognize his own shortcomings for their confession to be worthwhile. It sometimes proved to be a tricky achievement. Children possessed fantastic imaginations. They could rationalize anything. Once they realized their mistake, Father Nguyen did not ask them to succumb to any humiliation of apologizing to the ones they offended. Learning through their discussions was penance enough. For a child, it is hard to admit they erred. Most kids enjoyed their conversations and exited the dimly lit box feeling more confident about themselves. A dose of five "Our Fathers" and ten "Hail Marys" did not hurt them either.

The hardest sins he endured to listen to were from the destitute. These were from the junkies, alcoholics, and gamblers. No matter how many times their sins were forgiven, they still slipped further down into depravity. There was not much he could do for them from the confessional seat. Their salvation resided in their own hearts. He prayed with them for the Lord to shed mercy upon their self-destructive paths and to give them the strength to abolish their habits. Their salvations lie outside the confessional. The priest made mental notes about who he spoke to. He vowed to assist them to attend AA meetings or to find a detoxification center whose doors were open to the indigent. His nightly prayers always included this group. Some overcome the demons living inside a vodka bottle or those nagging at them to spend their mortgage payment at the blackjack table. Most did not until they reached the point of no return. To do so called for the community to embrace them and to let the person know they were not alone in their plight. Nonetheless, he still absolved them of their sins and passed brochures offering free assistance to the afflicted soul under the partition's sliding shade.

The souls entering his confessional that evening presented a mixed bag of issues. A wife confessed she slept with another man while her husband was away on business. A school superintendent admitted he received bribes to steer work towards a general contractor. A prostitute confessed her sinful ways but said she liked doing it. Last before Butcher Bill, a young man confided he was a homosexual. Each visited him to receive forgiveness from their sins. He pardoned each for their transgressions and sermonized to the first three. What they were doing was just plain wrong and they knew better. If they did not, they would not have come to see him. Father Nguyen did not mince his words. He called a spade a spade. Thus, the reason so many people sought his wisdom. He possessed a talent that made people realize their faults yet not to be intimidated by him for judging them. The gay young man sought comfort. He struggled with his identity. The Roman Catholic Church denounced homosexuality. Nguyen believed the church's philosophy in principle. However, he preferred to have a parishioner who realized his sexual preference for the same sex was not evil. He just wanted the man to be happy and to share his joy. It was better than having him hide who he was, end up miserable, and shunning his Lord. God created homosexuals. They were his children just as much as the heterosexuals were. In Nguyen's mind, if the person found comfort with a person of his own sex then so be it. He made it clear to the young man not to be frightened but to embrace the Lord who would give him comfort. Nguyen did not share this opinion amongst his fellow clergyman. The only person who knew he felt this way was his own confessor who absolved him of his own sin for preaching against church doctrine. Plus, his confessor was a happy camper right now because he was about to chow down a hot dog, a bag of peanuts, and a beer while he watched the Mariners battle the Yankees. Their God was a good and righteous fellow.

The church bells tolled announcing the time. It was six thirty. The bells chimed every half hour. Everett, Washington had three major professions. Either you logged and cut timber, you worked for the military, or you were a professional mariner. The latter built Saint Michael's church. It was a mariner's practice to announce time passing every thirty minutes.

The last bell reverberated through the church as Chief Medina ducked into the confessional booth. The air chilled Father Nguyen. His skin prickled with goose bumps. He need not slide back the confessional's shade to know a demon entered his sanctuary. The devil was in his midst. His eyes slowly shut to summon his Savior's grace and strength.

"Good evening Chief Medina," he softly spoke as he peeled back the rectangular partition separating good from evil.

"Bless me Father for I have sinned," uttered the murderous mariner.

"That is enough of the rote repertoire Chief. We both know why you are here. You tread on holy ground to report another repulsive act and desire to get it off your soul," Nguyen said calmly. "You're not here for redemption Chief. I believe you came here because you want to revel in your egregious acts." He purposely called him Chief to confirm to him he knew who is was and where he hid out. The priest decided a few days ago he would go head-to-head with hell's jackal. Too many innocent people died because some priest before him clung to his religious vows not to break the confessional's sanctity. Nguyen would not break his own oaths; but; he was resolute in his conviction to stand up and fight the monster in his midst. He flirted with danger and possibly even death.

"You are a brave man to speak to me like that Priest," growled Medina. "I came tonight to confess my sins and you are turning me away like a mangy dog."

"I am not turning you away Chief. Your murders are trophies and the confessional is the only venue you have to show them off. My vows force me to listen to your ugly tales. I do not have to sit here and be complacent about it Chief Medina. What innocent young lamb did you slaughter this time? Was she a librarian who wanted to help children learn to read? Was she a waitress who was working while she drafted melodic tunes on a guitar with aspirations of recording her music for all of God's children to enjoy? Was she a prostitute who desperately wanted a way out of her despair? Was she a feather light ballerina who graced the stage with the nimbleness God gifted her with? Tell me Chief Medina, what wrong did you witness in this new victim of yours?"

"You are quite cagey tonight, Priest. You think your being onboard my ship changes anything? Yes, I sacrificed a pretty, blond girl. She was not any of those you mentioned. She was a slut who deserved to die just like all the rest. That harlot flashed her tail around luring men to defile her. I did her one better. I taught that slatternly Jezebel a real lesson. I captured her three days ago and she is now lying in the marshes of a Stanwood Slough. The whore tried to pass herself off as a student. I saw through her charade. She was like my prostitute mother. She dolled herself up and was just begging to be someone's fuck toy. I saved her the trouble. The trollop is in hell burning and will suck devil cock for eternity."

Nguyen did tread on thin ice. He riled the beast just as he planned. Father Nguyen needed to calm the animal before the situation melted down. The beast wanted to boast of his imaginary triumph over evil. Nguyen's control of the dialogue with the demon was imperative. Enflaming the beast's rage could have untold and immediate consequences. Not predicting Medina's reactions correctly placed many more lives in jeopardy than his. Father Nguyen had to control the conversation's tone. Keeping Medina calm proved a daunting task.

"You do realize God never enlisted you as his agent. You are a demonic puppet of Satan. How did it feel to kill again, Ignacio?" asked the priest. "When she died did she scream for mercy? If you really were performing a service for God, how did he communicate his desires to you? You must feel some euphoria when the Holy Spirit envelopes your body and soul. That is how I feel when I help a person. God works through me you know. Through his divine manner he has led you to me. I can help you if you let me. But, first the killings have to stop and you must reconcile your deeds with humanity. Does that make sense to you, Ignacio?"

"Of course God relayed his desires to me. Why else would I be doing my part to exterminate filth from the face of the Earth? Humanity is better off now they were sacrificed in his name. They no longer have the opportunity to spread their diseases. I am preaching to the choir, Father. How many people's confessions do you hear of men cheating on their wives, using and abusing women to satisfy their own sexual perversity? You must acknowledge I am an instrument of God's will."

Nguyen wanted Medina to hear out loud someone calling him a monster and telling him his acts were wrong. He had to set the stage inside the murderer's warped brain.

"Tell me about your latest conquest, Ignacio. Who was she?" Father Nguyen learned a long time ago to use his first name. It soothed the beast in him. Practicing this technique made the individual feel like they were speaking with a confidant. That was

Nguyen's goal. He wanted the demon to vocalize his deeds. Once done, he could whittle away at the conscience every time he saw him in the hope Medina recognized his sins.

"She was a nobody. I seized her at her school. She never saw me coming. Surprise engulfed her when she woke up in her cell." Medina described the entire murderous episode, except how he had ejaculated on her body. For some unexplained reason he thought that was not a sin. Just like the priest, Medina considered himself one of God's chosen mortal warriors. He was placed on Earth to rid it of people like his mother and those who patronized her.

"You understand I cannot pardon you from your sins. You believe you are performing righteous work. But, really, you are committing the most grievous of sins. Until you decide to repent, your soul is lost and damned. I do not believe our Lord who volunteered his own life to save us from ourselves is the same God you pray to. I want you to think about that. Come back in a few days to talk again. I know you won't talk to me on the ship. I am here to help you," stated the priest.

Medina understood the confessional conversation was over and he was being summarily dismissed. Wordlessly, he rose and departed the booth. Father Nguyen dropped to his knees, tears flowing from his eyes. He prayed for the young girl whose soul the demon remorselessly extinguished.

Nguyen concentrated on saying the evening mass. The evening's service etched itself into his mind for ever. The rituals he administered to the church attendees seemed more significant than at any other time he performed them. His breaking of the bread and blessing of the wine helped him fortify for the coming storm. He understood he did not have any impact upon the killer. What he did do is find out where the victim lay. He needed to figure out a way to signal the authorities on her whereabouts. He was forbidden to expose the demon to law enforcement personnel directly. However, just like anything else in life, there were choices. He decided to bend the church laws a bit. Nothing prevented him from giving the police a path to follow. All he had to do was figure out how to do it without betraying the confidence of the holy penitential sacrament.

The churchgoers lined up to receive communion. The devil took his spot in the line. Father Nguyen saw his short form mumbling prays while he waited to commune with Christ. Medina reached the priest and presented his open cupped hands to receive the Eucharistic wafer. Father Nguyen stepped back from the murderer and silently refused the demon the sacrament. A tear dribbled from Medina's left eye. Hate beamed through the other.

The priest watched the wicked man turn, storm down the aisle, and walk through the church doors. Relief washed through Nguyen's body. It was time to take another walk in the forest. God showed him the first path he needed to chart to combat Satan's disciple. Maybe he would do so again. He prayed it would be so.

CHAPTER SIXTEEN

The phone call came to the Seattle 911 dispatcher at ten thirty in the morning. It was made anonymously from a public telephone. Tracing it back to its origins did not take long. The emergency phone system tied directly into the telephone networks database. It originated from a public telephone located near the Seattle Space Needle near the carousal. Whoever made the report wanted to remain undiscovered. Smart man.

On a typical weekend, the area around the Space Needle teemed with people. Hundreds of people visited the area for the good food, fresh air, and for the view from atop the city's land-mark structure. The view of Seattle from the tower delighted thousands every year.

Raphael repeatedly listened to the recorded conversation. The caller was calm. The report sounded rehearsed. Whoever made the call thought about what he wanted to say and how to say it without appearing distressed. What interested Raphael was the background noise. A phrase at the end of conversation captured his attention. Try as he might, Raphael could not discern what was said. He would pass it to the Colby's and the FBI Task Force for analysis. Their sophisticated spread spectrum equipment would easily break the signal down, remove the noise, and amplify what he so urgently desired to hear. The faint words just might deter-mine who the caller was or why he made the call. Raphael knew the caller was not Butcher Bill. A serial killer would have gloated more. Plus, if it was Bill, making a call to report the location of his latest victim did not fit his pattern.

"No," thought Raphael. "He wouldn't start bragging about his conquests after sixteen years of killing in the shadows. Bill liked killing too much to expose himself so easily. Someone out there has information regarding Bill. Whoever the caller is he's probably terrified of the information he possesses. Getting involved directly put him square in the killer's sights."

"I'd be frightened too if I knew what Bill was capable of," mumbled the detective.

The caller was an amateur, good intention or not. The 911 system recorded every conversation. It logged the time and date it was made too. The Seattle Space Needle Commons were a high-volume tourist attraction and an area where many local citizens liked to visit. To maintain security the Seattle Police Department mounted surveillance cameras. Hopefully, if they got lucky, Raphael would be able to match the voice to a picture of the anonymous caller. Collecting the video feed sat on the tip-top of his to-do list. They must retrieve the surveillance video before it was recorded over. Standard police protocol stated the video would be stored for seventy two hours. Three days was long enough to keep the recorded material. If a crime occurred, the police knew to secure the video feed long before it was erased.

Raphael removed his headphones and called the urban surveillance division. It took the detective twenty minutes to find the person he needed to talk with. He was connected to Doris Figby. On the phone, Doris sounded like a stereotypical government bureaucrat hired to manage her division with less than excitable enthusiasm. She told Raphael the surveillance tapes remained in her custody until she received the appropriate evidentiary paperwork that released the tapes to whomever in the department wanted it. Mrs. Figby sounded irritated when Detective Raphael stated to her he was granted full authority from the Chief of Police to cut through any red tape. That is all she needed to hear. The aged civilian government worker informed the police officer the tapes would be available for pick up in four hours. Copies were required to be made first. If the recordings captured a crime, the originals were sent to the evidence department for classification and processing. An evidence chain violation derailed many cases in the past. Therefore, the police department observed strict guidelines when it came to evidentiary collection procedures.

The information the mysterious caller reported involved a young woman. He never mentioned her name, only that she could be found in the Stanwood Slough. A search and rescue dog team, thirty Washington State Highway Patrolmen, sixteen Island County Sheriffs, and Detective Raphael combed the Slough's high grass for six hours until the dogs caught her scent.

The 911 telephone operator tried every trick she learned to entice the caller to reveal his identity, relationship to the murder victim, location, and job…anything to help the case. The tipster ignored all of her questions. He hung the phone up as abruptly as the call began.

One look at how the body lay in the towering green marshy grass convinced Raphael they found another Butcher Bill victim. His immediate reaction was to check for life but her chalky appearance convinced him otherwise. The female victim lay in a tranquil repose just like all the rest of Bill's female conquests were left. Naked head to toe, her breasts gravitated to the outer forms of her body. Her golden blond hair reflected the light beams from a Trooper's heavy black flashlight. Charlotte lay rigid. Her hands and arms folded neatly over her vagina protecting her modesty. The surrounding grass framed the body and made her appear peaceful in her final slumber. The only thing the detective planned to do with the newly discovered corpse was to sit tight and wait for Israel Colby to show up. He called the young CSI scientist as soon as he realized they had stumbled upon another murder by Butcher Bill's hands. Israel reminded him Ishmael was in Washington D.C. with Detective Hendricks presenting data to the FBI taskforce. Raphael ignored the reminder but made a mental note to make his second call to Hendricks. With any luck, any information processed from the crime scene could be immediately forwarded to the task force for review. The younger Colby jotted down the body's location and told the homicide police officer it would take him approximately two hours to respond. He was on Whidbey Island. Catching the ferry, driving through Seattle to Stanwood would be time consuming. Mercifully, the weatherman forecast a dry evening. He insisted that Raphael keep the crime scene as uncontaminated as possible. The opportunity to collect relatively fresh evidence resided foremost in both of their thoughts. They might have a chance to tighten the dragnet upon Butcher Bill to end the homicides. From the enormously long list of murders, this was the first time the police possessed a fresh crime scene. With luck, the dead woman would shed light upon her attacker. Hopefully, Israel was well rested. Raphael needed his A-game. No matter how long it took.

The moon peaked over the horizon and shone down upon the grassy slough. The same moon reflected off the water making the ferry ride from Whidbey Island serene. He refused to request assistance from other CSI technicians in the office. Israel did not relish the idea of spending the night processing the crime scene alone. However, the situation called for extreme attention to detail. Besides his brother, Israel was the only other CSI tech intimately acquainted with Bill's signature. As a boy, besides being outside traipsing about Washington's thick evergreen forests or fishing for trout in its clear water brooks, he loved reading Sir Arthur Conan Doyle's Sherlock Holmes stories. The nineteenth century fictional detective used rudimentary science and logic to solve heinous crimes. The stories molded Israel and his adult life. He too relied on science and logic to catch criminals. Though Holmes was just a character bound by leather he was also a superb teacher. The biggest lesson Israel learned from the Englishman was every criminal, no matter how much they attempted to hide their essence, always left behind a calling card.

It could be a lock of hair, a partial fingerprint, a dab of saliva, or a spot of glue from the tape they used to bind their victims. He delighted in the thought of filtering the mundane criminal traces to find the key to unlock this case. His mind coolly calculated how he intended to process the murder scene.

Red and blue police lights splashed the dock with colorful brilliance. Passengers clustered together on the observation deck trying to discern what was happening. The ferry inched its way into its mooring as it repeatedly did sixteen times a day. Israel's cell phone chimed in its holster clipped to his belt. Israel did not recognize the number. It had a Seattle area code though.

"Hello," he answered.

"Israel Colby this is Officer Daniel Crate from the Washington State Patrol. We have already spoken with the ferry's captain. You will be the sixth vehicle exiting the ship. Those preceding you will be directed to a position so you can have clear access off the boat and onto the access road. Two Washington State Troopers have been assigned to escort you to Stanwood. Are you comfortable driving your CSI van at a high rate of speed?" asked the officer.

"Raphael sure knew how to make things happen when he wanted to," pondered Colby. A police escort would slice through the city traffic and give him a clear path to the crime scene. That alone shaved thirty minutes off his estimated time of arrival.

"Yes, Officer Crate. Drive as fast as you want. Just tell your men to watch the corners. The van is top heavy and will tip over easily if I take a corner too fast. I appreciate the assistance."

"You bet Mr. Colby. Detective Raphael wants you on the scene pronto. In all of my fourteen years on the force I never received this type of order before. You must be pretty special to rate this type of treatment. We were led to believe the murder you are processing was a dump and run job. Not this one though. You guys must be working on something special. Would you care to tell me what?"

"No can do Trooper. The less you know the better. I will tell you your assistance will save many lives down the road. What you also need to know is to make sure your team keeps what they know about this crime close to the chest. It would really suck if any information leaked which torpedoed this investigation. The cop that leaks any info will be the first in the breadline."

"Roger, sir," replied the policeman. "We're waiting on the pier. After you disembark, head towards the blue flashing lights."

"Okay, see you in a few," answered Colby.

Israel departed the observation deck and walked down the ship's inner stairwells to where he parked his van. Ferrymen wearing hunter orange reflective vests stationed themselves at the exiting ramps. One approached Colby, verified his identification and informed him how the boat crew planned to speed up his departure. Whatever the State Trooper ordered the ferry's captain to do, he was making sure he cooperated to the fullest extent. A minivan, two pickup trucks, a van shuttling a high school baseball team, and a plumber's truck needed to be off loaded before he could clear the ramp. Each driver received a brief from a ferry sailor. The sailors apologized for the delay but the cops were calling the shots. The delay would not be long. Their patience was rewarded with a round trip ferry ticket. None complained.

The ferry smoothly moored to the pier and lowered the auto ramp. Colby rolled his truck off the boat and headed towards the flashing police lights. Upon arrival, he presented his credentials to the officer-in-charge of the escort detail, jumped back into his van, and followed the lead police cruiser to the northbound highway. Traffic proved light. The troopers cruised down the highway at eighty miles per hour. Their flashing blue lights kept the lane ahead clear. The drive took fifty-five minutes to make. An Island County Sheriff directed him to Detective Raphael who sat under a tree sketching the crime scene in his notebook and maintaining watch on the murdered corpse. Since he arrived, no one came near the scene. He made it perfectly clear that any Curious Georges who wanted a better look at the site would immediately be put on administrative furlough awaiting discharge from the force. His authority was not questioned. The cops understood his desire to maintain the dumpsite's evidentiary integrity. One wrong step could potentially damage critical evidence.

"Hello Detective," announced Colby.

"You made good time Israel," replied the plain clothes police officer.

"That escort did the trick. Without it, the drive would have been twice as long," Israel said as he visually canvassed the crime scene. "What are we dealing with sir?"

"As you can plainly see, there lies a Caucasian woman. My guess is she is between twenty two to twenty eight years old. We received an anonymous call giving us the general location of the body. The search lasted six hours until we found her. To me, she's Bill's latest victim. The way she is laying suggests he laid her to rest out here. Therefore, if he committed the murder and stashed her out here, I wanted you to conduct the crime scene analysis. You know what we are looking for."

"Did you check if she is alive?"

"No. There was not any need to. You can tell she has been dead for a good couple of days. Do your magic my friend. I will be right here if you need me. How long you think it will take?"

Detective Raphael recognized when it was time to let other people do their jobs. His job right now was to support the CSI guy doing his thing.

"I will examine and process the girl first. It will take about an hour. The most difficult and time-consuming part is canvassing the surrounding area for trace evidence. Give me three hours to complete the area recon and evidence collection. In the meantime, please get the names of the officers on the search team, their shoe sizes, and a statement describing the role they played in the search. Once I am finished, the coroner will take the body to the morgue for an autopsy. All told, including the autopsy, the evidence review should not take more that seventy-two hours."

"Okay, man. Good hunting and good luck. Holler if you need help."

"Will do boss," answered Colby.

Israel dove into his duties. Retrieving powerful battery powered lamps from his truck he illuminated the area where Charlotte laid. The scene was as bright as day. Camera in hand, the Sherlock Holmes wannabe silently started canvassing the crime scene.

CHAPTER SEVENTEEN

Processing the newest Butcher Bill crime scene took Israel double the time he anticipated. He originally estimated four hours to complete the job. Once he started, he decided the task needed extreme attention to detail. The tall grass yielded nothing. No discernible footprints or any other evidence was evident. He hypothesized how the murderer transported the body. The road to Stanwood was a two-lane country road. This far from the city the area was devoid of street lamps. Butcher Bill chose his dumping site well again. The best Israel could figure, Bill must have stopped his vehicle near the bridge passing over the slough. Probably late at night. During the day, the road was too well traveled by workers commuting to Seattle and Everett to work or mothers shuttling their children to their activities. According to the sheriffs charged with the Stanwood area beat, nighttime traffic dwindled to practically nothing. The area's residents chose to live in the country setting for the peace, quiet, and the complete lack of the city life hustle and bustle. The black Pacific Northwest darkness provided perfect cover for a murderer disposing his victim. Only the anonymous caller's tip led them to this place. If the call was never made, the dead girl would have slowly rotted for months before her remains were discovered. If she was found at all. The only people who ventured into the slough were hunters in the fall when the Canadian Geese headed south for the winter. The body was discarded a quarter of mile from the road. Where the girl lay, it proved impossible for a hiker along the road or a passenger in a car to spot the body in the tall grass. Israel proved his theory by having police officers station themselves at different points along the road to see if they could spot Colby standing perfectly erect near the corpse. No one could. An obvious clue was confirmed. Bill was fit. Only a healthy and strong person could carry a human adult body through the rough tundra. Israel imagined how Bill did it. Throwing the body on his shoulder using the fireman's carry was the easiest method.

The forensic scientist finally gave up looking for any traces. Bill covered his tracks too well. His best option rested with the evidence he collected from the body. It was not much though. Like Amanda Jackson, the dead girl was naked. The blood vessels burst inside her eyes made Israel believe she died from suffocation. The coroner would confirm his own observations. The county coroner promised a thorough yet expeditious autopsy as soon as he received the body in the morgue. No tape residue or any other type of physical evidence existed on the body. Following standard protocol, Colby took samples from under her fingernails and toenails. He swabbed her vagina, anal cavity, ear canals, nose and mouth for human secretions. Doubtful those samples would provide any help. He wrapped up his business, turned the body over to the coroner's crew, and headed back to the lab. It had been a long day with no end in sight.

Capturing his interest were the locks of hair he cut from her hair. The hair had a distinctive tasteless odor. Her hair did not smell like any of the shampoos or conditioners women used. It was obvious she took great pride in her hair. It was soft, supple, and had a beautiful sheen. But, it smelled sterile, antiseptically sterile. What made the distinctive aroma intrigued Colby. Fragrance was absent. He extracted three small samples from the baseball card sized manila envelope containing the hair. Three test tubes holding a bluish reactive agent were neatly lined up in a stainless steel rack on his workbench. Using tweezers, he added the hair to the tubes, stoppered the glass vials, and placed each into a centrifuge. Shutting the door Israel set the device's rotation speed. The tubes whirled around at one hundred thirty revolutions a minute until chemical equilibrium was reached. He needed three samples to compare the results to determine the chemicals used on the dead girl's hair. The centrifuge slowed to a stop. Israel methodically placed the spun samples in a shallow Petri-dish and placed one-by one in the analysis machine. The results feed into a computer holding an FBI program designed to identify chemical compounds. More impressive, the program pinpointed how the chemicals were used in the commercial world. The program's conclusion surprised the crime scene analyst. Her hair held traces of an industrial strength and biodegradable soap. The funny thing was the soap used was a common shampoo used by pet groomers.

Odd, Israel thought. *Why would the murderer use a pet shampoo?* He silently answered his own question. *Pet shampoos don't damage the hair but the soaps kill bacteria. Using pet shampoo was similar to using bleach. The difference is the pet shampoo caused no harm to the animal but destroyed DNA.*

Crafty bastard came to Colby's mind. *Bill used the soap to sterilize her hair. Israel and Ishmael might be able to trace it back to the manufacturer he bought it from. It was a long shot, but a shot nonetheless.* Tracing the sample to the store that sold it might prove the shampoo hunch. More labor-intensive work lay ahead. The twins would get the police to contact the product's local distributors. The stores computers recorded clients who purchased the product.

The last items on his task list were to see if the fingerprint database search turned up anything. He started the search six hours ago. As he worked in his lab, he monitored the computer's progress of comparing the victim's prints to those held in the FBI database. Sure enough, the database search completed its data mining while he finished the hair analysis. The results were disappointing. No hits emerged. The girl did not have her fingerprints on file. Hopefully, the police review of the missing person reports would turn something up useful.

Israel needed to sleep badly. He was running on caffeine and sugar to keep him going. Junk food and coffee were not his food groups of choice. Israel maintained his stamina by leading a healthy lifestyle. Not a lifestyle hard to achieve, he swam daily and ate a lot of vegetables, chicken, turkey, and pastas. The extreme pressure he put himself under to deliver quick results from his analysis demanded he occasionally alter his eating habits. The stimulates kept him awake for the twenty nine hours he just endured. Now, a quick catnap would let his mind filter the information it processed so he could draft a concise and accurate report. The blue leather couch in the office he shared with his brother beckoned him. Just long enough allowing him to stretch out his long legs, his eyes sealed shut when his head hit the pillow. It had been a long night.

His eyes fluttered open three hours later, Israel felt like a new man. Knowing exactly what he wanted to write in his report, he quickly tapped it out on his computer. He explained how thorough the murderer was and how the nonappearance of physical traces was just as significant as if there was a smoking gun found. When an experiment was completed, having it fail from the predicted results sometimes provided more insight than a perceived success. He understood who his audience was, the FBI behavioral science task force. He believed the task force would draw the same conclusions he did. They were looking for a nimble efficient character. The murderer planned every detail. The only useful information resulting from his hard work was the knowledge that the murderer washing the victim's hair with pet shampoo. The detail provided sound information the team could use to whittle the truth from the forest of seemingly useless information they gathered thus far. Fact: he used a white van to transport his victims. He probably used it to capture his targets as well. Fact: he had small feet telling them his height. Fact: he worked in the maritime industry. More likely than not, he made his living in the Puget Sound area.

Israel thought how the shampoo clue could be useful. The FBI or Seattle PD could develop a list of every pet store within a one hundred mile radius of Seattle. The process would be slow. But that was the fashion in which mountains were moved-one shovel full at a time. Contacting the companies who distributed the shampoo might narrow the margin even more. They would have a list of local stores with the soap on their shelves. Identifying the shops selling the shampoo would cut the overall search process down. The magnitude decreases rapidly after that. Then, it would be old-fashioned police work. Door-to-door, foot-pounding interviewing within the community was the only way. Task force members would visit the stores and start asking questions. It was tedious but effective. And, one step closer to flushing out the murderer from his lair.

The sad fact Israel admitted was he could not identify who she was. That was another job for the police. Whoever, the young, blond woman, was, she was pretty and most likely *had* a bright future ahead of her. Still, she was a Jane Doe.

CHAPTER EIGHTEEN

Hendricks and Raphael scoured the missing persons reports submitted by distraught parents, worried wives, and concerned husbands who turned to the police as their last bastion of hope. Their search encompassed counties within a three hundred mile radius with Seattle its epicenter. It never ceased to amaze either detective how many people went missing. Many were simply spouses having a long protracted fight with one of them leaving for a few days to find themselves. They typically turned up within a week. Children came up missing most often. Where they went was any ones guess. Some were abducted and murdered. Some were taken out of the country and sold into the sex and slave trade. Others vanished without a trace never to be heard from again. Some were eventually found on city streets hooked on drugs, eating out of dumpsters. Wrecked beyond repair. Just like Bill's victims. No one knew who they were or where they came from.

The two cops filtered through the reports for missing young women. Culling through the smaller listing in the police department's database, they eventually made a match to their latest victim. It may have come sooner if they allowed the rest of the department in on their investigation. The FBI kept close holds on who they let into their inner circle. Hendricks, Raphael, and the Colby's knew of the Task Force existence. The officers and members of the coroner's staff were sworn to secrecy. If any details leaked to the press, heads would surely roll. Retirements would vanish and the only law enforcement work available would be as a security guard at the local mall.

They were on the scent. Ohms did not want their prey tipped off. He wanted to pounce on the homicidal maniac before he had any idea he was being hunted. The girl's death was regrettable but her loss was another lead to capturing Bill. If it took an extra day to figure out who she was, then so be it. Security would not be compromised.

Dr. Ohms's theories proved correct. Charlotte Channels' missing person report identified a young Washington University student reported missing by her parents. The photo was an identical match for the woman found in the slough. A visit to the college was fruitless. Her fellow classmates and study-buddies told them the same story they told the campus police. The last time they saw Charlotte was during a study session at the library a couple of weeks ago. She was a new girl, bright, and liked by the few people she hung out with. No one knew if she dated anyone. The campus police were of little help except they told the two detectives what their patrol schedules were. Both policemen recognized the campus security ran on a rigid and predictable schedule. Any professional killer who knew how to kidnap his victims without causing a ruckus could easily bypass their patrols.

Charlotte's Malibu still sat in the library parking lot. The car collected a fair amount of dirt on it over the period it sat. A search of the car revealed nothing. Nonetheless, it was impounded and sent to the Colby twins for an examination. Neither detective believed they would find anything wrong with the car. Bill was too smart to leave simple tracks like that. The campus rent-a-cops possessed the library's surveillance film. The video tapes showed Charlotte leaving the library. Disappointment came when they realized the surveillance cameras did not cover the parking lots. Lost was any fleeting hope of seeing the face of her kidnapper. The tapes time stamps confirmed the time the study session broke up. Charlotte was abducted around 11:00 PM. Right after she finished her studying. The poor girl never had a clue what happened to her.

The local police and the Seattle detectives searched her apartment. Any sign of foul play or struggle was non-existent. They found stale bread with green mold taking over and a refrigerator filled with rotting fruit and vegetables. Her mail was typical of a young student. Offers for credit cards, gas and electric bills, and some fashion magazines. Nothing strange. She lived alone and only for a short period. Interviews with her neighbors yielded squat. Sometimes she had a few friends over to study or to visit. They never saw her with a man nor did they notice anyone weird hanging around. Hendricks did find something of interest. Plugged into the wall socket and sitting on her desk was a laptop computer recharging plug. The computer was nowhere to be found. She had it with her when she was abducted. It was the only logical conclusion to be drawn. After canvassing her apartment, Raphael and Hendricks admitted an evidence collection team. They wanted the entire apartment dusted for prints. It was a long shot. They might get lucky, but; they were not about to bet their paychecks on discovering anything useful.

While the two detectives searched the girl's place, the manhunt continued. Dr. Ohms cut through red tape and started the process Israel Colby suggested. There were fifty-two stores who sold the pet shampoo used to wash Charlotte Channels' hair. Local city cops received their assignments to investigate whether an average height male had recently purchased the soap from their shops. The beat cops were required to interview every employee. No stone would go unturned. The manhunt was gathering momentum.

Actually, it was two manhunts. The first was for Butcher Bill. The second search involved a priest. The video tape and voice analysis came back from the FBI. The soft voice Raphael heard in the background of the anonymous call that alerted the police of Charlotte's whereabouts was filtered and amplified. The sophisticated FBI voice communication equipment used analog to digital conversions. Every sound in the recording was reviewed by National Security Agency analysts. What they found surprised the team. The voice in the background said only three words.

Those three words made complete sense to Dr. Ohms and Agent Sherman. "Good morning, Father," was what they drew out from recording's white noise. A priest was the one who tipped them off. How could he though? If he was told something in the confessional, canon law stated that was where it was supposed to stay. A confession in the Catholic religion was sacred communication between the sinner and God's conduit. Apparently, a rogue clergyman put humankind before his vows of silence.

Reviews of the Seattle video surveillance tape were made easier knowing the caller was a priest. An Asian priest garbed in the traditional black suit and white collar made the phone call from a payphone outside the Seattle Metro Center's carousal square. The image captured by the cameras came out clear and undistorted. A full view of the holy man's face appeared on the analyst's TV screens. The face was quickly processed into a still shot and forwarded to Raphael for action.

There were twenty Catholic churches in the metropolis of Seattle. The city's suburbs supported just as many. Hendricks collaborated with Raphael. Sherman paired up with Amecii. The holy man search was divided in half. Amecii wanted to make the decision about who searches where but she knew better. It was the Seattle homicide detective's home turf. They would visit the city churches. The two FBI agents would start their search in the towns surrounding the city. Localizing the priest meant coming real close to the killer. Butcher Bill's freedom would soon be snuffed out. Dr. Ohms made his thoughts known to the team before they proceeded. The priest is not to be molested or approached. Doing so might place him into danger. The killer trusted him because he was a priest. The man relied on him to keep his vows. If he trusted him once, he will trust him again. All they needed to do was to find the priest and to watch him from a distance. The murderer apparently felt some guilt and remorse about his crimes. Why else would he seek out a priest? It also confirmed why Bill killed. He was performing a ritual or sacrifice. He must have been raised Catholic to feel guilt forcing him to want to be absolved of his sins. It was perfect. Once they caught the sick serial killer, he could not claim insanity. His going to church and entering the confessional proved Bill knew from right and wrong. Entering a confessional is where sinners went to be forgiven. Convincing a jury and a judge of that meant Bill had a date with the executioner. It did not matter what state he was caught in. He killed in enough states sanctioning the death penalty, the feds could pick where he was to be tried. Old Sparky or a magic death cocktail had Bill's name written on it waiting to be served hot or cold. Execution was certain for Butcher Bill. But, only if they could drive him to ground.

CHAPTER NINETEEN

Father Nguyen researched the Catholic Canon law governing the confessional again. He searched for a loophole releasing him from his vows of silence. He found nothing. The matter was between the sinner, the priest, and God. He struggled with his dilemma. He could not leave another soul left to rot. Letting the monster use him for his personal purging had to end. He left the answer in God's hands. The almighty sent him a sign once. Nguyen faithfully believed another sign would come along. Every unused minute of his day was spent on his knees in prayer. Even as he walked down the streets, he spoke to his Lord for guidance. He did not plead with him. The priest knew an answer would come. Patience was required. He believed the answer would be revealed to him somehow. And, it did.

Two days after the demon entered his confessional, the Asian clergyman sought relief on the stone littered banks of the Puget Sound beaches. He walked in the rain. The cool heavy drops crashed down on him but he did not feel the liquid seeping into his clothing. His body felt warm as he pondered the issue and attempted to let his mind free itself from the thought of the dead girl lying in the wilderness as fodder for animals and bugs. God's protection blanketed him from the elements. Transcended in thought, Father Nguyen focused on a bald eagle gliding from the heights into the trees where its nest was built. He watched the wind gently rock the evergreens back and forth. The gusts whispered and whistled gently throughout. It was a serene sound. The eagle landed softly in its nest, perched itself on the outside and fixed its stare upon the priest. Father Nguyen stared back in wonder at the majestic bird. Its head seemed so solid. The white feathers upon its head contrasted beautifully against its dark plumage. That is when he realized God answered his prayers. Since he could not overtly divulge what he heard, might he be able to covertly send a signal to people who could capture the murdering beast. Like the wind carrying a message through the forest, he could whisper his message. Only those who were listening for it could hear. Making an anonymous phone call telling the authorities to look somewhere was not violating the confessional. He did not turn in the killer. Making a phone call would only lead to the victim's discovery. It was a whisper in the forest. What happened to the whisper once it entered the trees was another story. If the wind died or increased in strength was entirely out of his hands. All he needed to do was to provide the wind.

It was the second time God answered his prayers using an animal. The first was a brook trout. Now the sign came on an eagle's wings. Many cultures believed an animal contained spirits of fallen men. To Nguyen, that was nonsense. Souls went to heaven or to hell. Peoples souls did not return to Earth reincarnated as animals. However, God does work in mysterious ways and using an animal to provide a sign was not unheard of. In biblical history, animals filled stories. Animals were his creation too. What better way to answer a prayer than delivering it on the wings of an eagle or the tail of a fish?

Nguyen recognized his whisper was heard when he saw two official looking men sitting and chatting with Father Paul in the back of the church. Growing up on the streets of Cambodia, you learned to recognize the police no matter how hard they attempted to blend in. They always appeared a bit too stiff. Unlike everyday people, cops were on guard twenty-four hours a day. Cops looked at their environment differently. It was a skill separating rookie police officers from the veterans. Some called it street-wise knowledge. Peace Officers simply referred to it as staying alive. They worked in war zones. The average Joe American was ignorant of the filth and ugliness police officers witnessed. And he liked it that way. Thus, the reason the cops were around. Their job was to keep the thugs, thieves, junkies, rapists, pedophiles, and murderers contained so they could go about their business. He sorrowed for their souls but he knew the devil never stopped working.

Seeing the two cops sitting in the back talking to the parish's head priest confirmed they received his sublime message. It was odd he did not read anything in the papers about discovering the girl. He searched the newspapers every morning for a story about a young girl found lying in a ditch. Unbeknownst to Father Nguyen, it never will until Bill was locked behind bars. Now, the cops needed to do a simple bit of two-plus-two math. He wanted the cops to identify him and to follow him. If they did post surveillance on him, eventually they would catch a glimpse of Chief Medina. It was as far as the priest could go short of personally turning the wicked murderer into the authorities. His vows were safe. He understood he stretched the limits of the confessional. Nowhere in the Canon Law did it say he could not tell anyone where a body could be found. He held a clear conscious. If the cops found the madman by staking him out then that was just good police work.

Father Nguyen prepared himself for the conversation he knew was coming. Father Paul trusted his fellow priests to be faithful to their religion and to respect the flock. It was not the first time the law came knocking on the church's doors. They always received the same answer. The church was a sanctuary especially to those who committed grievous sins. Violating the principle would shatter the churches legitimacy. Policemen knew it too and respected it. However, it never stopped them from trying. Sometimes they found a clergyman who was committed more to saving lives of innocent victims than the souls of criminals.

Father Paul sat in the pews and listened intently to the police officer's single question. They wanted to know if an Asian priest worked at the church. Without hesitation, the clergyman silently turned his head and looked in the Cambodian priest's direction. Later he would inquire why the policeman wanted to speak with him. But, for now, the best thing he could do was to acknowledge an Asian priest was part of his spiritual team.

Father Nguyen watched intently as the two plain-clothes policemen shook the elderly reverend's wrinkled hand. Knowing they would follow him, the angelic warrior turned and headed into his office. Taking his seat behind his desk, he neatly folded his hands together in his lap and waited for the detectives to enter.

"Father Nguyen," Hendricks hailed from the door accompanied by a knock.

"Officers, please come in and have a seat," replied the priest. He surprised himself with how calm he was. His heartbeat maintained a steady flutter unlike what it did when Chief Medina entered the confessional. He had nothing to fear from these men. They were on his side and were acting upon his orchestrations. Undoubtedly, they would attempt to manipulate or even coerce his cooperation. Nguyen would stand by his vows.

Hendricks entered first, hat in hand followed by Raphael. Being a Catholic, Raphael started the conversation as preplanned by the duo.

"Father, my name is Detective Paul Raphael and this is my partner Detective Benjamin Hendricks. We are from the Seattle Homicide Division. Do you mind if we ask you a few questions?"

"Gentlemen, welcome to Saint Michael's Church. I would be delighted to answer any questions you have to the best of my ability. First, may I offer you a cup of coffee? The nuns at my last parish taught me how to brew the best coffee in town. Priests from all over the city come to this office just for the java." replied Nguyen.

Hendricks entered the conversation as he and Raphael took a chair in front of his desk. "Father, that is most gracious. A cup of coffee after all the searching we have done for you would be most welcome."

The priest positioned three mugs in front of him and retrieved the coffee pot from the small table stationed behind him. Pouring the hot aromatic Columbian brew into each mug, he gestured for the officers to help themselves to cream and sugar.

"You were searching for me Detectives? Why would you be searching for a priest? Do you need spiritual advice?"

"Father, being a Catholic myself, please bless us and bless our work before we continue this conversation," asked Raphael.

"By all means Detective Raphael," Father Nguyen outstretched his hand to cover his guests. "Blessed and Most Benevolent God, keep your holy watch over these two peace officers who tread into danger to save the souls that I cannot. They are servants of your will. Keep them safe from all peril and bless their loved ones for allowing them to serve you and your people. Amen."

"Amen," came from both policemen whose heads were bowed in receipt of the tidings.

"Now, gentlemen…you were saying you were looking for me. Obviously, it was not for a blessing though I certainly am glad you desired one. What are your questions?"

Hendricks took over again. "Father, it has to do with the phone call you made reporting where the police should search for a murdered girl." Hendricks waited for some type of surprised reaction from the priest. He found known. Nguyen remained calm.

"It does?" he asked.

Raphael believed the priest made a statement vice a question. The priest in front of them knew what he was doing. Surprise was not on their side.

"I am going to be forthright with you Padre," spoke the senior detective. "You made an anonymous call reporting a murder. Who killed the girl Father Nguyen?"

"If I knew a person was a murderer you know that my position as a priest is protected gentlemen. I am sorry but I cannot answer your question. Yes, I did make a phone call. That is all I can tell you officers. Please do not press me for more information."

Gazing into Raphael's soul through his eyes, "You are Catholic Mr. Raphael. You know the church is a sanctuary. What happens in the church; stays in the church. Anything I may know; I cannot divulge to you."

"Then why did you make the anonymous phone call?" retorted Raphael.

"I cannot help you with what you seek gentlemen. I made the call to make sure the young woman was discovered. She deserved better. Her family deserves to mourn her loss knowing she was stolen from their lives," evaded the Holy Man.

"You realize Father, we could arrest you for withholding evidence or as a material witness?" answered Hendricks.

"Yes, Detective. You could and the church will bail me out or have a Writ of Habeas Corpus drafted and presented before your courts quite quickly. Your argument has been broached countless times before. And, each time the church has won. So, please, I am glad you were able to track me down and I am relieved you found what you went searching for. Have you spoken with her parents? I have not seen anything in the papers about your discovery?"

Gulping down what remained in his coffee cup; Detective Hendricks rose from his chair acknowledging the priest's correct assessment of the situation.

"Thank you, Father, for the coffee, your time, and your assistance. You were right. You do make the best coffee in town." Handing him his business card Hendricks continued. "If you decide you need help Father Nguyen, call me anytime. Day or night. We will be here in a flash. Good day, Sir."

"Thank you, officers. May God guide and bless your quest. Have a good day."

The priest's last comment threw Hendricks off guard. This priest knew exactly what he was doing. He wants to be watched. The cagey S.O.B. The priest knew he could not violate the confidence he had given the murderer. Nonetheless, he did provide them an opportunity to catch the murderer.

Raphael and Hendricks stood, walked out of the office, strolled down the center aisle and exited out the ornate redwood doors built from the strong local timber. Mission accomplished. They found their tipster priest. The news breathed fresh life into the task force. Within an hour, the entire church will be staked out. Sooner or later, the madman would show up to unburden his guilty conscious.

CHAPTER TWENTY

Sherman watched the church from afar tucked into the city's shadows. His weather beaten façade, lost eyes, ragged clothing, disheveled appearance, and lethargic posture transformed the strong, iron willed FBI detective into an everyday, invisible, and worthless street bum. Anyone passing him saw him. None acknowledged him. He immersed himself into the world of the insignificant. He wanted to be there but not there. He used this disguise before. Criminals never spared a second look to a homeless alcoholic junkie. They were as commonplace and annoying as the city's pigeons. Crooks watched too much TV. They expected cops to watch them from an unmarked van or spying upon them from a rooftop. It was too mundane to think that a common street bum was their worst enemy.

Ohms's and Amecii's profile depicted Butcher Bill as highly intelligent and methodical. He perfected his system over sixteen years of murder and torture. He became a creature of his own habits and devices. There was no doubt he would return to the church, sooner, or later. They all hoped sooner so they could rip the animal from his killing fields and encase him in a four by six foot prison cell where he could be studied like a lab rat for the rest of his wretched existence. Bill's methodic psychopathic nature spawned his eventual doom. The bell was beginning to toll for he.

If the FBI and Seattle P.D. staked out Father Nguyen's parish using normal surveillance methods, surely Butcher Bill would sense their presence and disappear into the ether. Ohm's team concluded Bill studied police tactics and learned to evade detection. He blended well into the public throng. Nothing flashy to focus attention upon himself. To those who know him, he is considered trustworthy and dependable. It was the only logical conclusion why he remained anonymous for so many years.

Sherman started his sentry duties six days ago. He ate his meals on the street. He used the local park restrooms when nature called. His bed was a tattered sleeping bag. He sought refuge from the rain in an abandoned storefront across the street from the church. His shopping cart carried the various worthless treasure trove veteran street people cherished and ruthlessly protected. It was their little bit of stuff that every human needs for whatever reason.

The team believed Bill would seek absolution for his grievous ways just like he did with his most recent conquest. Bill was on the hunt for a male victim to complete his devious cycle. The team desperately wanted to catch him before he killed again but they readily admitted they were not close enough. They knew about him but nothing of him. It was a sad affair to maintain such a morbid and gruesome watch. But, to snare the demon they needed to wait for him to take further action. Spooking their prey weighed heavily on their minds. This was the best chance they had to identify him. The surveillance called for every resource they could muster. State of the art visual equipment was brought in. Instead of the normal surveillance package the FBI offered, Ohm's tapped into the National Security Agency's and Central Intelligence Agency's surveillance expertise. This was a calculated decision by Ohms. Despite his fervent desire to keep the existence of Butcher Bill closely under wraps, he concluded the NSA's and CIA's Directors could be completely trusted. After all, they were in the secret keeping business. None of either agency's technical teams who set up the equipment knew who or what they working on. The nice thing about working with the two federal agencies, their employees knew not to ask too many questions. They were used to working in the black world. All they needed to know was what kind of intelligence they wanted to collect, where the site was, who would maintain the gear, and for how long. The two agency's surveillance experts established a surveillance grid that rivaled ones used to ferret out terrorists.

Sherman wanted video cameras watching every entrance and exit and all of the streets in a six block radius with the church at the center. Bill wouldn't drive his vehicle and park it in front of the cathedral. He was too cagey to do something so stupid. He had to blend in. Sherman believed the killer would park a few blocks or more away and make his way to the church on foot. High fidelity cameras captured every moment for twenty-four hours a day. Ohms established an analysis cell whose sole job was to review the live feeds and recordings and highlight any potential targets. They hoped his arrival and departure would be captured so they could pinpoint his vehicle.

Amecii and Ohms sought different information. Both agreed to the penchant for video surveillance. They also wanted something they could use to characterize the murderer even further. Infrared cameras filled that bill. The two behavioral scientists wanted to capture his heat signatures before and after he arrived to seek penance. Recording his body's thermal representation supplied insight into his state of mind. They guessed he would arrive slightly agitated and eager to make his confession. But, the more important images they desired were those following his meeting with the priest. Agitation produced a high body heat signature. If Bill's heat signature was elevated after Father Nguyen refused his absolution, it proved he yearned for forgiveness. Not receiving it would enflame his persona. If it did not, it would lend credence to a completely different set of conclusions. They wanted to characterize his thought patterns and mental stability. The same heat signatures before and after the confession would conclude he was even more methodical than originally thought. Ohms theorized the murderer believed the acts were God's will and he was His conduit.

The team had a single regret. They could not station surveillance equipment inside the church, especially the confessional booths. The Supreme Court recently ruled that doing so egregiously violated the separation of church and state. A church, synagogue, temple, mosque, or any other form of worship house could not be bugged. It was considered a sanctuary. The court ruled a citizen maintained a belief that speaking with a holy man or going to a house of worship provided them shelter from persecution from the state. This ruling manifested itself from recent cases against suspected Muslim terrorists who used mosques as places to plan their violent strikes against the infidel. Law enforcement officials regularly tapped mosques thanks to the Patriot Act. However, the FBI botched a case so badly where a suspected terrorist was arrested based upon the surveillance done inside the holy building. The accused terrorist was backed by deep pockets and top-notch American left wing attorneys. The evidence against the accused was thin. Arrested shortly after the 9-11 attacks, it took seven years for the terrorist's case to reach the Supreme Court. When it did, the Court ruled in favor of the defendant. The five to four ruling decided that any communication within the walls of a worship structure was protected. The state could not encroach upon the sanctity of the church. The two had to be separated because people believed the religious discussions were private and protected. A definite separation of church and state was pronounced. It was a place they could go to shed burden, seek comfort, or to solicit spiritual advice. Any gain received from monitoring was considered fruit from the poisonous tree. The task force possessed a loop hole. The ruling didn't prevent law enforcement officials from going inside the building to watch or to listen. They could not make an arrest. That was why Sherman covertly stationed himself outside and the Seattle PD staked out the interior.

Sixty-two cameras covered every aspect of the church and the surrounding area. All were remotely controlled and wirelessly linked to recording stations. Cameras were posted on rooftops, in windows, in trees, in vehicles with tinted windows. The NSA and CIA experts knew their business. They even asked if the team wanted an unmanned aerial vehicle to follow whoever needed to be followed. The offer was compelling but Ohms rejected the notion. It required an entire cadre of pilots, equipment specialists, and people who maintained the gear. It was too many people to handle.

The hunt was getting closer and they hoped to catch their prey unawares. Just like he stalked his victims from afar and then pounced. They would do the same to him.

Sherman's patience was inexhaustible. He didn't mind being covered in grime or being intentionally ignored by the city's downtown citizenry. Long ago he developed methods to keep his mind sharp while waiting for a criminal. He used his time wisely to hone his senses about people.

Ohm's and the FBI developed their profiling expertise by studying captured criminals and past horrendous crimes. Sherman perfected his innate understanding of the human mind in a different way. He watched people. If observed long enough, he discovered you could develop the persona and learn why a person behaved the way they did. Sherman eventually was able to predict their actions. Sitting in the dank, empty store front afforded him ample time to study his subjects. The people passing wore their worries on their faces and body. They were consumed in their worlds. The FBI agent reveled in trying to decipher what made a person. For the past six days, he watched many of the people making up the landscape surrounding the church. There were business men and women who worked in the high rise buildings up and down the street. There were the old ladies who shuffled into the church to say a rosary or attend the daily morning mass. There were others who serviced the local businesses selling office supplies, food, or other common everyday stuff.

This stakeout seemed different. His concentration was skewed. His normal quick observational powers were hard to focus. His thoughts were clouded and jumbled. Getting the sweet scent of Catherine's perfume out of his mind hindered his thoughts.

Six days went by as he watched the people go about their normal routines. He picked three people who were regulars in the area to study. The first was an overweight, thirty-something, and cheap suit wearing accountant who frequented the corner bakery three or four times a day. It was obvious his escape from the mind numbing number crunching and manipulation of the tax code was found in a strawberry cream cheese pastry. Sherman surmised the rest of his life was just as dull. He probably wasted away in front of the TV screen or surfed the web for free porn to jerk off to.

His second subject was a young woman strumming a guitar on the corner down the street. Her arms and legs were festooned with tattoos. The girl's ears, eyebrows, nose, and lips were pierced with silver bolts and hoops. Sherman's inquisitiveness drove him to abandon his perch to listen to her music. He wanted to get a better look at her tattoos and to see how she would react when the 'homeless bum' tried to speak with her. She arrived on the street corner every afternoon around two o'clock. The street musician opened up her guitar case, placed it in front of her feet, and started strumming tunes from the past and present. The tattoos adorning her appendages were themed. Leafy jungle vines were etched up, down, and around her arms and legs. Embedded in the vine's helixes were pairs of jungle and forest creatures. Each set included an adult critter with its off spring. There was a black panther and cub, a chimpanzee and baby, a kangaroo and her joey, and a various collection of exotic birds with their chicks. A bull elephant shepherding a calf took up the left calf muscle. An alpha grey wolf carrying a pup by the scruff decorated the right.

Her name was Anna and she came to Seattle from Pennsylvania by Greyhound bus. She attended college in Seattle and studied classical violin. Playing guitar on the street helped her relax and shed her pent up emotions. Her music was divine to listen to and people passing by slowed their pace to capture a snippet of her tunes. At times, she attacked the guitar with unbridled energy releasing a powerful melodic message into the air. Other times, she strummed the instrument gently making soft, colorful tones that floated in the ever present Seattle mist. Anna stopped playing on numerous occasions to observe the people around her too. Sherman studied her studying him. Fear of the unknown didn't prevent her from striking up a conversation with her bum audience. He found it refreshing someone else liked to learn about other humans. The guitar's girl carefree appearance sheltered an extremely complicated individual. She was a thinker. Her mind raced with thoughts and always needed to be occupied. Anna was also very kind. On two occasions, the musician showed up for her daily gig with tuna sandwiches. One for herself and one for her new found hobo groupie. Sherman made a mental note to return to the street corner when the case was over. For some odd reason he planned on telling Anna who he really was. He believed she would appreciate how her small and random acts of kindness help keep his sentinel watch from being mundane. She needed to be rewarded for her part in capturing Butcher Bill. Most of all, he just wanted her to know she was truly a good person and he hoped she never felt sadness or despair. People like her were rare gems in a human mine of cold rock.

The third person the undercover agent watched was another bum named George. Like the majority of homeless creatures, George toted his possessions around in a shopping cart. What made George more interesting than the other bums around him was he continuously cleaned the block on which he lived. From dawn to dusk, George would pick up litter from the street; sweep the sidewalks, wipe down the parking meters, scrape gum off of the pavement, and countless other little jobs demanding his cleaning skills. George spoke little. Sherman attempted conversation on three different occasions but received nothing except "mmm-hmms" for his troubles. He was not rude about it. Talking was not in his repertoire. He had too much cleaning to do. He listened to Sherman's utterances and wordlessly excused himself to continue his cleaning regimen. The local community accepted George as one of their own too. Rarely did he have to search out the trash cans or dumpsters behind the throng of restaurants for something to eat. The local small business owners appreciated his efforts and routinely fed him breakfast, lunch, and dinner. George earned his keep. His life seemed dull to many, but to Sherman, George found his purpose in life and was happy. When the sun began to drop below the horizon, Sherman watched George push his cart purposefully down the street as if he had finished his work for the day, punched his time card, and headed home for supper and a cold beer. He always lost sight of the bum when he turned the corner around the church. The thought of where George went for the evening occupied his thoughts. Did George live inside somewhere? Did he shuffle down to the park and live in the bushes? Did he sleep in an alcove like Sherman? It drove him a bit mad because he could not leave his post to find out. He made another mental note to find that out too when the case was completed.

Sherman felt lucky to have Anna and George to occupy his mind. The accountant was boring to watch but he was regular. When he was not watching the three citizens, his mind wandered down a different path. He always liked to stay in tune with his thoughts. His goal was to try to understand why his mind thought about certain things. What he discovered was shocking to him. Images of Catherine Amecii pleasantly haunted his mind. Fantasies of he and Catherine sharing a cool drink, listening to music in the fall sun made a pretty picture in his daydreams. Women aroused him in his past and he had his share of trysts. Catherine was different though. He not only longed for her sexually, he desired her for her. She captured Sherman. Her logical yet compassionate manner of thought, the way she spoke, and how she handled herself in the male dominated world intrigued him. Often throughout the day, images of the two of them ravaging each other's bodies sporadically popped into his thoughts. His daydreams erotically explored her body. Sometimes the two had their sweaty bodies joyfully intertwined. Other times, soft candlelight enveloped them while he explored ever crevice of her flesh with his tongue, lips, and fingers. The images were random yet told the same story over and over. Sherman lusted for Catherine. These were foreign emotions for him. He sat listening to Anna's soft serenades, trying to understand and determine what course he should plot with this woman he so desperately wanted to explore. How could they though? He led a life of loneliness and danger. She lived a more functional and regular lifestyle. Could the two somehow come together and meld? For that matter, Sherman first had to know if she felt anything for him or was the infatuation one sided? He was determined to find out at the earliest moment.

Sherman's thoughts were interrupted by a vibration in his pocket. It was a prearranged signal with Dr. Ohms, Hendricks, and Raphael. When the surveillance team picked up a subject of interest, they agreed to call the cell phone stuffed deep in his pockets. It signaled Sherman to insert his earpiece to connect with the team. The undercover bum rapidly uncoiled the wiring and switched on his radio.

"Bum," reported Sherman over the radio.

"Roger. Surveillance team three reports a white panel van pulling into a parking garage two blocks from your location. They couldn't ID the driver and the license plate is obscured by a tinted cover and dirt," reported Dr. Ohms over the command net frequency.

"Roger," was the only thing Sherman said to acknowledge the report.

Ohms continued. "We dispatched a two man team to investigate the van. The garage entrances and exits are not covered by surveillance. We believe the driver is either still in the garage or has left unseen. I wanted to give you a heads up to be alert."

"Makes sense," responded Bum. "Keep me updated on any men who fit the profile. We still don't know what Bill looks like."

The FBI and local Police Department team reached an agreement they would not pick anyone up at the church. They wanted an open and shut conviction. Their goal was to identify the man, follow him, and monitor his movements. They wanted to watch him. He was far too dangerous to approach without taking precautionary measures. Plus, too many cases were overturned on the slightest procedural error. The evidence compiled against Butcher Bill had to stand on its own merits. The number of people he murdered demanded the best from the task force team.

"Concur. The whole team is on full alert. Raphael and Hendricks reported Father Nyguen is milling about the cathedral's alter. Confession is scheduled to begin in twenty minutes. The appearance of a white van at the same time confession is to start is an omen we cannot ignore. Good luck and call if you need help," responded a female voice over the net.

Hearing Catherine's voice gladdened his heart. He liked to believe he heard an unspoken message in her transmission. The thought evaporated once Sherman's iron discipline brought him back to task. Catherine would have to wait. His attention was on the people walking towards the church.

Sherman pushed his hobo cart down the street and positioned himself across the street from the church. It gave him a better vantage point to watch for the man's arrival. The usual people he witnessed during his vigil shuffled into the church. It was mostly old men and ladies. Sherman forced himself to act his part. He was the first line of defense. He needed to appear as unobtrusive as possible and naturally blend into the city's backdrop. Any awkward behavior might tip off their prey to the surveillance. If

Butcher Bill realized he was being watched he would vanish as easily as he appeared.

Sherman had memorized the church's schedule. Daily morning mass started at seven. Rosary prayers commenced at eleven thirty. The church held mass on Saturday nights and Sunday mornings. Confession was held routinely every day of the week except Wednesdays and Mondays. The church had a rather large congregation. Seattle was populated by a diverse group of people. Filipinos, Italians, Asians, Anglo-Saxons, Hispanics, and many other cultures practiced their faith at Saint Michael's. The cadre of three priests and six nuns handled the church's business very well. All nine maintained rigorous schedules and were kept even busier working a homeless shelter and soup kitchen in a church out building. Luckily, the church had a lot of volunteer support. Without it, the three holy men and six frocked women would be overwhelmed.

Amecii alerted Hendricks and Raphael to the van's presence too. The detectives maintained their vigil inside the church. They agreed at the beginning of the stake-out where they would post themselves in the cathedral. The two plain clothes officers religiously showed up at the church an hour before the observation of each Sacrament of Reconciliation. Detective Raphael blended in wearing the clothes of a blue-collar construction worker. His post gave him a clear view of the church's entire interior, its entrances, and the confessional booths. Hendricks chose a less obtrusive nesting spot. The cathedral was built based on Renaissance architecture. Inside, the high walls were surrounded by a mezzanine and a choir's loft spanning the structure's rear and sides. Pantheon like columns carried the tier's weight. When the choir sang the cathedral reverberated with exultation and reverence.

Hendricks slid into the dark shadows. Immediately behind him was a circular staircase winding its way down to the mighty white oak alter. The stairs gave him quick access to the floor beneath and the confessional closets. In his hand he held a pair of miniature binoculars. From his vantage point, he could observe a person up-close and personal without them knowing. If and when Butcher Bill showed up, he wanted to see Bill's face. He needed to know his enemy. His perch did possess its druthers. Hendricks sight of the secondary exits was limited, but he trusted Raphael to cover those. It must have been his surroundings because prayers flowed from his lips as he waited patiently for Bill to expose himself.

Seeing the killer first hand helped Hendricks' know who he was up against. He held a mental picture of Butcher Bill's face but it would be entirely wrong. The police were more often than not surprised at how *normal* serial killers actually looked. People pictured predators with demented eyes, nasty teeth, and an overall nasty disposition. The stereotype was regularly shattered. What the PD normally found was a psychotic cold-blooded killer who blended in well with their community. Hendricks rationalized that seeing the killer would help him realize the good guys were making progress. Until now the case was filled with ugliness without any relief in sight. It was a laborious, tedious, and fright filled task. They sifted through the reapers path and found a field of death and decay.

The macabre vigil ate at him. When Bill appeared at the worship house to talk with the courageous clergyman it meant one thing—another innocent soul departed the Earth in a most horrible and painful fashion. Their morbid vigil was a necessary evil. The sole way they could find out who Bill really was, was to maintain their ghoulish watch. His arrival at Saint Michael's equated to another heinous ritual performed. But, they needed evidence to prove he was the killer.

Hendricks stood deathwatches before. No matter how many of these stakeouts he was assigned to, he never developed the callous and uncompassionate demeanor like many of his fellow officers did. He could not shake the powerless feeling he had. The police force had a lot of resources at their disposal to solve this crime but it was for naught. The psychotic killer covered his tracks too well. He became an industrial grade-killing machine. His process was perfected over many years of practice. Hendricks believed God made a divine intervention. Sometimes the free will he gave man got too out of hand and He had to step in to solve the trespass. In this case, his instrument was Father Nguyen.

With his senses on full alert and busy waiting, he began to pray for the poor bastard who Bill killed and tossed in a garbage heap or dumped deep in the forest after having his breath beaten from his body. Hendricks did not consider himself an overly religious man, but; he discovered solace having a conversation with God while he waited. He asked for strength, calmness of mind, wisdom, and prayed for the latest victim butchered by Bill. The team needed all the help they could get in capturing the deranged menace stalking his city. It never hurt to ask God for a bit of help.

Sherman sighted the perp first. He was unlike the rest of the people shuffling down the walkway. His demeanor differed from the throng of people surrounding him. Dealing with bad guys for many years gave him a sense about who was dangerous and who was not. The man's eyes kept scanning the scene. Most pedestrians plodded forward trying only to navigate their way through the street unmolested by the street vendors, bums, or the blanket of humanity itself.

He wore plain clothing. Nothing flashy. The white tennis shoes, blue jeans, blue and gray striped rugby shirt, and Seattle Mariners baseball cap made him into the average Joe. He tread lightly on the pavement. Sherman memorized every feature. The perp's skin was a light tan. His hair was short, black, and neatly trimmed. Standing five foot eight and clean-shaven, he blended in easily with the local community. Sherman focused on his left hand. He wanted to know if the guy wore a wedding band. The Behavioral Task Force surmised the man was unmarried. The unbelievable number of murders Butcher Bill committed made it impractical for him to be hitched to a family. Bill was single and would be for his entire life. His extracurricular activity required a lot of time and energy away from home. The clandestine stalking, kidnapping, and torturing consumed every second of the killer's free time. Any wife would rightly become suspicious of what swallowed up her husband's free time. If he was married, it would not take long for his wife to deduce something was squirrelly. Sherman wanted confirmation. He asked the surveillance crew to zoom in on him and report what they saw. Everything was the same as he witnessed. They confirmed he did not wear a wedding ring nor did he have a ring tan on his fourth left digit. Sherman knew he saw something in the man's appearance that would help. The thought nagged at him as he watched the man open the church's doors and enter. The man-of-interest paused and entered the temple with his left foot first. Sherman finally realized what caught his attention. It was the man's haircut and his gait. His hair was neatly trimmed around his ears. He wore it the way professional military men kept their hair. The second and third traits tugging at him were the man's posture and walk. He didn't stroll, he marched. His arms swung rhythmically and kept time with his natural cadence. When military men learned to march, they learned to step off with their left foot. It was ingrained into serviceman from the first moment they received close order drill in boot camp. After that, it became second nature and the habit stuck with them for the remainder of their lives.

Sherman rapidly scrolled through his mental list of military bases located in Washington. The Army had Fort Lewis but that was a four-hour drive away. There were many National Guard units in the area but the man's swagger and clean cut appearance made him reject that conclusion. Guardsmen and Reservists were top notch, but they tended to trim their hair a day or two before actively drilled. That left the Air Force, Navy, and Coast Guard.

It would be easy to find out who he was if he was in the service. Lifting finger prints off the church and van's door handles was the first order of business Dr. Ohm's directed over the radio circuit. A Colby was dispatched to the van and the other to the church. He wanted the finger printing done cleanly, professionally, and as efficiently as possible. Having the twins recover the fingerprints meant it was going to get done right. From his perch, Sherman monitored Israel's movements. With the tan complexioned suspect inside the church, Israel followed quickly behind. He did not want any overlying fingerprints contaminating the sample. He dashed up the steps and dusted the door handle with finger print powder. The powder adhered to the oil residue left behind. Within thirty seconds, the dark haired twin captured the man's fingerprints onto a clear piece of tape. He applied it to a laminated evidence card and stuffed it into an envelope. Turning on his heels, he bolted down the stairs and dove into a car waiting to whisk him away to a mobile forensic lab.

Ishmael was busy processing prints he collected from the white van. They dared not break into the van. Ohm's pondered it momentarily when the two man FBI team arrived at the vehicle. The behavioral specialist knew his police protocol. Searching the van without a warrant was forbidden. They did not have probable cause to request a warrant. Searching the van without one would torpedo the use of any evidence they might find. Any cheap ambulance-chasing lawyer could easily have any evidence collected thrown out for being collected illegally. A set of finger prints would suffice.

Sherman alerted Amecii he was shifting his position to the other side of the street. He wanted to meet the man they were watching. No one liked being accosted by a homeless street bum. It was the perfect opportunity to see how the man handled himself when confronted with a potentially violent scenario. For now, like Catherine, his only recourse presently was to wait for his opportunity. The surveillance operation was now in Detective Hendricks' and Raphael's capable hands.

CHAPTER TWENTY-ONE

Raphael spotted him first. He texted the suspect's approach from his smart phone alerting Hendricks. Hendricks did not need the alert. From his perch high in the mezzanine, he kept a close eye on the stranger's movements from above. Nonetheless, he acknowledged Raphael's message with a single K from his own screen. Words were not needed. He and Raphael had worked many cases together. They had learned how to communicate with the least amount of words when they stalked a predator.

Hendricks thought the man was on edge not unlike many other parishioners going to church to free themselves from their sins. They frequented confession for a reason. It helped them cope. Having the ability to shed their guilt, no matter how severe, somehow made the world more bearable. The priests sanctioned to hear their flocks sins were not normally shocked at what they heard. Some came to shed sins of adultery. Some wanted absolution for sins committed many years ago but still haunting their soul. Many just liked the comfort of talking to someone freely without any reservations or consequences. A handful made the trip just to have a kind voice listen and stave off their loneliness. That was what normally happened in the confessional. The abnormal situations the priest encountered were why the clergy were really there. The hardened sinners were the ones who needed the Sacrament the most. A person captured by the devil needed an outlet to vent their hate. Darkness crept over everyone sooner or later. It was the priest's job to open the curtains to let the light in.

Bearing their sins did not automatically mean their sins would be forgiven. God granted his children free will and a sinner chose to violate his rules. That same free will had to be exercised to set themselves free of their real and imaginary bonds. This was Father Nguyen's goal with the killer.

Hendricks watched the unidentified male doff his hat when he entered the church's nave. He dipped his fingers into the holy water basin anointing his forehead, heart, and shoulders. He walked to the front of the church, entered a pew, kneeled, and meditated. His lips moved silently as he prayed to his deity.

A tiny red lamp embedded in the wood over the confessional booth was lit, indicating the priest was busy hearing a confession. The light turned green after a young, pregnant Asian woman pulled apart the curtains and left the booth. Her place was replaced by the praying maniac. He was anxious to enter.

Hendricks wanted so badly to be at Father Nguyen's side. Anxiousness and fear swept his thoughts. The priest was a courageous man, he thought. Coming face-to-face with the most notorious serial killer America has ever faced was the bravest act he had ever witnessed. Untrained and a dedicated pacifist, Father Nguyen could easily be struck down before the two detectives could arrive to help him. The confessional booth truly was a sanctuary. To be a fly on the wall and to hear what was being said, is what Hendricks prayed for now. The best he could do was watch Detective Raphael move to a position directly outside the confessional and pretend he was asking forgiveness while awaiting his turn to see the priest. It put him in position to intervene if he heard any ruckus from within.

Time crept by. Several minutes later the booth's curtains separated and out stepped their subject of interest. Raphael stared into the man's eyes. They acknowledged each other's presence with a simple slight head nod. Hatred, pain, and turmoil emanated from the murderer's pupils, making Raphael involuntarily flinch. The surrounding air temperature suddenly dropped, causing a cold chill to run through the detective's body.

Hendricks watched the repentant individual head towards the front of the church. He stopped at the center of the church's altar where he reverently genuflected and crossed himself again. Turning right he walked towards a statue of the Virgin Mary. Digging into his pants pockets, he extracted a few bills and deposited them into a metal strong box paying for a candle. Blessing himself again, he lit a white candle and placed it at the statue's feet. Head bowed and fingers interlaced, he lingered for a moment staring at the female figurine in front of him. After relishing the tranquility, he rose and marched down the aisle towards the exit.

"Suspect moving," tapped the veteran detective into his iPhone keypad.

Raphael remained where he was. He relied on Hendricks to let him know when the man left the church. He dared not turn around to watch him himself. He knew he had been made when the two locked eyes and Raphael flinched.

The team had enough personnel and surveillance equipment for them to be confident of not losing their suspect. At the moment, the man was Raphael's secondary focus. He needed to speak to the priest. He worried for his safety. The light over the confessional remained red, worrying Raphael. Why would the priest leave the light on? He did not hear any commotion during their conference.

Raphael pealed the plush, black velvet curtain aside and stepped into the dimly lit closet. The curtain fell back into place creating a silent meditation chamber. His eyes took a few moments to adjust to the blackened space as he kneeled down on the cushion. Out of the darkness came a sliver of light from the other side of the partition. Cocking his head to the side he strained his senses for any movement. Faint, muffled sobbing reached his ears.

"Father Nguyen?" he whispered.

"My child, I'm not ready for your confession. Please come back tomorrow or have another priest help you. I know it is an odd request to make, but; I ask that you honor my wishes without any questions today," came a somber voice from behind the veiled wall.

Raphael paused to compose his thoughts. The priest was definitely shaken and upset. The policeman urgently wanted to help the hallowed man. Catholic himself, he empathized with the immense pain he must be experiencing. A police officer takes an oath very similar to the priest's. Both vowed to protect their fellow man. The moment a person joins the law enforcement community, the general populace treated him differently. Policemen witness many of the injustices human beings inflict upon one another. Similarly, a Priest hears their sorrow and grief on a daily basis and yet, he must manage to provide salvation, kindness, and forgiveness. It is a hard task to do on a day in and day out basis. Harder even still was dealing with cold-hearted villains who deserved to go to jail and to hell for their horrible deeds. Hearing a relentless list of evil is bound to tax even the strongest wills.

"Father, it's Detective Raphael. Are you injured? Do you need a doctor?" he asked. He wanted to make sure the priest's last client did not harm the kindly gentlemen.

"Detective, my body is whole but my soul has been severely injured. It is not often I unburden myself in my own confessional. I bear a terrible weight only I can carry."

"What happened, Father? Who was the man you saw last? What did he confess to you?"

"My son, you know I'm bound to silence. The anonymity offered within these narrow confines is a foundation pillar of the church. Whatever transpires in this booth is between God, man, and I," responded the bereaved clergyman.

Raphael knew coaxing or coercing the priest was fruitless. Pressing him would strengthen his resolve. He needed to take a different path. Hearing the priest cry and proclaim he could not discuss the man's confession was enough to make Raphael believe the latest confessor was Butcher Bill.

"I am sorry for your pain, Father. If there is anything I can do for you, just ask. You're not alone."

"Thank you, Detective Raphael. May God bless and guide you on your quest. You are a good man. Before you leave our Lord's House today, I want you to pray to Saint Michael the Archangel for courage. He's your patron Saint. You're going to need his help."

"Yes, Father. I will pray to Jesus too to help you carry your cross as resolute as he carried his."

Raphael understood the Cambodian clergyman was dismissing him. Father Nguyen had his moment of weakness and recovered. He would pray as the priest mandated. His team could do without him a few extra moments. His duty was done for time being.

CHAPTER TWENTY-TWO

Hendricks reported the suspect was on his way outside. The man was not panicky; he just appeared to be a man who wanted to get somewhere quickly. The team acknowledged the alert and focused on their surveillance screens. The only officer on the ground near the cathedral was the undercover bum. Sherman maneuvered his cart across the street in front of the church's façade. He made himself busy rummaging through a trash can for bottles and cans. Any good bum knows how to scrape together a few coins to buy himself a dollar meal at McDonalds.

The confessor exited the cathedral doors twenty seconds after Hendricks sounded the alarm. Sherman watched him from afar, as he marched down the stone stairs. At the bottom, he paused and glanced up and down the streets. Sherman expected him to head back to the parking garage. His prediction was entirely incorrect. Instead, the man walked briskly the opposite way. Sherman picked out Pepsi and Snapple bottles, dropping them haphazardly into his shopping cart. He wheeled it around to follow. He knew the surveillance cameras monitored the man's movements; however, the coverage distance was limited to two blocks. The undercover bum tacked his cart down the street wanting to maintain his cover. He was barely able to keep up with the walking suspect.

The man scanned the streets. He arrived at Anna-the-street-musician's corner where she happily strummed her guitar and sang a Cold Play tune. The man stopped at the intersection, gazed at Anna. She sensed his presence and looked up. Normally she continued playing to entertain her new audience, but; the look the man gave her cause to stop playing. She felt something different about the man standing in front of her. It prevented her from playing. It was the first time in six days Sherman had ever seen Anna frown.

The man quickly turned away and glanced at the traffic signal. It turned red and the crosswalk sign illuminated the white "man walking" signal. He waited until the sign started to flash and dashed across the street. There was no way Sherman could catch up without looking obvious. He had to let him cross without being tailed. The FBI agent reported the abrupt movement. The man climbed into a taxi waiting for a fare. Before he could do anything about it, the red and white checkered cab sped down the street. The surveillance cameras recorded his escape. It would help later to track down the cab and find out where he dropped his fare off; but, their suspected eluded their grasp.

Sherman replayed the last minute in his head. Somehow, the suspect knew the church was under surveillance and decided to abandon his van. The tracking device installed by Ishmael would never be used. The team needed a new plan. And fast.

Sherman shook his head watching the cab disappear around the street corner heading for the interstate on ramp. If they had a helicopter in the air they could have followed the cab from afar. The covert operation demanded unobtrusiveness; thus, Ohms dictated no air cover. The camera surveillance team reported losing the cab as it entered the highway heading south towards Tacoma.

Detective Sherman turned his bum cart away, pushed it to an empty bench located near Anna, and listened to her play a delicate song about a horse, a little girl, and spring. Her soft voice helped curb his frustration as he forced himself to calm down before he rejoined the team to debrief the operation and plan their next moves. Seeing her bum audience, Anna's smile returned to her gentle face.

CHAPTER TWENTY-THREE

Dr. Ohms was distraught. Wrinkles formed on his forehead. He combed the surveillance plan to ferret out the weak link that spooked Butcher Bill. The cause evaded him. They were up against a very crafty criminal who had a sense for evading capture. No wonder he went unnoticed for so many years.

While Ohms combed the surveillance tapes looking for flaws, Catherine debriefed the team on the day's botched surveillance effort. No one had to say it. They let a notorious serial killer slip through their grasp. Each fingered a picture of the suspect in their hands. Their thoughts remained private as they studied the monster's photo. At least they now knew what he looked like. Their work suddenly had more focus.

The crime scene duo lifted good fingerprints from the van and church doors. Israel and Ishmael wasted no time entering the data into their computers to compare against the world's databases. Dr. Ohms sent the impounded white panel van to the Seattle Police Department crime analysis center. The twins followed the van's delivery and pounced on the vehicle as soon it was removed from the flat bed tow truck. They discovered a whole bunch of nothing. The inside was spotless. The van was two years old, but only had six thousand and forty three miles recorded by the odometer. The interior looked showroom clean. The twins applied every forensic technique they had in their bag of tricks. Not a single fiber or strand of hair was discovered. Nowhere inside the vehicle were any signs of struggle uncovered. They were certain they would find telltale traces of bodily fluids inside the unseen crevices of the van. Nada. Even the engine compartment and undercarriage withheld its stories. Both were spotless save for some light mud that splashed on the van from driving on the wet Seattle roadways. The only evidence they discovered were finger prints matching those lifted from the van and church. Tracing the registration, license plate and vehicle identification number came up empty. The van bore California license plates which were registered to Sharon Sikorsky of Anaheim. It would have been a good lead, but; a call to the California DMV revealed she was a ghost. The VIN turned up the same results. The van was built and sold in Mexico. The Mexico City dealer who sold the car told the Mexico City police Juan Rodriguez purchased it two years ago. A name as common in the Hispanic world as John Smith is in the English world. It was a cash transaction. No other records regarding the purchase were available. In essence, the mysterious owner knew how to forge identifications and buy his merchandise under the radar. The twin's only hope to discover anything about the unknown owner was his fingerprints.

While the men searched for clues in the van, their computer servers hummed. Another six hours would pass until the search yielded a result. They told Dr. Ohm's it was much more thorough to search all the databases in parallel instead of individually. They had to be patient. It took time for their science to work. Dr. Ohm's chose another lead to pursue.

Tracking down the taxicab was easy. The surveillance team captured a superb shot of the cab, its driver, and the license plate number. Hendricks and Raphael were dispatched to the cab company. Their interview yielded little. The driver said the fare told him to get on the highway and take him to the rail station. The drive took twenty minutes and cost nineteen. The man paid him twenty-five bucks and took off fast watching him disappear into the crowd until another passenger jumped into his cab.

The two plain-clothes officers headed to the commuter terminal's security station to review the surveillance video. It showed the suspect purchasing a fare card from the kiosk station and disappearing on a north bound train. From there they completely lost the scent. He could have got off at any number of different stops. The man was lost in the crowd again. Their only hope to locate him rested with the Colbys again. Ohm's and Amecii used the investigatory pause to allow people to get some sleep, a good meal, and a shower. They needed a respite from their vigil. If the Colby's did turn something up, Ohm's wanted a fresh team ready to move out smartly.

CHAPTER TWENTY-FOUR

Sherman fielded Ishmael's phone from call at 1530 on Friday afternoon. The crime scene investigators' expertise and perseverance were not used in vain. Check the fax machine he was told. The fingerprint search bore fruit. Ishmael worked the fax machine while they spoke. Israel told Sherman the team would be surprised at the man's identity and if he was Butcher Bill, it would explain a lot of the murder's geographical disparity.

The FBI agent eagerly hung the phone up and raced across the room to the bank of three fax machines. The light hum of the fax's printer churned and spit out a page. The three seconds it took for the paper to materialize seemed like three hours. Sherman controlled his breathing to arrest his anxiousness. The data being received might allow them to end the needless butchering and suffering that spanned over a decade and a half.

Studying the faxed data sheet, Sherman eyes focused on the picture embedded in the information. It was a close resemblance to the man who visited the church. A much younger version, but definitely a match. A FBI digital photography specialist would be enlisted to virtually age the facsimile picture. It would be a formality since the likeness was so great. The agent continued to study the information. The fingerprint information came from the Department of Defense database. For over forty years, the DOD had fingerprinted their soldiers, sailors, airman, and marines upon entering military service. The military used the fingerprints to identify a warrior who fell in battle. In this case, it yielded Butcher Bill.

Their suspect enlisted in the United States Navy in 1996 from a recruiting station in the Philippines. The data sheet did not say anything about his current rank or duty station. That would be easily determined later. The man served in the Navy for seventeen years. With that type of seniority, it would make him a First Class Petty Officer, a Chief Petty Officer, a Warrant Officer, or a Mustang Commissioned Officer. The information sheet provided a plethora of other useful information. It listed every duty station he had ever been associated with. California, Virginia, Florida, Illinois, Washington, and Idaho were all listed. The man was even stationed overseas in Great Britain and Italy. What interested Sherman was the training and jobs the sailor held. The man became a US sailor when the Navy recruited Filipinos to serve. Since the end of World War II, America maintained a strong alliance with the Philippines. The Philippines government rightly understood their freedom from Japanese oppression was directly related to American heroics in the Pacific theatre. To the United States, the archipelago was strategically valuable. The Philippines equally desired a close relationship with the US. It provided national security and economic stability. One method to solidify the pact between the two allies was to allow Filipino men to serve in the US military. It bound the two nations together. For the Navy, the majority of Filipino recruits entered in logistics or engineering jobs. This was the case with Naval Recruit Ignacio Medina. He signed his enlistment papers on 27 September 1996 and agreed to receive technical training as an electrician. On 14 October of the same year, Medina was transported to the Great Lakes Recruit Training Depot just outside of Chicago. Boot Camp lasted eight weeks where he received top grades in all of his training. Then, Seaman Recruit Medina moved on to receive another six months of training that made him an Electrician's Mate. He apparently did well at A-School. Instead of being immediately assigned to a ship, the Navy sent him to continue his electrical education. The novice electrician received an additional year of training to work on nuclear reactors. It was 1998 by the time the budding sailor reached the fleet and reported for duty aboard a ship. Aircraft carriers, cruisers, and submarines were being built with nuclear reactors to power the vessels. The need for talented personnel was great. Sherman gleaned as much as he could surmise from the scant information in his hands. The sailor was dispatched to serve on a ship at the Naval Station in Norfolk, Virginia. From there the man's path was the same as countless other career sailors. It included numerous moves throughout the country for training and service. With this service came high operational tempos with multiple deployments overseas on ships. The deployments definitely would involve stops in foreign ports for replenishment, maintenance, liberty, and, above all, to show American resolve. Showing the flag through Gunboat Diplomacy was a highly effective strategy.

Sherman picked up the phone, called Catherine and explained the situation. Her excitement burst from his cell phone receiver. She and Sherman agreed who they would need the team to start tracing and profiling their target. The exchange lasted less than three minutes though Sherman subconsciously wanted it go on longer. His feelings for Catherine had to remain suppressed until after the investigation. Muddying the waters with romantic overtures was poor form. He knew his feelings were genuine and he knew the redheaded FBI profiler felt the same. First things first. The evil menace was their priority. One thing was sure. Sherman knew he would go undercover again. Chief Boatswain-mate Sherman was going back to sea.

CHAPTER TWENTY-FIVE

The War Room's energy could power a city block. The team was electric and humming. Telephones were ringing. Conversations toppled over each other creating a constant chatter. Agents collected information, collated data, processed it for relevancy, and posted the information on the numerous bulletin boards populating the large hall's sidewalls. The most salient facts were culled for Ohms's to give an overall brief to the team.

Dr. Ohms used his FBI special investigation hammer to beat open the Department of the Navy's bureaucratic doors. Official orders relayed from the Secretary of the Navy to the Chief of Naval Operations made vast quantities of data available from the Naval Criminal Investigation Service. The NCIS forwarded it to the FBI grudgingly. They were given strict orders to provide information only and not to ask any questions why the naval electrician named Ignacio Medina was under the FBI microscope. Orders or no orders, the NCIS agents unsuccessfully inquired about the case. All they received from the FBI was a polite thank you for their assistance and a door slammed in their face.

The Navy's electronic databases made the information transfer occur quickly. Sherman, Amecii, Hendricks, Raphael, the Colby's and a few select supporting agents sifted through the new material. They learned Ignacio Medina was a recently promoted to Chief Petty Officer and he served aboard the nuclear powered aircraft carrier *USS ABRAHAM LINCOLN*. Abe, as sailors called her, was home ported at the Naval Station in Everett, Washington. Everett was a short drive from Seattle. A drive north from Everett to where Roosevelt, the German shepherd, found Amanda Parker's beautiful yet lifeless body took a little more than an hour. The Navy also informed them that the *ABRAHAM LINCOLN* was scheduled to leave port in two days. The ship had orders to deploy back to the Indian Ocean and Persian Gulf in support of the Seventh and Fifth Fleets efforts in the Global War Against Terrorism. The ship had only been home for three months. No one had to drive the team any harder. The urgency beyond their diligent work was rhetorical.

Ohms decided to send both Agent Sherman and Agent Amecii under cover on the ship. Chief Petty Officer Sherman would go aboard as part of the ship's crew working in the Deck Department. The Navy agreed to allow Amecii to deploy under the guise of a liberal arts teacher contracted to teach college courses to the sailors while they toiled out to sea. Most naval ships were coed; so, having a female college professor onboard was a perfect cover for the intellectual agent.

Ohms understood the importance of having Sherman getting close to Medina. The mission was ripe with danger. A ship at sea was a good place to kill a person. A correctly timed shove on a moonless night would cast a person easily overboard. Falling from an aircraft carrier's lofty decks was akin to jumping off a ten-story building onto a slab of concrete. Even if the person survived the fall, he would be unconscious and drown. Seldom was the splash from a man overboard at night heard by the ship's lookouts. The ship would steam along its course and no one would know a person went over the side until the next morning when the crew was mustered.

Their evidence on Medina was thin. The only option they had was to place him under surveillance. Butcher Bill covered his tracks well. There was not any physical evidence connecting him to any of the murders. Overall, their case was built entirely on theory, coincidences, and circumstantial evidence. To ensure Sherman's back was covered; Ohms decided Amecii would be his partner. This did two things. Her pull as the team's deputy director allowed her to request and receive immediate and unfettered access to resources ashore while they were out to sea. The ability to communicate by satellite telephone and classified networks allowed them to reach back for assistance and information. Amecii's presence also gave Sherman physical back up if things got ugly while Sherman investigated the errant sailor. The FBI took great pride in Catherine Amecii's profiling ability. In a pinch, Catherine could protect herself too. Holding a Second Degree Black Belt in Tae Kwon Do made her a formidable adversary. Putting a 9mm pistol in her hand made her extra deadly. She aced every weapon qualification exercise the FBI ever threw at her. She was a pretty yet deadly opponent to criminals dumb enough to mess with her.

An hour passed and the team took a ten-minute break for a breath of fresh air or to make phone calls home to their loved ones. They reassembled to discuss the new information pieced together.

Dr. Ohms stood in front of three projection screens. The left screen displayed a full-face photo of Chief Petty Officer Medina. Absent was the Charles Manson fifty-mile death stare. He looked normal. Anyone would chat with him while standing in the supermarket line. Medina was a brutal killer disguised as an average citizen. A wolf amongst sheep.

The right screen showed charts containing Medina's biographical information. The center screen was the focus of attention. It exhibited a world map entwined by a spider web accented with yellow stars. Ohms marched to the podium, shuffled through his notes while he looked out amongst his team.

"Ladies and Gentlemen, let's get started."

Silence echoed through the auditorium. Twenty-six agents, policeman, and criminal forensic experts focused their attention on their boss. They knew this was the next chapter in their investigation and Ohms would brief them about how the new pieces of the puzzle they feverishly collected would come together.

"We have refined our profile on Butcher Bill. What you see before you is Chief Petty Officer Electrician's Mate Ignacio

Medina. We believe he is also Butcher Bill," he began. The room was hush.

"Chief Medina was born in the Philippines to an alcoholic and junkie prostitute whose clientele were the local shipyard workers. We possess high confidence Medina's mother abused him severely. The abuse was most likely a combination of physical, emotional, and environmental abuse. More likely than not, Medina was sexually abused on a routine basis. That's why he kills women 'politely' and tortures the men. Every murdered female represents a surrogate mother. But, always striving to be a good son, he shows his victim-mother respect by not defiling them. On the other hand, every man who died a brutal death at his hands experienced the vengeance he has bottled up inside him. He blames the men for his anger, the debasing of his mother, and the lack of maternal love," he said.

The team listened intently to the briefing. Some jotted notes into their tablets. Others leaned forward to ensure they captured every detail. Sherman listened with his arms crossed and his chin resting on his thumb. He needed every bit of information Ohms and Amecii could drum out of the data they received. The Cobly twins were enthralled. It was their hard work that started the investigation. After Bill was captured, they would be immortal within the forensic science community.

Ohms continued. "Medina is thirty four years old. He stands five foot eight, weighs approximately one hundred sixty five pounds. Brown eyes. Black hair cut military style. He serves in the Navy as a nuclear power plant electrician. To the Navy, that makes him very intelligent. To us, that makes him methodical, patient, and extremely detailed oriented. The Navy trained him how to think logically, to plan his every move, and to clean up after he was done. If Chief Petty Officer Medina is Butcher Bill, he has applied that same training in a most sinister manner."

Ohms turned and pointed to the center screen to preface his next thoughts.

"Chief Ignacio Medina has traveled far and wide. He has spanned the globe, visited more than forty countries, territories, and possessions. The yellow stars represent all the naval bases or ports he has visited. The black lines depict his travels from a specific base. As you can see, when he departed on a deployment from Norfolk, Virginia in 1998, Medina traveled to Great Britain, Spain, France, Italy, Greece, Crete, Turkey, Egypt, and Africa. We suspect he left a trail of carnage in his wake. Much like he did here in the States. Next slide please," he commanded.

Instantly a series of neon green coffin-like shapes appeared on the slide with red circles surrounding many of the green icons. Each circle's center was a yellow star.

"This is a most telling and chilling picture. Every green shape you see is where either a body fitting his M. O. was discovered. Ladies and Gentlemen…what you see in front of you is Butcher Bill's killing fields."

Ohms paused to drink from a water bottle. The crew knew he was not done and understood not to interrupt the Doctor with questions until he finished.

"Medina is devoutly religious and believes his acts are sanctioned and ordered by God. His heinous brutality is not committed to curb a sexual appetite. He kills because he's on a mission from God. He is placid around authority. His aggression he unleashes on his victims. To Bill, the men represent the people who dominated and abused him as a child. The women, he pretends they are compassionate versions of his mother. The polar opposite of his mother. What Bill sees is his mother not a different woman. So, he strikes out and kills the person who should have loved and protected him as a youth."

"Catherine and I also concluded Butcher Bill's primary weakness is his faith. It frustrates him when he confesses his sins and the priests refuse him absolution. It torments him because he seeks solace from the church as he did as a boy. As a boy, he probably received comfort from people, like nuns and missionaries, who were associated with the Catholic Church. Not receiving relief from the church pains him deeply. We based this conclusion on the heat signatures we collected. Before he went in, he seemed slightly agitated and anxious. Following his visit to Father Nguyen, his heat persona was brilliant blue. His whole aura was hot…hot….hot. Father Nguyen's outright refusal to participate created a furnace inside him. This is the weakness we want to exploit," preached Dr. Ohms.

"I want you to look deeply into the map. He has gotten away with murder for over sixteen years. If you think his homicide tally here in the United States is high, I guarantee the total tally will increase when we start receiving information from all of the nations he traveled to. He is about to disappear for another six to eight months unless we take action to follow him. The ship he is stationed on deploys in two days to Asia and Arabia. He is returning to killing fields he has already grazed upon. This time, he is going to have a surprise waiting for him. Our team will be there in force wherever he lands. The Navy has agreed to keep us abreast of the ports the ship intends to visit. But, our most important asset at this point is Agent Sherman and Agent Amecii. Both are going onboard the *USS ABRAHAM LINCOLN* to get close to him and learn his habits. They will feel out his personality and how to exploit it further."

"It's Agent Sherman's job to go undercover as a fellow sailor. Besides being the worst serial killer we have ever come across, he's also a sailor. And sailors are traditionally distrustful until you gain their respect. That is going to be a hard nut to crack for Agent Sherman."

Taking one last breath, Ohms concluded, "That is all I have to say. The information displayed before you is what each of you has diligently investigated. We are way ahead of where we were a month ago. You should all be proud. Take the next two days off. See your families. Recharge your batteries as much as you can.

There is a lot of hard work in store for us in the very near future. Are there any questions?"

Seattle Police Detective Hendricks commented first. He started with praise.

"Dr. Ohms, from the Seattle PD perspective, I echo everything you said. This team has uncovered more than I have ever seen in my many years investigating homicides. I applaud the team's efforts."

Ohms and the audience respected Detective Hendricks. He was a good and honest cop. Whatever he was about to say would hold merit.

"With Medina leaving the country, it is obvious the FBI has the resources, tools, and relationships established around the globe to pursue the investigation. The local team here has put just as much into this investigation as our FBI brethrens. We would not be where we are in this investigation without the Colby brothers or Detective Raphael. Their professionalism and intelligence revealed Butcher Bill for the first time," said the plain clothes cop.

Looking directly into Ohms's eyes Hendricks' continued. "Doctor, I want your absolute word you intend to take the Colby brothers, Detective Raphael, and I wherever this investigation leads us. I possess the authority to speak for the Seattle Police Department and we insist to follow this case to the bitter end. Do you concur?"

His questions spurred whispered side discussions amongst the team members. All of them were nodding their heads up and down in agreement with Hendricks's observation.

Ohms quickly spoke up. "Absolutely. I have no intention of breaking this team up now. Everyone in this room has devoted tremendous energy to get us where we are at right now. Leaving you, Raphael, Israel, and Ishmael behind is a recipe for disaster. We started as a team; we will finish as a team," replied Dr. Ohms.

Satisfied, Hendricks retired to his seat.

It was the only question posed. All recognized their job just got tougher. The details of Ohms's plan would be worked out in more detail in the next few days. The team respected Dr. Ohms's judgment and left it at that.

CHAPTER TWENTY-SIX

The *USS ABRAHAM LINCOLN* shifted her colors, charting her course to the other side of the world. The sun peaked over the horizon lighting the path over the black water. Eight tugs assisted the massive grey hull depart her moorings and point her hurricane bow towards the Strait of Juan de Fuca. It was a good day to go to sea. The air was crisp but not cold. The winter rains let up to give them a pleasant and calm passage through the Strait to the open ocean. Once she entered the Pacific Ocean Abe's first objective was to embark the airplanes she would take to war. They needed three days to recover the F-18 Super Hornets, the Electronic Attack F-18 Hornets, the E-2 Hawkeye radar planes, and the squat propeller driven Carrier Onboard Delivery airplanes. In between recovering the airplanes, HH-60 and SH-60 helicopters would orbit the ship ready to recover any pilot who had to ditch in the cold sea.

Bringing on the air wing was deep in the back of the flattop's CO's mind. Captain Russell was a direct descendant from two naval heroes, Rear Admiral Russell and Colonel Russell. They were two brothers who plied the seas when iron men served wooden ships. Going to sea came natural to him despite being an aviator. Congress mandated that pilots command aircraft carriers. Russell cut his teeth flying F-14 Tomcats. It was in the Tomcat cockpit he earned his two Distinguished Flying Crosses. The first was for operations against the Soviet Union. People at home had no idea of the danger imposed during the Cold War and the Soviet Union. He and his wingman were awarded the DFC for intercepting and escorting a sixteen ship Russian Bear Bomber flight from Alaska to Asia. It took twelve hours and ten in-flight refuelings to make it happen. The added stress of having Soviet MIGS flying wingtip to wingtip who wanted him to bump one of them to create an international incident did not help much. It was this mission when his squadron commander officially changed his call sign from *Gecko* to *Ironman*.

His second Flying Cross was awarded at the end of the first Persian Gulf War. When the alert came down to launch for the attack, he was recently promoted to Commander. Being such, he was now the squadron commander. His squadron launched in the dead of night, were vectored to their orbit position until they received word the Stealth Bombers and Tomahawk Cruise Missiles' strikes were carried out. With the Iraqi enemy on full alert, his squadron entered a hornet's nest to deliver the two five hundred pound bombs strapped to their F-14's belly. They made their approach against the Iraqi surface-to-air missile emplacements, radar stations, and communications towers in pitch-black darkness. GPS and the E-2 Hawkeyes vectored them to their targets.

Delivering the bombs was a skill the pilots practiced often. Even so, the intense anti-aircraft artillery fire and surface-to-air missiles made it difficult. As the squadron's most experienced pilot and commanding officer, he decided he would be the last airplane to deliver its bombs. It was considered the most dangerous place to be in an air-to-ground attack with an enemy on full alert. His Radar Intercept Officer, or RIO, rode in the airplane's back seat. The two had flown together for six years. Lieutenant Commander Henry Builder manned the aircraft's radar, comm gear, and weapons while *Ironman* flew the airplane. When it was *Ironman*'s turn, he had to run an iron gauntlet. Commander Russell waited for his turn for the attack and commenced his run. The explosions in the air from the AAA bounced and shook his fighter jet. He could not use afterburner because the speed would upset the ground targeting solution. Reaching the target, Builder, a.k.a. *Mason*, delivered the bombs on target and on time. That's when things got dicey. *Mason* pushed the button and dropped the bombs. Cockpit alarms blared inside their flight helmets from the electronic warfare equipment picking up the fast pulses of surface-to-air missiles locking onto their plane. *Ironman* went into evasive mode while *Mason* dispensed flares and chaff. The missiles never scored a direct hit but the two aviators felt the anti-air missiles bursting around them. An engine was knocked out before Russell piloted his plane out to sea where he expected to find his home plate, the *USS EISENHOWER*. He made a dicey landing catching the flight deck's number one wire. The aircraft was quickly covered in firefighting foam by the flight deck's emergency firemen. A crippled two million dollar fighter jet carrying highly flammable aviation fuel was not a good thing to have exploding onboard a ship at sea. If the damaged plane set fire to the ship, it would be difficult to extinguish. It meant time and energy lost from performing the mission the floating airport was designed to execute.

The two airmen were ripped out of the cockpit and were quickly surveyed by medical corpsmen for wounds. None were discovered.

Later that night the flight deck's maintenance department presented the damage report. Besides one of its engines being destroyed, the aircraft mechanics told him a piece of his right aft stabilizer wing was sheared off and the landing gear doors were peppered with AAA. It flabbergasted everyone the landing gear even worked. Chock one up to hearty American engineering and ingenuity. Three months later, a formal ceremony was held by the Battle Group Commander who awarded the Distinguished Flying Cross to both aviators. *Ironman* lost track of *Mason* six years ago. *Mason* left the Navy after serving his twenty years. He had enough of risking his life to soothe his adventurous spirit. Over a beer one night in Hong Kong, *Mason* told his lifelong friend and colleague he was leaving the service to make sure he saw his kids grow up. *Ironman* understood and bid him "Fair Winds and Following Seas."

Russell liked the adventure, as did most men or women who joined the military. They are always doing something different, something out of the ordinary. A dull day was rare. He never really appreciated how hard the Black Shoe Officers worked. They chose careers working the mighty warships that make up the backbone of the Navy. He assumed command three weeks ago. He only had her out to sea on two occasions. The first was for sea trials to test the ship's machinery after being in the shipyard for two months. The second was a brief five day jaunt receiving ammunition and fuel from an auxiliary ship. He had to admit, commanding the largest and most sophisticated warship in the world was exhilarating but it came with a completely new set of dangers. Grounding or running into another ship haunted his thoughts. Launching and recovering planes at night or angry seas brought forth their own unique worries.

Training a green crew of five thousand sailors for war seemed impossible. Sleep was a luxury to the *ABRAHAM LINCOLN's* Captain. Captain Russell thought he had a handle on all of the challenges he would experience. That is, until he met Boatswain-Mate Chief Petty Officer Sherman and Professor Amecii. Prior to their departure Admiral Shiloh summoned Russell to his office where he was told two undercover FBI agents were joining his ship. Russell pressed for details but none were offered. The Admiral told Captain Russell he was in the dark as well. "Orders straight from the Secretary of the Navy," said the Flag Officer. "Complete secrecy was to be observed. They were the only two people in the Battle Group who knew who Sherman and Amecii really were." Not even the Naval Criminal Investigatory Service was aware. That proved to be an odd fact. The FBI must be looking for something big and super sensitive if NCIS was not involved.

Admiral Shiloh relayed the rest of his orders to Captain Russell.

"We are not to recognize or offer any special treatment to the two undercover agents. Chief Sherman is a reservist. He knows his job on the decks. Agent Amecii will teach philosophy classes to the crew. However," he continued, "Amecii is to have unfettered and secure communications capability to shore. She will use my personal office without anyone present when she wants to use the satellite telephone. That means we have to pay extra particular attention in the radio room. We will station officers in the Command Communications Center to ensure no one is listening to her comms."

Russell was baffled. "What case were they working on that demanded such high scrutiny? Especially since the phones were used to pass highly classified information already," he thought to himself.

Admiral Shiloh was not finished. "Whatever they need, without question, we are to give to them. If they need a helicopter, they get a helicopter. If they need fifty sailors, they get fifty sailors. If they need weapons, they get weapons without a bat of an eyelash from us. I know it sounds strange and it is the weirdest thing I have ever come across in my twenty eight years plying the oceans. But, we're just like Sailor Timmy; we will give the Secretary of Navy a cheery Aye-Aye and carry out his orders. Do you understand the orders and will you acknowledge them Captain Russell?" questioned the Admiral to make certain ambiguity did not cloud Russell's judgment.

"Yes, Sir, I understand the orders and I will comply," replied Russell.

Captain Russell departed the Admiral's stateroom office with a thousand questions bouncing through his mind. The frustrating part was he knew those questions would never be answered any time soon. A warship's Commanding Officer was obligated to know everything going on within its steel frames. Having two undercover FBI agents onboard his ship and having to ignore them wrinkled his brow. He theorized the two agents were investigating espionage, potential terrorists amongst his crew, or smuggling operations. He was recently briefed on the huge drug bust carried out onboard the Aegis Destroyer *USS ILORETA* a few months ago. The story he was told described the NCIS performing the investigation with FBI assistance. Was that FBI assistance Chief Petty Officer Sherman? Russell could speculate on the what-ifs for hours. Hours he did not have time to waste. If the Admiral said *"mums-the-word"* about the two FBI people, then he would carry out those orders to the letter. The saying *"Loose Lips Sink Ships"* rang true. The secret would go no further than him. Besides, he had a crew to train before they started launching airplanes headed into harm's way.

The FBI obviously believed the two agents could fend for themselves; therefore, he would not second-guess the Bureau's actions. Whatever they were doing was for the good of his ship and his country.

CHAPTER TWENTY-SEVEN

Chief Sherman studied a great deal of philosophy in his life. The subject enthralled him. He admired great men like Lincoln, Gandhi, Martin Luther King, Jr., the Great Dali Lama, Socrates, and countless others. Taking *Professor* Amecii's, shipboard 'Ancient Philosophy' class peaked his interest. Taking the class was a much welcome respite for him. Both were undercover, but it seemed when they were in the class discussing a subject they both enjoyed, it was more date than an undercover mission. At times, Sherman shut his eyes, kicked his feet out, and listened to Catherine's sweet voice as she discussed Augustus Caesar who ruled the Roman Empire. Sometimes, he caught himself fantasizing that he was kissing the sweet nape of her neck and listening to her lightly whisper for him to continue. His fantasies went further when he lay in bed trying to sleep amongst the other snoring chief's in the bunkroom.

Taking Catherine's class served a more pressing need. The two agents used the class to communicate with one another without arousing any suspicion by Chief Medina. Their class was held every other day in the ship's library. Catherine made sure the homework assignments included written essays on the literature the sailors studied. For Sherman and Amecii, it provided a good opportunity for her to forward information funneled to them from Dr. Ohms ashore. When she handed the graded essays back to her students, Sherman's papers always had a note about the continued investigation back home. He read the latest note sheet standing on Vulture's Row while observing the carrier's ballet of recovering the F-18 airplanes. The noise was thunderous from the thirty knots of wind whipping over the ship's flight deck and the high-pitched whine of jet's engines as they descended at 130 knots to drop onto the flight deck. For the moment, all of the noise was drowned out by the latest news Catherine provided. Ohm's communiqué said the team had found another male victim severely beaten to death. He was a long shore man who had been reported missing by his sister twelve days ago. A Tacoma Boy Scout Troop on a weekend hike discovered his corpse rotting in a ditch along a hiking trail in the Olympia National forest. His name was Norman Hook. He was thirty-eight, five foot nine, blondish hair, single, and known to frequent prostitutes plying their sultry wares near the Seattle harbor. The victim's body fit the pattern of Butcher Bill's conquests. Norman Hook lay naked, covered in blood, bruises, and beaten to death. Whatever Boy Scout made the discovery, the image would haunt him for the rest of his life. Butcher Bill stayed true to form. The autopsy revealed severe blunt trauma over his entire body. Teeth were missing. His nose was broken and wedged to the left side of his face. An ear lobe dangled by fragments of skin. The note sheet told the story of a grim and painful death. Dr. Ohms's report surmised it was the reason Medina sought Father Nguyen. He killed again and desired absolution from the Church. He also wanted to brag. His ego was getting in the way. Butcher Bill needed recognition for his conquests.

The shore team was running down any evidence the Colbys managed to collect. Being left out in the open, the damp weather reduced their chances of finding a link tying Medina to the crime. They had to process the scene nonetheless. They would forward their discoveries within twenty-four hours.

Lastly, Catherine's information stated she had contacted Dr. Ohm's to inform the investigators that the *LINCOLN*'s first port-of-call would be Pearl Harbor. Hendricks and Raphael were busy preparing for their arrival to the island. Round the clock and redundant surveillance would be established to watch Chief Medina's every move.

Sherman neatly folded the covert message and placed it into his shirt pocket. Later, he would rip it to pieces and flush it down the marine head. Out to sea, human waste was pulped and discharged overboard. Having a note like that fall into the hands of some unsuspecting sailor would tip Medina. The aircraft carrier was essentially a small town floating on the ocean. Rumors circulated constantly. Gossip helped sailors cope. Everyone knew whose spouse was cheating on them back home. Everyone knew what their next port of call was. They knew about arguments in the officer's wardroom mess. Rumors ruled the ship. A piece of paper like the one neatly stowed in Sherman's pocket, would run rampant below decks.

During the week's time onboard, Chief Sherman quickly assimilated to his new role. A sailor's respect had to be earned and Agent Sherman achieved it quickly. He knew his job and he treated his charges with respect and tough love. The American sailor was different than the rest of the world's navies. Their desire to work, their passion to excel, and being given authority at young ages made them effective. Unlike many navies, they performed brilliantly when asked to do something. Giving them direct orders on a continuous basis shut their creative thinking down, reduced their morale that impacted their ability to be an effective and fluid team.

They liked Chief Sherman. His speech was not grandiose. When they needed guidance, he gave it to them plainly. Picking up a tool to help finish a taxing task was not beneath him. He listened to their sea stories and he shared his own. To the sailors, Chief Sherman was one of them. He climbed the promotion ladder and maintained his compassion to be a sailor first, leader second. Sherman recognized it and relished in the quick acceptance. It made his true mission much easier. Now, he could concentrate on getting to know Chief Medina.

On past missions, Agent Sherman posed as an American sailor on the Aegis destroyer, *USS ILORETA* and only one other ship. He had never really seen how an aircraft carrier worked. Watching the planes land on the black flight deck amazed him. It was a well tuned machine. He thought to himself that a well-oiled machine did not depict what was actually happening. The high tempo flight deck operations were more ballet than machinery. Every sailor knew his job and the importance of doing it right. As an airplane landed, it needed to be connected to a tractor and towed off the flight deck. Sailors wearing brown vests did that job. Once parked off to the flight line's side, purple vested sailors refueled the airplanes tanks while green vested men and women started doing mechanical spot checks to the planes components. Red vests stood by with firefighting equipment and pilot extraction tools in case of an emergency. Corpsman wearing white shirts and helmets adorned with red crosses stood ready to give immediate medical care. Leading the dance were sailors donned in yellow shirts and vests. They were the most experienced of the flight deck crew. Last but not least were the safety officers who monitored the entire operation for everyone's safety. They were senior non-commissioned and junior officers clad in white vests with green crosses. Danger and mishaps were defeated through redundancy and vigilance. Everyone watched out for everyone. It was a fascinating play to watch observed Sherman. He lost himself watching airplanes being recovered every sixty seconds, while other pilots boosted the fuel being burned by the jet engines to maximize thrust. Once achieved, they signaled their readiness to launch to the yellow shirts who gave the signal to engage the catapult. Within a flash, the airplanes jetted down the short runway at 190 knots per hour and were flung into the air from the steam-powered slingshots. The engines flamed bright orange from the planes afterburners. Thirty knots of wind sustained them in the air as they accelerated and climbed.

Sherman shook himself from his concentration. Other 'Lookie-Lous' had amassed on Vulture's Row to witness the same spectacle. He estimated roughly two hundred sailors and a small mix of civilians were captivated by the flight operations drama. He scanned the crowd and fixed his gaze on a black clad Asian male. Sipping from a steaming mug of liquid stood Father Nguyen. His appearance startled Sherman. "*What in the hell is he doing here?*" were his first thoughts.

Father Nguyen turned slightly and looked directly into Sherman's eyes. The priest's lips parted slightly and formed a gentle smile.

The flight deck operations were idling down. The last jet was recovered. The flight deck crew kept busy by preparing the deck for its next cycle. The spectator mass broke up with most ducking back inside the skin of the ship. Two minutes later, only Father Nguyen and Agent Sherman remained outside. Sherman stood his ground as he watched the priest stroll to where he stood.

"You clean up well my young friend. The last time I saw you were camped out across the street from my church," said the priest.

Sherman kept his rock solid composure to the clergyman's words. He did not know how the priest knew.

"You're not the only one who likes to watch people. It is my occupation too. Do not worry my friend. Your secret is safe with me. I believe the Almighty has destined us to be teammates."

"Father Nguyen, you should not be here," was the only reply Agent Sherman gave.

Father Nguyen stood his ground. His eyes smiled with delight. His decision to join the ship's crew terrified him. Not because he was going to sea as a favor to the ship's chaplain and to the Navy, but because of the real reason he wanted to join the ship. He decided a month ago, that where Chief Medina would go he would go. His inner self tried to protect itself when he made his decision. His mind kept conjuring up thoughts of the danger he was exposing himself to. Being the only one in the world, until now, who knew Chief Medina's secret, he placed himself in a situation fraught with terror and pain. What else could he do? The demon was leaving for at least half a year. Leaving the United

States would not stifle the evil spirit. He knew from the killer's confessions he would continue his debauchery overseas. In the end, his thoughts of self-preservation were overcome by his need to pursue his God's will. God put Medina in his confessional for a reason. If it demanded courage, than he would summon the strength to overcome his fear, somehow.

"What is your name my friend," came the priest's answers to Sherman's observation.

Sherman assessed the situation. Here was the priest who led them to Medina. He could screw up the entire operation. Or could he? The agent remembered Dr. Ohms profiling of the killer. "The weak link we need to exploit was Butcher Bill's fear of the church and its wrath," Ohms had said. Sherman believed his first action was to contact Amecii to arrange for a helicopter to whisk the priest off the carrier. Thinking over what Ohms had stated, Sherman concluded having the priest along would help work in their favor.

"The sailors call me Chief Sherman," he replied. "Obviously, you know different Father Nguyen. We are here for the same purpose."

"Yes, it seems God has sent an angel to watch my back as I engage the devil."

"Father, I hope you understand how dangerous this man is. He has no compassion. His soul is filled with hate and he will not have any problem killing you, me, or anyone else in the world. But, if you are going to be here, you have to play by my rules. Okay Father?" stated the FBI agent clad in sailors clothing.

"Chief Sherman, do you have a first name? And yes, I agree with what you ask. I will rest better at night knowing God and Saint Michael are helping me."

This priest was something else. Untrained in any type of self defense or surveillance techniques, this man struck out on his own to battle pure evil and had placed his entire safety in his religious faith. Sherman witnessed remarkable feats of courage before but this was the bravest thing he had ever come across.

"My name is Andrew Father. Now that you're onboard, what are your intentions?"

"Thank you Andrew. I always like to become acquainted with my flock. It is always easier to help a friend than a stranger. My plans? That is a good question. I really do not have any plans except to keep a close eye on Chief Medina. I figure if the evil incarnate knows he's being watched, he might not commit the horrible acts he does. That's the only plan I have."

"Thank you, Father. We cannot stay together much longer. I have to think about what your being here does and how it can help. I want you to go do whatever you plan on doing, except keep out of Chief Medina's path. Steer clear of him for the time being. I will come and find you in a few hours to talk more."

"Very good, my son. God bless you. I look forward to our talk."

Father Nguyen's soul leaped with joy as he turned away from Agent Sherman, opened the access door, and entered the ship's interior. His prayers were answered again.

Sherman waited fifteen minutes before he departed. He watched the sun set over the horizon while his brain developed a plan. The first thing he needed to do was contact Catherine. He longed to see her beautiful eyes again and this new turn allowed him the excuse to do so. His hearted skipped at having another chance to spend time with Catherine. It was not the most charming time but it was better than nothing. He would have time after Butcher Bill was behind bars to explore his feelings for her.

CHAPTER TWENTY-EIGHT

Catherine possessed the same remorse when she learned Father Nguyen was onboard the *LINCOLN*. With an air wing embarked onboard, the floating city's population reached above five thousand sailors. The massive steel vessel operated its own hospital, pharmacy, convenience stores, cafeterias, gymnasiums, machine shops, libraries, post offices, and chapels. Father Nguyen and Catherine shared a common theme with two hundred and fifty civilians onboard. They were all brought onboard to assist the sailors with faith, education, or work. Besides herself, three other college professors, and the priest, the rest of the civilian contingent were equipment technicians hired to repair shipboard equipment and to train the crew. She thought it was funny she did not discover his presence sooner. He was keeping a low profile.

She and Sherman discussed their options. They could send him ashore to protect him from danger. They could arrest Medina on the scant circumstantial evidence the team already assembled. They could let Father Nguyen stay and fend for himself. Or, they could bring Father Nguyen into their confidence and trust. Catherine called Ohms. His reaction took Catherine off guard. He rapidly dismissed the first three ideas without comment. Removing Father Nguyen from the ship would narrow their ability to exploit their nemesis' fear of displeasing God. Arresting Medina was out of the question. They had good reason to believe he mercilessly killed hundreds of people. But, he could not be linked to any specific crime. Without connecting him to the victims, the evidence was superficial and any student directly out of law school would get him off. The third option was certainly out of the question. Leaving Father Nguyen to battle Butcher

Bill alone equated to a death sentence. Father Nguyen understood Medina much better than they did. He knew his thoughts, his motives, and his weaknesses. Partially bringing him into the fold would help baiting Bill into exposing himself. The danger demanded vigilant caution. It was up to Sherman to coordinate Father Nguyen's efforts. They wanted to control the environment of when and where Medina came into contact with Nguyen.

Father Nguyen received Chief Sherman in his office. It was the best place to meet. No one would bother them during a private conversation between a Priest and parishioner.

He and Sherman discussed his involvement. He concurred with the agent to proceed with caution. Stepping onboard the *LINCOLN* took amazing courage. During the murderer's latest confession, Medina bid Father Nguyen bon voyage. His ship was pulling out for six months or more. The monster confessed his latest evil conquest. It galvanized Nguyen's spirit. At the moment, he heard the filth spewing out of the killer's mouth; Nguyen knew the time for positive action was at hand.

A month before, the ship's senior Chaplain, Commander Riley, asked him to embark for the deployment. Father Nguyen had done such a wonderful job helping his office and the ship's crew that the Chaplain wanted him to continue his work. Becoming a Navy Chaplain was not a prerequisite. The day after the confession, Nguyen solicited the Diocese Bishop's advice. He spoke about the Navy Chaplain's request but not the real reason why he wanted to go. The Bishop agreed with Father Nguyen's desire to deliver spiritual guidance to the sailors heading to war and immediately approved his request to deploy.

Commander Riley was surprised yet thrilled to hear Nguyen agreed to go. He made the offer more lightheartedly and did not believe the Priest would entertain the idea. There was a remote chance Nguyen would deploy. The odds a civilian priest would join the deploying crew were slim to none. But, it never hurt to ask.

He embarked onboard the ship just prior to the brow being lifted for departure. The priest desired his appearance onboard to be an utter surprise to Medina. He had steered the cops as best he could. Alerting the authorities to where the murderer's latest female victim rested was the best he could do without violating his vows of secrecy. Their presence at the church certainly was encouraging. Meeting Agent Sherman on Vulture's Row was another sign his Lord backed his hand.

The meeting with Sherman provided his mission focus. The conversation lasted twenty minutes. Sherman did most of the talking. Nguyen agreed to everything he suggested. Sherman explained who he was and why he was onboard the ship. He wanted Nguyen to maintain the relationship he already developed with the crew. Appearances were vital to insure the crew did not notice any special attention given to their target. Father Nguyen's personal contact with Medina demanded control. Sherman identified specific times and methods he desired Nguyen to make his presence known to Butcher Bill. The two would never be alone.

Coming aboard made him an instant target. It would be difficult but the priest had to make a concentrated effort to be in the company of another person. If Medina felt threatened by the Priest, he might decide to take matters in his own hands. Making something or someone disappear was a synch. All it took was a moonless and starless night, a walk outside to one of the exterior decks, and a good shove. The ocean's deep would do the rest.

CHAPTER TWENTY-NINE

Running a naval ship and having its crew respond to eminent danger required good order and discipline. Despite the close quarters, a sailor's world revolved around military protocol. The Captain's dinners were made in a private galley by a cook whose sole duty was to serve him. The Officers ate their meals in the Wardroom off fine china and silver cutlery. The *LINCOLN*'s crew received their meals by going through the cafeteria-style chow line. They ate communally on the mess decks. First Class Petty Officers did not warrant a private setting like the officers or chiefs but they improvised. No sailor dared to take their tray and sit in the forward corner of the mess decks where the senior non-khaki sailors carved out their own clique.

The real place where more than dining occurred was in the Chief Petty Officer's Mess. Otherwise known as the 'Goat Locker', the CPO Mess was an informal gathering place for the vessel's senior enlisted sailors. The ship's Chiefs ate, read books, watched TV, and played chess or other games in the only part of the ship allowing them to escape the rest of the crew and the demanding officer cadre to unwind from their jobs demands. Most of the time, the Chiefs huddled over a cup a coffee coordinating the ship's business amongst their fellow Chiefs. It was a place strictly off-limits unless you were formally invited in. On occasion, the CPO Mess invited the Captain for dinner. A Captain who needed the cooperation of the Chiefs to run his ship knew to decline an invitation to the Chief's Mess would be an outright insult. Work would suffer. Productivity would decrease and discipline problems amongst the crew would likely increase. Captain Russell looked forward to his first invitation to dine with the backbone of his crew. Russell liked to engage his sailors as often as possible. Some Commanding Officers preferred to be aloof from his crew to maintain the mystical aura of the ship's CO. Russell was the opposite. He walked the carrier's decks often and expected his officers to do the same. His leadership cadre had to be accessible to the crew. It was the only way they could effectively lead such a large group of people. He made that expectation abundantly clear during a meeting with the Officers and Chiefs after he assumed command.

His change of command was a formal affair. It was a sunny July day and the entire crew wearing their dress white uniforms assembled on the flight deck. According to tradition, the old CO delivered a speech highlighting the vessel's accomplishments during his tenure. The relieving Commanding Officer comments were supposed to be kept short and sweet. Captain Russell observed the tradition. The following day his first action was to address his leadership cadre. It was the venue where he established his command policy and vision. His policies were clear and simple. He expected his officers and chiefs to engage the crew. Proactive leadership and tutelage was the key to preparing the ship to go into harm's way. The only way to achieve that goal was to train, train, and train some more.

He needed his entire crew focused. There was a schedule to keep and a war to fight. A successful deployment depended on successful maintenance, training like they fought, and solid communications efforts.

Being delayed in the shipyard would have cascading affects to the Battle Group schedule. As it turned out, his speeches were not needed. The crew responded magnificently, especially his Chief Petty Officers. So, when the Command Master Chief Petty Officer, the highest-ranking enlisted man on the ship, showed up in his stateroom the day after they got underway with an invitation to dine in the Chiefs Mess, Captain Russell gladly accepted. The dinner would be a formal affair. All were expected to wear their Service Dress Blue uniforms. The CPO galley's Culinary Specialists planned an elaborate dinner of lobster and filet mignon. *LINCOLN*'s Chief Petty Officers compliment consisted of three hundred men and women. Besides the Captain, the invitation requested the CO to bring ten of his officer cadre. It was up to Russell to decide who attended.

Captain Russell and his officers arrived at the door of the Chiefs Mess promptly at two bells during the evening watch. Commanding the mighty warship *ABRAHAM LINCOLN* did not give him, carte blanche. Like her sister services, the United States Navy was steeped in tradition traceable back hundreds of years.

Captain Russell straightened his tunic and rapped heavily upon the aluminum door. Command Master Chief Swanson swung the door open. Behind him stood the entire senior enlisted cadre festooned in their service dress blue uniforms. Yellow, red, and white chevrons decorated their sleeves advertising the years each sailor served the Navy and their nation. Adorning their jackets, the Chiefs displayed a cornucopia of medals and ribbons earned during their service.

The lights were dimmed. The tables were set with blue table clothes, fine china and crystal, and silver cutlery. The meal consisted of five courses. A cold cucumber soup, a fresh vegetable salad, lobster and filet mignon dinner followed by an around-the-world cheese tray and a scrumptious dessert of bananas foster was served. The elegance of the dinner rivaled the finest five star restaurants. It was no small wonder that the White House traditionally selected a Navy contingent to prepare and serve all of the President's private meals and state dinners. The Navy prided themselves upon preparing the best meals for their crews. It was a small consolation of making a warrior leave his family and float about the oceans in total isolation from the world for months on end.

Master Chief Swanson escorted Captain Russell and his officers to the main table. Captain Russell's setting was in the middle of the dining room. He and Chaplain Riley sat together. Russell chose the Executive Officer, Operations Officer, Air Wing Commander, and the ship's senior nuclear Engineer to attend. He left the other four attendees up to the XO who chose the Fire Control Officer, the Main Propulsion Assistant and the Communications officer. The first two officers were Warrant Officers. Both were ex-Chief Petty Officers who applied for and received an Officer Commission. The XO believed it would be good for morale in the Chief's Mess and Wardroom if former enlisted men who ascended the ranks to become officers returned to their roots. The Communications officer was a mid-grade Lieutenant Commander who everyone liked to work with. He was well on his way to commanding a ship of his own. Exposing him to the senior enlisted traditions helped him learn the importance of the enlisted leadership.

The last person the XO extended the invitation to was based on a recommendation from Chaplain Riley. Inviting Father Nguyen to the dinner at first seemed unorthodox. But, he listened to Commander Riley's reasons why the civilian priest was a good choice to attend the nautical banquet. Father Nguyen volunteered to embark the *LINCOLN* to continue the work he started back in Everett. The crew respected the priest who was certainly a morale booster. Of all of the civilians onboard, Father Nguyen was their favorite. He often dined with the crew. He attended the training sessions they endured and he actively reached out to help those in need. Riley wanted to make sure their holy guest learned as much as he could. Plus, it was good sign to invite a civilian crew member to share in the rich tradition. It was good politics.

Chief Sherman watched with great intensity as the Officers sauntered into the Chief's Mess. Father Nguyen alerted him that he was asked to attend. The invitation was a coincidence. Sherman learned after a few days onboard the ship Chief Medina was recently promoted. Medina was a new chief. Sherman's life became a whole lot easier. Trying to find an excuse to place him in a position to monitor a sailor in the engineering department would have been awkward. Now he was a Chief and part of the onboard clique made it much easier. The CPO '*dining-in*' proved a good opportunity to observe Medina's reactions when he learned the priest was onboard the ship.

Getting the priest seated at a table near Medina was not a simple task. He could not just go up to a sailor and pull out his FBI badge. Maintaining his cover was paramount.

Volunteering to help the Senior Chief in charge of the event, Sherman manipulated the table seating charts. He sat Father Nguyen two tables away from Medina's assigned seat. Both sat on the same side so neither would have direct eye contact with the other. Sherman strategically placed himself across from both tables. He wanted to agitate Medina to cue his defense mechanism. A person under stress was more apt to make mistakes. Sherman wanted to up the ante and apply pressure.

The suspect already knew something was afoot from how he quickly disappeared from the church. For years, Medina avoided detection and practiced his evil ways without fear of detection. He went to great lengths covering his tracks and not leaving an evidence trail. Over time, he developed a false sense of security and invincibility. It was time to shake that attitude.

Sherman observed the moment Medina spotted the priest. The killing-sailor was chatting with another Engineering Department Chief and stopped talking in mid-sentence when he noticed the Asian Padre ushered to his seat. The usher walked in front of the clergyman. The two approached Medina's table. Father Nguyen knew exactly where the murderer was located. As he passed Medina's table their eyes met. The priest acknowledged Medina with a head bob and making a sign of the cross in the air over Medina's table.

The killer watched the black-clad catholic pastor stop at his assigned table setting and stand in front of his chair like all the rest of the sailors. Sherman watched both of them. Father Nguyen prepared himself mentally for this moment. If the meeting bothered him, he hid it well. Nguyen casually stood at his table and introduced himself to his new messmates. He purposely chatted up Chief Petty Officer Noble who stood to his left. As he spoke, Nguyen focused his gaze past Chief Noble's shoulder toward Medina.

Medina felt the priest's scrutiny. He no longer had a place to escape. The priest invaded his comfort zone, his sanctuary, and his private world. Medina stared back at the priest. He wore expressions of surprise and utter contempt. He wrung his hands, shifted his weight from one foot to the other, and took multiple sips of water. Sherman was pleased. The tactic worked. They succeeded in throwing the killer off balance.

With Captain Riley seated at the main table, the rest of the CPO Mess's guests were ushered to their seats. Master Chief Swanson struck a ceremonial bell two times. It quieted the mass of sailors. Swanson welcomed the officers to the Chief's home. Captain Russell expressed his gratitude for the invitation. He signaled Chaplain Riley to say grace. Chaps asked his audience to bow their heads and receive God's blessing for the meal and a safe deployment. The Captain was the first to sit down. The rest of the crew followed his lead.

Stewards dressed in white shirts and black pants served the dinner while the mess hall filled with conversational energy. The Chiefs enjoyed the opportunity of having their Captain dine with them. The tradition traced itself back to times of wooden heavily armed ships-of-the-line when the senior leaders invited their Captain to dine with them on the gun deck where they lived and ate their meals. The modern navy embraced technology but it was tradition and good discipline that provided its mortar.

Sherman monitored the nonverbal communication between Medina and Nguyen. A war was being waged between evil and righteousness. The priest ate his meal heartedly and enjoyed the event tremendously. On the other hand, Medina barely touched his meal and only spoke with single word answers to queries from his messmates. Nguyen's presence visibly upset the murderous sailor. So much so, that in the middle of the main course, Medina rose from the table and vectored himself towards the Captain's and Command Master Chief's table.

"Captain Russell, sir?" said Medina.

"Good evening Chief…Chief Medina right?" replied the CO.

"Yes sir, Chief Ignacio Medina, Electricians Mate. Sir, I respectfully request to be dismissed from the mess to relieve the watch?"

It was a routine request the Captain had heard many times over his service in the Navy. "Permission granted Chief Medina. I am sorry you will not be able to enjoy the rest of the party."

"Thank you Captain. I have some junior electricians standing a watch in the engineering plant and I want to check up on them."

Captain Russell turned to the Master Chief Swanson. "Well done Master Chief. That is the type of dedication that will keep our ship ready for operations. Permission granted Chief. Keep up the good work," stated the Captain who returned to extracting the meaty flesh of the lobster from its spiny shell.

Medina turned on his heels and headed for the exit. On his way to the door, the killer's path took him past Father Nguyen's table. As he passed, he placed his hand upon Nguyen's right shoulder and slightly squeezed. Nguyen snapped his head around in response. "Welcome aboard Father," he said. Medina, who did not wait for a reply, continued for the door. Sherman scrutinized the whole affair. If the encounter caused any angst in the padre, he hid it well. He just followed Medina's exit as a zebra watches a lion stalking across a field. For now, the zebra was safe from

264   ERIC W. HERBERT

the predator and could continue its grazing. It was not time for a confrontation.

Father Nguyen looked towards Agent Sherman. The priest licked his finger, raised it in the air and scored a tally on an invisible sheet. Sherman ignored the gesture and went back to talking to the sailor seated across from him. Inwardly he was celebrating. The reaction the priest solicited from Medina was better than he anticipated. Medina was shaken. His mysterious world was finally being fractured. The game suddenly became more dangerous. The FBI agent intuitively recognized the priest's courage. Many men would have fallen apart when confronted with the type of pressure the priest was under. Sherman realized he was dealing with two extraordinary men. One bent on destruction and evil pursuits. The other followed a righteous path. Before they went any further, Sherman wanted to get Amecii's and Dr. Ohms's opinion on how to proceed. They entered a new dimension in the investigation. The wild animal was being cornered in his den and his only defense mechanism was to attack.

CHAPTER THIRTY

Medina stormed down the passageway. His rage blinded him from seeing the sailor carrying an armload of cleaning supplies until he careened into him. The collision caused the fledgling seaman to pitch backward while his cargo flew in the air and scattered about the deck. Medina did not care. He plowed through without bothering to stop. The sailor yelled to the shaken Chief Petty Officer to watch out and swore as he got up and recollected the items.

The killer had to get away from that damned meddling priest. He had visited many priests over the years to describe his ugly deeds. Two never recovered. The burden placed on their minds and souls was always too great. Both voluntarily sequestered themselves to a monastery in upstate New York. Feeling powerless to confront the evil visiting their doorstep, the confessions drove them mad. Others refused him absolution just as Nguyen refused.

How in the hell did he get aboard my ship for the deployment? thought the killer. He could handle him showing up on the naval base, but this was a new problem.

That troublesome priest will not stop meddling unless he is taught a severe lesson not to interfere with God's servant. What was he going to do? raced through his mind. Realizing he did not control himself well after meeting the priest he searched for an isolated place to regroup and calm himself down. *That obstinate holy man made me lose control* was all he could think of. His chest tightened. Anxiety ripped through his body. He craved fresh air. The cool sea air would calm his rage. He slowed his pace through the ship. He ended up in the Super Hornet hanger bay aglow with soft yellow fluorescent lighting. The airplane elevator doors were open ventilating air into the bowels of the massive vessel. His body craved the night air. It was a feeling he had not felt in a long time. Losing his composure was foreign to his mind and body. He vowed not to be caught off guard again. Now that he knew the priest was aboard, he could handle it. Priest or no priest, his relentless pursuit to answer God's call would not be subverted.

Medina lifted the steel handle unlocking the door leading to the ship's exterior decks. He found himself standing on the scaffolding surrounding the carrier's flight deck. Stars riddled the night sky, providing the scantest illumination. The moon had not risen yet so it took a few moments for Medina's eyes to adjust to light's absence. His lungs sucked in the air until his breathing returned to normal. His body needed a release of the pent up energy. Surprisingly, he realized his member was stiff and aching. Touching it made his body shudder uncontrollably. He undid his pants and let them fall to his ankles. He began to madly pump his uncircumcised organ. The pressure was unbearable. What he found ironic was meeting the meddling priest aroused him. All his life he looked towards priests for comfort and acknowledgement of his service to God. It dawned on him the church was too rigid in its ways and never saw his actions as serving God. His sole refuge from the sorrows of his life was no better than living with his tortuous tramp of a mother and the filth she serviced. Medina stroked as he dribbled spit into his palm to lubricate himself. The sensation made him stroke his shaft harder and faster. He ejaculated his evil seed violently over the railing into the sea. His body stood motionless with the sea spraying light salt mist over his shaking torso.

If the church wanted an enemy, the church has found one. If Nguyen wants to meddle; then he'll pay for his interference. Medina sensed a stir in his world. He first felt it in Seattle while he confessed his sins to Nguyen. There was no way the priest could violate the confessional without compromising his vows. But something was amiss. Abandoning the van was a necessary precaution. When he exited the church that morning, Medina knew he could not return the way he came. He could not see anything out of the ordinary at the church or in the street. All he knew was he felt like he was being watched. Maybe it was the way the construction worker in the church looked at him. Now, mysteriously, the man he confessed his sins to magically appeared onboard the aircraft carrier.

Things were set back to normal in Medina's mind. In twenty days the ship planned to visit Thailand. More than enough time to plan. This time he would have a most attentive audience to witness his Abrahamic sacrifice to God. Then he would disappear forever. Something inside him told him it was time to do so.

CHAPTER THIRTY-ONE

The Chief's Dining-In ended promptly at four bells or eight PM. All attending were in high spirits and sad to see it end. But, work on a naval ship never ceases. The officers migrated to their staterooms to prepare for the late evening watches. Chiefs not on duty changed into their working uniforms and assisted the mess attendants in cleaning the dining area. In an hour's time, you could not tell a formal gathering was held in the senior enlisted dining facility. It was reformed back to the sterile cafeteria it was before.

The Captain went to the bridge to check the ship's position and the Battle Group's stationing. The voyage across the Pacific Ocean to the Indian Ocean took seven days traveling at fifteen knots. The battle group, all except the *USS CHANCERLORSVILLE*, which was the carrier's shotgun escort, steamed silently towards Asia while the carrier and Aegis cruiser made a brief stop in Pearl Harbor. The Battle Group Commander, Admiral Shaw wanted to discuss the flotilla's operations with the Commander of the Pacific Fleet. Plus, three days in Honolulu was a good respite for a crew who worked tirelessly for the last three months. Once they departed the Hawaiian Isles, Captain Russell estimated their arrival into Phuket, Thailand would take seventeen to twenty days depending on if the seas cooperate.

Before entering the Afghanistan and Iraqi operational theatre, Admiral Shaw wanted to show the flag. A bit of gunboat diplomacy to keep China, North Korea, Iran, Syria, and Russia on their toes. He scheduled the armada's ships to visit numerous ports. The *USS HOPPER*, an Aegis Destroyer, was headed to Australia. Two other combatants, the *USS LAKE ERIE* and *USS*

RUSSELL, Aegis ships equipped with Ballistic Missile Defense technology sailed for Cambodia. Captain Russell thought it ironic a ship named after his great-grandfather made up part of the battle group protecting his ship. The family naval legacy was immortal.

The newest addition to the United States Navy, the *USS FREEDOM*, a Littoral Combat Ship or LCS, steamed towards the Philippine Archipelago. The *USS SAN ANTONIO*'s Captain, a new amphibious warship, wanted to take his crew of sailors and marines to Japan. The fourth of the San Antonio class ships, the *USS INCHON*, steamed for South Korea. The final ship, the *USS WAYNE E. MEYERS*, otherwise known as TFA or the "The-Father-of-Aegis", set her course for China.

The Navy was unfurling America's flag far and wide. The Secretary of the Navy who received his guidance directly from the President cleared all of the port visits. Unlike other Democratic Presidents who sat in the oval office, President Talbert wanted to use his military to make sure the world still saw America ruling the world's vast high seas. He preferred non-confrontational negotiations and friendly relations with other sovereign nations, but he was also a realist. Talbert was the only Democratic President since FDR to boost spending on military hardware and infrastructure instead of slashing and burning through its budget. He rightly surmised that to achieve American goals in peacetime it had better be backed up with a big punch. Otherwise, his legitimacy amongst America's rivals would diminish. So, he took a special interest in where and how the military deployed around the world.

Admiral Shaw's Battle Group deployment was the President's first in his tenure. So, he wanted to send a message throughout the world that he commanded the most technologically advanced and capable military ever amassed. The visits were tended to be peaceful. Formal receptions and visits by foreign delegations onboard the ships were tightly choreographed. State Department officials paved the way for the ship's arrival into China and Cambodia. Sending the rest of the ships to visit American allies in the Philippines, Australia, Japan, and South Korea sent an equally powerful message. The Pacific Rim was important to America. She would protect her allies in the time of need. Plus, going to China and Cambodia spread American good will by strengthening the tender ties between the nations.

Sherman debriefed Catherine on the evening's activities and how Medina reacted to the priest's presence. They hit a weak spot in the suspect's armor. Now, they needed to continue to jab at until he made a mistake. Catherine relayed the information ashore. Dr. Ohm's received the information in his normal fashion. He analyzed both sides of the equation. They were playing a dangerous game by including an untrained and unprepared civilian. Those in the FBI had seen their fair share of trauma and ugliness. Father Nguyen, on the other hand was a gentle and compassionate man who was putting himself in front of a highly volatile criminal. Anything could happen if they didn't take the necessary precautions. Ohms still beat himself up for the mistakes his team made in Seattle when Medina escaped their surveillance. That error would not be made again. On the flip side, Ohms recognized the future reward outweighed the risk. Too many innocent people suffered a brutal and dismal death at the hands of Butcher Bill. Father Nguyen understood the risks he took. The murderer must be stopped at all cost. If placing the priest into danger helped silence Medina's evil rampage and if he got hurt in the process, so be it. God was directing his hand. He refused to shirk his destiny.

LINCOLN navigated the Pearl Harbor channel at dawn. It slowly twisted and turned its massive hulk through the narrow channel. Tugboats stood off the port and starboard sides to insure she didn't venture onto the coral laden bottom. LINCOLN's and CHANCELORVILLE'S crew smartly manned the ship's rails dressed in their best blue uniforms. They stood rigidly at attention ready to pass the only battleship still on the Navy's active commission roster. The *USS ARIZONA*, sunk with all hands onboard during the Japanese surprise attack on 7 December 1941, was a reminder of war's reality. Every ship passing the grim memorial rendered honors to the watery grave and those encased in her watery steel tomb.

A whistle sounded over the ship's 1MC general announcing circuit. Thousands of hand salutes were presented in unison. Two more whistle blasts ordered the salutes to be dropped. A third blast told the crew to carry on with their duties.

The ships glided into their moorings against the piers. Cranes quickly installed the steps and steel planking connecting the vessels to land. Sailors with approved leave chits and hotel reservations in Waikiki raced down the stairs for cabs waiting to take them to the beach, a cold Mai Tai, surfing, and pretty young women strutting around in bikinis.

Catherine joined the mob departing the carrier. She waved to her star philosophy student. Sherman smiled, returned her wave, but stayed onboard. He wanted to keep tabs on Medina and Father Nguyen.

Prior to their arrival at Pearl Harbor, Ohms established surveillance teams to follow their suspect wherever he went. Sherman discovered Chief Petty Officer Medina requested and was granted three days leave. His leave papers showed he had a reservation at a hotel on the island's windward side near Diamond Head Crater. Sherman and Amecii left the surveillance to the FBI team. He and Catherine were scheduled to meet Dr. Ohms, Hendricks, Raphael, and the Colby twins to strategize in a secluded bungalow resort hotel on the North Shore of the island.

The FBI had already installed listening devices and surveillance cameras in Medina's hotel room. Ohms enlisted the CIA and NSA to assist again. This time, he accepted their offer to use unmanned aerial vehicles. Two were at his disposal. Each UAV carried enough fuel for twelve uninterrupted hours of flight. CIA civilians established control high in the mountains of Oahu. Oahu was part jungle and part desert. They did not want to lose control of the pilotless drones if they had to dip down into the island's jungle valleys. Sherman was to alert Ohms when Medina left the *LINCOLN*. The UAVs would scramble and be on station to commence surveillance once Medina departed.

Eight teams of three people stood at the ready to follow by car or on foot. If Medina struck out on foot somewhere, the third person in the car was designated to follow. Whoever it was, he or she had to be able to run long distances and have strong stamina. Ohms vowed not to lose the suspect again. Especially since he has was in new killing grounds.

Sherman stood in the hanger bay pretending to work on a yellow tractor used to maneuver airplanes around the deck. He watched Father Nguyen standing near the end of the brow. Next to the priest stood a medical corpsman passing out plastic bags containing a small tube of sunscreen, aspirin for hangovers, and condoms to protect the sailors from sexually transmitted disease.

Father Nguyen passed out business cards with the ship's telephone numbers printed on one side and a prayer for their safety on the other. Sherman recognized the civilian clergyman enjoyed the task. He smiled and blessed each crew member as they passed his station. He had found a new flock to shepherd. When he and Sherman met before the Chief's dining in, it was Father Nguyen's idea to stand at the brow. The FBI agent had told the priest that Medina was taking leave when they reached Hawaii. He did not tell him where he was staying. The decision was made by Catherine not to allow Nguyen to pursue Medina on leave. The FBI had enough surveillance to watch his movements. Sherman readily agreed. Poking the evil bear onboard the ship was one thing. Taunting the murderer too much could spell disaster. Thus, the idea came to Nguyen to make sure Medina came into contact with him right before he left. Sherman and Amecii wanted Medina agitated before he left the ship. Stirring the pot might cause him to be reckless and remiss in covering his tracks.

Satchel in hand, Butcher Bill entered the far side of the ship's hanger bay. Sherman saw him first. He picked up a hammer and struck a forklift's steel forks three times. Everyone looked towards his direction but paid it no mind. He was a sailor working on his gear. Business as usual. Work on a navy ship never ended. However, to Father Nguyen, it was a prearranged warning from Sherman to him. It gave him time to steel himself for his next encounter with the demonic sailor. The priest turned towards Medina and intently watched him make his way towards the brow. Medina wasn't fazed by Father Nguyen's presence. Medina collected his "goodie bag" from the corpsman and stopped in front of the devout Christian.

"Good morning Father."

"Good morning Chief Medina. By the bag in your hand, I surmise you are taking a little time off on this most gorgeous of God's islands."

"Yes, I am. I need some time to relax and some time to release some pent up energy. I suggest you be very careful if you visit the city. At night, Honolulu can be as dangerous as any other big city," said Medina with a wink of an eye.

The gesture slapped Nguyen in the face. Medina was warning him to avoid his path. The warning came in loud and clear to Father Nguyen. It did not matter anyway. He had no intentions to birddog Medina. The FBI took care of that.

Nguyen handed Medina the emergency business card and made the sign of the cross over Butcher Bill. "May God bless you and shed his light upon you. May you and *all* those around you be safe and free from evil spirits," came the blessing.

A menacing grin emerged on his face but Medina did not engage the clergyman any longer. He crossed himself, saluted the Officer-of-the-Deck, and requested permission to go ashore. The Officer granted his request and watched him stroll off the ship.

The corpsman watched the short exchange between the two men. "I don't like Chief Medina, Father," he said. "He's an odd sort. Rarely does he speak to anyone except about work. I don't believe he is close to anyone on the ship. If you wanted to visualize a person being a lone wolf, that sailor is the epitome."

If you only knew the breadth of your observation son thought the priest.

Sherman observed the short conversation. He pressed the number two on his cell phone, listened to it ring until the other end answered the call. One word came from his mouth. "Execute," he stated.

"Roger," replied the unseen recipient. No further communication was needed. Butcher Bill's twenty-four hour surveillance commenced.

CHAPTER THIRTY-TWO

Agent Sherman left the ship and picked up the Jeep Wrangler Ohms arranged for him. Before he left, he and Father Nguyen covered the priest's plans. He passed the surveillance baton of the evil menace to Ohm's crew. Medina could not make a move without someone watching him. Sherman wanted the priest to enjoy Hawaii as much as he could, given the present circumstances. The pressure on Father Nguyen was about to rise. Sherman knew how valuable a respite to prepare oneself and to steal his nerves for a mission could take. Even for a seasoned trained undercover agent like himself. For a pilgrim like Father Nguyen he could only hypothesis on the level of stress placed upon the man's nerves and lean shoulders. He suggested Nguyen go snorkeling in Hanauma Bay to swim with the turtles, visit a pineapple plantation, or lounge on the beach at Waikiki. Anything to keep the man's mind occupied on something besides Butcher Bill.

As Sherman was rapidly discovering, the steely-eyed priest beat to his own drummer. Nguyen had his own agenda. There was a monastery located deep in the North Shore's jungle. It opened once a year for pilgrims to worship a sliver of the cross Christ was nailed to. Otherwise, the monastery shut its doors to everyone except to priests, monks, and nuns. He planned to meditate and seek the Lord's guidance amongst the monastery's seclusion and comfortable surroundings. Nguyen would enjoy Hawaii another time when he could relax. For now, he needed spiritual comfort and a quiet place to reflect on his task. There was too much at stake for him to go and play. An evil presence was roaming the Earth and he had to recharge to continue the fight.

The Jeep's blue digital dashboard clock displayed ten thirty in the morning. Ohms scheduled a team meeting at four in the afternoon at a North Shore resort not far from where Father Nguyen took his retreat. A team meeting in the afternoon gave Sherman and Amecii a bit of time to unwind, eat, and prepare their thoughts. They knew Medina the best. Ohms wanted them to share their knowledge with the team so they could progress on his behavioral profile. Ohms seriously doubted Medina would make any type of aggressive move during the day. If he wanted to kidnap another victim for sacrifice, Ohms believed Medina needed to scope out his surroundings to pick a target. That would take time. The surveillance team would tip them off if he started acting quirky.

Sherman easily found the resort. It was off highway H-1, but set back a mile into horse country along the beach down a narrow paved road. The resort's no-vacancy sign was subtly lit at the entranceway. Ohms had rented all thirty bungalows for seven days. It was not an easy task. Lodging for the resort's current guests had to be found and found quickly. Most were transferred to the Turtle Bay Resort a few miles south. Some accepted accommodations at the Hilton Hawaiian Village, the Sheraton, and Marriott hotels located on Waikiki Beach. Two customers utterly refused until an FBI agent showed up at their homes in Wisconsin and Mississippi. After that, there weren't any more problems.

Three helicopters sat idle in the fields. The pilots napped under palm trees.

Sherman checked in and showered the ship stink off his body. Donning blue cargo pants, a white t-shirt, and running shoes, he headed to Catherine's bungalow to discuss the team's overall progress. The bungalows stood alone with twenty yards between each building. People came to the resort to escape and to reinvigorate their love lives. The landscaping relaxed the mind and rekindled the spirit. The atmosphere soothed Sherman. Being on edge all the time could cause irreparable harm. Taking a bit of time, even if it was for a few hours helped him maintain his sanity.

Catherine's cabin stood a hundred yards away from his. Reaching it, he gently tapped on the door. The door opened and Sherman's heart skipped a beat. She stood in complete dichotomy of who Sherman thought she was. Her deep auburn red hair flowed across her bare shoulders. She wore a white strapless sundress hugging her breasts and thighs. White bamboo sandals adorned her feet. A white and yellow sweet plumeria flower was gently tucked behind her left ear. Without a word, Catherine took his hand, tugged slightly to make him enter, and closed the door. Soft kisses came one after another upon Sherman's face and neck. He had wanted this ever since he saw her. His arms surrounded her thin torso and pressed her into his chest. Their mouths majestically met and explored each other's panting breath. Catherine moaned softly and squeezed him closer to her. He pressed into her causing a wave of euphoria throughout his mind. The two agents kissed hungrily while Catherine's hands explored Sherman's muscular body as he caressed the soft skin on her shoulders. Continuing to stroke Catherine, Sherman peeled the dress down, exposing her sweetness. Her nipples stuck out and begged to be kissed. Sherman kneeled down and firmly kissed her creamy breasts. Catherine ran her fingers through his hair in ecstasy. He continued kissing her torso while he removed the rest of her dress. She applied pressure upon his head and pushed his head into the crease between her legs. Her body shuddered as soon as he licked her with his wet tongue. Instinctively, Catherine parted her legs inviting him even further. A warm Hawaiian easterly breeze blowing through the bungalow's open windows engulfed the lovers. Sherman picked her up and carried her to bed. Stripping down, he stood throbbing in front of her. Reaching for it, she slowly scrapped her finger nails down its length. Grasping his firm buttocks, she pulled his member into her mouth. She engulfed him running her tongue down the purple shaft's sides. What she really wanted was for her man to join with her. Pulling him down on top of her, she wrapped her legs around him. Sherman easily slid into Catherine's hairless tropical avenue of euphoria. The two madly and softly hugged and shared each other over and over. Their hands, mouth, and feet explored each other with unbridled love and desire. Time stood still as they swayed back and forth upon each other. Closure came simultaneously. Catherine's locked her arms around his body, digging her nails deep into his back as he erupted deep inside her. The two lay in each other's arms snuggling and kissing. Not a word was spoken between the two during the entire affair. None was needed. Sherman looked down into her green eyes and told he loved her. She smiled and whispered she loved him too. Sherman fantasized about this moment often since the time he realized he loved Catherine. The fantasies did not compare to the love he just shared with his red haired beauty. He knew she felt the same about him. Only people in true love shared the type of blissful passion they just relished.

CHAPTER THIRTY-THREE

LINCOLN headed back to sea on the morning of September 11. Admiral Cable chose to leave on nine-eleven for symbolic and political reasons. American aircraft carriers movements were always of interest to other countries. The event was covered in the Honolulu Star. The Taliban, Hezbollah, al Qaeda, and their rogue sponsors had a sophisticated spy network established. He wanted the terrorists on the other side of the world to know he was coming for them to celebrate on his own terms the anniversary of the attack on New York City that shamelessly killed hundreds of innocent civilians. It was a small but powerful gesture.

LINCOLN's and *CHANCELORVILLE*'s crews were in good spirits. Having a few days to play in Hawaii recharged their spirits. The crew liked leaving on 9/11. They shared their Admiral's sentiments. The bombs they intended to drop were for those responsible for killing their friends, family members, and fellow countrymen. It was time for more retribution. Just like the Japanese learned after their shameless attack on Pearl Harbor in December 1941, the Muslim extremists had awoken a sleeping giant. The giant was hell bent on seeking out and destroying the hornets in their nest.

Sherman still reeled from the last three days with Catherine. They rendezvoused as much as they could during the time ashore with their secretive love increasing daily.

The surveillance team observed Medina the entire time. Predominantly, he did little except sit on the beach and read. He occasionally went out to eat but that was it. His hotel phones and internet connections were bugged, but recorded little. The murderous tourist used the phone in his room a single time to order his breakfast from room service. So, Catherine and Sherman had a lot of time to explore each other's personalities far away from the case.

The entire team met on three separate occasions. Ohms wanted the priest to continue making passive contact with Medina. However, he wanted either Sherman or Amecii present each time he did. The priest needed their protection. Some serial killers lived in strict adherence to their own established rules; however, they could also be insanely unpredictable when threatened. The next stop for the aircraft carrier was Phuket, Thailand. The team would be on the ground the week prior. Medina had prowled this turf before. Ohms believed Thailand was where Medina would strike. Another chance was not available for at least two more months while the carrier was on station conducting operations. The team knew the pot was starting to boil and it needed to release its steam.

Hendricks and Raphael arrived in Thailand first. They established their headquarters in the Grand Royal hotel. It sat atop the tallest hill overlooking Phuket beach. The Grand Royal was recently renovated just like the rest of Phuket after the Tsunami that ripped through the tourist area, devastating the economy for two years. Signs of economic recovery were finally sprouting and taking root.

Phuket's beaches were made of soft sand. Palm trees peppered the landscape and flowed back and forth in tune with the gentle shore breezes. The open air shops and restaurants serving fresh seafood were once again littered with American, Asian, and European tourists. Phuket was known for its beautiful seaside resort. The other draw was its cheap and liberal sex trade. The streets behind the city's main thoroughfares were jammed with strip clubs and brothels. Any fetish anyone wanted tickled was made available for a small price. Multiple women, domination, sadist acts, young boys, or pre-pubescent girls were constants on the sexual menu for a few American dollars or Euros. If you could fantasize it and you had money, then you could get it in Phuket. The girls and boys peddling their bodies were illiterate kids sold to the pimps by their destitute parents. Many were imported from Malaysia or other third world Asian countries. The sex trade had always been part of the Thai culture. It was considered the norm.

Hendricks and Raphael surveyed the city. Surveillance wise, keeping close tabs on Butcher Bill would prove difficult. There were so many back alleys or unseen doors a person could duck into. Hopefully, Ohms would receive permission from the Thai government to fly his UAVs in Thai airspace. If the request was rejected, the team would react on the fly. Only a limited amount of surveillance cameras were available. Wiring the entire city proved impossible and impractical. They had no idea where Medina would head once he left the ship. The team would have to rely on good-old-fashion shoe leather surveillance by tailing him everywhere he went. Hendricks called Ohms and told him they needed more men. He agreed. How much he could get was not guaranteed. The investigation still needed to balance its efforts against its operational security desires. Hendricks and Raphael expressed their concern over how they intended to keep Butcher Bill under their watchful eye. He sensed their presence once. If they overloaded the stake out, Bill might catch whiff of the cops and disappear altogether. The senseless brutality had to end here.

LINCOLN made good speed. With Pearl Harbor behind them, Russell kept the ship busy training. They practiced launching alert aircraft with less than ten minutes' notice. Countless fire drills, man overboard drills, quick draw gunnery exercises, and ship maneuvering operations were held. No notice emergency operations drills were executed at night forcing his sailors from their slumber to react flawlessly and without hesitation. He wanted a complete accounting of the ship's crew when the alert came announcing that a man fell overboard.

A ship the size of his took continuous practice to get all of the crew to respond promptly. Their first attempt when the ship came out of the shipyard took the crew forty minutes to determine who the staged missing sailor was. The best-recorded time they had in mustering the crew was twenty three minutes and sixteen seconds. Roughly surpassing his threshold by more than a minute Captain Russell was satisfied with the results and proud of his crew. By the time his ship reached Thailand, Russell demanded the time be shaved by eight minutes. It was a tall order to ask but he asked nonetheless.

Flight deck and aircraft maintenance operations were suspended for the last two days of the journey. The half of each was spent sounding the alarm that a sailor was lost at sea. After seven grueling attempts, the Captain settled for achieving sixteen minutes and four seconds. The rest of the day concentrated on refining the crew's ability to fight fires, solve equipment failure problems, and practicing first aid. No rest was given during the evening. The night watches were perfect opportunities for the vessel's engineers running the propulsion plant to practice scramming the nuclear reactors, restoring electrical power, responding to propulsion losses and other drills associated with failures to critical pieces of ship's equipment.

Working in the deck department, Sherman kept extremely busy with the man overboard drills. It was his division's responsibility for getting a helicopter launched with the rescue swimmer embarked onboard. Russell wanted the helo launched within ten minutes of the alarm being sounded. The order took a lot of practice and coordination, but; the deck hands and aviators exceeded his expectation on two occasions.

Father Nguyen never experienced this type of environment before. The vessel was always busy. It worked a twenty four hour seven days a week schedule. Every minute of every day was accounted for and used. It amazed him how much energy was cocooned aboard the ship. The busy pace also worried the priest. With so much going on, Agent Sherman was unable to help Nguyen plan his overt meetings with Medina. He wanted

Medina on edge as much as the FBI agents did. The pressure on the killer required sustainment. If Medina would not listen to reason, he wanted him to feel God's presence emanating from Nguyen. The murderer needed to understand the church would never forgive him unless he was truly repentant, surrendered to the legal authorities, and confessed his sins openly before God and man.

Nguyen enjoyed exploring the aircraft carrier. It was a modern day mechanical labyrinth. Luckily, someone taught him how to read a compartment's bulls-eye. Painted on all of the ship's bulkheads were pea green fluorescent squares with black letters. Spray painted over the luminescent square lie a series of three numbers. The first number represented the deck you stood upon. The second value told a person what the nearest longitudinal frame was. The third and final number was either an even or odd number. If it was odd, you were on the starboard side. An even number represented being located on the port side of the ship. As long as you had that information, you could find your way anywhere onboard.

The priest was headed to space number 12-356-6, the main engineering control room. The sailors called it Engineering Control Central. ECC for short. The ship's nuclear reactors, lubrication equipment, main engines, propeller shafts, steering equipment, electrical generators, fuel systems, air conditioning, and fluid systems were controlled remotely from ECC. Nguyen was excited about his tour. Since arriving onboard, he explored many areas of the massive warship. Sailors loved to talk about what they did and the priest liked to listen to them. He liked people embracing what they did for a living. It was one of the many things making them who they were. Arranging tours was always easy too. He predominantly took his meals on the mess decks to eat with the crew. During the meals, he chatted with the sailors he dined with. By the end of the meal, he would have a tour of where they spent their long at-sea hours. In the last two weeks, he visited the ship's massive bridge where the Officer-of-the-Deck navigated the ship from, the aircraft control tower coordinating aircraft movement and plane launches on the flight deck, the long hangers where the airplanes were stored, the ammunition magazines where bombs and missiles were stockpiled, and the Combat Information Center where the ship's external communications, radars, and defensive weapons were operated from. Chief Sherman took him to the flight deck and explained the catapult launching mechanism. It was a steam operated contraption. The nuclear reactors boiled water and siphoned off high pressure steam. The steam traveled through pipes and filled massive tanks under great pressure. With an airplane connected to a thick wire rope at the landing gear wheel, the pressure was released. The immense force behind the pressure's release shot the airplane into the air.

Father Nguyen discussed with Sherman the tour of the engineering spaces the ship's Engineer offered him. Commander White, a naval nuclear engineer for over eighteen years, invited him deep into the bowels of the ship when they met at the CPO dining in. The priest expressed great interest and enthusiastically accepted the offer. However, the last few days of drills, drills, and more drills prevented White from fulfilling his invitation. But, the drills were over for now and Nguyen jumped at the chance. There was another reason he wanted to take the tour when he did. Precisely from 1130 to 1630 hours, Chief Medina was scheduled to stand watch monitoring the ship's electrical generators and distribution centers. It was a perfect time to impart more pressure upon the demonic sailor. Nguyen arrived promptly in ECC at 1230 as Commander White had suggested. Waiting an hour after the watch turned over allowed the sailors to settle in and finish any work needing to be accomplished at the beginning of their watch.

Commander White stood speaking with the Engineer-of-the-Watch explaining what he wanted accomplished for the rest of the day. Father Nguyen entered the control room and was welcomed by a female sailor sitting in front of a bank of computer screens. She turned her attention to him and said, "Good afternoon sir, what brings you down into the land of pipe and pumps?"

"Good afternoon Petty Officer Zuwalski," replied the priest after reading the nametag stitched into her blue flame retardant coveralls. "Commander White promised me a tour of the Engineering spaces today. This is quite an impressive set up you have here young lady."

"It is a marvel of technology. Do you want to see?" the short blond girl asked.

Nguyen cast a glance towards Commander White. He was still preoccupied with his work.

"That would be lovely. My name is Father Francis Nguyen and I'm a visiting priest here to help your shipmates while we're on deployment," he said extending his hand in friendship. He used that standard introduction each time he met a new sailor onboard the floating haze gray metallic city.

Shaking the priest's hand, Petty Officer Zuwalski continued the conversation. "Welcome aboard Father. This may be a big ship but it is not. The entire crew knows who you are. Everyone likes you. Word travels fast especially when you do something good for a shipmate. It travels twice as fast if you do the opposite. What you did for Fireman Baker was fantastic. He has been a happy camper ever since. We thought he was a real slacker when he first arrived. Come to find out, he carried the weight of the entire world upon his shoulders and didn't know how to deal with it. Until you came along."

He remembered Fireman Baker. It was the case Riley suggested he cut his teeth on when he first volunteered his services. Baker had a huge dilemma. He was a new addition to the ship's crew. He was only nineteen years old when he joined the Navy to support his pregnant wife. The two did not expect to have a child so soon; but, like many youngsters, they were more enthralled with exploring their sexual universes than contemplating the consequences of their carnal desires. They had dated since their high school junior year. Then, his girlfriend, Annette, told him she missed her period and thought she was pregnant. Sure enough, the doctor confirmed her suspicion.

Both kids had Catholic roots. Baker's Father said he had to step up like a man and assume his responsibilities. Abortion was out of the question. Six weeks later, the kids became Annette and Roger Baker in a very hasty small church ceremony.

Unskilled, unprepared, and scared to death, Baker joined the Navy for a paycheck, a roof over his young family's head, and health insurance. After finishing eight weeks of boot-camp, he and Annette found themselves two thousand miles from home with little money in their pocket. They moved into a one-bedroom apartment provided by the Naval Station housing office. Baker started going to sea and his wife went through a lot of depression from being alone. The strain took its toll. They started to bicker and despise each other. Baker was at a loss on how to help his new bride with a baby coming soon. Chaplain Riley learned of the boy's plight during a command in-processing interview mandatory for all new arrivals. Since the couple was Catholic, Riley figured it would be a good case for Father Nguyen to work on. That is exactly what the volunteer priest did. He arranged for the young husband and wife to visit him at his church. He enrolled them in marriage classes, helped them find a good doctor for Annette, and taught them how to communicate. In the end, Baker's work performance turned around, Annette established friends through the ship's family network, and they gave birth to a healthy young boy who they named Francis.

Father Nguyen felt as proud as the newborn's parents when he baptized the child prior to getting underway. He helped them from a state of despair to one they could handle. Now, Annette was back at her parent's house in Texas while Fireman Baker finished the deployment. As sailors do, they talk about their accomplishments and troubles freely with their shipmates. Word spread throughout the ship about the assistance Father Nguyen provided. From that point forward, he was part of the *LINCOLN*'s crew regardless of what uniform he wore.

"All in a day's work. You are right; Baker needed a leg to stand on. The water was rising quickly over his head. Now, he, his wife, and little baby Francis are doing great." Nguyen shifted the subject, "So, what do you have here?" he inquired about the bank of controls and computer screens in front of the young engineer.

"Sit down Father, I'll explain everything to you," she said.

The two spent a half hour discussing how the computer station controlled the nuclear power plant's sophisticated machinery. Each piece of equipment was backed by a redundant piece of machinery in case of failure. Riley sat watching Petty Officer Zulwalski from his office. He sauntered over realizing she was almost finished with her explanations.

"Petty Officer Zulwalski is one of the best engineers we have onboard," he said. "I'm glad you found something to keep you occupied while I finished some work. Many apologies for my tardiness" he told the priest. "Shall we walk around the plant to give you an even better impression about what we do down here?"

"If your entire group is made up of people like Ms. Zulwalski, you will never have a problem," observed the clergyman. "Yes, I am eager to start our tour. Now that I know how your power plant is controlled I am anxious to see the equipment itself."

"Great, let's get moving then. Did you bring your holy water like I asked?" inquired the Engineer. Commander Riley wanted Father Nguyen to bless his equipment. No matter how educated they could be sailors were a superstitious lot. If there was a way to ward off trouble, they welcomed it. Even if it meant believing in luck, omens, and spirits.

The two stuffed ear plugs into their ears to protect their hearing from the high pitched sounds the machinery made and headed into the power plant. Riley showed him the nuclear reactors and how the uranium rods heated the water surrounding them to generate steam. The steam was funneled into massive turbines turning the ship's shafts and propellers. Nguyen stopped every so often, sprinkling holy water on the machinery and whispering prayers as he went along.

Commander White continued the tour. Leaving the main prolusion spaces, he directed them to where the ship's electrical generators and switchboards were kept. The door he entered had large yellow lightning bolts painted on it. The two men stepped inside the massive space with White explaining how the steam generated by the nuclear power plant turned even more turbines producing thousands of kilowatts of power. During a national crisis, the electrical generators could power a small city. Finishing the tour of the equipment, White escorted the priest towards the Electrician-of-the-Watches space. There they found Chief Medina logging information into the ship's engineering computer.

Butcher Bill turned to see who entered the electrical control room. Spotting Father Nguyen, a menacing frown replaced the warm smile he initially wore.

It's that damn meddling priest again, thought Medina.

Commander White sensed the tension between the two men. He tried to uplift the mood.

"Chief, this is Father Nguyen. He is a civilian priest who volunteered for the deployment. I am showing him around the plant. Can you take some time and explain what you and your team of electricians do?"

"Yes, sir. Not a problem. I know you are a busy man. I can bring the good Father to ECC after I am done. That way, you're not locked down hearing stuff about the electrical plant that you already know."

"Capital idea," exclaimed White who was already contemplating how to occupy the time that was just liberated from his imposing schedule without realizing the true danger he thrust the priest into. "Father, I hope you enjoyed your tour. This is where I leave you in the capable hands of Chief Medina." After shaking hands, Commander White zipped out the Electrical Distribution Center heading back to his office to grind out some paperwork. White was oblivious he was leaving a defenseless sheep in the clutches of a hungry wolf.

Butcher Bill stood two yards away from him. Anger radiated from his cold eyes. Fear rippled through Father Nguyen's body. His body hair stood on end. A cold sweat engulfed him. They were not in the sanctity of the church anymore. Nor were they surrounded by a group of people. Here they were face to face and alone for the first time outside of the confessional. Medina's eyes ripped holes into his soul. Father Nguyen had never felt fear like this before. Less than six feet away breathed the most evil force he had ever encountered.

"Welcome to my other sanctuary Priest," whispered Medina. "I used to find comforting solace at church until you decided to break your vows. Now you are nothing but a man dressed in cheap black cloth. You should be ashamed of yourself."

Nguyen's body prodded him to flee from the angry beast's talons. Something compelled him to stay. He wanted to escape. He wanted to put as much distance between he and Median as humanly and as quickly his feet could carry him. Another force kept him there. The same force calmed his thoughts. Nguyen shut his eyes, drew in and expelled three large breathes. The sweating stopped. He relaxed as quickly as he had developed the urge to flee.

"I am not ashamed of anything Chief Medina," spoke the priest with a clear strong voice. "I have not broken my vows nor do I ever intend to. I love my God and will do his bidding. However, unlike you, what God asks me to perform is truly from his hand. Not like the perverted rationalization you use for the unholy acts committed in his name at your hand."

The words stung Medina. The priest did not waiver. He expected the man to fear for his life as he certainly well should. The only thoughts going through Medina's mind were how to murder Nguyen without making it appear hostile and intentional. There were many ways he could accomplish it. Fatal accidents happened all the time on navy ships. A sailor could stumble on a ladder, fall, and break his neck. He could electrocute the priest to death. The navy invested a great deal in educating the sailors about the dangers of electrical shock. The monthly navy safety newsletter always told a tragic tale about how a careless seaman was electrocuted because of his negligence to follow electrical safety protocol. A person could have a tool dropped on his head striking him dead. It was why when men working aloft had their tools attached to a lanyard and tethered to their body. The options were limitless. Sailors worked and lived in a highly dangerous industrial environment seven days a week, three hundred and sixty five days a year. Extraordinary precautions were taken, but, nevertheless, industrial accidents still occurred. The only problem was how Butcher Bill could take action, when, and by what method. Medina needed a few minutes to think it through.

"You should have stayed in Seattle and tended to your flock Father. You are the only one who knows of my sacrifices to our Lord. I have told many other priests things similar to those I have confessed to you, Father. Never had any of them done anything as stupid as you refusing me absolution and lecturing me that my soul was going to hell if I did not stop and repent. I even drove a couple of your peers crazy with the tales of my deeds. They were too weak to handle my confessions. They deserved their madness. They were not worthy to serve our Lord like I do. It took a great deal of courage for you to come onboard this ship. I think you already worked it out in your thoughts and prayers that there was a very high potential for your never returning home."

The ruthless killer continued. "I do respect you though Padre. You are placing trust in God to protect and deliver you from evil. He won't, you know? People keep expecting him to intervene and to squash the miseries that plague the Earth. God granted man free will; therefore, it is up to man to determine his own destiny.

Yes, he works in mysterious ways. I am proof of that concept. I have been charged by our Maker to wage a silent war against sin."

"There lays the problem my son," Nguyen said. "Your conception of our Lord is warped. It forces you to commit horrible, horrible atrocities upon your brothers and sisters. God performs miracles every day. A sickly child is rescued from abusive parents by a neighbor. An elderly person goes and lives with her children instead of being left to age and die alone and unhappy. A drug addict walks into a homeless shelter and asks and receives help to overcome his weaknesses. You just need to look around you to find goodness. However, instead of goodness that I see now, I see only the devil using you as his puppet."

Nguyen had to keep him talking and philosophizing. The longer he could keep him talking, the better chance someone might appear so he can escape the loathsome beast's lair.

"Devil's work, huh! All those people I dealt with deserved what they got. The women were all sluts who gave their sex freely to whoever wanted it. The men were the worst of all. They sought out disease-infected crack whores to fuel their addictions and perverse desires. Where were your miracle workers then?"

"Thus we come to the central problem Ignacio. You are a hypocrite who kills and tortures people for no other reason than thinking you are God's instrument. It is the devil who has captured your soul, not God. When you were a young boy, God intervened and saved you once. Then you turned away from him many years ago. What happened then to make you seek revenge for the treatment your mother gave you?" inquired Nguyen.

"What right do you have to preach to me about who is God's instrument and who is not. Just because you studied theology and was ordained does not automatically make you His vessel for His grace to channel through. You of all people know God works in mysterious ways. I am just one of his more unorthodox mannerisms, not a tool of Satan."

"You tortured and abused hundreds of innocent people. Can you righteously state you are His instrument? God is good, kind, and gentle. He does not invoke the pain you suffer onto innocent people."

"Is that right priest?" inquired the mass murderer. "What about the great flood. God executed the entire human race save Noah, his family, and a bunch of animals. The great medieval plagues, mass genocides by Hitler and Stalin, the slaughter of thousands by Saddam Hussein are not examples of a just and kind God. God does not like his subjects ignoring his wrath. Thus, he commissioned me to do his bidding. Those like my mother who abused their children in seek of their own hubris must pay the ultimate price. They must die and be cast down into hell as quickly as possible."

Medina's brow furled and crinkled. Years of pent up rage started to release from his mind. He was no longer acting like the good sailor. Butcher Bill was emerging from his dormant solitude.

Nguyen's fright returned temporarily. He had to figure out how to escape the situation. He vowed not to move from this position. An engineering security camera was capturing the entire saga between the two. As long as the camera covered him, he knew he was safe. Petty Officer Zulwaski stood a taut watch.

Medina caught the priest's glance to the camera encapsulated in a half glass domed enclosure. He figured the best way to get rid of the priest was to throw him down a ladder. Such a fall would certainly snap his neck. If it didn't, stomping on his head would do the trick. No one would question his word about what happened. The story line he would use to explain the accident would be simple. The simpler the better. How to get him out into an engineering space while the camera captured everything would prove difficult. The priest understood he was safe right where he was.

Sherman finished the inspection of his division's equipment for anchoring the ship in Phuket Bay. The young men and women did a great job. The heavy and cumbersome tools used to manipulate the chain and windlass were all in order. The communications lines to the bridge were checked and double checked. Having the anchor windlass on the inside of the ship instead of on the forecastle weather decks never appealed to any ship's captain. They like to see their crews working the equipment to make sure the anchoring commands were promptly carried out. Anchoring a ship was a dangerous evolution. A specific anchoring point was selected by the navigator. He had to ensure the currents, tides, depth of water, bottom composition, wind, and anchor chain swing circle, all worked harmoniously together to keeping the ship exactly where it dropped its hook. Too many ships ran aground due to faulty foresight by a ship's navigator and CO.

With the anchor inspection completed, he had one more task to accomplish before the day was done. The Admiral's Barge, Captain's Gigs, and the rest of the ship's boats would be used to ferry personnel to and from shore until the water taxis started running. The most important were the barge and gig. Both boats would launch just prior to anchoring to shuttle the Admiral and CO ashore to pay respects to the local government officials. Strolling down the passageway he caught sight of Commander White walking towards him. An odd feeling overcame him realizing Father Nguyen was not following him. The priest and he discussed the previous evening that Commander White extended an invitation to him for a tour the engineering machinery rooms. The two rapidly closed each other.

"Howdy, Chief."

"Hey, Sir. How goes it? I thought you were scheduled to give the civilian priest a tour of the engineering room?" inquired the undercover agent.

294   ERIC W. HERBERT

"I gave him a tour of most of the plant. But I left him with one of our Electricians Mates to finish it off. Always better to get something explained to you from the horse's mouth than one who knows barely enough to be dangerous," replied Commander White with a grin.

Sherman's stomach flipped upon hearing the comment from the Engineer. Sherman did not like the way this sounded. His reflexes kicked in. "Whose hands did you turn Father Nguyen over to sir," came a quick and terse response.

The Engineer was not ready for Sherman's stern question and he answered it automatically. "Chief Medina has the watch right now," he said.

Without another word to the officer, Sherman bolted down the passageway. He made it to Engineering Control Central in less than five minutes muttering, "Damn, damn, damn," the whole way there. Stepping into to ECC, Sherman spied Petty Officer Zuwalski scribbling notes on a clipboard.

"Petty Officer, do you know where the civilian priest Father Nguyen is? He's late for an appointment with the Executive Officer and I was asked to fetch him."

"Sure, Chief, he's down in Electrical Control with Chief Medina. Look on that monitor over there. That priest sure is inquisitive. He and I spent some time together before the Engineer took him through the spaces. Father Nguyen kept peppering me with questions. I think that's why the crew likes him. He is surely a genuine person".

Sherman peered at the video monitor. There was not any sound for him to listen to. Father Nguyen stood just out of arms reach from the killer. He could tell they were engaged in a serious conversation.

"Zulwalski, we need to get Father Nguyen up here ASAP. Can you go down and get him?"

"I can't leave my station Chief. You can go get him if you want. Just make sure you wear ear plugs," she responded.

"I'm new here like Father Nguyen. I would get lost and the XO is not accustomed to be kept waiting. Is there anyone you can send to get him?"

"Sure, that's not a problem." Picking up a phone located on the console desk, Petty Officer Zulwaski punched in a few numbers and spoke into the phone. Her voice echoed throughout the lower tiers of the engineering compartments. "Fireman Crabtree this is the EOOW. Head over to the switchboards and escort Father Nguyen back to ECC. Be quick please because the XO wants to see him."

A young male voice responded back over the loudspeakers. "Aye, aye. Headed that way."

Both Nguyen and Medina heard the announcement. Nguyen shoulders slumped with relief to learn someone was going to extract him from this unplanned confrontation with Butcher Bill.

Medina spoke first. "You're lucky this time priest. I guarantee the next time we meet you will not escape quite so easily" sneered Butcher Bill. He had been poised to make a move on the priest but was foiled by an unexpected witness coming towards his way.

Father Nguyen turned to the right and saw his sailor savior scampering down the ladder.

"Father, I was sent to come and get you. Apparently, the Executive Officer desires your presence sir. Will you follow me please?"

"Gladly, son, I am right behind you. Lead the way. Ah…hold on a second."

Turning back towards Chief Medina, the priest bowed his head, said a quick prayer to God, Jesus, Mary, and all the Saints to thank them for the strength they just provided. Outstretching his right hand, he rapidly threw his arm down vertically followed by a horizontal line making the sign of the cross upon Medina. "May God help you find strength from the Lord and may he illuminate a path out of any darkness you may find yourself in," he

296 ERIC W. HERBERT

prayed. Finished with the blessing, Nguyen rotated on his heels and followed Fireman Crabtree away from the brink of hell.

Medina stood silently watching his prey elude his grip. There would be another time very soon.

Sherman sighed with relief watching from the close circuit TV screen as Fireman Crabtree escorted the priest away from the monster. The boy will never know he just saved a person's life. The five minutes it took Crabtree and Father Nguyen to arrive in ECC seemed likes days to the FBI agent. Visions of how cruel Butcher Bill could really be occupied his thoughts until Fireman Crabtree sauntered in with the priest in tow. Relief washed over his body. Sherman recognized Nguyen was a different person. His face seemed aglow. He expected to see fear rippling through the frail man. What he saw was a man on a mission. His back was rigid, head held high, and the ever present Nguyen gentle smile tattooed on his face.

"Chief Sherman, it is so nice of you to fetch me for my appointment with Captain Benefield. I was so captivated by my discussion with Chief Medina I simply lost track of time. It was my lucky day you came along."

Before Sherman could reply, Petty Officer Zuwalski piped up.

"Did I not tell you Father Nguyen was the inquisitive type? He probably got Chief Medina going on and on about how electricity was generated and distributed throughout the ship. That is the longest I have ever seen Chief Medina talk to anyone on the ship. How did you get him to talk so long?"

"Chief Medina and I had a most interesting discussion. Thank you Ms. Zuwalski for noticing. I sensed that too. We talked about his interests and the conversation just kept flowing. But alas…" he paused, "I have another appointment with yet another interesting *LINCOLN* sailor. Thank you so much for being kind to me. God Bless you."

Father Nguyen turned and headed out the door with Sherman close behind.

They strolled down the passageway. Sherman broke the silence. "Are you okay Father? What happened down there? What did he say to you?" inquired the undercover FBI agent.

"God came and filled me with his spirit. I know Chief Medina wanted to kill me and was planning on how to do it right then and there. The Holy Spirit entered my soul and gave me Saint Michael's strength to stand my ground. That man is truly a minion of the devil."

"I am sorry you had to go through that Father," Sherman said.

"Chief Sherman, you do not have to apologize to me. It was the best spiritual experience I have ever had in my life. That episode has galvanized my spirit. We will stop this monster before he strikes again."

Butcher Bill did not feel the same way Father Nguyen did. The meeting upset him and he had no way to release the negative energy flowing through his veins. He had the priest in his grasp and he was ripped out of his hands. Someway, somehow, he would teach him not to interfere with him. Medina had to figure out how and when he would extract his revenge. It had to be while they were in Phuket. Anytime after that would be impossible. Medina planned on deserting the Navy and disappearing.

CHAPTER THIRTY-FOUR

The *LINCOLN* Battle Group steamed along at fifteen knots plowing through calm deep blue seas. The nine ships rendezvoused in the middle of the Pacific Ocean six days after the carrier and her escort cruiser left Hawaii. When they met, Admiral Cable stationed the ships to maximize his sensors and weapons coverage for the trip across the great Pacific pond.

Two Aegis destroyers, the USS *WAYNE E. MEYERS* and *USS HOPPER* led the charge. Both ships were ordered to take station two hundred miles in front of the battle group and two hundred miles apart from each other. The other Aegis destroyer, *USS RUSSELL*, was stationed two hundred miles behind the aircraft carrier covering the rear. The destroyer's powerful radars and sonars created overlapping coverage of the entire air, surface, and under water battle space. Battle space supremacy was achieved through technology, good leadership, sound tactics, and dedicated sailors. Any information gathered by any of the ship's sensors was transmitted to satellites orbiting the Earth. Then, the surveillance data was retransmitted from the military satellites to the rest of the flotilla. What the destroyer's saw on their radar scopes was seen on all of the battle group's combat system display systems almost instantaneously. The battle group's protective umbrella spanned well over an eight hundred mile radius.

The aircraft carrier, the two amphibious ships, *USS SAN ANTONIO* and *USS INCHON,* the AEGIS cruiser, the *USS CHANCELORVILLE,* and the Littoral Combat Ship, *USS FREEDOM* steamed together for most of the journey. The two LPD ships made up the van. All ships maintained their relative position to the aircraft carrier and cruised along at a steady speed of fifteen knots.

On the eighth night, Admiral Cable ordered his three destroyers to close his position. Before the ships dispersed and traveled to their respective ports-of-call, he wanted a picture to capture the historical moment. When he arrived on the bridge, he found everything as he ordered the night before. The ships were trekking along nicely on their westerly heading. The *LINCOLN*'s bridge team was busy transmitting orders using signal flag hoists and semaphore lights. The messages could have been sent using radios but every good naval warrior liked to keep radio traffic to a minimum. Over two hundred years ago, the famed British Admiral, Horatio Nelson, known for crushing Napoleon's French Fleets, used signal flags to communicate his orders to his ships. The methods had improved greatly since then, but the basic use of flags representing different commands remained the same. Plus, it kept the sailors on their toes. If they ever had to stealthfully attack an enemy, using the ancient methods still proved valuable.

LINCOLN's signal crew bent-on the multicolored flags to the halyards. Admiral Cable was sending messages for his ships to form lines based on relative bearings from the aircraft carrier. With signal flags flapping in the wind, the officers scanned the horizon to ensure the other ships acknowledged their orders. They did so by displaying the same flags hoisted on the carrier. Once seen, the *LINCOLN*'s Officer-of-the-Deck ordered the flags hauled down signaling the silent signal's execution. Cable watched as each ship in the battle group increased speed, turned their rudder hard over, and headed to their assigned positioning. It took thirty minutes for the vessels to reach their predetermined destinations. Once on station, every ship unfurled a massive American battle flag from their highest yardarm.

The sight was impressive. The aircraft carrier had its entire aircraft compliment stationed on deck. To the north and south of the flap top in a 'V' formation sailed the cruiser, amphibious ships, destroyers, and LCS. Helicopters flew around the ships snapping pictures. Once onboard, the digital images would be instantly processed and beamed to the Navy's website. The pictures sent clear and powerful messages to the world. America commanded the seas. They could reach out and touch an enemy easily anytime they wanted to.

The photo exercise was completed by mid-morning. The signalmen received another order from Rear Admiral Cable to send up the signal flag message for "All ships proceed on duties assigned." The messages were silently acknowledged. Each ship spurred their engines to flank speed, shifted their rudders, and headed to their destinations. The ships would meet again in two weeks time to start supporting the Global War on Terror in the Middle East, Arabian Gulf, and Indian Ocean.

LINCOLN and *CHANCERLORVILLE* altered their courses to the northwest when the carrier battle group dispersed. They arrived in Phuket at precisely fifteen hundred hours. The ships anchored in twenty fathoms of water and paid out one hundred and sixty fathoms of anchor chain.

Thai boats ferrying the port liaison officer, custom officials, local merchants, and repair personnel flooded aboard the ship once the accommodation ladders were lowered and the ship was ready to receive them. Once aboard, crew members with approved leave chits scrambled down to the waiting water taxis. For an American sailor, Thailand was a playground. Hotel rooms cost less than thirty dollars a day. Beer was a buck. Beautiful Asian women would service all of their needs for the entire stay for two hundred greenbacks. Jungle excursions, scuba diving, surfing, sailing, and Thai cultural tours were set up for the sailors onboard for relatively low cost. It was no wonder the crew departing the ship were in good spirits.

Dr. Ohms learned of the interchange between Father Nguyen and Butcher Bill from a telephone call he had with Amecii and Sherman. Sherman summarized to Ohm's what was exchanged between the good guy and the bad guy. Ohm's sensed the paradigm shifting. It did not surprise him Medina was on the verge of doing something horrible to the priest in his own back yard. Butcher Bill was starting to buckle under the pressure. When it came to stalking his victims and covering his tracks the killer was an expert. Now, he found himself in a different zone. Someone was coming after him. Medina sensed something was amiss in Seattle at the church causing him to deviate from his plan and abandon his vehicle. With Father Nguyen confronting him in his sanctuary, Bill was a man starting to worry who believes his only recourse was to kill his pursuer as soon as he saw an opportunity. He had to exterminate the only link between him and his victims.

Medina left the ship with the first wave of liberty hounds heading to the beach. The FBI surveillance team picked him up when he stepped ashore. Bags in tow, he scrambled into a Tom-Tom truck, a colorfully adorned truck with bench seating in the back. The Tom-Toms squeezed ten sailors and their donnage in the truck bed and made stops at various hotels along the main beach-front strip. The agents Ohm assigned to trail Medina reported he got off the truck and registered at the Phuket Bay Hotel. He had a bite to eat and then headed to the beach to get an open air massage by a young Asian woman who charged him five bucks to walk on his back. After, he went back to his room. No phone calls were made and he did not connect to the hotel's internet server. Six FBI agents dressed as American tourists watched all of the hotel's exits. The room remained quiet. They used infrared sensors to monitor his movements inside. Bill remained low key by showering and lying down in his bed to take a nap.

Agents Sherman and Amecii and Father Nguyen found a van waiting for them two blocks away from the beach. Ten minutes later, they were sitting in a penthouse at the Phuket Grand Royal Hotel. The three-bedroom loft suite had been transformed into a living, breathing FBI operational cell. It had a bank of twelve telephones, fax machines, copiers, computer terminals and large screen surveillance monitors. All of the information boards they had in the United States were transported to Thailand.

Father Nguyen was amazed at what he saw. At one time, he thought he was the only person trying to stop Medina. Then he met Hendricks, Raphael, Amecii and Sherman. The weight on his shoulders lifted slightly. Looking at the massive effort in front of him, he realized heavy resources were being levied to bring Butcher Bill down. God sent an army of angels to help him.

Ohms saw the three enter the room. "Welcome Father Nguyen. My name is Jeff Ohms. I lead this investigation and I am glad to see you are safe and well."

"Thank you. I hope we can end this nightmare very soon," replied Nguyen.

"If you are not aware, we would love to pick Medina up right now. We have already cleared it through diplomatic channels here in Thailand. But, we still don't have any direct evidence linking Medina to any of the homicides. We know it is him based on circumstantial evidence but it won't get us very far for an indictment. That's where you come in," preached Ohms.

"With the strength of God, I will do anything you need me to do."

"You've already contributed a great deal Father. Amecii and Sherman filled me in on your experiences on the ship with Medina. We are starting to rattle his cage. I would like to keep that pressure on."

Father Nguyen understood what he was being told. Ohms wanted to use him as bait. If it was God's will and baiting the killer to halt the horror was what was needed, then he would summon the courage to continue.

To make the plan work, it would take extreme measures. The original thought was to place GPS transmitters in Nguyen's clothes. Ohms wanted to discuss another idea with the Priest.

"Father, I am going to ask you to go into the lion's den. We know Medina wants to harm you; however, we believe he wants you to bear witness to him killing someone else. He'll stick to his pattern; one girl and one male victim. We are going to let him do exactly that. But, in this case we'll be there to stop him. It is risky but I do not know any other way to catch him."

Nguyen's face slumped once he realized what was being asked of him. Could he do it? Did he have enough will to press forward with the dangerous cat-and-mouse game? The fear that gripped him on the ship was debilitating. He could not imagine being left alone with the serial killer again. "Who else would do it then?" he thought. The maniac had to be stopped. God chose him to wage this private war of good versus evil. Nguyen steeled himself for the challenge. He called upon Saint Michael for protection.

Father Nguyen breathed deeply and relayed his thoughts to Dr. Ohms and the team. "I will do what you ask. From what Chief…um… I mean Agent Sherman has told me, Medina slipped your surveillance coverage in Seattle. Gentlemen, how do you intend to keep me safe?"

Sherman looked at Ohms who nodded his head approving him to answer the question.

"Father, like Dr. Ohms said we wanted to put GPS transmitters in your clothes. However, if Medina captures you like we want him to; he will search your clothes as soon as possible. We want to do something a bit different."

"Okay, gentlemen, we beat around this bush twice now. Just tell me what your plan is," scolded the priest.

Sherman paused to create the words he wanted to use. He decided the best way was not to sugar coat the truth but to tell him man-to-man the plan they envisioned.

"Father, we want to insert GPS receivers under your skin." There it was. Plain, simple, and to the point.

The priest was stunned. He never had dreamed something like this was possible. Better yet, how would it be done and where in his body would the devices go?

Sherman knew the priest was silently questioning what he just said. He decided to continue the explanation.

"I have one of the transmitters in my hand Father. As you can see, it is small and thinner than a dime. Our surgical team will cut two small incisions near your armpit and place the devices under your skin. The inserts are medically safe. The incisions will be closed with a single stitch, and covered with a protective flesh adhesive." Sherman said and continued. "We want to insert two devices just in case one should fail. We will know your exact location within five meters at all times."

"Are you guaranteeing me I will not be harmed?" questioned the shaken clergyman.

"You know as well as I do Father I cannot strictly guarantee your safety. But, we will be able to extract you immediately. The odds are low any harm will come to you."

"How low Agent Sherman?"

"Seventy-thirty," he replied recognizing the odds were not as low as they should be.

"As I said before ladies and gentlemen, God has given me a mission. It is the most important thing I can do for the good of humanity. If I choose not to do this, then I am hypocrite like the animal you are hunting. I will help you in your quest. And God willing, he will help us all."

CHAPTER THIRTY-FIVE

Medina knew he was under the microscope. He could not see them. He felt their presence. How did they find out about him and who were they? There was never a shred of evidence left for anyone to follow his tracks. His studies of criminal forensics were at a senior crime scene analysis level. Only one solution came to mind. His exposure came from Father Nguyen.

Gathering up his backpack, Medina left the hotel. There were arrangements to be finalized. He exited the hotel and walked the three blocks to a Thai Bank. Over the years, he had stashed money, bogus passports, and open ended one way airplane tickets in safety deposit boxes around the world. Here in Thailand he had stashed one hundred thousand dollars. Being single and the great bonuses the Navy paid him allowed him financial freedom. He could live like a king in Indonesia or Malaysia with a hundred grand in American dollars. Departing the bank, he dashed into a liquor store and purchased a disposable cell phone. In the store's bathroom, he made two telephone calls, removed the SIM card, and threw the phone into the trash.

Medina's activity was closely tracked by the Ohms agents. Still, they could not move in. Butcher Bill had to make the first move.

Leaving the liquor store, Medina strolled down the main street thoroughfare. He was hungry and craved Thai tiger prawns for dinner. As he sat eating his food, he thought how he was going to find the priest and snatch him away. He fantasized how he was going to teach the menacing priest a lesson. But, his immediate desires needed to be met as well. He scanned the street for the right target just as he did countless times before over the last sixteen years. Almost giving up, he spotted her. He did not want an Asian woman. The woman he stalked was white. She looked so familiar. Where had he seen her before? Then, it hit him. The red headed woman taught the philosophy classes onboard the ship. Professor Amecii was her name if he recalled correctly. Sitting directly across from her drinking a coke and eating Pad Thai Noodles was Chief Sherman, a fellow shipmate from the *LINCOLN*. He could not be involved. The two had to be separated.

Medina finished his meal, drank the last of his Tiger Beer, paid his tab, and left the café. As he left, he spotted a Thai man dressed in shorts, a blue stripped short sleeved shirt, and flip-flops reading a paper outside of the café. Their eyes met. Butcher Bill nodded and shifted his gaze towards Professor Amecii. The Thai stranger looked in the direction Medina hinted towards and nodded his head. Medina's plan was starting to coalesce.

Finding the priest was already taken care of. Before he left the ship, he found out the priest had arranged for a hotel through the ship's morale, welfare, and recreational program. Father Nguyen was staying at the Star Villas on the beach located two miles down the road.

Perfect, thought Medina. He would wait to execute his plan until dark. Early morning would be best.

Sherman, Hendricks, Raphael, and Ohms were anxious and jumpy. The warrior values they lived with rhetorically forbade them speaking about how they felt at that moment. The team was deployed in and around Father Nguyen's villa. Another team watched the place Medina holed up in. None of them liked what they were doing. Luring the killer with Father Nguyen in seemed wrong and went against their best senses. They all agreed that other options left too many loopholes the killer could use to wiggle out of the inevitable. This time, Ohms did not make the decision to use the priest as bait. Operational protocol demanded he inform his superiors of his plan. He explained his reasoning. He described the dilemma confronting his team. Ohms relayed the team's belief that Butcher Bill was aware the net was closing in on him; therefore, he needed to escape. His mind was too crafty to maintain the status quo. He would develop a plan to elude the team and disappear into the back country of some third world country. Being Filipino enabled him to blend into any Asian third world country without raising suspicion. Not taking any action came with a high potential of losing the suspect all together. Drastic and risky measures were necessary.

The decision went directly to the FBI Director who consulted the Secretary of the Navy. He funneled it to the President's office. Arresting an American on foreign soil had its challenges. Arresting the most notorious American serial killer ever discovered would be media frenzy. Arresting a serial killer who was a highly decorated American sailor brought an entirely new set of political ramifications. Presidential advisors advised against performing the sting operation. They remembered the international backlash experienced when a low ranking Marine raped and killed a native Japanese girl in Okinawa a few years back. The incident received international attention to the point the United States was called to close its military bases in Japan. The doves lost that bid by the slimmest of margins.

POTUS understood his advisor's recommendations. But, he also agreed with the FBI. The killer had to be captured and undergo American prosecution. The president told the White House team to give him time to think over the matter. Knee jerk decisions were not his forte. He wanted to evaluate the problem without people whispering into his ears. The clock ticked off thirty minutes and the President called in his staff and communicated his approval and direction personally to the Secretary of the Navy. He understood all of the potential ramifications associated with his decision to execute the risky plan. But, as he explained to his staff, he sometimes had to make decisions based more on morality than on politics. It was a case of doing the right thing for humanity versus the right thing for the Oval Office.

Inserting the GPS transmitters under Father's Nguyen skin was completed quicker than expected. A surgeon working for the CIA performed the minor operation. He injected a local anesthesia numbing the two locations where the GPS units would be inserted. Cutting two small incisions in the side of the priest's upper torso near his armpit he quickly inserted the devices and the stitched the wound closed. The surgeon stayed until the local anesthesia wore off to assess Father Nguyen's pain level.

Father Nguyen needed to be steady. If he had any pain the doctor would provide enough pain medication to dull it but keeping the priest alert. After the surgery, Ohms sent Father Nguyen to his hotel to wait. A deadly cat-and-mouse game started.

Sherman sat in a white jeep with the canvas top up. A GPS receiver unit showed a small dot on its screen which had not moved for eight hours. The sun set three hours ago and the moon peaked over the horizon. Streaks of silver shone upon the tumbling ocean. The lightly crashing waves made him daydream about making love to Catherine on the soft sandy beach in Hawaii. The moonbeams reflecting off the water reminded him of looking out on the ocean and seeing the same silvery luminescence on the water while she slept in the cradle of his arms.

Catherine did not witness the Father Nguyen's surgery. The last time Sherman saw her was when they shared a dinner on the waterfront. A few sailors walked by and said hello. Some knew Chief Sherman was her class pet. It was obvious the two were attracted to each other. She was not part of the crew so having a dinner date didn't violate the ship's fraternization policies. They liked seeing a sailor with her too. Many of the young sailors passing by envied Chief Sherman because the professor was a sexy woman. It dawned on Sherman he had not heard from her since. She was probably working with Dr. Ohms at the command center waiting to hear news of the trap.

Medina woke at midnight. He dressed quickly in blue jeans, a red shirt, and black sneakers. He inventoried his back pack sitting on the dresser. It contained a black lightweight jacket, flashlight, collapsible blackjack club, a can of pepper spray, a leather-man multi-functional tool, duct tape, his laptop computer, another disposable cell phone, and a collapsible hunting knife. In a sealable folder, Medina inserted ninety thousand American dollars in cash, three fake passports, birth certificates from the Philippines and Malaysia, and a plane ticket from Bangkok to Indonesia. Escaping the past in this part of Asia was easy for a Filipino. Many of the archipelago's citizens left their island nation in search of work. Their ethnicity spanned the globe. He blended into the crowd very easily.

Medina assumed the worst. His senses told him he was being watched and followed. By whom he did not know. He also wondered why he wasn't being confronted. Special effort on his part was needed for his escape. Gathering his backpack, Medina sat on the bed meditating to control his thoughts, body, and anxiety. A step out the door meant he could never return to the navy life he loved. Joining the navy so many years ago saved his life. But, he was willing to give it up for the best reasons. Continuing God's work was his main priority. Nothing would stand in his way from accomplishing the most unholy of holy missions.

Medina armed himself with the short bladed hunting knife, threw on his pack, and slowly opened the hotel door. He rode the elevator from the fourth floor to the lobby and headed outside the building. The Phuket streets teemed with people having a good time. Bringing an American aircraft carrier and a cruiser to port unleashed four thousand thirsty and horny sailors upon the town. It created a drunken chaos. The streets were one great big street party. Bars, strip clubs, brothels, and eateries lining the main thoroughfare and its alleys bristled with energy. Disco, heavy metal, rock, and country music blared from the bars and mixed in the air making the noise level high. The party scene rivaled any New Orleans Mardi Gras celebration. Melting into the crowd would make it very difficult for anyone to monitor him.

Hendricks spotted Butcher Bill first. His watch showed twelve forty five in the morning and the killer was on the move. His first priority was to alert the rest of the team.

"Bill is on the move. Suspect is wearing jeans, a red shirt, and is carrying a black backpack. He's headed North on foot towards Raphael. I will follow him on foot," he reported over the radio net.

"This is Raphael. Copy all. I am in front of the Trident Café two blocks north of your position. Agents Drum and Bridger have the side streets covered."

"This is Bridger. Suspect in sight. He's moving forward with the crowd."

Dr. Ohms's voice was heard over the communication circuit.

"You guys be on your toes. I am betting Butcher Bill knows we are here. He is a crafty bastard. He is going to do something to escape your surveillance."

Medina walked down the street with the flow of the foot traffic. Each time the crowd slowed to a stop, he stole a glance behind him. He could not tell if anyone was following, but sensed they were there. No matter, he will lose them shortly. The crowd picked up its pace and he moved along with the drunken throng. Looking forward, he spotted a man looking directly at him and touching the Bluetooth device affixed to his ear. Now he had an idea who was tailing him.

Sherman started the jeep's engine. The team had Butcher Bill's surveillance under control. Placing the car's gear into drive, he headed towards the Star Villas to Father Nguyen.

"Suspect turned west onto a side street. I am in pursuit," reported Agent Bridger.

Butcher Bill formed a plan in his mind. He wished he did not have to do this on the fly but he needed to know who was tailing him so he could assess the situation. The people keeping tabs on him were professionals. How many there were he did not know.

The street he turned down was more alley than thoroughfare. Drunken sailors and tourists stumbled down the road. Strip clubs, bars, and street vendors hawking food littered the street. He glanced into the first club he passed. Three naked Asian women were on an elevated platform hugging a pole and gyrating their bodies for the customers in the bar. One girl bent over, spread her legs and started fingering herself madly. The drunken sailors cheered her on. Sexual mania was in the air. He passed another shop and glimpsed another Asian woman on her knees blowing a man while another man took her from behind. The bars normally used their back rooms for the sex to occur but those were full to capacity. So, the girls, eager to make as much money as they could practiced their professions right where they were. They had screwed so many men it did not matter to them where they earned their money. In private or in public, there was not any difference. The entire scene brought flashbacks into Medina's mind of his early life with his mother. His blood boiled in his veins. The desire to strike again was stoked by the images he was seeing. He walked into the next bar he saw. An Asian girl who dyed her hair blond sat on a bar stool with her legs open displaying her wares to whoever wanted to look. He reached for her hand and she smiled thinking she was getting a customer. With the faux-blond girl in tow, Medina made his way to the back of the bar where he knew rooms with old stinky mattresses for the girls to get their customers off were located. It was the same arrangement he grew up in.

Agent Bridger still had Bill in sight when he scooped up the girl. He watched him take the whore to the back of the bar. "Butcher Bill is headed to the back rooms at Tully's Bar with a blond Asian prostitute. If I go in there he'll know he's under surveillance. I'm going to wait outside. Someone should cover the back door," he reported.

"This is Drum. I am on the road just north of you and behind the bar. I got the rear covered."

Hendricks chimed in next. "Good plan. Drum takes the back. Bridger covers the front. Raphael joins up with Drum. I will meet Bridger in the front."

Medina let the girl lead him to an empty room. Once there she lay down on the bed and spread her legs, waiting for him to mount her. Butcher Bill walked over to her, whipped out his knife slicing open her throat with a single slash. Horror screamed from her eyes. Blood spewed out of her wound while she frantically tried to stop it with her hands. She rapidly passed into unconsciousness and death in a pool of her own blood. Bill watched her die. It had not been his plan to kill her but he realized he had to leave and didn't want any commotion when he did. Wiping the knife off on the mattress, Bill left the room and headed down the dimly lit hallway. Someone looking into the darkness from the bar would be unable to see who he was. He found the back door and pushed it open carefully. He scanned the area for signs of surveillance and saw a white male speaking into a blue tooth headset heading his way with determination. Medina put on his black jacket and melted back in with the crowd of people. Whoever was following him was looking for a guy in a red shirt. Donning the jacket would throw them off ever so slightly. Moving across the street he dashed into another bar waiting for the man to pass.

Agent Bridger kept his eyes to the right side of the street. It was the third bar he was looking for. Spotting it, he reported he was in position. He took up roost across the street and leaned against a palm tree to wait. The pain he felt in his kidneys felt like a hot iron shaft being thrust into his body. He wanted to scream but could not. The fire traveled up his chest. Turning his head, he realized Butcher Bill punctured his diaphragm. Without any air, he could not scream for help. Blood gurgled from his mouth. His killer reached up and took the blue tooth headset from his ear.

Bridger hugged the palm tree and slide to the ground. No one witnessed the attack. No one came to his rescue.

Medina withdrew the knife from the Agent Bridger's body and let him slump to the ground. No one screamed. People would see the agent passed out against the tree and conclude he had too much to drink. It was not an unusual sight in Phuket. An added bonus was the blue tooth device he took from his stalker. He placed it over his ear and listened.

"Bridger this is Raphael. Where are you? I'm at the end of the street coming your way but I can't see you. Call me when you see me."

Medina turned west to escape the crime scene. He was free to do what he wanted now. Tapping the blue tooth's transmitting button, Butcher Bill spoke into the microphone. "I am afraid your friend Bridger is not going to be able to see you," he said.

"Who is this?" questioned Raphael.

"I do not know how you found me, but you'll never be able to find me again."

Medina had compromised their communications and it would cause enough commotion to keep his pursuers busy while he escaped. Killing the agent was risky but it had turned out to be beneficial. He had two more errands to complete and then he would be able to commence the sacrifice to appease his god.

Agent Sherman heard over the radio what happened. Raphael found Agent Bridger lying in a pool of blood. Butcher Bill had taken his head set and escaped. Hearing Raphael's discovery, Hendricks entered the strip club with his gun drawn but concealed. He checked every room for Medina and discovered the hooker with her neck sliced open. Butcher Bill had escaped. Sherman knew where he was headed though. Medina wanted the priest. He had been resourceful and ruthless in his escape from the surveillance. Now he was free roaming and headed Sherman's way. Butcher Bill desperately wanted his revenge upon Nguyen. The method of how the killer would attempt to get to

Nguyen escaped Sherman. It tugged at him. The team knew surveillance in Thailand would prove difficult. They did not imagine him being able to identify the agents and then to stalk and kill one. It was the second time they underestimated Butcher Bill. So, the murderer wanted the priest and he had to come and get him. Sherman decided to wait for the killer with Father Nguyen.

He called the priest from his cell phone and told him what happened. Surprisingly, Father Nguyen remained calm and reaffirmed his commitment to capturing Butcher Bill. The priest had more courage than most seasoned battle veterans. He said he would pray for Agent Bridger's and the poor girl's soul and families. Sherman told him his plan and Nguyen readily agreed. They would fight the demon together. The next call he made was to Dr. Ohms who was angry over Bridger's ambush. The first mistake the team made cost them nothing. The second mistake was fatal. A good agent and another innocent life were snuffed out because they wanted desperately to capture the killer. At any cost. The investigation's leader concurred with Sherman's assessment. The priest was in Butcher Bill's sights. How he intended to move on him was a mystery to both agents. Ohms ordered Hendricks, Raphael, and six other agents to converge onto the priest's hotel. The rest of the team he wanted in the city looking for Medina. All except Catherine Amecii. Sherman assumed Amecii was at the command post. He had asked Ohms what her thoughts were. Ohms responded with surprise.

"Catherine isn't here with us," Ohms stated. "We thought she was with you. She's not?"

"No, the last time I saw Catherine was when we grabbed a bite to eat after our meeting this afternoon. Are you telling me no one knows where she is?" questioned Sherman. Sherman hung up on Ohms and dialed her cell phone. All he got was her voice mail telling the caller to leave a message. He started to worry. *Where did she go?*

CHAPTER THIRTY-SIX

Medina located the van easily. It was stashed behind an abandoned warehouse as agreed with the guy he hired. It is amazing what ten thousand dollars would buy in a third world country. If he pushed it, the thug would have done it for much less. He did not have time to haggle price. Ten thousand dollars in Thailand would let anyone live in luxury for a few years. Unless, he gambled it away or spent it on booze, drugs, and whores. What happened to the money was of no concern to him. He made the arrangements using the disposable cell phone. The first call he made ordered a van. The second call went to the man he saw outside the restaurant.

It was a blue, late 1980s panel van. Rust ate away at its body. Medina found the keys stuffed under the rear bumper. He unlocked the driver's door and climbed in. A package lay on the passenger's seat. He tore it open and found two 9mm semi-automatic pistols, four boxes of ammunition, and a cell phone. Medina's attention was drawn to a slight noise in the back of the van. He switched on the van's light, turned to the rear, grinning devilishly.

"Hello, Professor Amecii," he said.

Catherine saw who it was and thrashed about the van's floor. Tears streamed down her cheeks. She was kidnapped and sold to Butcher Bill. How in the hell did he pull that off with so many people watching him?

"If you remember, we met on the *LINCOLN*. My name is Ignacio Medina. I have been watching you closely and you are perfect for a ritual I am performing very soon. You are very beautiful and would make a nice sacrifice to God."

Agent Amecii tugged at the bonds holding her legs, feet, arms, and hands fast. It was wasted energy. The plastic wire ties trundled her without any chance of escape. All of the pictures she studied profiling Butcher Bill flashed before her eyes. She tried to remain calm. Medina escaped the surveillance team and she realized only she could help herself survive. The killer driving the van had no idea who she was or who his customer was. Medina believed he had a beautiful alluring white helpless woman to sacrifice. Amecii understood his thought process. He was definitely out of his element. Everything he did now was not preplanned. Medina was operating on the fly driven by his need to placate the urges in his mind. He would eventually slip up. He would make a mistake. No matter how minor, Catherine prepared herself to capitalize upon it. She needed to remain in control and seize the opportunity when it presented itself.

Medina originally planned to infiltrate the priest's hotel and kidnap him somehow. It might have taken killing more cops but he wanted that priest. Another plan came to mind. He pulled the van over and pulled out the cell phone from the box. Switching on the van's light provided enough lighting to take a picture of Catherine bundled up in the van. Pointing the cell phone towards his captive he snapped the picture. Medina would not have to capture the priest by going into the hornet's nest. Father Nguyen would come to him.

He put the blue tooth phone back on his ear. He tapped the transmit button and said, "Are you there?"

Immediately, Dr. Ohms replied, "Yes, we are here waiting for you."

"Good. I want to send you something. Give me a cell phone number that can receive pictures."

Ohms was skeptical. But he had to keep him talking. "Why do you want to send me something? That is unlike you Ignacio. You normally do not like people discovering your sacrifices. Have you already killed again?"

"Didn't you find my last two sacrifices? More comes later. Now, tell me the number." he ordered.

Knowing he was beaten again, Ohms complied with the madman's orders. "Where are you Chief Medina? You cannot elude us much longer. We have finally found you. Give yourself up." Ohms knew the plea for Medina to surrender himself was useless. He wanted to give his team enough time to trace the cell phone's position.

"Look to your phone Officer. I want the priest and I want him alone. You have one hour," demanded Medina.

An agent brought the cell phone to Ohms. He opened the photo. What he saw made him gasp. The photo showed a tearing Agent Amecii tied up and gagged on a rusted metal floor. She was being held captive by Medina. Amecii was his hostage and he was using her in exchange for the priest. What Medina did not say was whether he knew she was a FBI agent. Ohms forwarded the picture to Sherman and Hendricks. Now they knew how Medina planned to get at Father Nguyen.

Sherman opened the picture. It was the first time since he was told his Mother died that his eyes welled with tears. Catherine was in the hands of a monster. Seeing her hog tied with duct tape over her mouth scared the living hell out of him. Terror was etched into her face. The first woman he ever truly loved was in serious peril. His soul ached to save her. Her eyes pleaded for salvation and mercy. His mission now had even more meaning than before. At all costs, Butcher Bill shall reap what he sowed upon his hundreds of victims.

Hendricks looked at the photo and gasped for air. One of their own had already died. Now another was in the killer's grasp. This case will not have a happy ending. He dialed Ohms cell phone number to ask for guidance. Hendricks knew what he would do but he wanted to know what the director wanted to do.

Ohms told him they were to continue with their plan. It was originally set for Father Nguyen to be taken by Medina and

318   ERIC W. HERBERT

tracked for capture. The hunt had not changed, just the rules. They would play by Butcher Bill's rules for now.

Ohms phone rang once more.

"Have you made up your mind?" spoke the voice in the receiver.

"We have. Father Nguyen has agreed to go with you in exchange for the woman."

"Very well," replied the demon in human form. "Have the priest meet me at the Dole pineapple plantation in two hours. When he arrives, tell him to take the northerly trail. Make sure he's not followed or the woman dies a slow and horrible death." Ohms paused. "He'll meet you there," he replied sadly. Butcher Bill was running the show. He was putting two people of his team in the destructive path of the crazed maniac. There was nothing he could do about it except to comply with the Butcher's demands.

CHAPTER THIRTY-SEVEN

Agent Sherman and Father Nguyen left the hotel and joined the investigative team at their ad-hoc operations center in the hotel penthouse. It took fifteen minutes for the agent and priest to travel to the hotel overlooking the Phuket beaches. Dr. Ohms, Officers Hendricks and Raphael, the twin criminologists, Israel and Ishmael Colby, and eighteen other FBI agents were present. Sherman noticed an entirely new set of characters were also there. They were there at Sherman's request. The agreement between the FBI and the Navy stated he could call upon any resource the aircraft carrier had onboard. This was why Rear Admiral Cable, Captain Russell, and four other of his officers were in the room.

Sherman went directly to Rear Admiral Cable and Captain Russell. "Gentlemen, I'm Agent Andrew Sherman from the Federal Bureau of Investigation. You know me as Chief Petty Officer Sherman from the *LINCOLN*'s Deck Department. Thank you for coming."

Rear Admiral Cable spoke first. "Agent Sherman, we know who you are. Before we left Washington, the Secretary of the Navy informed us you and Agent Amecii were onboard conducting a covert investigation. If and when the need ever arose, we were ordered to provide you *ANY* assistance you needed." Captain Russell stood to the Admiral's left, nodding his head in full agreement.

"Thank you, gentlemen. We do not have much time. I want to give you enough details regarding what is going on and what we need from you. Our target is Chief Petty Officer Medina. The information you see displayed on the walls and boards within this room covers sixteen years of a serial killer's rampage. The person responsible for the murders of hundreds of innocent men and women is Chief Ignacio Medina. Over the last six months we slowly unraveled his gruesome story. All of the direct evidence leading us to Chief Medina was circumstantial and would have crumbled if we arrested him. Then, he would have vanished."

"Now I understand the reason behind all of the secrecy. What can we do to help your fight?" responded Captain Russell.

"Before we stumbled across Chief Medina, we named him Butcher Bill. He is ruthless and has no regrets killing. He escaped our surveillance this evening by murdering Agent Bridger and a Thai prostitute. Medina is on a rampage and is desperate. Butcher Bill is a different kind of serial killer we are accustomed to tracking down. Dr. Ohms developed Butcher Bill's psychological profile. I would like him to explain to you what we're up against."

Ohms continued the discussion. "Everything Agent Sherman stated skims the surface of Medina's cold blooded prowess. He is a man who has felt persecuted his entire life. He released his anger and bitterness on the public worldwide. The ability to travel around the world has made him a global serial killer. Butcher Bill believes he is working directly for God. His vengeful acts stem from an abusive childhood. Therefore, the sins committed upon him as a boy are being avenged in his mind as God's work. Now, he feels even more betrayed because the God he serves is not supporting him. Thus, the reason he wants Father Nguyen."

Captain Russell focused his gaze upon Father Nguyen. "We did not know Father Nguyen was involved. How is our volunteer civilian priest mixed in with your investigation?"

Father Nguyen placed his hand upon Sherman's arm signaling that he wished to answer the question.

"I cannot go into the details behind my involvement Captain for spiritual reasons. We are dealing with pure unadulterated evil residing in Chief Medina. In essence, we are in a battle between Lucifer and the God almighty. Medina is a puppet whose strings are manipulated by the fallen angel. This is how Satan works. He has captured the murderer's soul and convinced him he is on a mission for God. Chief Medina is a pious man who has committed atrocious acts against his fellow man. He has strong religious beliefs conflicting with what he is doing. Every time he murders, he seeks absolution for his egregious sins but is refused every time. Now, God is using me as his instrument to wage battle against evil."

Sherman took back control of the conversation. "Until we boarded your vessel, Father Nguyen was trying to intercede by himself with Butcher Bill. He has waged a personal pacific campaign against Medina. His presence has severely unsettled Medina. Revenge against the church he loved and trusted is now his ultimate goal. He sees Father Nguyen as a traitor to his spiritual cause. He feels betrayed. For that, he wants Father Nguyen to suffer for his betrayal. Medina wants to sacrifice Father Nguyen."

"Agent Sherman, you stated we're under a deadline. Can you explain the deadline and how the Navy can assist you in bringing this madman down?" asked Rear Admiral Cable.

"Yes sir, I will. Butcher Bill's sacrificial pattern is to kill in pairs. He always murders a woman and a man. The woman is killed gently as if he being reverent to her. However, the man is always brutally tortured and made to suffer great pain. Dr. Ohms has linked his modus operandi back to Medina's childhood. When he grew up, he was constantly abused, neglected, beaten, and molested. The anger and resentment developed as a child but manifested into a killing spree when he became an adult. He still wants to maintain that sacrificial balance. We received information he already has a female captive and now he wants Father Nguyen to complete the set."

Dr. Ohms displayed the picture of Agent Amecii lying in the back of a van completely immobilized by her captor. Sherman choked back tears. Rear Admiral Cable and Captain Russell looked stunned.

"You are saying Butcher Bill has kidnapped Professor Amecii, is that what I'm seeing here?" said Captain Russell.

"Yes. Medina was under constant surveillance here in Phuket. He must have hired someone to abduct Agent Amecii. However, he doesn't know she is an FBI agent. We believe he thinks Agent Amecii is a Professor of Philosophy. His female sacrifices are always beautiful and exotic women."

"This tale gets worse and worse by the moment Agent Sherman. If you would, please answer Captain Russell's previous question. Are we on a timeline and what can we do to help?" asked Rear Admiral Cable.

"I apologize for not answering your questions directly," replied Agent Sherman.

"It is now 0230 in the morning. Butcher Bill wants us to deliver Father Nguyen to him at a pineapple farm twenty miles north of here. If we do not comply, he will kill Agent Amecii. We have no doubt he'll keep his promise. Father Nguyen has agreed to meet with Medina. Inserted into the priest's body are GPS transmitters. We will know exactly where he is at all times. With that information, we will look for an opportunity to attack Butcher Bill before he has time to slay either Father Nguyen or Agent Amecii."

"That is a very dangerous plan young man," stated Rear Admiral Cable.

"I agree. That is why we asked you to bring Lieutenant Commander Echols and his *SEAL* teams. After Father Nguyen is exchanged for Amecii, we will follow them using your helicopters. His plan involves sacrificing Father Nguyen and Agent Amecii. We believe he has a site already picked out. He is cornered and he knows it. I believe Medina expects to die or to disappear today. But, before he does either, he wants to make two last sacrifices. Our goal is to capture Butcher Bill and save Agent Amecii and Father Nguyen."

"Father, are you sure you want to do this? This sounds like suicide," said the SEAL commander.

"Yes, it does sound like suicide Commander. It is not. I am the only one who can pinpoint Medina's location for you to swoop in and save the day. Please don't be tardy. I believe in my faith. If I am killed, it is inconsequential. All of my life I have devoted my work and deeds to God. God has given me a most Jobian task to test my resolve and faith. I know, if I am murdered, I will immediately go to heaven and sit next to the Lord Jesus. My soul is prepared."

Dr. Ohms broke into the conversation. "We have to be at the pineapple plantation in ninety minutes. Your *SEAL* teams need to be ready to take off in one hour. Five helos will be used. The first will be used by me for command and control. The second helo will transport Father Nguyen and Agent Sherman to Butcher Bill. The third will carry a *SEAL* team, deploy to the ground and approach the pineapple plantation from the South. *SEAL* team two with my FBI team and Officers Hendricks and Raphael on helo four and five will approach from the East and deploy as Lieutenant Commander Echols sees fit. Once Father Nguyen is delivered, we will storm Medina's hideout and capture Butcher Bill. Snipers need to be ready on my or Agent Sherman's command to pull the trigger and put a bullet between this murderous letches' eyes."

The Navy *SEAL* Team leader, Lieutenant Commander Echols wanted more details. "We need a layout of the pineapple ranch. If you want us to help, we have to know the ground."

Hendricks was prepared to answer the question. "Gentlemen, we have all the details you need. We have satellite photos of the farm. The Thai government approved your helicopters to fly anywhere within a two hundred mile radius. No clearance required. The Thai police are interested in nabbing this creep too. Butcher Bill has been to Thailand before. A while back ago we asked the Phuket PD if they ever had murders like those we saw in the states.

Sure enough, they provided info linking the American murders to many overseas. To say the least, they want this creep bagged."

Echols replied, "Roger that Five-O. Let's start looking at those plans with my team and the pilots. We'll figure out how to cover the ground."

"Team, we are up against an extremely desperate and dangerous adversary. He already has one of our own and he will have another very shortly. The rules have changed. I want to take Butcher Bill alive, but one false move and he is going to meet his maker. Does anyone have any questions before we get started?" asked Ohms.

Silence enveloped the room. Father Nguyen cleared his throat. Everyone turned their focus towards him.

"Dr. Ohms, before we begin, I have one wish."

"Certainly Father, if I can provide it, you can anything you desire," said Ohms.

"Thank you, Doctor. Please locate a priest and bring him here."

The request intrigued Rear Admiral Cable. "May I ask why we need to bring another clergyman into the equation? We want to keep the amount of people involved in this operation to a minimum."

Father Nguyen nodded and pondered the question. "I understand your concern Admiral. My religion has seven Holy Sacraments. I desire to observe three of those before I face Chief Medina again. The first is the Sacrament of Reconciliation. Penance. In layman's terms, the priest will hear my confession. I also want to receive Communion before I enter into the Devil's liar. The other is the Sacrament of Last Rites. He shall anoint my forehead, eyes, and lips with sacred oil, pray over me, and prepare my soul for death."

Silenced again engulfed the command center.

CHAPTER THIRTY-EIGHT

The FBI agents, Seattle PD, and Navy team listened intently to the *SEAL* Commander's plan. The pineapple plantation had a single entrance off the main road. There were four back roads traversing across the farm. However, the roads were not paved. Tractors used the roads. The farm tracks were rough and not suitable for streetcars.

Commander Echols described his plan. "*SEAL* Team One is assigned to protect the priest. Three, two man sniper teams will provide a triangular crossfire zone. Wherever the target is standing one of the fire teams should have a clear shot"

"SEAL Team Two is being split up. Fire Team Alpha will cover the pathways leading in and out of the plantation. Fire Team Bravo will be hovering overhead for the unexpected. Five SH-60 Blackhawk helicopters are fueled and waiting for us on the hotel's lawn. Helos one through three will carry the *SEAL*s. Helo number four is the command platform. Helo number five is the Holy Helo carrying Father Nguyen, Agent Sherman, and Seattle PD. Are there any questions?"

Dressed in black combat uniforms, the SEALs checked their weapons and their partners gear one last time. Their faces were painted black. Each carried an M-4 rifle, 9mm pistol, night vision goggles, body armor, miniature binoculars, ammunition, a razor sharp bayonet, and a radio. Going in light improved their agility. The snipers carried .50 caliber rifles with a night vision laser sighted scope attached.

The team escorted Father Nguyen outside to the waiting helos. He marched between the heavily armed warriors. Agent Sherman, Hendricks, and Raphael waited for them. Reaching the Holy Helo, Rear Admiral Cable motioned for his team to take a knee around the priest. Father Nguyen looked around at the confident men. He wished their kind was not needed. Alas, it was and always will be only a dream. There would always be evil in the world. With the warriors huddled and kneeling in front of him, Father Nguyen led the men in prayer.

"Dear Lord, bless these brave men who are champions to your cause. Keep Catherine Amecii strong and safe. May you guide this holy quest in its fight against Satan and his minion. In your name, we pray for you to shine upon us your grace and everlasting love."

The men replied in chorus. "Amen."

Lieutenant Commander Echols stayed with Agent Sherman until Father Nguyen was safely buckled into his seat. The two shook hands. Words were unnecessary. The two warriors knew exactly what to do. The helicopters started their engines making the rotor blades rotate.

The command helo lifted off first carrying Rear Admiral Cable, Captain Russell, and Dr. Ohms. The helicopters were outfitted with secure communications equipment the SEALS used during their combat operations behind enemy lines. Cable thought his battle group assets would be used to strike fear in the terrorists bent on America's destruction. He never dreamed his forces would be used to hunt one of his own sailors.

The helicopters flew in a serial formation, one behind the other skimming the palm tree tops. They were going in fast and low. The command helicopter separated from the others and rose to eight hundred feet. At that altitude, it covered the entire operation with enough time to swoop in to provide assistance. Each helo came equipped with door gunners manning M-60 machine guns.

The pineapple plantation parking lot was empty. Lieutenant Commander Echols' helo circled the plantation searching for

Butcher Bill with its high intensity search light. The halogen lamps turned darkness into day but Butcher Bill evaded detection.

Echol's deployed his perimeter teams. SEAL Team Two's helo flew in fast and hovered over the landing zone. The first fire team fast roped to the ground and reached their assigned positions within thirty seconds. Their night vision goggles turned night into day. The second and third helo performed the same maneuver with fire teams Alpha and Bravo. Fire Team Bravo's helo rose to one hundred feet and hovered above the parking lot. The SEALs reported ready for action within two and a half minutes.

Sherman held Father Nguyen's hand while he gazed into the night's darkness. His lips moved slowly in prayer. He envied the priest. The clergyman was the most courageous human being he had ever come across. What type of person willingly put his life in the hands of a brutal killer? He did not have any stake in this except for his faith and beliefs. Agent Sherman thought he possessed strong convictions and beliefs. The mental fortitude seen in the five foot seven, hundred and sixty seven-pound pacifist came from one source. His faith.

The undercover agent was not overly religious. Next to him and holding his hand was a living, breathing miracle. A unique individual surrounded by a sea of average people. A living saint.

Dr. Ohms's cell phone rang. It could be only one person.

"Yes," he answered.

"I see you brought in the heavy guns. Five helicopters are overkill for one man, don't you think."

"We are at the plantation. Where are you?"

"Well, I am not at the plantation. How stupid do you think I am," Medina sarcastically replied. "The helicopter carrying the priest has ten minutes to travel six miles due north. Land the helicopter on the bridge and make him get out. Once he is on the ground, the helicopter will take off," he ordered.

"No. You wanted us at the plantation and we are here. If you want the priest, you come and get him," replied Ohms sternly.

"Do not test my patience cop. By now you found the cop who followed me and that whore in the bar. I will not wait long. When I leave, I will take Professor Amecii with me. She is quite lovely, you know. A real shame to waste a piece like her just because you want to be defiant."

Ohms had to think fast. "Okay, we will send the priest to the bridge."

"You have nine minutes. A flare is lit for the pilot to recognize the landing zone. Land the other helos at the plantation and shut their engines down. I am watching your every move. Do as I say or this white trash gets a bullet in her eye. That is all."

The telephone line went dead. Ohms contacted Sherman and told him what to do. The Holy Helo veered to the right to follow the road north. Its search light illuminated the two lane road cut through the dense jungle. The pilot had eight minutes to fly to the LZ. He pushed the aircraft's nose down and accelerated the aircraft to ninety knots. If the pilot worried about hitting power lines or striking a tree with the rotor blades he kept it to himself.

The command ship pilot pushed down on his helicopter's collective stick. The helicopter fell like a rock towards the earth. SEAL Team One's helo landed and shut its engines down. Echols commanded the other helos to land and pick up the fire teams.

Sherman thought something like this would happen. Medina was too crafty to allow a force of armed men to land and surround him. Butcher Bill was savvy. Forcing them to first come to the plantation provided him the chance to assess the firepower levied against him. The best way to get troops on the ground fast was by helicopter. The plantation land was flat. Sighting how many helicopters in use could be done by a child with a pair of binoculars.

The Holy Helo's pilot alerted Sherman he spotted a red flare burning on the road near a bridge. Sherman commanded the pilot to do a fly-by to check out where he was going to land and the FBI agent wanted to reconnoiter.

The flare burned brightly in the middle of a bridge. Sherman strapped night vision goggles onto his flight helmet. The dark night transformed into florescent green. The pilot banked the helicopter hard left and came quickly about. Sherman hastily searched the area surrounding the bridge. His searched discovered nothing. It puzzled him. Trekking through the jungle on foot with two hostile captives was impractical and thus improbable. There were not any cars hidden in the bush. So, how did Butcher Bill plan on escaping? The pilot flew down the bridges length again and banked left so Sherman could search out his open door. Sherman switched his goggles to infrared mode. He did not want to look directly at the flare. The flares brilliance would swamp his goggles with heat and shut them down. Sherman picked up two heat signatures hiding in the bushes at the bridges end. The reddish yellow glowing shadows were human in form.

"Ohms…Sherman, we are getting ready to land. There aren't any cars in the area. I got two people hunkered down in the bushes at the west end of the bridge." "Roger…be careful. How's Father Nguyen holding up?"

Sherman looked to the priest. It was impossible to tell what was going through his head. Sheer terror was obvious. Undaunted determination was etched upon his face. His hands were folded in silent prayer. Rosary Beads dangled down swaying with the helicopter's motion. It was a biblical corollary of David versus Goliath. However, this David did not have a sling or a rock. His deep faith was his only weapon with Navy SEALS as a backup. He had no idea what was in front of him. He blindly trusted his maker to see him through the perils in his path.

"Holy Helo on the ground," reported the pilot. Sherman armed with an M-4, 5.56 mm rifle with a night scope jumped out of the helo motioning for Hendricks and Raphael to cover the priest from the other side of the helicopter. Both Seattle Police Officers carried rifles identical to Sherman's with night goggles attached to their helmets. Crouching in the thicket surrounding the bridge's end, Butcher Bill watched the men deploy. A high pitch hum emanated from the helicopter when the pilot reduced the throttle and applied the rotor brakes. The powerful turbine engines hummed to a stop.

A figure stood up from the brush where Sherman knew Butcher Bill was concealing himself. It was Catherine completely naked. Her white skin reflected the moon's rays. She contrasted heavily against the jungle's dark texture.

Sherman whipped off his goggles. Butcher Bill stood behind the frightened and exposed FBI agent enveloping her body crushing her to his chest. A cocked nine millimeter caliber pistol was shoved against the right side of her temple. Tears streamed down her face.

"Send me that treacherous priest," screamed Medina. "Send him to me now. He and I have unfinished business to attend to."

Sherman hollered back. "It's over Medina. Let the Professor go and you won't be harmed."

"I know you, don't I? Where do I know you from?" Butcher Bill pondered aloud. "It's Chief Sherman, right? All this time you have been watching me. You're a cop? Mark my words you filthy bastard. After I am done with Father Nguyen, rest assured I am hunting you. It won't be tonight nor the many nights that follow. You'll have to keep looking over your shoulder for the rest of your life, but I will come for you," he shouted.

"Medina, I'm a FBI agent. You know you cannot go anywhere. Throw away the pistol and let the woman go," Sherman commanded.

More anger pulsed through Medina. He jammed the barrel of the pistol harder against the captured agent's temple causing Amecii to cringe and cry out in pain. Tears cascaded down her reddened face. She tried to wriggle free from her captive but Medina closed his arms tighter about her chest. "It's an even trade," Medina shouted back. "This whoring tramp for the traitor priest!"

Sherman knew what had to be done. Butcher Bill possessed the advantage. They only had one choice. They had to give the murderer what he wanted.

Father Nguyen approached Sherman, made a blessing over the agent's head, and calmly walked towards the madman with his shoulders squared and his chin held high. He hummed "Amazing Grace" as calmly as if he was amongst his parish congregation.

An evil grin overcame the killer's face. He will have the vengeance that consumed his thoughts since the first time Nguyen showed up at the naval base. The meddling clergyman was going to pay for violating his vows and betraying him.

Nguyen stopped in front of Catherine. Her nakedness was invisible to the holy man. "Catherine, you are in God's hands, my daughter. Fear not this beast. He is a wicked and tortured soul who is going to hell very soon."

Catherine turned and locked her eyes with Father Nguyen's. She felt warmth and comfort in his presence. All fear she previously felt vanished and dissipated into the wind. Her strength returned. For some reason, she no longer felt panic, anxiety, or terror.

"Turn around priest and put your hands behind your back," commanded the madman.

Nguyen did as instructed. Medina used Catherine and the clergyman as human shields. He whipped out a circular white plastic zip-tie with his left hand, slipped it over the priest's hands zipping the fastener tight. Nguyen grimaced as the plastic bit into his skin. Now he knew a little piece of how Christ felt as he was being captured and abused.

Medina shoved Catherine to the ground and grabbed Nguyen's captured hands. He harshly pressed the gun against the priest's right temple. "Run you unholy scank. Run to your saviors. You would have made a good sacrifice but now I have something more valuable. God will reward me greatly for executing a priest who violates his holy vows."

Catherine sprinted towards Sherman. The twenty-five yards felt like twenty five miles. Without warning, she heard a thunderous crack and felt fire ripping through her back. The bullet penetrated her skin just below her left clavicle and exited her body in her lower back. A second bullet struck her on the right side of her neck. Her skin turned cold. The strength in Catherine's legs evaporated. She felt herself crashing to the ground.

Neither Hendricks nor Raphael had a chance at Medina without hitting Father Nguyen. All they had were front row seats watching the murderous bastard outstretch his arm and pull the trigger of his 9mm pistol. The shot's sound waves bounced off the trees reverberating through the jungle valley. The dense foliage soaked up the pistol's report.

"No!" screamed Sherman restraining himself from returning fire. His FBI training kicked in. The FBI agent threw himself to the ground. He aimed towards the target darting down the jungle hill with the priest in tow. His vision captured two images. Catherine tumbling to the earth and Medina cutting a swath through the jungle. His love's soft red mane cascaded in front of her face. Her arms were open and outstretched yearning to be caught by his strong arms. It all happened so fast. Catherine's naked body plummeted to the ground. Her head ponged off the bridge's unforgiving pavement. She lay motionless less than ten feet in front of Sherman.

Medina needed a diversion. Shooting the pretty professor as she ran towards safety provided him the perfect opportunity. The cops would take cover and try to attend to the wounded victim. The few seconds the shooting provided gave him enough time to escape with Nguyen. It also touched off his murderous cycle of killing in pairs.

Sherman bellowed "Hendricks, Raphael go after that bastard. Shoot him if you have a shot."

The two police officers dashed to where Medina disappeared into the jungle. Bullets slicing through the fragile jungle foliage hampered their pursuit. Butcher Bill's distance between him and the officers expanded rapidly. Hendricks and Raphael only saw the muzzle flashes from a pistol firing at them. The shots were wild but had their affect. Their pursuit slowed to a crawl.

Medina dragged Father Nguyen down the hill. The priest realized how Butcher Bill planned his escape. A blue speedboat was tied up to a stake at the bottom of the hill. The river led to the ocean. And, the ocean led to many sites on the Thailand mainland or a plethora of small islands along the coast. Medina thought out his escape plan well. Making the small police force first go to a wide open field so he could assess their forces, then diverting them to a isolated bridge, shooting Agent Amecii to cause a diversion for his getaway, and now a boat to whisk them away to wherever Medina planned on torturing him. The plan was brilliant. The cops did not have a home field advantage and did not know the lay of the land.

Sherman cradled Catherine in his arms telling her he loved her over and over. Blood drenched his lover and spilled over the cold hard concrete. Catherine tried to speak to Sherman. She desperately wanted him to save her. Her legs were numb. Shivers encapsulated her flesh. Sherman knew she was dying and there was nothing he could do except hold her and comfort her. Their tender love was snuffed out in a flash. His fingers combed her soft red mane petting her gently to comfort his fallen lover. Catherine fell deeper and deeper into a deathly abyss. Her breathing shallowed and finely ceased altogether.

The helicopter's pilot kneeling next to him shouted and gestured with his hand but Sherman was oblivious to everything around him. Catherine's sudden death stunned the veteran police officer where he could not hear nor see. Agent Andrew Sherman was numb to the activity going on around him. The cranking of a boat engine and its throttle pushed to the maximum snapped him back to consciousness. Rifle shots echoed from below the bridge. Hendricks and Raphael had opened fire on the boat trying to hit its engine as it sped away.

He picked up Catherine, her legs, arms, and head dangled heavily from her body as he placed her in the back of the helicopter. There was nothing in the helicopter to place over her blood covered naked body. He did the best he could. Sherman lay her down and pushed her red locks away from her face. She was angelic. It was at that moment Sherman realized Butcher Bill had claimed his next female victim. The irony washed over Sherman's thoughts. The way he positioned her body with her hands folded neatly over her blood drenched corpse reminded him of how Butcher Bill left his females victims.

Turning to the pilot who stood next to him with his sidearm drawn, "Get this bird cranked up and in the air," he commanded.

"Right," was the only reply the Navy Lieutenant said. He climbed into the Blackhawk's cockpit and fired the engine's igniters. The spinning rotor blades beat the air around them. The two Seattle police detectives sprinted up the embankment and threw themselves into the helicopter.

"Ohms, this is Sherman. Medina shot and killed Catherine. He escaped with Father Nguyen on a speedboat. They are heading down the river towards the ocean. Get your team in the air and lock onto the GPS signal. Wherever Butcher Bill is taking Father Nguyen, he will know we will be close behind. He wants to kill him quick and take off. If he does that, the murdering bastard will disappear forever."

Ohms heard the gunfire. Being in the fields waiting for information was grueling. He never fathomed Butcher Bill killing Catherine. As he thought about it, he realized the murderer played them like a flute. Everything they did reacted to his motions. This would be their final chance at capturing Butcher Bill. No matter how much he liked the priest, they could not let the killer escape again. Even if it meant attacking and causing the saintly priest's death. Butcher Bill's murderous rampage ended tonight.

CHAPTER THIRTY-NINE

Shooting the redheaded female professor had not been the way he wanted to sacrifice her. It turned out to be good enough. Stripped of her clothes, she was made to feel her humility and shame just like Eve felt after she enticed Adam to taste her fruit. Firing on her as she ran for protection to her godless protectors filled his innards with strength. Killing her made capturing the priest and escaping much, much easier.

The speedboat sped done the black river. Acquiring the boat had been child's play. Boats moored near Phuket beach made it easy to steal one. During the day, the boats embarked tourists for parasail rides, water skiing, snorkeling, or scuba diving the vibrant underworld of the nearby islands. The boat he chose looked new and in good working order. Hot wiring it was elementary for the experienced electrician. After stealing the boat, Medina backed the van down the pier and loaded Catherine, still gagged and bound her to the gunwale. He had to hurry but he wanted to exploit his sacrificial lamb a bit. Medina drove the boat out of the bay and headed north. He saw the river's mouth easily and steered into the jungle tributary. The urge overcame his senses. Edging the boat near the riverbank, he fastened a rope to a boat clew and tied the other end to an overhanging branch. Kneeling at Catherine's side, he clasped his hands together in silent prayer. Clearing his mind of anxiety, he withdrew the knife he carried and opened the blade. Catherine madly kicked and whipped her body ferociously in an attempt to escape. It was useless. Medina pinned her down and leveled the knife's sharpened edge in front of her eyes. Her thrashing ceased. She was more docile than a broken stallion. Medina rolled her over onto her back and sliced her shirt down the center. Pulling on the center of her bra he slid the knife under its strapping. The cold steel blade touching Catherine's skin made her freeze inside. One rapid slash cut through the woman's bra exposing her tits and raised nipples to Medina's touch and gaze. Medina did not ravage her breasts or harm her. He just wanted to touch her young feminine skin. Butcher Bill spun around on his sacrifice's chest and sliced away the skirt she wore. Underneath, she wore sheer white panties. Medina ran his rough hands over her legs and massaged her. His favorite spot was petting the inside of a woman's thighs. To him, it was the most tender part of a woman's sex. Time forbade him from carrying out his normal murderous ritual. Feeling her fear emitting from her body served his purposes.

Leaving Catherine naked and bound on the boat's deck, Medina recovered the line making the speedboat fast to shore, backed the boat into the black river, gunned the throttle, and headed towards the bridge. The rest of the night was history. Using Catherine as bait and as a shield worked perfectly. The priest was his ultimate prize. His Lord God, will reward him greatly for serving his wrath upon the clergyman who broke his sacred trust. He placed a lot of trust in God and each step of his plan tonight was rewarded with His grace. It was executed flawlessly. However, the cops had helicopters and would soon be on his tail. The sun was about to rise over the horizon so he had to be under cover soon.

The boat sped down the river pushing forty-five knots. Traveling with the current and tide made the craft skim across the inky waveless surface. Exiting the river's mouth, the boat slowed a bit when it plunged into the denser salt water. He vectored the boat northeast. Five minutes later he slowed to a crawl near an abandoned fish cannery. It still had a covered mooring used to protect boats from the seasonal monsoons. Pulsing the engine slowly, the boat slid into the boat garage skimming its starboard side against the wooden docking. Only as a seasoned sailor could do, he switched off the engine, scrambled over the side and lashed the boat tight to the pier. The only sounds heard were the gentle lapping of the ocean waves against the wooden pylons. Darkness was beaten back by the moon's reflection off the sea.

Father Nguyen laughed heartily. "This is your sacrificial temple," chastised the holy man. "I thought you were God's servant who presents great gifts in an offering to his Holiness and might. For all of the decadent brilliance you have demonstrated over the years, you still are bent on destruction and cannot see the devil has consumed your being."

Medina stood motionless listening to his captive preaching. "You of all people should understand it does not matter how the offering is made Priest. It matters only if the sacrifice is made in His name."

"Whose name are you referring to when you say those words Ignacio Medina? I know you believe it is our Savior's name but it truly is not. Do you know why I have never granted you absolution?" quizzed Father Nguyen.

The question caught Medina off guard. He expected the Catholic shaman to start weeping and begging for his life. The man in front of him was steadfast but definitely not afraid.

"Because I have committed mortal sins violating the church's protocol and commandments. I have heard it all before. Save your paltry spiritual rhetoric," he replied. "The priests before you peddled the same message. Follow the code and you will be given absolution. I have given up on your false promises. The only way to serve God is to show Him you are willing to do the extreme for Him. Just like Abraham and Job. That's where faith lies, not in your rituals and dogma."

Nguyen continued to sit in the boat. The longer he stalled and kept his captor occupied, the sooner the cavalry would arrive. His life no longer mattered to him. If Medina killed him, it was God's will. But, this night would see the end to the demon's rampage. Sacrificing his life for the countless other lives this butcher

338 ERIC W. HERBERT

snuffed out was the price he was willing to pay. His savior did the same over two thousand years ago.

"No, my son," whispered Nguyen. "You will never receive absolution because you cannot feel remorse inside your heart. Being truly penitent and contrite is the path towards the Light. Satan holds the reins over your life. The demonic angel is the master and you are his wicked puppet. Drop to your knees now and shout to God that you beg his forgiveness, I will then grant you absolution."

Butcher Bill jumped back into the boat. Nguyen flinched from Medina's rampant and uncontrollable aggression. "God's grace courses through my veins, Priest," screamed the maniac. "No words of yours will sway me from the task our heavenly Father placed upon my shoulders. He thrust this cross onto my shoulders to carry. He demands blood to be spilled to make up for the blood Jesus spilled trying to save man's worthless and manipulative existence. Sinners must be punished not forgiven."

Father Nguyen began to speak but Medina's seized him by the throat, dragging him onto the dock. Barely able to keep his feet under him, the monster propelled him forward. Medina seized a wooden bat from the boat used to thump fish. Nguyen suppressed his urge to flee when he saw the weapon being swung at him. Running away did nothing. Staying with the murderous leech was the only way Sherman could find them. Everything seemed to travel in slow motion. The bat waved high above the killer's head came crashing down onto Nguyen's right thigh shooting stabbing pain through his nervous system making him cry out in pain.

"Now priest, get your holy ass up and start walking down that pier before I take this bat to your skull," ordered Medina.

Father Nguyen wiped the tears from his eyes, slowly pushed himself erect, and stood searching for his balance. The leg was not broken but the blow made him limp. The killer struck him in the leg to make sure he could not run if he wanted to. If he tried, Medina would be on top of him in a flash.

Drops of water fell from the sky with a strong breeze blowing in from the west signaling a rapidly approaching storm. Yellowish blue lightning bolts flashed from the heavens to the Earth. The previously sedate palm trees rustled in the wind dancing in time with the electrical arcs racing across the pre-dawn sky. Father Nguyen stared at the light show.

"Do you see this weather Ignacio?" the priest asked. "It's a sign from God. He is not pleased with your ugly deeds and what you've done and what you intend to do. Give yourself up to the police, face your just punishments, and pray for Christ's mercy. If you do not, I guarantee your soul will pay the price for all eternity."

"Shut your mouth priest. This is just a seasonal monsoon. It is good weather for your sacrifice. Think of it like being a dramatic backdrop to an awful tragic play."

Nguyen did not respond. His mind was fixed on what Butcher Bill said about an awful tragic play. Just like his Lord in the immortal passion play, he had his own part in a tragic play to act out. He marched from the wooden pier onto a path leading to an open grass thatched pavilion. It used to be where the fishermen brought their daily catch, weighed it, packed the fish in ice, and loaded the seafood onto trucks for the local market. The building sat disused and discarded for more modern facilities located nearer town. Just like the dock, the place was deserted. It smelt of rotting fish. The dirt floor was hardened from fish blood spilled over twenty years of dead fish cuttings. Time and hundreds of feet stomping on the jungle soil turned the ground into a stone like surface. Wooden fishing processing tables lined the right and left side of the pavilion. Teak pillars supported the palm thatched roof. Six lined the outer portions of the enclosure with others providing the support from the inside. Medina pushed the priest towards the center pylon.

"Wrap your arms around and hug the column, Father," the murderer commanded.

Nguyen peacefully complied. He felt Medina grasp his wrists tightly. Butcher Bill wrapped black electrical tape around his hands binding him to the pole. The demon then thrust the priest's ankles against the poles and bound those with the tape too. Lastly, Medina circled his waist with the tape immobilizing his victim against the pole. To Nguyen, it reminded him of the pillar Jesus Christ was lashed to at the orders of Pontius Pilate. The priest prayed to Christ to give him the same strength he possessed when the barbarous Roman torturers unleashed their lashings on his mortal flesh. In albeit a smaller scale, like Christ, Father Nguyen rightly believed he was sacrificing his life for the good of man.

"We have a strong signal from the priest's GPS transmitters," reported a FBI technician to Dr. Ohms and the other teams over the helicopter's command radio frequency. "The signal was moving at forty knots five minutes ago. They're stationary and most likely on foot ten miles up the coast from where we are."

The five helicopters hovered at two thousand feet. The command helicopter carrying Dr. Ohms, Admiral Cable, Captain Russell, and the SEAL team commander watched a FBI agent work the tracking equipment. Helicopters two through four carrying the camouflaged SEAL Teams One and Two patiently sat in their jump seats ready for action. The SEALS knew who the target was. The best use of the most highly trained warriors in the world meant they always had to be trusted with information. Leaving small yet significant details out typically got one of them killed. Their lives and unique skills were too expensive to waste by not giving them all of the pertinent facts and dangers associated with a special op.

The last helo carried Agent Sherman, Detective's Hendricks, and Raphael. Agent Catherine Amecii's bloodied corpse lie coldly on the helicopter's metal deck. Her blood seeping from her body made the aircraft floor sticky. Her deathly pose was covered in a silver thermal survival blanket provided by the aircraft's pilot.

Sherman's guts churned inside but he suppressed his need to grieve. Right now, the best way to avenge his lover's death was being focused and steely-eyed. After it was over, he would mourn and honor her presence in his life properly. Butcher Bill remained his primary focus. Sherman made his mind up. It was time for an eye for an eye. He did not share those thoughts with any of his teammates. Not that they would disagree with him. When Medina targeted his lover, mercilessly defiled her, and gunned her down. The battle lines were redrawn. The murderous madman's decades old rampage was going to end today with his death delivered at Sherman's hands.

Each helicopter waited for the plan. Ohms and Rear Admiral Cable handed the tactical operations reins over to Lieutenant Commander Echols.

Echols studied images of the areas topography from satellite images taken from high overhead on his battlefield laptop. The images were taken from a reconnaissance satellite, transmitted to the CIA, and forwarded to the Navy in less than three minutes. The photos showed an industrial fishing compound with three sets of docks and piers, four open air roofed structures, and a staging area where metal bins and fifty-five gallon drums were stored. A single dirt road approximately a half mile long snaked through the jungle from the main highway. Besides that, the Thai jungle swallowed up the rest of the Earth for a five mile radius. Butcher Bill picked a very remote spot.

"Gentlemen, *Operation Butcher's Block* will go down like this," Echols said over the radio. All Navy operations had a name assigned. It was tradition. Echols liked it because in this operation Butcher Bill was going to be taken out of the general population one way or another. After learning of Medina's homicidal resume and the recent cold-blooded murder of Agents Bridger and Amecii, he didn't care if his team extracted him dead or alive. His only concern was the safety of his men and saving Father Nguyen from a horrible death.

Each helicopter carried a military field laptop computer onboard. The respective crew's huddled around the screen to follow along with Lieutenant Commander Echol's plan.

"We're going to use a three pronged triangular offensive. SEAL Team One approaches from the sea. A quarter a mile away SEAL Team One deploys into the ocean and swims the distance to the dock. You will deploy in a line and approach the pavilions from the West. SEAL Team Two fast ropes to the dirt access road. You will be deployed about a mile up the road from the fishing complex. I estimate a steady run allows you eight minutes to reach your dispersion point. At that point, you will divide into two sub-teams making two lines of the triangle. Everyone understands so far?" the Commander asked.

Silence in his headset meant no one had any questions.

"This is a combined Navy, Federal, and State operation," Echols continued. "Agent Sherman, Detectives Hendricks and Raphael will fast rope after SEAL Team Two. Hendricks will accompany one sniper team while Raphael teams up with the other. Agent Sherman goes with Lieutenant Foley and Master Chief Zucher. Foley is in command but takes his kill orders from Sherman on the ground. Everyone got that?" Thirty seconds passed and again there was only silence.

"Good, it is a simple plan. We got storm clouds rolling in providing good cover. I want us deploying in five minutes. Check your gear, lock and load, be safe. Let's get this bastard and save the *Saint*."

Saint was the call sign the team gave Father Nguyen. It seemed fitting. None of the battle hardened warriors knew of a braver act of courage than what the *Saint* volunteered for. Before the mission started, Father Nguyen had said a prayer over each of the team members. Navy sailors are naturally a superstitious bunch. The superstition was amplified tenfold within the SEAL community. To them, receiving a blessing from the *Saint* felt like being personally touched by the hand of God.

Rear Admiral Cable nodded his head in approval and gave the command to execute the mission. The four helicopters carrying the SEALs and police officers dove towards the ocean and flared up when they were ten feet above sea level. The pilots were permanently assigned with the SEAL teams to perfect their special ops flying skills. The three lead choppers buzzed over the water veering left to make their approach to the insertion point behind the fishing compound.

The fourth helicopter's pilot pulled up on the aircraft's cyclic controls causing the forward speed on the aircraft to be siphoned off. A few more adjustments to the throttle, collective stick, and foot pedals had the helicopter hovering five feet above the blue water below. With their weapons safely stored on their backs, masks, snorkels and fins donned, the fifteen members making up SEAL Team One jumped into the inky ocean. The aircraft's crew engineer tapped the pilot on the shoulder signaling the team deployed safely. The pilot veered to the right, increased his speed and started to gain altitude. He would rejoin with the command helicopter hovering three miles out to sea at one thousand feet.

Land was roughly a quarter a mile away. Rain poured down from the heavens concealing the SEALS kicking madly to get ashore in time to be in position. Trained to swim long distances, the warriors effortlessly swam through the water making their amphibious assault.

SEAL Team Two's and the plain clothes cop's helicopters dashed over the jungle treetops, banked hard right making the helicopter's sides point down toward the earth. The SEALs were used to tactical approaches trusting their seatbelts to hold them in place. Sherman, Hendricks, and Raphael gripped their harnesses tightly. The helos leveled above the dirt road leading to the fishing compound while the helo's crewmen tossed out inch thick manila ropes. One by one, the naval strike team members gripped the ropes with their glove-covered hands and slid stealthily to the ground. The fast roping insertion operation lasted three minutes. On the ground, the team members formed skirmishing lines and jogged down the muddy road.

Satellite imagery showed a large bend in the dirt road before it opened to the fishing compound. The SEALs decided to enter the jungle at the road's bend ignoring the thunderous storm raging around them. They preferred stormy weather because it concealed their positions.

Lieutenant Commander Foley keyed his throat microphone. "All teams report status," he commanded.

"Team One manned and ready," said the SEAL Team One leader.

"Team Two-Alpha manned and ready," was heard by Foley. Two-Bravo reported the same message.

"Roger, observe and report," he replied.

Nguyen did not resist Medina. He accepted his destiny as doing God's will when he embraced his dangerous journey to halt the maniac's killing. He watched silently as Medina reached into his knapsack and withdrew a silver metallic object. The clicking of the lock blade startled him back to reality. The killer circled around his immobilized victim. Grasping Nguyen's black shirt by the collar he raised the stainless steel blade and slashed down through the texture of the priest's shirt. The knife blade's tip creased his skin. Agonizing pain pulsated down Father Nguyen's spine from the laceration feeling his hot blood flowing down the path of his backbone. Medina thrust the sharpen edge back against the man's shirt, slicing it open to reveal his sacrifice's bare skin.

"Father, don't fret over the small wound I just gave you. Think of it as the least of the pain you are about to receive. I first thought about beating your body senseless with the bat but your words on the dock gave me a better idea. A more fitting tribute to the twisted version of faith you persist to believe in. I am going to show you how Christ felt. When it's over, you will tell me if you still believe in a just and loving God. I guarantee you that you will believe God wants men who disregard his teachings punished like I'm going to punish you. The pain you are about to receive will open your eyes to see what God really wants from his servants."

Father Nguyen gathered the strength he needed to reply.

"In the end, you will most likely hear what you so desperately desire to hear. Remember this though, it was coerced from me. I admit the human flesh is weak. But, my God is all knowing, all seeing, all loving, and all powerful. Killing people in his name is wrong and you will never join him in his kingdom. You are a product of Lucifer and to Lucifer's fiery hell you shall go. God knows my faith is strong and the bond between him and me will never be severed."

The priest's reaction inflamed Butcher Bill's raging internal fires. He whipped off his belt from his waist. The long strip of leather had pyramid steel studs riveted into it the thick black leather. The belt whirled in the air and crashed down on Nguyen's back tearing the holy man's skin. Blood flowed from his wounds and knocked the wind out of Nguyen's lungs forcing a scream out from within. Medina raised and crashed the metal and leather belt onto the man's flesh again and again. The lashing peeled the soft human texture from the priest's body in irregular strips. Dents and holes formed where the metal studs penetrated the skin. Nguyen hands involuntarily balled into fists in a futile attempt to control his screaming. More blood seeped from his mouth when the priest bit into his bottom lip.

Medina continued the flogging. He slashed at his sacrifices legs, feet, arms and head. Bits of scalp and hair flew across the room after being ripped away by the metal studs. Nguyen panted heavily trying to draw in lost air. The tears he shed mixed with the blood streaming from his head wounds.

"Where is your God priest? Give me absolution Father and the pain will stop. Forgive me of my sins and I will cease crushing you into a bloody pulp. If you do not forgive me now, the pain will continue. You will force me to keep the scourging going," screamed the madman.

Father Nguyen barely heard Medina's words. The pain rippling through his mind and body stabbed at his senses. The world whirled about him as he fought to remain conscious and alert. His eyes blurred from blood, sweat, and tears rolling down his face whilst the thunder and lightning storm raged around them. Any movement made him flinch from the excruciating pain. Raindrops forced into the pavilion from the storm's winds landed heavily upon his skinless back. Every time thunder cracked or a lightning bolt flashed, its energy slapped at his tender wounds. Despite the hurt he felt, Nguyen mustered enough energy to reply to the madman's demands.

"Your whipping will make me stronger, Lucifer," gasped the priest. "I am empowered by Christ to battle you. Do what evil you must, but I will never absolve you from your horrendous sins. The fleeting pain you inflict on me is not even a fraction of the pain you are inflicting upon yourself for all eternity. Hell awaits you with its gates wide open." The speech sapped his energy. Thirst overcame his senses. He wished for a taste of water followed by a quick death. Neither would come. The demon sailor was just getting started.

Sherman heard the report made by SEAL Team One. He scrambled to the sniper's position focusing his binoculars on the pavilion. What he witnessed sickened him. Father Nguyen was barely conscious and lashed to a pole. The weight of his body made him slump but his bonds kept him erect. Medina was mercilessly thrashing the priest's flesh with a blood-covered strap. Butcher Bill was covered in blood. He was whipping the man to death.

The agent focused on the valiant clergyman. Great chunks of skin, muscle, and tissue were brutally torn from his body. Throwing down the binoculars, Sherman dashed through the jungle racing to the pavilion. The rainstorm covered the noises of his rapid approach. He had to get to the priest. Adrenalin pumped through his body. Hopefully the priest would still be breathing by the time he reached him.

Butcher Bill spotted the charging agent but was too late to react. The priest's blood that spattered into his eyes clouded his vision. He was in a sacrificial frenzy. The more blood he shed the more numb to his surroundings he became. Medina was a killing machine in blood lust. All he wanted to do now was to transfer his own emotional pain into his victim's body.

Sherman threw his shoulder into the killer's body forcing Medina to tumble to the ground. The sudden impact awakened him from his torturous trance. He sprang up quickly and drew out the knife he used to cut away the priest's clothing.

"You are not stopping me in God's work. I told you I'd kill you too," he cried.

Sherman charged the madman again. Medina swung his blade madly at his assailant slashing a deep cut along Sherman's face. He never felt the wound. The agent's rage fueled his body. Tackling Butcher Bill, Sherman pummeled him with heavy punches to the murderer's face and body. Medina tried to fight back but he had expended too much energy torturing the priest. Sherman landed blow after blow. It was the first time Sherman ever lost control. The loss of his lover murdered within ten feet of him and the horrific sight of Nguyen being mercilessly whipped against the wooden pillar caused his heroic hysteria.

Medina lay in a crumbled bundle on the ground. Sherman looked down at the madman. His face was bruised red and purple. Blood dripped out of his mouth from where the FBI agent knocked out some of his teeth. Picking up the knife, Agent Sherman ran to Father Nguyen. Sherman surveyed the man's wounds from the brutal whipping. Blood dripped from the man's body pooling around the pillar. Agent Sherman feared he was too late. Laying his fingers on the man's throat it was difficult to feel a pulse. His hands kept slipping off from the slickness of the blood. A faint heart beat pulsated. The *Saint* was alive.

"Corpsman, he's alive," he bellowed but the SEALS were already cutting away the tape releasing Father Nguyen from his bonds. The wounds would have to wait. The naval medic wanted to pump fluids into the priest's body. He had lost a lot of blood. The man needed hydration quickly before his heart pumped the rest of the blood out of the *Saint's* body into the parched Earth.

He thrust a needle into Nguyen's arm attaching a saline solution bag to its end starting the slow process of keeping the man alive. Reaching into his medical kit, the young lifesaver pulled out an ampoule filled with a clear liquid. Filling a syringe, the medic mouthed to Sherman *"Morphine"*. If the priest woke up, the torture he suffered would make the pain unbearable. The best thing for him to do now would be to stay asleep. The man was a true hero. He went through all that pain and agony to defeat the evil killer. The medic told Sherman they would have him aboard the *LINCOLN's* sickbay in less than thirty minutes. The ship possessed a medical department more sophisticated than most major city hospitals. Father Nguyen would be provided the best care until he was stabilized and able to be moved to a hospital stateside.

A deep groan roused Sherman's attention. Butcher Bill began to stir from the intense beating he received. Eight guns manned by SEAL Team were leveled at his head. The FBI agent crossed over to the serial killer, flipped him onto his stomach, pulled his arms behind his back and tightly secured his hands with handcuffs. Before he could do anything else, Lieutenant Commander Foley stepped forward, leaned down to Chief Medina and stated, "Chief Petty Officer Medina, you are under arrest for three counts of murder and one count of attempted murder. Your court martial is in two days as prescribed by the Uniformed Code of Military Justice."

Sherman was stunned. "What the hell are you doing sailor?" exclaimed Sherman.

"Orders, sir," was his reply.

CHAPTER FORTY

Lieutenant Commander Foley's actions first upset Sherman. Arriving back on the *LINCOLN*, Medina was carted away in shackles by four of the biggest Marines he had ever seen. The immobilized criminal was inspected by a Naval Medical Corp Captain who declared Medina fit for duty. It was the military's way of saying Medina was not injured enough to prevent him from performing his military duties; thus, he was able to participate in his naval court martial which was already scheduled to take place in two days. The Navy doctor's declaration had an underlining proclamation as well. Declaring Medina fit for duty also said his mind was sound. He knew right from wrong. He was not delusional or hearing voices. He could participate actively and coherently in his defense at the court martial. Pleading *not-guilty-by-reason-of-mental-defect* would not be entertained whatsoever.

Things were different on a naval ship when it was forward deployed. The usual constitutionally guaranteed protections provided the average American citizen at home, were usurped by the Uniform Code of Military Justice. The rights of due process were not applicable if you were in the military. Once a person enlisted or accepted a commission as an officer, many of the amendments he or she went to battle for were stripped away. Military justice was swift; thus, maintaining good order and discipline. The only way to accomplish that tenet was to handle problems expeditiously.

In all rights, Butcher Bill should have been arrested by the FBI and immediately flown to the United States for arraignment and trial for the hundreds of murders he committed. Instead, the military took over. Dr. Ohms expressed the same frustration his team felt to his superiors. His hands were tied. The Department of Justice's acquiesced to the Department of Defense's might.

The orders came straight from the White House to arrest the murderer under military authority vice federal authority. Rear Admiral Cable received the orders directly from the Secretary of the Navy. The two star Flag Officer was commanded to preside over a court martial comprised of Battle Group's ship captains who were solely responsible with determining Medina's guilt or innocence. Two Judge Advocate General Attorneys were flown in from the Pentagon. One served as the prosecutor while the other assumed the role as Medina's defense attorney. The outcome was already decided before the martial litigation began. The court martial was merely a formality.

The political ramifications surrounding the events in the last day shocked the world. The United States needed bold and decisive action to save its respect within the international community. An American sailor, identified as one of the most brutal serial killers ever to prey upon humanity, had been routinely transported across the globe onboard United States war ships where he committed numerous acts of unfettered violence. Killing the Thai prostitute, two American FBI agents, and attempting to kill an American Catholic Priest on foreign soil had to be expeditiously addressed.

While the combined Navy, FBI, and Seattle Police Department hunted Butcher Bill, the Pentagon legal gears churned. The Naval Judge Advocate Office scoured the military regulations, martial laws, and precedents. The results were presented to the Joint Chiefs of Staff, the Supreme Court, and select members of Congress. Their opinion was overwhelming unanimous which made the President's decision easier.

The United States was embroiled in a war against terrorism. The naval combatant Chief Petty Officer Medina was stationed aboard the USS ABRAHAM LINCOLN which was at sea and at war. Citing tradition and precedent rooted as far back as the

Continental Navy, a sailor in time of war could be tried, convicted, and if found guilty, punished at sea. Sentences handed down by a court martial at sea were to be expedient and befitting the crime. A sentence carried out with haste maintained good order and discipline throughout the fleet. In days past, if a violation of military orders was not severe enough or not carried out quickly it sent a signal to impressed sailors that they could violate the rules without recourse. Eventually, it might lead to mutiny. So, punishments were harsh, severe, and quick. The most extreme punishment a convicted sailor could receive was death.

Over the next two days, Captain Decker, Medina's defense attorney, attempted on many occasions to discuss Medina's case with him. Each time, Butcher Bill refused to speak with him. Instead, choosing to legally represent himself. As prescribed, Medina was afforded the opportunity to review the evidence to be used against him. Most of the time, Medina sat silently in his shipboard cell, relishing in his exploits over the last two days.

The Court Martial lasted a mere eleven hours. Medina sat in front of the seven naval officers chosen to judge him. The officer panel listened to all of the prosecutorial witnesses. They listened to Medina's court appointed attorney who unsuccessfully tried to convince the naval tribunal the serial killer was insane and unfit to stand trial. While Captain Decker was attempting to defend his client, Chief Medina stood up from his chair and stated he did not wish for Captain Decker to represent him. The court advised him that his decision was unwise. Medina did not care. He relished in his guilt.

Standing in front of the panel, Medina voluntarily recounted slicing the Thai prostitute's throat, gutting Agent Bridger, kidnapping, torturing, and shooting Agent Amecii, and whipping Father Nguyen nearly to death. Remorse was foreign to Butcher Bill.

Rear Admiral Cable halted Medina's testimony to ensure Medina understood that anything he said to the court was official testimony and it could be used against him. Chief Medina acknowledged that he understood and continued his diatribe.

The Court Martial panel listened intently to Medina. They sat stunned at the man's callousness and complete contempt for human life.

After Medina finished speaking, the court adjourned for three hours while the Court Martial Panel discussed their verdict. They unofficially conceded Chief Petty Officer Medina was insane. That observation would never be committed to paper only through spoken words amongst the sea captains whose thoughts vanished with the salt mist. Any man who believed he received orders from God to brutally kidnap and kill his fellow man was definitely not in control of his thoughts. Only one conclusion could be reached. The man was not in command of his faculties, *non-compos mentis*. However, justice had to be done and carried out swiftly. Sane or insane did not matter. The world and Medina's hundreds of victims demanded decisive action.

Rear Admiral Cable collected the court martial panel's votes. The judgment was unanimous. Cable called for the Marine's to deliver Medina back to the court. Shuffling in with shackles attached to his hands and feet, he stood at rigid attention dressed in his Service Dress Blues uniform ready to hear the court's decision.

"Chief Petty Officer Electrician's Mate Ignacio Medina," stated Rear Admiral Cable from behind a green clothed covered table. "You have been tried by a Military Court Martial in accordance with the United States Naval Uniform Code of Military Justice. The charges against you are three counts of First Degree Murder, one count of Attempted Murder, three counts of Kidnapping, one count of Larceny, and one count of Conduct Unbecoming a United States Navy Non-commissioned Petty Officer. Do you understand what I have stated to you Chief Petty Officer Medina?"

Medina stepped towards the green table where the panel sat. His Marine guards quickly grasped him by the arms preventing him from approaching the naval officers any further.

"I understand the charges you have levied against me. However, I do not recognize your authority to judge me. There is only one who can judge me for what I have done. I am sure I will soon meet the ultimate Judge and He will reward me for doing his holy bidding," replied Medina.

Cable sipped from a glass of ice water and rose from his chair. The six Naval Captains who presided over the proceedings stood in unison. They were united in their findings. The seriousness of the event demanded proper military protocol.

"Chief Petty Officer Medina, a panel comprised of this Battle Group's Commanding Officers and I, Commander of the USS *ABRAHAM LINCOLN* Battle Group, Task Force Twenty-Three performing gallant duties in the Seventh Fleet area of operations find you guilty on all counts of the charges read. I hereby sentence you to death by hanging. Punishment will be executed at dawn on the morrow. That is all. This court martial is dismissed."

The Marines harshly grabbed Medina by the arms, brusquely turned him about, and marched him out of the shipboard courtroom.

Medina was afforded a last meal of his choice. He asked for Thai spicy beef panang with white sticky rice. He asked for a Budweiser beer but settled for a Coke. Alcohol was forbidden onboard US Navy warships ever since Josephus Daniels ordered alcohol removed from US Navy ships during his tenure as Secretary of the Navy. For dessert, he requested and received fresh, ripe papaya with sweet rice.

His final request was for a priest to visit him. Specifically, he wanted Father Nguyen. Medina's Marine Corps guards immediately summoned Captain Russell and Commander Riley. Riley took the request to the ship's medical bay where the *Saint* was recuperating from the wounds Butcher Bill inflicted upon him.

Unbelievably, Riley found Father Nguyen sitting up in his bed reading his bible despite having the majority of his body covered in white bandages. Slight dots of blood were evident from where the severe wounds he received at Medina's hands seeped through. Instead of being in a surly mood like any other person would have been after undergoing the torment he suffered, Father Nguyen was quite chipper. The painkillers the navy medical staff prescribed helped as well. However, Riley did not believe his priest friend was entirely free of pain. What he found was a man who emanated grace and courage.

"Hello Commander Riley. I'm glad you have come to visit with me," remarked Father Nguyen as if he never went through the ordeal he had experienced three nights before.

"Father, I'm so glad you're feeling better. The last time I saw you, you were still sleeping and just out of surgery."

"I heard Chief Medina has been captured, tried, and convicted for his evil deeds. That is such a relief my friend," said the priest. "My prayers have been answered."

"Yes, we are all quite relieved. We are still reeling from the fact a serial killer was living in our midst. Your faith and bravery brought him to justice. The Naval Court Martial found Medina guilty. His execution is tomorrow morning," said Riley.

"I heard the same thing. Agent Sherman told me the outcome less than an hour ago. May God have mercy on his evil soul."

"That's why I'm here Father. Chief Medina has asked to see a priest. He wants you."

Father Nguyen answered quickly. "Yes, I will see him Chaplain Riley."

"Are you sure Father?" asked Riley.

"Yes. I am still a priest. I told Medina if he was truly repentant I would absolve him of his sins. Now, when he departs this world and if God thinks differently, then Medina is bound to the fiery pits of hell where he belongs. What kind of priest would I be if I refused a sinner on his deathbed? Everything I fought for over the last few months would be for naught. I would be a hypocrite. So, yes, I will speak to Chief Medina."

"Very well Father. I'll have it arranged," replied the ship's senior clergyman.

Medina sat on his bunk in the holding cell when a corpsman wheeled Father Nguyen into the ship's brig. Father Nguyen wore his rosary beads about his neck, held a crucifix in one hand, and the bible in the other. In his lap was a small plastic vile of holy water.

"Wheel me next to Chief Medina's cell please, Petty Officer Ropp," commanded the priest.

The corpsman looked towards a Marine Corps Gunnery Sergeant for direction. The muscle bound Marine nodded his head approving the request. Agent Sherman stood nearby silently.

"Chief Medina, I was told you desired to speak with me. What can I do for you?"

"I want to confess my sins, Father," Medina replied.

"Are you ready to truly confess your sins?"

"Yes Father, I killed a young Thai whore and two FBI agents. I am sorry I can no longer perform our Lord's holy orders. I ask you to forgive me for not fulfilling God's tasking to me."

"I see," said the priest. "I cannot forgive your sins. You are still not sorry for the pain and suffering you caused over many destructive years. You have killed so many people and you still maintain God was directing your actions. I cannot absolve you of your sins. I will pray for your soul which is going to be cast into the depths of hell when you die tomorrow. I was hoping you were repentant but I see you are still unwilling to recognize that Lucifer commands your spirit. I believe after sunrise tomorrow when Satan's demons are viciously tormenting you, you will regret your decision."

"Then I will be waiting for you there, Priest. God will surely send you to hell for breaking your vows."

"My son, I never broke my vows. All I did was make an anonymous telephone call to alert the authorities where Charlotte Chambers was. They did the rest. They followed you into my church and deduced you were Butcher Bill. You have no one to blame but yourself demon."

Medina went silent. He held his hands over his face. The discussion could go no further.

"Corpsman, please push me back to sickbay please," asked Father Nguyen. "My business with this beast is complete."

Captain Russell recalled the entire *LINCOLN* and *CHANCER-LORVILLE* crews from their liberty ashore. The day after Medina was found guilty; the two ships weighed anchor at dawn and headed to sea. Fifty miles over the horizon and out of sight of any land, the ships stopped their engines in calm water maintaining two hundred yards apart. The crews were mustered on the main decks in full uniform bearing witness to an extraordinary event that had not occurred onboard a United States Naval ship in more than a hundred and fifty years.

LINCOLN's crew stood in military formation on her massive flight deck with the sun still below the horizon. The brightest stars in the sky began to fade away as the orange globe started to turn night into day.

CHANCERVILLE's crew gathered on her weather decks too. Many held binoculars to their eyes trying to see what was going on. Others impatiently stood by those who did pestering their shipmates to explain what they were seeing on the carrier's decks. The cruiser's crew knew they were watching naval history unfolding. Cameras were strictly forbidden.

Fireman Recruit Medina stood at the end of the flight deck facing forward toward the ship's hurricane bow. In front of him stood a Marine Corp Captain wearing his dress uniform and carrying a sword. Four Marines armed with M-14 rifles boxed Medina in. A lone drummer started to rap on his drum. At the sound of the drumbeat, Medina's guards marched him from the back of the ship's flight deck through the four thousand sailors assembled. He wore the uniform of an unrated seaman. Besides the sentence of death, the Court Martial Panel stripped him entirely of his rank. He proceeded to receive his punishment as an E-1, Fireman Recruit. The Marine Guards held Medina by the arms and marched him solemnly through the assembled sailors. *LINCOLN*'s crew stood at attention watching their evil shipmate heading to the gallows. At the end of the formation, the Marines took Medina through the carrier's steel island and proceeded up to the ship's signal bridge.

Fireman Recruit Medina stood in front of Command Master Chief Blye and the ship's Master-at-Arms. Rear Admiral Cable, Captain Russell, and all of the ship's officers stood one deck above him. Agent Sherman, Dr. Ohms, the Colby twins, and Detectives Hendricks and Raphael stood with them. Next to Command Master Chief Blye was Father Nguyen. Despite the overwhelming pain Nguyen suffered at the hands of Butcher Bill, the priest insisted that he was the Chaplain who presided over the man's soul at his execution.

"Fireman Recruit Ignacio Xavier Medina. You have been found guilty of First Degree Murder, Attempted Murder, Kidnapping, Larceny, and Conduct Unbecoming of a United States Naval Chief Petty Officer," read Master Chief Blye from the execution order in his hands. He continued, "For crimes against your fellow man and for the disgrace you have brought against the United States Navy you are sentenced to die by hanging. Today, precisely at sunrise, you will be hanged from the neck until you are dead. After, you're wretched body will be committed to the deep. May God have mercy on your soul."

Father Nguyen, encased by the bandages covering his wounds, limped forward.

"Ignacio are there any last words you would like to say to your fellow man before God judges you for your actions upon this Earth?" he asked. The ship's crew knew of the priest's torturous ordeal suffered at Medina's hand. None of them believed they could stand in front of the murderer like he was doing now. The man was filled with bravery as an example for all.

Medina raised his head. Remorse was foreign to him. He lifted his head to the heavens and spoke "Dear God, oh merciful Lord, I have done your will. Accept your most obedient servant into your kingdom with grace. Lift up your mighty hand and swallow these ships into your mighty oceans deep."

The ship's crew remained silent. Though sailors were superstitious, they knew the demon's curse was useless. In front of Butcher Bill stood God's pacific soldier holding a rosary in one hand and clutching a Bible in the other. Father Nguyen's presence protected them all. No harm would come to the Navy's ships that day.

"Brother Medina, you still refuse to confess your evil deeds. You will never reach the gates to heaven. Satan and hell's fires await your arrival where you will be tortured for all eternity," preached Nguyen. "May you feel only the pain and agony you have inflicted upon the hundreds of innocent souls you unjustly extinguished," prayed the clergyman. Father Nguyen stepped aside to clear a path to the gallows.

Master Chief Blye spun on his heels, saluted Rear Admiral Cable, and formally stated, "Sir, request permission to carry out the punishment as ordered?"

Crisply returning the sailors salute, Cable replied, "Request granted. Carry out your orders Master Chief. Execute the prisoner."

"Aye, aye sir," replied the Chief Master-at-Arms.

The two Marine guards marched Medina forward. The hemp line noose made with thirteen coils hung down from the warship's highest yardarm. Medina was placed directly below the rope. Master Chief Blye stepped forward, slipped the noose around his neck, and tightened the hangman's knot about Butcher Bill's neck. Stepping back, the military policeman placed a whistle between his lips and stared at his watch. It read 0651. Official sunrise was at 0652. The second hand clicked away each passing second until it reached the apex of its travel. Master Chief Blye blew one long, loud blast on the whistle reverberating over the ocean.

Sailors manning the rope made fast around Medina's neck swiftly ran aft with the line. The rope whizzed through the series of pulleys it was threaded through. Butcher Bill's body smartly rose into the air. Fireman Recruit Medina's body kicked and jerked as the noose constricted around his neck and gravity pulled his weight back to Earth. Rear Admiral Cable and his mixed entourage of uniformed officers and civilian guests watched the life ebb from Fireman Recruit Medina's body. Butcher Bill's face reddened. His movements slowly faded away as the noose constricted his airway. Medina's suspended body twisted slightly in the stale air as the drumbeat and Butcher Bill's heart ceased to play. Final justice and God's will had finally been done.